TOR BOOKS BY CHARLES STROSS

the
REVOLUTION
BUSINESS

BOOK FIVE OF THE MERCHANT PRINCES

CHARLES STROSS

A TOM DOHERTY ASSOCIATES BOOK
NEW YORK

This is a work of fiction. All of the characters, organizations, and events portrayed in this novel are either products of the author's imagination or are used fictitiously.

THE REVOLUTION BUSINESS

Copyright © 2009 by Charles Stross

All rights reserved.

A Tor Book
Published by Tom Doherty Associates, LLC
175 Fifth Avenue
New York, NY 10010

www.tor-forge.com

Tor® is a registered trademark of Tom Doherty Associates, LLC.

ISBN 978-0-7653-5590-4

First Edition: April 2009
First Mass Market Edition: February 2010

Printed in the United States of America

0 9 8 7 6 5 4 3 2 1

For Gav
Better read than dead

the
REVOLUTION
BUSINESS

PROLOGUE:
EMPTY QUIVER

❦

The inspectors arrived before dawn.

A convoy of six gray government cars pulling up at the east gate to the complex was the first warning anyone on site was permitted—and the two security police officers in the gate booth took it. "Call Ops," the older cop grunted, narrowing his eyes as the cars dimmed their headlights and queued up between the concrete barriers for inspection. "Tell them we've got visitors."

"Protesters?" The younger officer straightened up as he reached for the secure handset that tied the booth to the Operations Center. They'd had a problem with the peacenik protesters earlier in the year, some new folks from outside who'd tried to block traffic outside the perimeter, but mostly the protesters stuck to the Peace Farm round the far side of the site.

"Not likely." He opened the door and stepped out into the twilight. After dark it cooled off—the open-oven-door temperatures of summer in Carson County had subsided to an arid stillness. Five hundred hours was dead time; the other eight officers who worked the entrance during the morning rush would still be signing in and getting their kit. His hand went to his two-way radio. "Sergeant Brady on east gate two, requesting backup. Over." He walked towards the first car. A silver-gray Continental with a minivan behind it. As he approached, the driver's door opened. Some instinct tipped him off. He straightened his back: "Let me see your badge, sir!"

The driver stepped out and held up a badge. Blue, for Q-level access, Brady saw. "I need to touch that, sir."

"Of course."

The driver was in his early thirties, with a certain look to him that gave Brady unpleasant flashbacks. The passenger seats were occupied, too. "Everyone out." Brady peered at the badge, and at the other federal ID the driver was holding. His handheld scanner said the badge was the real deal, so . . . "There y'are, Agent Cruz." He handed the badge back. There, let someone in Ops deal with this. "I need to check everyone in person."

That meant checking three cars and three minivans, and by the end of it Brady was in a cold sweat—not because of the work, but because of what it implied. Six FBI agents and four federal agents from the NNSA's Office of Secure Transportation was one thing, but there were another five close-faced men and women who didn't have any ID for him other than their Q-level site badges, and they seemed to be running this circus. *Not my job to ask,* Brady reminded himself dubiously, *but someone's about to get a nasty shock.* "Welcome to Pantex, sir," he said, walking back to Agent Cruz's car. "Do you know who your assigned escort is? You're not on my roster."

Cruz smiled humorlessly. "I think it'll be whoever that is, over there." Brady glanced round. The car was coming from the direction of Ops, clearly in a hurry. "Meanwhile, our business is in Area Twelve and we will be wanting security to secure a particular building. You and Officer Nelson are due to be relieved in half an hour—sooner, now."

Brady's two-way crackled: "Brady to secure line, over."
"You're coming with us."

Rich Wall hung as far back as he could behind the NNSA
muscle and the local Agency staffers, doing his best to people-
watch without attracting the attention of the local officers,
who were clearly not happy about their shift being extended
without warning. *Fascinating*, he decided. *They're all acting
out.* Nothing surprising there, of course—everyone from the
NNSA agents to the site security commander would be on
tenterhooks and trying to look as professional as possible—
but if the colonel's tip-off panned out, it would make his job
somewhat harder. He fingered his Q-level badge again, and
waited for the RWI staffer to work her way along the line
outside Access Control, pinning dosimeters to the visitors'
jackets.

"Y'all been cleared for this visit already," the staffer announced, her voice flat. "Ah'm therefore assuming y'all have
read and signed the radiological training test books. Ah just
want to remind y'all to keep your hands to yourselves. Ah
mean that. The things we store in this building are not toys.
Sergeant." She nodded at the older, grumpier security cop—
who in his forage cap and desert camo looked a lot more
like a soldier than a police officer. Wall noted the M16 on
his shoulder. *Definitely* a soldier.

*Maybe the colonel's wrong. Maybe it's just a bookkeeping
error.*

Having been thus admonished, it came as a minor anticlimax to be told to climb back in the car. "Where now?"
Rich asked as Lisa Chavez pulled on her seat belt.

"Now we play follow the leader." She stared at the people-
mover full of serious-minded FBI agents from Utah. "Hope
someone in this clusterfuck knows what they're doing. Hope
somebody's wrong."

"Why isn't Rand on this case?"

Chavez glanced at him sharply. "You ask too many questions."

Rich leaned back as she started the car's engine. "Asking questions is my job."

The convoy moved off slowly, hugging the shoulder of the narrow road in the thin dawn light. They drove for some minutes before stopping for another checkpoint in a chain-link fence. *Sixteen thousand acres,* thought Rich. More cops dressed as soldiers, armed like soldiers, checking badges and waving vehicles through, one at a time. *Looks like Fort Meade, without the office blocks.*

A big barn of a building loomed up on one side. Chavez followed the convoy into a wide doorway, then into an enclosed ramp—a corridor about five meters wide, lined with pipes and branch routes leading off to other buildings. Walls rolled past at walking pace. Air monitoring units at head height glowed steady green, like traffic lights: no tritium release, no alpha radiation. The Pantex plant sprawled across the Texas landscape north of Amarillo, almost the size of a city in its own right. But the inhabitants weren't anything you'd want for a neighbor.

After a half-hour-long eternity they rolled back out onto a strip of blacktop road, past a clump of low earth berms, and halted again outside another chain-link fence. This, too, was guarded: "Everyone out," crackled the radio on the dash.

"You heard the man." Chavez opened her door. "Come on."

They were queuing up at a gate in the fence, being individually checked by officers with metal detectors. For a moment, Rich's spirits rose. *Real security?* But no. *The colonel's right. They'd be totally unprepared.*

There was a brief argument over some of the monitoring equipment, but in the end the NNSA specialists said something—Rich was too far away to hear—and one of the guards headed for a windowless hut at the double, and when he came back they were allowed to proceed after opening the heavy cases for inspection. *It's not as if we're taking anything out of here, after all.*

"Welcome to Area Twelve," said one of the NNRT staffers. He gestured at the low earth berms around them. "Doesn't look like much, does it?"

"Cut it out," Cruz grunted. "Which is Building Sixteen?"

"You're standing on its roof." Cruz looked down as the staffer gestured at a windowless bunker. "This way."

Rich glanced back beyond the fence. "Are we expecting visitors?" he murmured to Chavez.

"I don't think so." She followed his gaze. "Huh. Someone in Operations has finally woken up."

Rich shook his head. "Let's catch the floor show. This should be good."

The secure storage vault was a concrete-lined tomb with two rows of six coffin-sized trapdoors in the floor separated by aisles a meter wide. A small forklift truck waited patiently under the ceiling, ready to lift the lids and raise their contents. Yellow guidelines painted on the concrete promised dire consequences for anyone who crossed them without due caution; more air filters and warning lamps hung from the walls, quiet sentinels keeping a graveyard watch.

With this many people this close to their charges, the guards were clearly edgy. "If you all could stay behind that red line, this will go much easier," the sergeant from the gatehouse announced. "Three at a time. Who's first on the list?"

"Agent Moran, Major Alvarez, and Captain Hu," said one of the NNSA staffers, reading from the checklist. "Step forward and present your credentials." Everything, Rich noted, was scripted as closely as the protocol surrounding an execution. With the gate cops and the regular guards and now a group of officials from Control who included the site administrator—looking distinctly unhappy about having his usual morning routine upset like this—the vault was getting crowded. "Sergeant, your turn." The to-ing and fro-ing over identity verification went on for almost half an hour as checklists were exchanged and a bulky procedures manual—one of the NNSA agents had brought along a rolling flight case crammed with files—was thumbed through.

Finally: "Open storage cell number one, please." Someone in the back row coughed; Rich nearly jumped out of his skin. The duty technician drove his truck into position, skillfully threading its forks through the rings in the top of the lid before lifting the heavy trapdoor off the storage cell. The guards were clearly tense. Rich leaned forward to get a view of the narrow crypt below, taking care to stay behind the red line on the floor.

The contents of the crypt didn't look like much: a pair of olive-drab containers, one briefcase-sized and the other more like a dwarfish oil drum, swathed in canvas straps, with a pair of grab-handles on top. "Major Alvarez, Captain Hu, please identify the items."

The two army officers placed their equipment case on the floor, knelt by the side of the crypt, and peered at the objects within. "Storage cell one appears to contain an H-912 transport container and a D-902 detonation sequencer," Alvarez reported. "Released for active inventory under special executive privilege as per Executive Order 13223, secret codicil A."

"I concur," agreed Hu.

Hang on, Rich noted, *"Released for active inventory"? What the hell? . . .*

"Please determine whether the H-912 is active."

"We'll need to enter the storage cell." Alvarez's tone was matter-of-fact, almost bored.

"You may enter when ready," said the lead NNSA inspector.

One of the guards tensed.

"You may enter," repeated the inspector; the chief administrator cleared his throat.

"Sergeant Jackson? If these inspectors' authorization isn't good enough for you, then put it on *my* tab."

"Sir, I—" The guard subsided, clearly unhappy.

"Thank you, Mr. Ellis." The NNSA inspector raised an eyebrow at the chief administrator.

"We've all got our jobs to do," Ellis grunted. "And unauthorized access *is* an issue here." He fell silent as Alvarez and Hu climbed down into the crypt and bent over the cylinder, their heads nearly touching.

As with all nuclear weapons procedures, two commissioned officers were called for. There was a small inspection window on the top of the cylinder; if an actual core were installed, a colored reflector would be positioned right behind it. "I can confirm that the H-912 inspection window is showing code orange," said Alvarez. "Captain?"

Hu echoed him: "I concur with the major."

The minder of the checklists ticked off another box.

"Next, uh, if you could verify that your instrument is working using the test sample, we can proceed to step six—"

More to-ing and fro-ing as Alvarez and Hu proceeded to calibrate their portable detector. "It's working alright," Alvarez confirmed. "We're going to check the H-912 now." More to-ing and fro-ing as he fastened a stubby cylinder to the top of the olive-drab container and pushed buttons. A minute passed. "I'm not getting anything."

"Agreed. Something not right here. . . ."

Someone swore. "Agent Moran, if you'd like to try your instrument now?"

Rich felt an unpleasant numbness creep over him, a resignation to the unfolding process of discovery and the horrors that it promised to reveal. Everything that had happened to bring them to this situation had taken place weeks, months, or even years ago; nor was he implicated in it. Other people would have to defend their actions, possibly in court—not Rich. But that didn't make things better. *Nothing* made things better, not when they were the kind of things that were the bread and butter of his occupation. Agent Moran was unpacking his detector as carefully as a forensic tech attending a particularly gruesome murder scene. "Nothing," he announced.

"Right." The NNSA inspector sounded as unhappy as Rich felt. "Mr. Ellis, with your permission, I think we ought to proceed to open the H-912 and see what's really in there."

"You're sure those detectors"—Ellis nudged forward— "let me see that. McDonnell, if you could check this reference sample—"

More to-ing and fro-ing as Ellis and his staff confirmed (not to anyone's relief) that the reference samples the inspectors were using were, indeed, the real deal—"Alright, on my authority, Willis? Unseal this carrier for internal visual inspection."

"Sir." The senior guard made it sound like a cough. "Opening a device on inactive inventory is a security—"

"Sergeant, I am very much afraid that this is not, in fact, a device on inactive inventory. It's something else. In which case, the regulation you're about to quote at me doesn't apply, does it?"

"Right." The guard looked unhappy. "Will you put that in writing, sir? Because if not, I'll have to . . ."

Ellis took a deep breath. "Yes, I'll put it in writing." He jerked a thumb over his shoulder. "Now, are we going to keep these people waiting?"

Rich felt an elbow in his ribs. "Have to *what?*" whispered Chavez.

"Shoot somebody," Rich grunted. "Probably us."

"Captain Hu . . ."

"I'm on it."

The audience in the storage room fell silent as Captain Hu set to work, unfastening catches and then going to work with a torque wrench under Alvarez's watch. He took barely five minutes, but to Rich it felt closer to five hours. Finally, the lid of the carrier came free.

"Well?" asked Ellis.

Hu held the carrier open as Alvarez reached down and pulled. "We've got an empty quiver," he said laconically, and held up his catch: an object which, from the way he held it, had to be unusually heavy. "Unless we've taken to storing lead bricks in nuclear weapon carriers. . . ."

The transportation of mobile phones—let alone camera phones—into the secure areas of Pantex was more than slightly discouraged. Rich stayed with the crowd scene for the next two hours, as the inspectors ripped through the other eleven storage cells in the facility with increasing desperation. Then, with the final tally—six H-912s filled with the sleeping FADM lightweight nukes, six H-912s empty but for lead bricks and a slip of red paper taped inside the inspection window—he slipped outside.

Chavez followed him. "The colonel will want to know," she said as the door closed behind them.

"Yeah," he agreed. He nodded to the guard on duty outside, then presented his badge. "We have to make a call. Where can I find a phone?"

The cop looked at him with barely concealed suspicion. "You don't get to go anywhere until I confirm you're free to leave the area, sir."

Chavez snorted. "You have no legal authority over us, soldier." She held up her warrant card. "C'mon, Rich, we're—"

The guard tensed. "You're not leaving!" he repeated, louder.

Rich spread his hands. "Whoa! We don't need an argument and we don't need to leave the area, we just need to make a phone call. Is there a voice terminal we can use nearby? Preferably secure?"

"You want an outside line?" The guard looked aghast.

"No, just one that can put me through to Operations Control. Operations Control? Come on, there must be one—"

"Internal phone's over there." The cop pointed at a box on the wall. "Just don't try to leave the area until you've been cleared, sir, ma'am. I don't know what's going on in there, but nobody's to leave. And I don't care what your badges say, I've got my orders and I'm sticking to 'em. Don't put me in a position where I've gotta do something we'll all regret."

"I don't intend to." Rich tried to look as unthreatening as possible. "I just need to talk to someone in Operations Control. We're not going to be any trouble."

He could feel Chavez's eyes drilling a hole in his back. He glanced round. "You want to make this one?"

"No, you go first." Chavez grinned humorlessly. "I'll just watch your back."

"Shit." Rich picked up the handset and dialed a four-digit number. "Ops? This is a call for SERENE AMBLER. Yeah, that's SERENE AMBLER. They're expecting you to connect me immediately . . . good. Colonel? Rich here."

The voice at the other end of the line sounded alert. "What's the news?"

"Our FADM inventory is fucked, and it's worse than we feared. We're out by another five, in addition to the one we found in Boston. That one was on forward deployment when it went walkies, but the ones we're missing here were supposed to be in secure storage. Turns out they've been tampered with in the meantime—someone has gotten inside the storage cells. I slipped out while they were declaring an official Pinnacle Empty Quiver so I could warn you; the missing items are all from the covert resource allocated to SECDEF and VPOTUS back in 2001, so somebody needs to brief WOLFMAN and WARBUCKS urgently to head it off at the pass before the shitstorm hits the National Command Authority and confuses the president."

"I see." The colonel fell uncharacteristically silent for a few seconds. "And what does the scene look like to you, right now?"

Rich paused, glancing at the guard, who was pointedly not listening—too pointedly, he thought. "The area's secured against normal threats, so your guess is as good as mine as to how they got in." Which was to say, not a guess at all—

they both knew perfectly well how these particular bad guys might sneak into a secure area. "The building's surrounded by a—the usual kind of security you'd expect—but it's AGL. The guards seem alert enough to"—yes, the guard was *very pointedly* not listening—"intruders. I'm not making any guesses how they managed to make the substitution, but the H-912 cases were full of ballast. Which suggests whoever took them knows exactly what they're doing with the contents."

Another pause. "Can you confirm six missing, and no more?"

That was an easy one to answer: "No, sir. I can confirm six empty quivers and six full ones, but I cannot rule out the possibility that there are more missing." He licked his dry lips. "I would be astonished if the site authority doesn't order a full lockdown immediately and commence an audit within the next hour or two, in anticipation of NCA's likely orders. Meanwhile, it looks like we'll be stuck here for a few hours, if not days. What do you want us to do?"

Silence. "Leave it to the NNSA," the colonel finally said. "I'll escalate it for WARBUCKS's attention immediately. Meanwhile, I want you back in Boston as soon as you can disengage. There's a problem with COLDPLAY. . . ."

1

ḃEIR APPARENT

❧

I *am not hearing this,* Miriam Beckstein told herself. The temptation to giggle, to laugh it all off as a bizarre joke, was enormous. *Pretend it isn't happening; yeah, right. Story of my life.* She tightened her grip on the valise holding her notebook PC and its precious CD-ROMs. Except that for the past six months, the mad stuff had made a habit of punching her in the guts whenever she least expected it. "Run that by me again," she said.

"It's quite simple," said the hard-eyed young debutante with the machine pistol. "Your mother wants to use you to consolidate power." She kept her eyes focused on Miriam as she twisted the magazine free of the gun, worked a slide to eject a cartridge, and swapped another magazine into place. "The duke agrees with her. And *we*"—the eloquent roll of her shoulder took in their companions, a cohort of young and alarmingly heavily armed Clan world-walkers—"intend to make sure you're not just there for show."

They look like students, thought Miriam. Students outfitted by North Face for a weekend hike; accessories by

Fabrique Nationale and Heckler & Koch. Of course they were nothing of the kind. Young aristocrats of the Clan nobility—born in the curious quasi-mediaeval kingdom of Gruinmarkt, and able to travel to other worlds at will—they might look like ordinary American undergrads, but the mindset behind those fresh young faces was very different.

"Oh, really?" she managed. The idea of her mother—and the duke—plotting to put her on the throne of the Gruinmarkt was pretty preposterous, on the face of it—but then, so were so many of the other intrigues the Clan seemed to generate. Then another thought struck her: *You said "we," didn't you?* So Brill had an agenda of her own, over and above her loyalty to the duke—or Miriam, for that matter? Time to probe. . . .

"Was this"—she pointed at her belly, quiet anger in her voice—"part of their plan?"

"Milady" Brill—Lady Brilliana d'Ost, a mere twentysomething—furrowed her brow. "With all due respect, if you think *that,* you're paranoid. Do you really think the duke—or your mother—know you so poorly as to think you a suitable mother for the heir to the throne? Much less, under such durance? Henryk and your—his backer—were fools for thinking they could manipulate you that way, and now they are dead fools. The rest of us are just trying to make the best of a bad deal. And if you want to talk politics, would you mind leaving it until later? I've got a splitting headache and it's about to get worse."

Miriam winced. World-walking took it out of a member of the Clan's inner families, those with the ability: Doing it more than once in a day risked migrainelike symptoms and a blood pressure spike. There were other symptoms, too: pregnancy, she'd learned the hard way, made world-walking under your own power impossible. But they'd come here from New Britain, escaping after the abortive ambush at a provincial railway station in that world's version of California, immediately after picking her up.

One of the young men pacing the perimeter of the clearing raised a hand, twirled it in a warning circle. "One hour to go."

"Yah." Brill glanced round again. The forest clearing was peaceful, unoccupied but for Miriam, Brill, and her three young bloods, but she never stopped scanning.

"Are we in any immediate danger?" Miriam asked, shifting her balance on the fallen tree trunk.

"Probably not right now." Brill paused to continue her inspection. "The Kao's patrols don't usually sweep this far northeast. Better not linger, though. We'll be ready to move in another hour."

"The Kao?"

"The Favored of Heaven's border troops. Most of the local tribes give them a wide berth. We should, too." A warning look in her eyes gave Miriam a cold shiver; if Brill was scared of them, that was enough for her.

"What are you planning on doing once we cross over?"

"We've got a hotel suite in San Jose. I plan to get us over there, then make contact with the duke and ask for further instructions. I imagine he'll want us back on the east coast stat—we've got a biz-jet standing by. Otherwise, we'll do what Security tells us to do. Unless you have other plans?" Brill raised a carefully shaped eyebrow. Even though she'd started the day with a brisk firefight, then a forced crossing into wilderness, she'd taken pains with her makeup.

Miriam shrugged. "I thought I did." Her hands were restless; trying to keep them still, she thrust them deep in the pockets of her overly heavy coat. "The political situation in New Britain is going to hell in a handbasket. Erasmus was on his way to meet a big wheel in the, uh, resistance." In point of fact, the *biggest* wheel in the underground, returning from exile after a generation—to whom he had once been a personal assistant. "It's too hot for comfort. I was only going along because I couldn't think of anything else to do; when I fetched up in London all I had was the clothes on my back."

"Well, at least you got away from the mess at the Summer

Palace with your skin intact," Brill observed. "And thank whatever gods you believe in for that."

She fell silent for a few minutes. But finally Miriam's curiosity got the better of her. "I can guess how you tracked me down," she said. "But what about Huw? And the other two? Who are they? You said something about a job I'd suggested, but I don't recall . . . and they don't look like Uncle Angbard's little helpers to me."

"They're not." Brilliana's eyes narrowed. "I just called in help and head office sent them along. Hey! Sir Huw? Have you a minute?"

Huw nodded. "Bro, cover for me," he told the tall, heavily built guy with the semiauto shotgun as he walked towards them. Huw was anything but husky: skinny and intense. "Has something come up?"

"Huw." Brill smiled, oddly cheerful. "We've got a couple of hours to kill. Why don't you tell her grace what you found?"

Her grace? But I'm not a duchess. Miriam blinked. Suddenly bits of the big picture were falling into place. *Heir to the throne.* "What you found, where?"

"We're calling it world four right now, but I think a better name for it would be Transition A–B," Huw said as he sat down at the far end of the fallen trunk. "It's where you go if you use the Hidden Family's knotwork as a focus in your world, uh, the United States." He grinned, twitchily. "Nobody was able to cross over in New England because, well, it's probably under an ice sheet—the weather there's definitely a lot colder than in any of the other time lines we know about."

Hang on, time lines—Miriam held up a hand. "What were you doing?"

"The duke tasked me with setting up a systematic exploration program," Huw explained. "So I started by taking the second known knotwork design and seeing where it'd take you if you used it in world two, in the USA, which the

Hidden Family had no access to. The initial tests in Massachusetts and New York failed, so I guessed there might be a really large obstacle in the way. There's some kind of exclusion effect . . . but anyway, we found a new world."

Miriam narrowly resisted the urge to grab him and start yelling questions. "Go on."

"World four is cold, as in, about ten degrees celsius below datum for the other worlds we've found. That's ice age cold. We didn't have time to do much exploring, but what we found—there were people there, once, but we didn't see any signs of current habitation. High tech, *very* high tech—perfect dentistry, gantries made out of titanium, and other stuff. We're still trying to figure out the other stuff, but it's a whole different ball game. The building we found looked like it had been struck from above by some kind of directed energy weapon—"

"Some kind of—"Miriam stopped. On the opposite side of the clearing, the young blond woman who'd come with Huw was kneeling, her weapon trained on something invisible through the trees.

Brill was already moving. "Get ready to go."

"But it's too early," Miriam started.

"What's Elena spotted?" Huw rose to his feet. The big guy at the far side of the clearing—the one Huw had called "bro"—was crouching behind the blonde, his shotgun raised: A moment later she turned and scrambled towards them, staying low.

"Riders," she said quietly, addressing Brill. "At least three, maybe more. They're trying to stay quiet. Milady, we await your instructions."

"I think"—Brill's eyes hardened—"we'd better cross over. Right now. Huw, can you carry her grace?"

"I think so." Huw knelt down. "Miriam, if you could climb on my shoulders?"

Miriam swallowed. "Is this necessary? It's too early—"

Brill cut her off. "It is necessary to move as fast as possible, unless you want another shoot-out. I generally try to limit them to no more than one before lunch on any given day. Huw, get her across. We'll be along momentarily."

Miriam stood up, wrapped her arms around Huw's shoulders, and tried to haul her legs up. Huw rose into a half-crouch. She strained to clamp her knees around his waist. "Are you alright?" she asked anxiously.

"Just a second," he gasped. "Alright. Three. Two." Something flickered in the palm of his hand, just in the corner of her vision: a fiery knot that tried to turn her eyes and her stomach inside out. "One."

The world around them flickered and Huw collapsed under her, dry-retching. Miriam fell sideways, landing heavily on one hip.

They were in scrubland, and alone. Someone's untended back lot, by the look of it: a few stunted trees straggling across a nearby hillside like hairs across a balding man's pate, a fence meandering drunkenly to one side. A windowless barn that had clearly seen better days slumped nearby.

Miriam rose to her feet and dusted herself off. Her traveling clothes, unremarkable in New Britain, would look distinctly odd to American eyes: a dark woolen coat of unusual cut over the mutant offspring of a shalwar kameez. Along with her temporarily blond, permed hair it was a disguise that had outlived its usefulness. "Where are you parked?" she asked Huw as his retching subsided.

"Front of. Barn." He staggered to a crouch. "Need. Pain-killers. . . ."

Something moved in the corner of her sight. Miriam's head whipped round as she thrust a hand in her coat pocket, reaching for the small pistol Erasmus had given her before she recognized Elena. A few seconds later Huw's brother Hulius popped into view, followed almost immediately by Brilliana. "Come on, people!" Brill sounded more annoyed than nauseous. "Cover! Check!"

"Check," Huw echoed hollowly. "I think we're still alone."

"Check!" trilled Elena. "Did they see you, Yul? Ooh, you don't look so good!"

"*Guuuh* . . . Check. I don't think so. Going. Be sick."

Brill clapped her hands. "Let's get going, people." She was almost tapping her feet with impatience. "We've got a safe house to go to. You can throw up all you like once we report in, but first we've got a job to do." She nodded at Miriam. "After you, milady."

In a soot-stained industrial city nestling in the Appalachians, beneath a sky stained amber by the fires of half a million coal-burning stoves, there was a noble house defended by the illusion of poverty.

The Lee family and their clients did not like to draw attention to themselves. The long habit of secrecy was deeply ingrained in their insular souls; they'd lived alone among enemies for almost ten generations, abandoned by the eastern Clan that had once—so they had thought until recently, so some still thought—cast them out and betrayed them. Here in the industrial heartland of Irongate there was little love for rich foreigners, much less wealthy Chinese merchants, at the best of times. And the times were anything but good: With the empire locked in a bewildering and expensive overseas war (to say nothing of multiple consecutive crop failures and a bare treasury, deflation, and high unemployment) the city was as inflammable as a powder keg.

Consequently, the Lees did not flaunt their wealth and power openly. Nor did their home resemble a palatial mansion. Rather, it resembled a tenement block fronted by the dusty window displays of failing shops (for only the pawnbroker's business remained good). Between two such shops there stood a blank-faced door, a row of bellpulls discreetly off to one side. It might have been a stairwell leading to the cramped flats of shopkeepers and factory foremen. But the reality was very different.

"Be seated, nephew," said the old man with the long, wispy beard. "And tell me what brings you here?"

James Lee bowed his head, concealing his unease for a few more moments. As was right, he went to his knees and then sat cross-legged before the low platform on which his great uncle, the eldest of days—and his companions, the eldest's younger sibling, Great-Uncle Huan, and his first wife—perched.

"The Clan has gone too far," he began, then paused.

"Tea for my favorite nephew," the eldest commented, and one of the servants who had been standing behind James bowed and slipped out through a side door. "You may continue."

James took a deep breath. "They resumed their scheme to capture the royal house. My understanding is that the chosen bride, the long-lost daughter of the western alliance, was not an enthusiastic participant: The architect of the marriage, her grandmother, allied with the conservative faction at court to coerce her."

He paused for a moment as the servant, returning, placed a tray bearing a steaming cup before him. "I considered the merits of direct action, but concluded the cost would outweigh any benefit. It would be interpreted as base treachery, and I did not feel able to take such measures without your approval."

"Just so." His great-uncle nodded. "What happened next?"

James chose his next words very carefully, aware of the tension in the room: There was no whispering in corners, and none of the usual cross-play between the ancients that was normal when the eldest held court. "The baroness and her coconspirators made a fundamental error of judgment when they arranged the betrothal of the heir Miriam to the youngest son of the King. They failed to see how this would be received by his elder brother. Prince Egon is not of the blood and therefore they ignored him; Creon, though damaged, was thought by them to be an occulted carrier"—one who carried the recessive gene for the world-walking ability, but was not able himself to world-walk—"and so they planned to breed from him a king who would be one of their own. Egon took as dim a view of this marriage as you would expect, and the result was bound to be messy. Although I did not realize how drastically he would react at the time."

He reached out and picked up the cup of tea, then took a sip before continuing.

"I intervened at the betrothal by presenting the eastern heir—Helge, as they call her, Miriam, in her own tongue—with a locket containing our house sigil. She had made it clear that she felt no filial piety, and wished to escape. I therefore concluded that there was no reason to kill her if it was her heart's desire to do what we wanted: I merely gave her the means. I confess that I did not anticipate Egon's attempt to massacre everybody at the ceremony—but by now either she's dead or in exile, so our goal is achieved without her blood on our hands."

"About the massacre." Great-Uncle Huan leaned forward. "You were present, were you not?"

James nodded.

"How did you escape?"

Another sip of tea: "The situation was confused. When Egon's men detonated a petard beneath the palace and then attacked, the royal life guards fought back. While this was going on, those of the Clan's leaders who were present made themselves scarce. They left their dead behind. I hid under a table until I could get out, using my spare sigil." With one hand, James reached into the sleeve of his robe. *Now or never.* He pulled out a small gilded locket on a fine chain. "Before I left, I removed this from the body of a dead baron. It's the authentic sigil of the eastern Clan. I have tested it myself." He laid it on the dais before the eldest. "I brought it here directly."

He sat back to wait, straining to reveal no sign of his inner tension. *It's like trying not to think of invisible elephants,* Helge's mother Patricia had told him with a twinkle in her eyes. *All you have to do is learn to ignore the elephant in the room.* Which was perfectly true, but when the elephant in question was the huge lie you'd just told the patriarch of your family, that was easier said than done. The background was true enough, if one chose to overlook some judicious omissions. But his escape—that was another matter. Yes, he'd hidden under a table, shivering and concussed. But it had been one of the eastern Clan's soldiers who'd carried him across to that strange doppelganger city of New York, and it had been a very much alive Lady Olga Thorold who had gifted him with the locket, in return for certain undertakings. Because, when you got down to it, sometimes treachery was a two-way street.

The elders stared at the locket greedily but with trepidation, as if it might bite. "This is definitely the sigil of the eastern Clan?" the eldest asked, in a tone of almost superstitious disbelief. "Have you compared it to our own?"

James stifled a gasp of relief. "Not directly, uncle," he admitted. "It allowed me to travel, and its bite is the same— I think it subtly different, but I thought it best to leave the comparison to someone who knows nothing of our ways."

The eldest nodded thoughtfully, then looked up. "Leave us," he said, encompassing everyone in the room but his brother, his brother's wife, and James. There was a mass exodus towards the doors at the back of the day room as various servants and no few guards bowed themselves out, but presently the shuffling and whispering died down. Finally, his great-uncle spoke again. "Do they know you live, nephew?"

The implied claim in his familial loyalty nearly made James overlook the implicit threat in the question. "I don't believe so, uncle, but I may be mistaken," he said politely. "I stand ready to return to them if you so order it." He might have said more, but instead bit his lower lip, waiting. He'd spent more than six months living among the eastern families as a hostage: His disappearance might be taken as a sign of treachery. *Might.* Except the events of that fateful night a week ago would make a perfect excuse for absence—one that would be accepted, unquestioned, if Olga was in a position to hold her patron to his side of their bargain. On the other hand, if he returned to the Clan too soon he'd be unable to make good his side of their pact. It was, all in all, a delicate situation.

"You broke their parole." Great-Uncle Huan's eyes narrowed accusingly.

"He had good reason," Number One Wife remonstrated.

"Humph." Huan slouched sideways on his cushion. "Still looks bad."

"Appearances are everything," the eldest agreed. "Nephew, we will think on this. I believe, however, it would be for the best if you wrote a letter to the eastern Clan's elders, perhaps to the white duke himself, explaining your absence. Apologize, remind him of the circumstances that caused you to flee, and ask whether their security will be able to guarantee your safety upon your return." He smiled, evidently amused. "Shame them for forcing you into an act of cowardice."

James bowed his head. "I'll do that." He paused. "Do you expect me to return?"

"Only if they can guarantee your safety." Eldest's smile widened. He picked up the locket. "You've done excellent work already, my nephew. I wish we'd been able to persuade them to provide bed, board, and bodyguards for our spies back in my father's day. It would have made things so much more entertaining. . . ."

The sun had long since set behind the battlements of the Hjalmar Palace, and the besieging forces had settled down to intermittent sniping, seemingly intent on making the defenders keep their heads down. Which might be good news or bad news, Lady Olga thought, depending on whether they were doing so to conserve ammunition for an attack, or simply planning on keeping the Clan security force bottled up indefinitely. The former seemed likely: The usurper had demonstrated a dismaying talent for keeping the Clan on the back foot.

Not that a prolonged siege was in any way preferable. The usurper's army had taken the castle by stealth, planted explosives, and nearly succeeded in mousetrapping the Clan's inevitable counterattack. Only the extreme paranoia of Clan security's leadership (who had prepared a secret way in, against the possibility of treachery) and the professionalism of their assault team (who had found and defused the explosive charges) had stopped them massacring the counterattack. But the situation was far from resolved. Egon's men had an unpleasant additional surprise for the Clan forces, in the shape of a handful of machine guns—presumably looted from some Clan arms dump earlier in the war—dug in on top of the castle's gatehouse. The enemy were still clinging on to the gatehouse—largely because Clan security didn't have enough spare troops to mount a frontal attack on what was effectively a small castle in its own right—and so they were forced to keep their heads down and stay away from the front windows of the inner keep.

What the enemy weren't to know was that the Clan's main mobile strength was bottled up in the castle: The doppelganger site in the United States was knee-deep in Special Forces troops, for the secret cross-agency task force set up to track down the Clan had spotted their hastily prepared operation and brought the hammer down hard.

And that was the *good* news.

Olga turned and paced back across the width of the stone-flagged hall, past the map-strewn table and the improvised command and control station where hollow-eyed radio technicians tried to pull useful information together from the walkie-talkie equipped guards on the outer hard-points, to the cluster of men standing around the foot of the table. "Earl Hjorth. Earl Wu. Lieutenant Anders." She nodded and smiled agreeably, trying to maintain a facade of confidence. *Angbard's valkyrie,* they called her behind her back; a nickname freighted with significance, and one she'd have to work doubly hard to live up to when they learned the truth. "What word from Riordan?" she asked.

"Nothing in the past ten minutes." Carl, Earl of Wu by Hjorth, and captain of the Clan's security service, rubbed his mustache. A blunt, bulky fellow, his usually ruddy features showed signs of sagging under the burden of responsibility that had landed on his shoulders. "Riordan tells me the plane's not equipped for night flying and they're running short of fuel—we're at the extremity of its flight radius, and they didn't have much stockpiled. It's not a real airborne detachment: We wouldn't have it at all except that Rudi pursued his hobby despite official discouragement. . . . Well, that's a question for another time. Right now, we're not getting anything in or out tonight. I've got guards with infrared sights on all four bastions and the gatehouse, with continuous radio coverage and M249 sections to cover the approaches, but the enemy have got the sally ports pinned down, and they brought down the riverside culvert so we can't sneak anyone out that way. All the early warning we've got is what we can see from the walls."

"That's going to do us a lot of good if the pretender shows up with an army in the middle of the night," Oliver, Earl Hjorth, said sharply.

"I don't think that's very likely," pointed out Sir Helmut Anders, a portly figure in the camouflage surcoat he wore over his body armor. "He can't be closer than Wergatsfurt and it'll take him a day to move a large force from there to here. Small forces we can deal with, yes? The real threat will arrive on the morrow. So it seems to me that we need to locate the usurper's main force, and then trap him between Riordan's mobile force and this stronghold." It all sounded so reasonable, until she reminded herself that Riordan's mobility owed itself to his ability to move his troops across to the other world, and that the United States was not hospitable territory for Clan security detachments right now. And the other complications . . .

"How is his grace?" Helmut asked, in a misplaced attempt

to divert Earl Hjorth. Olga tensed, hunting for an excuse, but then Oliver nodded emphatically.

"Yes, damn it, how is he?" They were staring at her, expecting an answer.

"He's hanging on." Olga glanced away from the table as she extemporized. "Ivar and Morgaine are tending to him in the baron's bedroom. If we weren't mewed up in here I'd have him in a hospital as soon as look at him—the apoplexy has taken his left side and left him sleepy." Which was a major understatement, but they didn't need to hear the unvarnished truth right now. Duke Angbard, the foundation stone on which Clan Security was built—the one professionally organized institution to which all five member families deferred—had managed to gargle a few words after his collapse, following the disastrous forced worldwalk out of their assembly area near Concord. He was enfeebled and incoherent, and it was well past the magic first hour in which advanced medical care might reap rewards. He wasn't exactly dead, but the likelihood of him ever making a recovery was very poor—especially if they couldn't get him to a stroke center. But the last thing they needed right now was to be leaderless, so . . . "He gave me instructions to resolve this situation, but it's going to take a little while to set up." She shrugged. "I don't suppose we could fly him out tomorrow morning?"

It was a faint hope, and Carl's shaken head told her all she needed to know. "The ultralight's not equipped to carry a passenger who's incapacitated. If we had a real airplane, maybe things would be different. I already asked. When this is over—"

She could finish the thought herself: *When this is over, we will have ultralight helicopters and jeeps with mortars and two-way radio systems in every stronghold. Even if it takes us a decade to carry them across.* And, of course, a chicken in every world-walker's pot. *But for now—*

"What are we going to do?" asked Earl Hjorth. To his

credit, there was no quaver in his voice. "What *are* these special orders of yours?"

"Sir Anders mentioned trapping the usurper's army, didn't he? We have certain weapons that aren't public knowledge. I'd rather not disclose the precise details, my lord, until we're ready to deploy them, but if we can locate the usurper I am certain they will make the job of ending his rampage easier. But for that, we need to know where the pretender *is*. And we need to get out of this mousetrap." She smiled happily. "None of which should be particularly hard."

"But we're doppelgangered—"

"Not in New Britain." She tried not to laugh at his expression. "And that's where we're all going, just as soon as the mail arrives."

It was late in the day: The sun had already set, and the evening rush of homebound commuters was well under way. Business was beginning to slacken off, which was fine by Jason. The sooner they all went home, the sooner the boss would shut up shop and *he* could go home. But for now . . .

The store was mostly empty: a couple of tired guys with handbaskets down by the discount stationery, a harried suburban mom riding herd on two preteens round the aisle of laptops; nothing much to do. Jason waited by the cash register, trying to look attentive. It'd be just like Bill to hang out in back and watch him on the CCTV, then jump on anything he did wrong. That was the trouble with this job— with a busybody like Bill minding the floor, you just couldn't fart without him noticing. One of the fluorescents overhead was flickering, its strobing glow reflecting off the glass cabinets. He shifted from foot to foot—sore as usual, after a day of pacing the aisles.

The doors opened. A few seconds later Jason glanced up, registered the two weirdly dressed men. "Can I help you?" he mumbled, taken aback.

"Yes." The younger of the two grinned. "We've got a shopping list. And we're in a real hurry." He held up a sheet of paper in one gloved hand.

That's armor, isn't it? Jason blinked. The glove was made out of ringlets of metal, knitted together as if by machine— dull gray metal, hundreds of ringlets. Both men were wearing chain mail suits under loose tunics. The tunics were speckled with camouflage dye, like army fatigues. The older man had a full beard and a livid scar drew an emphatic frown-line across his brow. "Uh, I can't leave the register, sir—"

The old guy—middle-aged, by the gray hairs speckling his beard—shook his head. "Call your manager, son. We do not have much time." His voice was heavily accented.

"Uh, I can't—"

"What seems to be the problem?"

Jason gritted his teeth as Bill materialized somewhere behind him. "These folks need a personal shopper."

"Well, you'd better look after them." He could practically *hear* Bill's shit-eating grin. "I'll mind the register for you."

"Let me see that list."

The young guy handed it over. Jason squinted. "A Hewlett-Packard 4550N? I don't know if we've got one of those in stock—"

"Please check." The young guy shrugged. "If you've got one, we want it *right now*. And the other items. If you do not have that precise model, we'll discuss alternatives. Whatever you've got."

"Okay, let me have a look."

Jason scanned the list. A laptop, a heavy laser printer, a scanner, software—all big-ticket items. Some cheaper stuff: a badge laminator, paper, spare toner cartridges, a paper cutter. And some stuff that didn't make sense: an uninterruptible power supply and a gas-fueled generator? He didn't bother to glance at his watch, he already knew the time: three minutes to closing. *Shit. I'll be here all evening.* But the stuff on this list was worth close to ten big ones; the commission on it was close to a day's wages. Plus, Bill would have his guts if he let these fish go. *Jesus.* "I'll get the big stuff out of the stockroom if we've got it, sir. Do you want to pick up the software? It's over on that aisle—"

"Hurry up, we don't have all night." That was Bill, grinning humorlessly at him from behind the register.

Jason shoved through the doors into the stockroom, grabbed a cart, and went hunting. Yet another fucked-up job to add to his list of eccentrics and weirdos who passed through the shop on a daily basis: *Did you hear the one about the two guys in chain mail and camo who came in to buy a DTP system at three minutes to closing?* They *did* have the printer in stock, and just his luck, the fucking thing weighed more than a hundred pounds. No scanner, so he picked the next model up. Laptop, check.

It took him just five minutes to rush round the stockroom and grab the big ticket stuff on the list. Finally, impatient to get them the hell out of the shop and cash up and go home, Jason shoved the trolley back out onto the floor. Bill slouched behind the cash register, evidently chatting with the older customer. As he followed the cart out, Bill glared at him. "I wanna take this sale," he said.

"No you don't." Bill laid one hand on the trolley as the younger guy appeared round the end of an aisle, carrying a full basket. "You want to go home, kid, that's the only reason you were so fast. Go on, shove off."

"But I—"Now he got it: Bill would log himself in and process the sale and claim the commission, while Jason did all the heavy lifting.

"Think I'm stupid? Think I don't see you watching the clock? Shove off, Jason." Bill leaned towards him, menacing. "Unless you want me to notice your timekeeping."

The younger of the two customers glanced at Bill. "What is your problem?" he asked, placing his basket on the counter.

"We get a commission on each sale," mumbled Jason. "He's my supervisor."

"I see." The older customer looked at Jason, then at the trolley, then back at Jason. "Well, thank you for your fast work." He held out his hand, a couple of notes rolled between his fingers; Jason took them. He turned back to Bill. "Put the purchases on this card. We will need help loading them."

Jason nodded and headed for the back room to grab his coat. *Fucking Bill,* he thought disgustedly, then glanced at the banknotes before he slid them into his pocket.

There were five of them, and they were all fifties.

"I am sorry, but that's impossible, sir."

Rudi paused to buy himself time to find the words he needed. Standing up in front of the CO to brief him on a tool they'd never used before was hard work: How to explain? "The Saber 16 is an *ultralight*. It has to be—that's the only way I could carry it over here on my own. The wing weighs about a hundred pounds, and the trike weighs close to two hundred and fifty; maximum takeoff weight is nine hundred pounds, including fifty gallons of fuel and a pilot. You—I, whoever's flying the thing—steer it with your body. It's a sport trike, not a general aviation vehicle."

Earl Riordan raised an eyebrow. "I thought you could carry a passenger, or cargo?"

The question, paradoxically, made it easier to keep going. "It's true I can lift a passenger or maybe a hundred pounds of cargo, sir, but dropping stuff—anything I drop means taking a hand off the controls and changing the center of gravity, and that's just asking for trouble. I can dump a well-packaged box of paper off the passenger seat and hit a courtyard, sure, but a two-hundred-pound bomb? That's a different matter. Even if I could figure out a way to rig it so I could drop it without tearing the wing off or stalling, I'd have to be high enough up that the shrapnel doesn't reach me, and fast enough to clear the blast radius, and the Saber's got a top speed of only fifty-five, so I'd have to drop it from high up, so I'd need some kind of bombsight—and they don't sell them down at Wal-Mart. Sorry. I can drop grenades or flares, and given a tool shop and some help we might even be able to bolt an M249 to the trike, but that's all. In terms of military aviation we're somewhere round about 1913, unless you've got something squirreled away somewhere that I don't know about."

Earl Riordan stared at him for a few seconds, then shook his head. "No such luck," he grunted. "Damn their eyes." The CO wasn't swearing about him, for which Rudi was grateful.

"So what *are* you good for?" demanded Vincenze, loudly.

Rudi shrugged. The cornet had maybe had a drop too much rum in his coffee. Not terribly clever when you'd been summoned into the CO's office for a quiet chat, but then again nobody ever accused Vince of being long on brains: That wasn't much of an asset in a cavalryman.

"Fair-weather observation. Dropping small packets, accurate to within a hundred feet or so. If you can find me somewhere to land that isn't under the usurper's guns I can carry a single passenger in and out, or up to a hundred and fifty pounds of luggage."

"A single passenger." Hmm. The earl looked distracted. "Hold that thought. Out of curiosity, is it possible to parachute from the passenger seat?"

"Maybe, but it'd be very dangerous." Rudi didn't need to search for words anymore: they were coming naturally. "It's a pusher prop so you couldn't use a static line. It'd have to be free fall, which would mean close to maximum altitude—I can only reach five thousand feet with a passenger—and if their primary chute didn't open they wouldn't have time to try a secondary, and I'd have fun keeping control, too."

"So scratch that idea." Riordan raised his mug and took a mouthful of coffee. "Okay. Suppose you need to land somewhere, pick up a passenger, and fly out. What do you need?"

"A runway." Rudi glanced into his own coffee mug: It was still empty, dammit. "With a passenger, depends on the weather, but a minimum thousand feet to be safe. I can probably get airborne in significantly less than that, but if anything goes wrong you need the extra room to slow down again. Ideally it needs to be clear-cut for the same again, past the end of the runway—most engine problems show up once you're just airborne."

"A thousand feet?" Vincenze looked surprised. "But you took off from the courtyard!"

"That was me, without a passenger," Rudi pointed out. "At two-thirds maximum takeoff weight you get in the air faster and you can stop a lot faster, too, if something goes wrong. If you want to take off with less than five hundred feet of runway, you really need an ultralight helicopter or preferably a gyrocopter—ultralight choppers are dangerous. Oh, and a pilot who knows how to fly them. It was on my to-do list."

"Noted." Riordan jotted a note on his pad. "Assume bad people with guns are shooting at you when you take off. How vulnerable would you be?"

Rudi shivered. He'd been shot at before, in his previous flight. "Very. The Saber-16 can only climb at about six hundred feet per minute. Takeoff is about thirty miles per hour. Handguns or musketry I could risk, but if they've got rifles? Or M60s? I'm toast. I'd be in range for minutes."

"So we won't ask you to do that, then," Riordan muttered to himself. Louder: "Right. So, if we asked you to deliver a cargo weighing about a hundred and fifty pounds into the Hjalmar Palace you could land in the courtyard—as long as we've got the usurper's men out of that gatehouse—you could probably fly out of it on your own, but if you had a problem on takeoff you'd hit the wall, and again, the usurper's men would have you in rifle range for a minute or two. You can't fly at night, and you can't fly low enough to drop anything useful on the enemy without them riddling you with bullets. Am I missing anything? Is that a fair summary of your limitations?"

Rudi blinked. "Yes, sir, I think so. Uh, that and, we need

more gas. Sorry." He shrugged. "I think we've got about five gallons left. Avgas, not regular."

"Damn." Riordan glanced round. "Steward? More coffee." He turned back to the table. "Have Joachim and Stefan reported in yet?"

Vincenze looked thoughtful. "Not unless they've come in since we started in here."

"Go and chase them up, then."

Dismissed, Vincenze rose. He nodded at Rudi. "Good luck, cuz."

Startled, Rudi watched him leave.

"The cornet has no need to know what I'm about to tell you," Riordan said quietly. He paused while the steward placed fresh mugs of coffee in front of them. "That will be all."

"Sir." The steward bowed then left the room.

Rudi waited until the door was shut. "Sir, you obviously have something in mind?"

"Yes." Riordan fell silent. Then: "I sent Joachim and Stefan out to buy some office equipment. Most of a print shop, in fact—a laptop, graphics software, a printer, a scanner, and equipment for making badges."

"Badges?"

"You know of our long lost cousins, I take it?"

Rudi nodded cautiously. "I've never met any of them."

"Hmm." Riordan raised one eyebrow. "You will, soon enough." He picked up his coffee mug and blew on it. "When Joachim gets back he's to run off two hundred laminated color cards with our lost cousin's knotwork seal on it."

"Their—"Rudi stopped. "It's not the same as ours, is it?" he asked.

"No." Riordan put his mug down. "According to the duke, they became lost two centuries ago when—you know the story about how the seventh brother went west, to make a home for himself in the outer kingdom, what the Americans call California? He fell on hard times, and lost his sigil.

Later, he tried to recreate it from memory, and got it subtly wrong. That's why neither he nor his descendants could visit the United States; they found themselves in another world, only slightly different at that time. Anyway, we have a copy of the lost family's sigil, and we are going to make enough duplicates of it to equip every world-walker in the Hjalmar Palace. As its doppelganger site in Massachusetts is crawling with federal agents, and we have not accurately surveyed the terrain in the other world, you're going to fly the badges in."

Rudi's thoughts spun. "So I won't need to fly out? . . ."

"No. The duke's men will help you dismantle your aircraft and carry it with them when they leave. Lady Olga is developing the evacuation plan and will organize your logistics. The larger goal is to present the usurper with a tempting target, and then give him a nasty surprise when he tries to take it. Do you understand?"

"Yes, I think so. But I thought he knew about our talent? And is clearly taking pains to avoid situations where we can use it?"

"Indeed." The earl grinned humorlessly. "I'm counting on it. Egon knows about world-walking, and plans his moves accordingly. Which makes his behavior predictable . . . and I'm going to use that fact to kill him."

Mike Fleming was trapped in the basement of his apartment, trying to figure out how to get out, when the phone rang.

It was the colonel's fault. "Son, I'm relying on you to stay home and convalesce," he'd said sternly, after handing over a brown paper bag containing an anonymous mobile phone and a semiautomatic pistol. "I want you back in the saddle as soon as you're fit for duty. But you're not going to be any use to me if you overdo it. So relax, take it easy, and try to remember your job is to get well, and maybe see to the other thing." (The *other thing* being his mission if the Mad

Grandmother or the Ice Princess made contact—but Mike had an uneasy feeling that this latter duty was more than slightly deniable.) But there was only so much sitting on his ass that he could do, and after a few days frittered away watching *Friends* reruns and reading pop-history books about the Middle East, he was ready to climb the walls.

Hence, the basement.

Most apartments don't have basements, but the one Mike rented in a converted brownstone was the exception to the rule: A steep staircase opening off one wall of the kitchen led down into the low-ceilinged cellar. With perfect hindsight, Mike had to admit, deciding to clean house while recovering from a broken leg and a nasty little infection was not one of his most sensible moves. But once he'd gotten down those steps, it turned out that filling garbage sacks and trying to figure out how to dismantle the dead drier that had been stranded down here for years was a whole lot more attractive than trying to figure out how to get back up the stairs. Especially because he wasn't sure he'd be able to make it around the tight bend at the top, and having to phone for help to dig him out of his own cellar would really do his self-image no end of good. *(You're a special agent working for a secret government organization and you had to call in help to* climb a staircase? *What is this, the CIA?)*

Hence, the phone ringing while he was stuck in the basement.

Mike swore. The phone rang twice as he disentangled himself from the cable of the defunct drier and hopped around the workbench, trying to find the extension handset behind the pile of rusting paint cans and the overflowing toolbox. "Yes?" He barked, making a one-handed grab for the phone and simultaneously putting too much weight on his bad leg.

"Is that Mr Fleming?" It was a woman's voice, a noisy office providing unwelcome background context. *If this is a telesales call . . .* Mike felt a hot flash of anger, echoing the pain in his right ankle. About a week and a half ago he'd trodden on a man-trap—a mediaeval antipersonnel mine, as Sergeant Hastert had put it—and with the cracked bone, torn ligaments, and nice little infection he'd picked up, he'd been lucky to keep the leg.

"Who is this?" Mike demanded.

"I'm Letitia, from Family Home Services. Can I speak to Mr. Fleming, please?"

The spark of helpless anger passed rapidly. Mike blinked. "Yeah, that's me." He glanced round instinctively. "Free to talk." No, *not* a telesales call; the background office noise was a recording and the company name a cover. "It's Tuesday today, isn't it?"

"No, it's Wednesday," said the woman at the other end of the line, who wasn't called Letitia any more than it was any day other than Monday. "You're late for your CAT scan. Dr. James wants to see you as soon as possible, and as it happens we've got a slot free right now—are you free now?"

Mike glanced round at the dusty basement again, his pulse quickening. "I believe I can fit you in."

"Good. An ambulance will collect you in fifteen minutes, if that's convenient?"

"I'll be waiting." The usual pleasantries, and Mike hung up the handset, staring at it in surprise. So the colonel wanted to talk to him? But the colonel knew damn well what shape his leg was in, and the boss-man was in the loop, so what could he want? . . .

Mike began to smile, for the first time in days.

The ambulance that pulled up outside his front door twenty minutes later resembled any other one, and the two paramedics made short work of wheeling Mike—sitting up, chatting, no need to alarm the neighbors unduly—into the back of their vehicle. The door shut, and there the resemblance stopped: Normal ambulances didn't have door gunners in black fatigues riding behind the one-way glass windows. They didn't roll like a foundering ship beneath the weight of armor, either; and they especially didn't come with passengers like Dr. James, whose specialty was distinctly non-medical.

Dr. Andrew James scared the crap out of Mike Fleming, with his Ph.D. from Harvard and the flag pin that had lately replaced the tiny crucifix on his lapel. Gaunt and skinny and utterly dedicated, James attended to the ills of the body politic with all the care you could expect of an apprentice engineer of human souls; and if an amputation was required, he could get a consent form any time he liked, signed by the office of the vice president. And he didn't waste time. "How's your leg?" he asked as the ambulance moved off.

"Still bad, but I can get about indoors. Last time I asked they said I'd be able to get the cast off in another five weeks, be back to normal in three or four months." *Why is he asking me this stuff?* Mike stared at him sidelong. *It's not as if he can't pull my medical records any time he wants. . . .*

"Not good enough." James frowned, his lips forming a bloodless crease. "There's a change of plan."

Shit. Mike shivered under the thin thermal blanket the "paramedics" had draped over him. He could see what was coming next, like a freight locomotive glimpsed in the side window of his crossing-stalled car. *He's cutting around the chain of command. Which means I'm in trouble.* James was political, and even in the flattened wartime hierarchy of the Family Trade Organization he was several levels above Mike. If he was descending from on high to give Mike orders in person, it meant that either Mike's boss, Colonel Smith, was on the out—or that Mike was being snipped out of the org chart. Spoiled goods, a deniable asset, disposable on demand. "What do you want me to do?" he asked, keeping his face as still as possible.

The ambulance turned a corner and began to accelerate, swaying from side to side as it shoved across two lanes of traffic. "We've made a breakthrough in the past week, and it's led us to review our existing programs." James was looking at him, but not meeting his eyes. "You speak the bad guys' language, much as anyone does. We need you as an interpreter."

"But—"Mike shook his head, confused. "What about the negotiations?" Miriam's crazy mother and her sidekick, the blond sniper who looked like a Russian princess: They were supposed to be making contact, negotiating over the stolen nuke. "Don't you want—"

"Son, don't be naïve." Dr. James smiled, and this time he looked Mike in the eyes. Mike tried not to shiver; he'd seen a warmer smile on the face of the pet alligator he'd once tripped over in a drug dealer's pad. "The missing gadget has been retrieved so the negotiations are over. We don't need them anymore. Our job is now to hit these people so hard they won't ever be able to mess with the USA again." The ambulance bounced hard across a pothole and Mike's stomach lurched as he felt it accelerate down a steep gradient. "I don't think your contacts will be back, but if they are, it's kill-or-capture time."

"The phone? . . ." Colonel Smith had given him an untraceable mobile phone to pass on to the ice princess if the Clan wanted to negotiate.

"It's a Kidon special." Made by Mossad's—the Israeli secret service's—assassination cell. "It works fine, but there's ten grams of C5 in the earpiece. If one of them tries to call us, that's one less bad guy to worry about."

"Oh." For a moment a vision of Olga's blond head flashed through Mike's mind, bloodied and slack-jawed. He bit down on his reaction: *That's assassination!* Quiet terror made him swallow, queasy. "If that's the way you're playing it." *(You're a cop, he's a spook. You knew these things happened. So why's he telling you now?)* "You said you want an interpreter, but you're not talking to the Clan. So what's going on?"

"There's been a breakthrough." Dr. James leaned back against the side of the ambulance, his death's head grin fading. "Pretty soon we're not going to need the freaks for transport anymore, so we're winding up to restart CLEANSWEEP. This time we've got the logistic support to set up a full-scale branch office on the other side. You'll be going over in about three months as a civilian advisor. But in the meantime, I've got a little extra job for you as soon as you're cleared for duty again. You've already got a clearance; you're going to need a higher one for this job. Unless you think there's something that might disqualify you? . . ."

Mike swallowed again. "Uh, what do you mean?"

James gestured irritably: "I can't tell you what you're needed for until you've been cleared. Additional background checks will be required. So this is your chance to come clean about anything you wouldn't want to disclose during a polygraph interrogation."

"You're offering me an amnesty?" Mike raised an eyebrow.

"Son, *I* don't care if you're f— sleeping with the Russian ambassador's grandson; all I care is that you're not keeping secrets from *me,* you're not going to embarrass me in front of an internal affairs polygraph, and you're up to, to listening in a bunch of conversations in gook-speak and translating them into English for me. And keeping a lid on it. So. Is there anything you really *don't* want to be quizzed about during your clearance interview?"

"I—" the penny dropped. "It's not CLEANSWEEP that's so damn secret, is it?" he said without thinking. "It's the content, isn't it? You've got some kind of source—"

"Mr. Fleming." Dr. James's stare was leaden. "What do we pay you for?"

Mike winced. "Sorry. Forget I asked." He took a deep breath. "As for your question, I'm not blackmailable. Nothing to hide here." He tapped his chest. "So. When do I begin?"

"Soon as you go back to the office, son. You'll be scheduled for a full security re-cert within a couple of days, then I'll have some extra work for you. Which will go on your worksheet as routine admin, incidentally." James nodded to himself. "That should keep you busy right up until the invasion."

"Invasion?" Mike echoed incredulously. "You're going to invade the Gruinmarkt?"

"We're going to have to sooner or later. Unless you've got any better ideas for how we ought to handle the existence of such a major security threat to American soil? . . ."

"But how?"

James cast Mike a knowing look. "Ask me again when you're cleared."

2

RECEPTION COMMITTEE

❦

Baron Otto Neuhalle was afraid of very few things; the wrath of gods, the scorn of women, and the guns of his enemies were not among them. He was, however, utterly terrified of one man—Egon the First, former crown prince and now self-proclaimed monarch of Gruinmarkt. Egon was a handsome-faced, graceful, hale, and charismatic young man who had all the pity of a rattlesnake for those who failed him. Even if Otto hadn't failed *yet*, failure nevertheless looked disturbingly possible in light of the witch-clan's continuing occupation of the Hjalmar Palace. And the cloud of dust he could see from his vantage point near the brow of the hill was almost certainly the vanguard of Egon's army.

"Another hour, sir," said Anders, who had materialized at his elbow while he peered through the witch-bought "binoculars."

"Nonsense, they'll be three at least—" He blinked. "Wait. *What* will be another hour?"

"The ammunition, my lord."

"*Scheisse . . .*" Otto turned back to the castle, barely visible behind its banked ramparts on the other side of the moat and the sloped killing apron. Bodies littered the ground before it, and clouds of smoke still billowed from the gatehouse his men had latterly abandoned. He'd gotten two of the witch-clan's machine guns out of the gatehouse to cover his soldiers' retreat, but things hadn't gone well: The enemy forces had laid down a stupefying volume of fire, and they'd brought some kind of artillery with them, not honest cannon but an arquebus-sized tube that belched fingers of flame that exploded on impact. And his gunners, undertrained, had burned through their ammunition too fast. *They weren't supposed to counterattack for at least a day. If it hadn't been for that flying spy . . .* he shook his head. The buzzing witch-bird would cut less ice with his majesty than the heat-warped machine gun barrels and prematurely expended stockpiles of valuable, irreplaceable cartridges. "What word is there from Hern?"

"The waterway holds so far, my lord. That's recent."

Otto nodded thoughtfully. The castle's dependence for fresh water on a buried culvert leading to the nearby river was a weakness. If the new defenders were foolish enough to rely on the well, or the casks in the cellar . . . *no, they're not inexperienced.* He glanced at a nearby soldier. "You, March. Bring me paper. And pen. I have a report to write."

"My lord." March bowed and scurried back towards the hastily established headquarters tent.

And if I write well, will it save my neck? Otto suppressed a shudder. All told, it had been a *good* plan, and the witches had been on the back-foot for the past several weeks as the king's forces harried their homesteads and burned their crops—the plan to force them to counterattack in a place of his choosing, where they could be chopped up by the king's stealthily stolen machine guns and mines, was a good one. But the upstart clan of witches-turned-nobles had struck back viciously fast, and shown a good few surprises of their own, from the flying spy down. *And they can walk through the shadow world,* Otto reminded himself. Evidence of witchcraft, but he'd also seen a couple of them vanish in front of his own eyes: Otto was a believer. *What could I do with an army like that?* He raised his glasses again and peered at the castle. "Sir Anders," he said quietly. "A general order. Be on watch for the dog that fails to bark in the night. If any man notices that the enemy have fallen silent for more than a quarter of a bell, they are to send word to me immediately, regardless of the hour of day or night."

"Sir?" Anders raised a craggy brow.

"Who are we fighting, again?" Otto grinned sepulchrally as dawning understanding—and fear—crept across his hetman's face.

The dust cast up by the royal army crept closer over the next half hour as Otto scratched an abbreviated report, then sealed it in a hide tube and sent a messenger careening towards the vanguard. Occasionally he had one or another of his troops' pre-prepared positions light up the walls, or take careful aimed shots at the windows of the castle: The returning spasms of automatic fire were reassuringly solid, evidence that the enemy was not yet melting into shadows and mist that could reappear in his rear at any moment. Otto didn't waste his reprieve. His men were beginning to grumble about the amount of ditch-work he was making them dig, but his periodic rounds of the trenches and foxholes they were preparing kept the muttering under control. With a high, fine overcast to keep the sun off their necks, and no rain to bog them down, the weather wasn't giving them much to complain about—but if the witch-clan staged a breakout, or the king arrived to find the works incomplete, they'd have something to moan about for the rest of their lives, however short.

The shadows were beginning to lengthen across the apron in front of the castle (putting his snipers at a considerable disadvantage) when the first column of riders thundered up the valley floor and came to a stop by the guards. They didn't pause for long: After no small amount of shouting half a dozen of them walked on, mounts breathing heavily, towards the headquarters tent. Otto, who had been checking the second gun emplacement, steeled himself as he walked back downhill towards the group. He'd been expecting this moment, trying not to allow it to get in the way of his urgent defensive preparations for most of the day.

"Your Majesty." He bowed deeply, but without flourish.

"Otto." The golden boy's face was calm, but his eyes were stony. "Your tent, please. We will have words." The guards behind him sported strange black weapons, machine-pistols looted or stolen from the clan's dead.

"Yes, sire." He gestured towards the tent. "If you would follow me?"

"Certainly," Egon said, easily enough, but Otto had a hard time pretending to ignore the two guards who preceded them, or the two who took up stations beside the tent.

Inside the tent, the young king turned to face Otto. "What happened?" he asked. "In your own words."

"They counterattacked too early." Otto frowned. "We took the castle as planned. But we'd only been there for half a day when a witch—flying beneath a wing like a bat's—flew overhead. My men shot at him, but he got away. High up, high as an eagle. I redoubled my efforts to prepare the grounds, but only two hours later there was an explosion, then witch-troops everywhere. They came from inside the palace, as your majesty predicted, but they arrived before we were ready for them. Seven hours, I reckon, from our entry to their arrival."

"Seven hours . . ." Egon stared at Otto measuringly, although Otto couldn't guess whether it might be for a medal or a noose. "This flying witch. Describe what you saw."

Otto felt himself burst into chilly perspiration. "It made a buzzing noise, as of bees, only louder. . . ." He described the ultralight haltingly, its arrival from the southwest and subsequent departure after overflying the castle.

"And three hours later they arrived in force," Egon said musingly. "What of your force did you recover?"

The next ten minutes were the hardest examination of Otto's life, as he explained the precise disposition of his withdrawal. "In the end, we lost two of the machine guns, and we have but four gun barrels left. We have also expended all but four belts of ammunition," he finished. "Of men, eighteen dead and twenty-three wounded. The defensive positions are nearly complete, although I do not propose to defend them past dawn tomorrow—too much risk of the witches infiltrating our lines. My men are at your disposal, sire."

Egon glanced at the rough map of the surrounding area on Otto's camp chair. "Flying spies. Some sort of artillery—that's a new twist." He nodded to himself. "They are still bottled up in there?"

"Yes, sire." Otto nodded back, reflexively. "I've detailed my men to tell me at once if the witches stop replying to our probing fire. But so far they're sitting tight. It's almost as if they can't simply walk away."

For the first time, the young king's poker face relaxed. "Well." His lips quirked. "You've done no worse than aught of our commanders might. And that flying witch—yes." He nodded briskly. "Bravely done, Baron Neuhalle." Then he smiled, and Otto's blood ran cold at the look in the royal eyes. "Something you might not know about the witches is that they have to use their magic sparingly—should they walk through the paths of the dead too frequently, they fall ill and die. By your own word it is barely a day since they retook the palace. Normally that would be enough time to allow them to escape, but I have intelligence that suggests to me a new possibility. Your men did succeed in dropping the culvert and poisoning the well, I trust?" Unsure where this was leading, Otto nodded. "Good." The king clapped his hands. "Krentz. Fetch Sir Geraunt and Baron Rolfuss."

"Sire." One of the bodyguards bowed, then ducked through the tent door; the other visibly tensed, watching Otto alertly.

"Your Majesty?" Otto tried not to let his own tension show.

"We're going to take them." Egon's eyes twinkled.

"Because, you see, they are not only under siege *here*. They may be able to walk through the realm of the dead, but the dead, I am informed, have taken a dislike to them. They won't be able to escape this time. All that remains to be established is how we may dig them out of that castle. And my other intelligence suggests a solution."

The house squatting behind the densely tree-clad hillside had seen better years, that much was clear: its wooden decking needed a fresh coat of paint, the shingled roof was silver and cracked behind the eaves, and the chain-link fence that surrounded the acre lot was rusted. But the padlock holding the gate closed was well-oiled, and as she followed Brill and her team of bright young adventurers up the front steps, Miriam spotted the discreet black dome of a CCTV camera lurking in the shadows of the verandah. That, at least, looked to be new and well-maintained.

"It's a safe house," Brill explained as she pushed buttons on an alarm system that was far fancier—and newer—than the building it was attached to. "We own a bunch of them, lease them out for short stays via a local Realtor, so there's a lot of turnover. There's always one free when we need it, and it doesn't look suspicious. We actually make money on the deal: We can buy the properties with spare capital and they're mostly going up."

Miriam glanced around as they entered the front hall. Dust tickled her nostrils; the husk of a dead beetle lay, legs upturned, in the middle of the floor. She wrinkled her nose. "What's the plan?"

"Oh, I just phoned the Realtor and told them I was a friend of the owner and we were taking it for two weeks." She held up a key. "There's some emergency gear stashed in the cellar, behind a false wall. Other than that, it's clean—the emergency gear's the kind of stuff a survival nut would have, nothing to attract special attention. The only real trouble we've

ever had with these safe houses was when one of them was
accidentally let to a meth dealer. We cleared them out good.
The Sheriff's department *like* us." She said it with such evident satisfaction that Miriam shivered. For a meth dealer,
setting up a clandestine lab in a Clan safe house was a bit
like a fox setting up house in a grizzly's den. "You may want
to take the front bedroom, milady. I'll get the air and hot water working and everyone else settled in, then we can talk."

Three hours later, Miriam felt a lot more human. Air conditioning! Proper showers! Toilets with lids and a handle
you turned to flush, rather than yanking on a chain! It was
almost like being home again. Brill had even, somehow, managed to find the time to scare up some clothes that fit her, so
she didn't look totally weird. Well, Brill had been her lady-
in-waiting for some months; as one of the jobs she did for
the thin white duke—Miriam's uncle—knowing her mea-
surements wasn't that odd. It was a shame she'd bleached
her hair blond while she'd been on the run, Miriam told
herself; the colors Brill had picked didn't match her new
look, and besides, her roots were starting to show.

But I'm home. So, what now?

She sat on the edge of the bed, one leg of a very new pair
of jeans dangling, and stared at the window. So unlike the
stony castle casement she'd spent weeks staring at in a state
of desperation, under house arrest and facing a forced political marriage as a lesser evil to paying the price of her
earlier mistakes, but it was still a window in a house guarded
by the Clan's traditions and rules. The formal betrothal had
gone adrift in a sea of flame and gunfire, as crown prince
Egon took exception to the idea of a Clan heiress marrying
his younger (and retarded) brother; then she'd been running
through the confusing political underworld of New Britain,
too fast to think. But now—

It all depends on what else has been going on since I left.
She sighed and began to work her other foot down the pants
leg. *Is Mom okay?* She paused again. *Brill said something*

about being under attack over here. Is Paulie *okay?* Paulette, her sometime PA, was an outsider to all this—but stuck in Cambridge, if the Clan was being attacked from outside, she could be in big trouble. Guilt by association: Some within the Clan would see her as a tool tainted by Miriam's low stock, while whatever agency was going after the Clan would assume the worst. *I've got to find out,* Miriam decided, and stood up just as there was a tentative knock at the door.

"Come in," she called, hastily buttoning up.

The door opened and Brilliana looked in. "Milady?"

"I'm nearly done here." Miriam glanced around. "Where did I put my shoes?" Handmade leather ankle-boots from New Britain wouldn't look too out of place, and shoes were the one thing Brill hadn't been able to buy for her. "Eh." They were hiding under the dressing table.

"I think we need to talk," Brilliana observed.

"Yes." Miriam bent over and began working on her left foot. "What exactly has been going on since the, the banquet?" Her brain began to catch up with her earlier thoughts: "My mother—is she alright? What about the duke? My grandmother—"

"It's a mess," Brill said wryly. She perched on the stool by the table. "We're not sure exactly how long Egon had been planning it for, but he used Henryk's scheme"—the plan to forcibly marry Miriam into the Gruinmarkt's royal dynasty—"as leverage to get a bunch of the backwood peers behind him. He's declared the entire Clan outlaw and placed a price on our heads, and is promising half our estates to those nobles who back him. It's turned into a messy civil war and Angbard's had his hands tied trying to defend individual holdings instead of going after the pretender's army. While all that was going on, we've had some disturbing— well, a couple of couriers have gone missing over the past six months. Missing with no explanation, no hint of trouble. Not only did the bastard Matthias rat us out to the Drug Enforcement Agency, now there's some sort of secret government cross-agency committee trying to hunt us down. Everyone on this side has had to activate their emergency cover plans. And the really bad news is that this agency managed to sneak a couple of agents into the Gruinmarkt, which means it's serious."

"Yes, I know." Miriam sat up and took a deep breath. "I told you about meeting Mike, didn't I?" She'd once had a thing going with Mike Fleming. Odd, it seemed an awfully long time ago. "He got me out of the palace alive." She shrugged. "He was unexpectedly honest." Another deep breath. "Told me that if I wanted to join the federal witness protection program . . ."

The words hung in the air for a few seconds. Finally, Brilliana nodded. "We know. And it will count for much when it comes to the Council's attention, I think," she said slowly. A longer pause. "Olga and your mother have been talking to him. Trying to negotiate a, a temporary ceasefire. But things are really bad. They believe we've stolen a nuclear weapon, and they want it back."

"Jesus." Miriam shook her head. "Why would they think *that?*" She looked at Brill, aghast. "Hang on. They *believe* the Clan has stolen a *nuke? Why?* Why would they believe that? Has Angbard— He'd have to be mad! Tell me he hasn't?"

Brill looked uncomfortable. "*Angbard* hasn't stolen a nuke. But they leave them in undoppelgangered bunkers; is that not a temptation?"

"Tell me." Miriam shoved her hair back from her face. "Has someone in the Clan actually gone and stolen a nuclear weapon? How? I mean, I thought they were too big to carry—"

"Not one," Brill said, then bit her lip. "Six, we think. Maybe more. They're backpack devices, part of the inactive inventory—the CIA asked for them, originally."

Aghast, Miriam stared at her. "Is that why they're all over us?"

Brill nodded.

"Then who—"

"Oliver, Earl Hjorth, is the key-holder designated by the Clan committee."

"Jesus, why *him?*" The thought of what might happen if the feds discovered the Clan had haunted Miriam ever since she'd learned about her own ancestry; what they might do if they thought the extradimensional narcoterrorists had nuclear weapons didn't bear thinking about. And Baron Oliver was about the worst person she could think of to be holding them—an unregenerate backwoodsman and dyed-in-the-wool conservative faction member. "And they can get their own people into the Gruinmarkt, can't they."

"There's more bad news," Brill added after a moment. "Why don't you come downstairs? Then Huw can deliver it himself."

Elena sprawled across the sofa in the living room, pulling an oiled cleaning cloth through the breech of her P90. "Find another channel, minion," she drawled without looking up. "I can't *stand Friends.*"

"As you wish, my princess." Yul, hulking and fair-haired as any Viking warrior, carefully squeezed the remote. Advertisements and sitcoms strobed across the eviscerated guts of the machine pistol on the coffee table until he arrived at MTV. "Ah, that is better." Marilyn Manson strutted and howled through the last tour on earth; Elena pulled a face. "Manly music for martial—" an oily rag landed on his head.

"Children."

Elena glanced round, pulled a face. "*He* started it!"

"Sure." Huw stood in the doorway, trying not to smile. "Did you get the Internet working?"

"Something's wrong with it," Yul said apologetically.

"Ah, well." Huw shrugged and walked over to the armchair, where a laptop trailed bits of many-colored spaghetti towards the wall. "I'll sort it out. Got to report in." Expect-

ing Yul or Elena to do anything technical had been a for-
lorn hope. *Am I the only competent person around here?* he
wondered. Dumb question: While he'd been studying in
schools and colleges in the United States under a false identity, Yul had been bringing joy to their backwoods father's
heart, riding and hunting and being a traditional son on
their country estate in the western marches of the Gruinmarkt; and Elena had been under the stifling constraints of
a noble daughter, although she'd kicked up enough of a fuss
that her parents had allowed her to escape into Clan Security, leaving them with one less dowry to worry about. Which
left Huw as the guy who knew one end of an Internet router
and a secure voice-over IP connection from another, and
Yul and Elena as the armed muscle to watch over him when
they weren't engaging in risky post-adolescent high-jinks—
risky because the older generation weren't many years past
fighting blood feuds over that sort of thing.

It took him a few minutes, some scrabbling with cables,
and a reboot to get everything working properly, but Huw
was setting up the encrypted link to the ClanSec e-mail hub
and looking forward to checking in when he heard footsteps.

"Yes?" He glanced round. It was Miriam. She looked—
not tired, exactly, but careworn. And something else.

"Brill tells me we need to talk," she said, then glanced
across the room at the sofa.

"She said—"Huw's larynx froze for a few seconds as he
stared at her. The first time he'd met her, gowned and bejew-
eled at a royal reception, she'd been turned out in the very
mode of Gruinmarkt nobility; then earlier, when Lady Brilliana had so rudely yanked him (and Yul, and Elena) away
from his survey, she'd been wearing an outlandish getup.
Now she looked—*at ease,* he decided. *This is her. She isn't
acting a part. How* interesting. "Ah. Well, she did, did she?"

"She said." Miriam leaned on the back of his chair.
"You've been exploring. Whatever that means." She sounded
bored, but there was a glint in her eye.

"Uh, yeah." Huw leaned forward and shut the laptop's

lid. "Why don't we go fix something to drink?" He glanced sidelong at Yul and Elena, who were sitting on the sofa, bickering amiably over the gun, their heads leaning together. "Somewhere quieter." The TV howled mournfully, recycling the sound track of a guitar in torment.

The kitchen was bland, basic, and undersupplied—they'd traveled light and hadn't had time to buy much more than a bunch of frozen pizzas—but there was coffee, and a carton of half-and-half, and a coffee maker. Huw busied himself filling it while Miriam searched the cupboards for mugs. "How did you go about it?" she asked, finally.

Huw took a deep breath. "Systematically. We haven't started de-convoluting the knotwork"—the two worlds to which the Clan's members could walk were distinguished by the use of a different knot that the world-walker had to concentrate on—"but I'm pretty sure we'll start finding others once we do. The fourth world we found—it's accessed from this one, if you use the Lee's knot. We couldn't get through to it in New England, but it worked down south; I think it may be in the middle of an ice age."

"Did you find anyone? People, I mean?"

"Yes." Huw paused as the coffee maker coughed and grumbled to itself. "Their bones. A big dome, made out of something like, like a very odd kind of concrete. Residual radioactivity. A skull with perfect dentistry, bits of damaged metalwork, fire escapes or gantries or something, that I'll swear are made out of titanium. It's clearly been there decades or centuries. And then there's the door."

"Door?"

"Yul hit it with an axe. Nearly killed us—there was hard vacuum on the other side."

"Whoops." Miriam pulled out a stool and sat down at the breakfast bar. "Too fast. *Vacuum?* You think you found a *door* onto another world?"

"We didn't stick around to make sure," Huw said drily. "But it didn't stop sucking after a couple of minutes. Last time we saw the dome, it was surrounded by fog."

"Oh my." Her shoulders were shaking. "God."

Huw watched her, not unsympathetically. He'd had more than a day to get used to the idea: If Lady Brilliana was right—and his own judgement was right—and Miriam was fit to lead them . . .

"That changes a lot of things," she said, looking straight at him. "If it *is* a door to another world . . . how do you think it works?"

Huw shrugged again. "We are cursed by our total ignorance of our family talent's origins," he pointed out. "But what we seem to have is a trait that can be externally controlled—that's what the knot's for—and I figure if it turns out that other knots take us to other worlds, then it's no huge leap to conclude that it was engineered for a purpose. I don't think anyone's looked inside us—I figure the mechanism, if there is one, has got to be something intracellular—but the fact that it's controllable, that we don't world-walk at random when we look at a maze or a fractal generator on a PC, screams design. This door? There's more stuff in that dome, lots more, and it looks like wreckage left behind by a civilization more advanced than this one." He pointed at the coffee maker. "Think what a peasant back home would make of that? You know, and I know, what it is and how it works, because we went to school and college in this country." He pulled the jug out and poured two mugs of coffee. "Electricity. But to a peasant . . ."

"Magic." The word hung in the air as Miriam poured milk into both mugs.

"So." He chose his words carefully. "What do you think it means?"

"Oh boy." Miriam stared at her coffee mug, then blew on it and took a first sip. "Where do you want me to start? If nothing else, it makes all the Clan's defensive structures obsolete overnight. One extra universe is useful, two is embarrassing, three extra universes implies . . . more. Which means, assuming there are more, that doppelgangered houses stop being effectively defended." Doppelgangering—the practice of building defenses in the other worlds, physically colocated with the space occupied by the defended structure, in order to stop hostile world-walkers gaining access—was a key element in all the Clan families' buildings. But you could build an earth berm or a safe house in one parallel universe—how could you hope to do it if there were millions? "And then . . . well. I tried telling the Council their business model was broken, but I didn't realize *how* broken it was."

"Really?" Huw leaned forward.

"Really." She put her mug down. "The—hell, I'm doing it again. Distancing. *We* got rich in the Gruinmarkt by exploiting superior technology—being able to move messages around fast, make markets, that kind of thing. And we got rich in *this* world"—she glanced at the window, which opened out onto an unkempt yard—"by smuggling. But what they were *really* doing was exploiting a development imbalance. Making money through a monopoly on superior technology—okay, call it a family talent, and it may be something you can selectively breed for, but if you're right and it's a technology, then *it's not a monopoly anymore.*"

"Uh." Huw took a mouthful of coffee. "What's your reasoning?"

"Well. You're the one who just told me you thought our ability was artificial? And we've established that someone else—let's take your door into a vacuum realm as a given—has a way of moving stuff between time lines—yes, I'm going to take the idea that we're in a bunch of parallel universes that branch off each other as a given. New Britain really rubs your nose in it—and I think if they can just *open a door* then we have to admit that what the Clan can do? The postal corvée? Is a joke."

Miriam closed her eyes for a moment. "The Council are *so* not going to want to hear this. And it's not the worst of it."

"There's more?" Huw stared at her, fascinated. *Have you figured out the other thing? . . .*

"Okay, let's speculate wildly. There are other people out

there who can travel between parallel worlds. They're better at it than us, and they know what they're doing. That's really bad, right there, but not necessarily fatal. However . . . we've been pointedly ignoring, all along, the fact that what we do isn't magical. It's not unique. It's like, after 1945, the government pretended for a few years that making nuclear weapons was some kind of big secret. Then the Russians got the bomb, and the Brits, and the Chinese, and before you can blink we're worrying about the North Koreans, or the Iranians. What the Clan Council needs to worry about is the US government—who they've spent the past few decades systematically getting mad at them—and who now know we exist. What do *you* think?"

"But we don't know how the world-walking mechanism works. It's got to take them time—"

Miriam took another mouthful of coffee. "They've had *seven or eight months,* Huw. That's how long it's been since Matthias went over the wall. And there's"—she paused, as if considering her words—"stuff that's happened, stuff that will turn hunting us down into a screaming crash priority, higher than al Qaida, higher than the Iraq occupation. They've got to be throwing money at . . ." She trailed off.

"I don't think they'll have got anywhere yet." Huw reached for the coffee pot again, emptying the dregs into their mugs. "It takes time to organize a research project and they'll be doing it under conditions of complete secrecy."

"Yes, but they've already got the big national laboratories. And if they've got captive Clan members they're *starting* from where the Clan stood, as of forty-eight hours ago. And they could have started months ago! It all depends on whether the problem they're trying to crack is a hard one or an easy one. If we've got some kind of mechanism that lets us do this, then it's designed to replicate, and there's got to be some sort of control system wired into our brains—are you telling me nobody has put bits of a Clan member under an electron microscope before to look for anomalies?"

"You've met enough of your cousins by now. How many

brain surgeons did you spot?" Huw looked defensive. "It wasn't a high priority."

"Well it is, *now*. Because if they can figure out what makes us world-walk, they're probably halfway to mass-producing it. Given they've got scouts in the Gruinmarkt—"

"They've got *what?*" Huw sat bolt-upright.

"Eh." Miriam cocked her head to one side. "Forget I said that?"

"Sure . . . can I finish your sentence?"

"Um . . ."

"Right now, any scouts they can send our way are going to be riding piggyback. Lightning Child knows how they're making the couriers cooperate, but nothing would surprise me: The current administration are so Machiavellian they make Prince Egon look like a White House intern. But what you're speculating about is how long we've got until there's a large-scale incursion." Her expression made him look for other words. "*Invasion*. Is that what you're thinking?"

Miriam nodded. "I— No, *we*—have got to talk to Angbard, and fast. Whatever the prince has been up to back, uh, home"—he spotted the moment's deliberation before she chose the word—"it's a sideshow compared to what's coming. I don't know how long we've got, but I'd guess it's going to be weeks to months, not months to years." She pushed her empty mug away. "Do you have Google on that laptop of yours?"

"What are you thinking of trawling for?"

"News items. Foreign stuff, not more shit about Paris Hilton's funeral; I want to hear about anything that suggests that State is planning a hasty exit from Iraq. They're not going to try and occupy Iraq and Afghanistan *and* invade the Gruinmarkt simultaneously, are they?" She slid off her bar stool, visibly jittery. *Iraq* had been a ghastly object lesson in what the current administration could do to people they didn't like: the increasingly desperate pleas of the coup plotters after they deposed Saddam, the cringing threats of

gas attacks in event of invasion—and in response, the huge
B52 raids on Baghdad. All of it had been calculated to send
a message, *this is what you get if you mess with us.*

"Depends." Huw reached over and switched off the coffee maker. "Don't they have some kind of doctrine about
being able to fight two wars simultaneously, anywhere on
the planet? And the supply lines to the Gruinmarkt are *real*
short, if they can build a world-walking machine. Or gate."

"And mostly they'd be up against irregulars with mus-
kets. They could roll over in their sleep and crush us, if—"

A door slammed in the passage. Moments later, Brill
darted into the kitchen. "Oh. There you are!" Visibly agitated,
she focused on the coffee pot. "Ah, you emptied it. Huw. Have
you brought the e-mail service to life?"

"Not yet, I was going to—"

"Scheisse." Brill glanced aside. "I'm sorry, milady. The
news is bad. I *must* get in touch right away. Huw, if you
would be so good—"

"What's happened?" demanded Miriam.

"My pager ordered me to call in, in the clear—maximum
urgency. It's the duke, my lady. I'm afraid there's been an
accident."

There was a room on one of the upper floors of the Hjalmar
Palace with a huge canopied bed in it, and the bed stank of
death and uncontrolled bowels. Lady Olga sat on the edge
of the bed and spoke to its occupant, as a medic cleaned
him and a soldier stood by waiting to replace the fouled
sheets.

He'd been strong once, and clever and ruthless, a bul-
wark for his allies and a terror to his faction's foes, during
the years of madness when the Clan's member families had
engaged in a bloody succession of mortal feuds. Then, as the
madness receded, he'd helped broker a series of treaties—
some on paper, others cemented by blood in marriage—to
disarm the worst of the remaining hostilities. He'd risen to

dominate the Clan's external security apparat, modernizing it and turning it into the glue that bound the new settlement together. The hammer of the council, his combination of force and guile had cowed the hotheads and brought the wily to his table. But he was just one man—now paralyzed on one side and barely conscious, lonely and adrift in what might be his deathbed.

"We're holding out," she said quietly, touching his immobile left hand, hoping against hope for a reaction. "Earl Fredryck's observers report that the federal presence at the doppelganger site is continuing, but all our people made it across ahead of the siege. We have plenty of ammunition. The monarchists dropped the culvert from the river, and attempted to poison the well, but the osmotic purifier is working. Earl Riordan reports that the pretender's army is encamped athwart the valley just downriver of the bend, 'tween here and Wergatsfurt. The scouts are already preparing a route for us through New Britain, once Riordan's men have manufactured a sufficiency of knotwork badges."

The duke made an odd noise in the back of his throat, something between a cluck and a gurgle. Olga leaned close, trying to discern words. His eyes rolled, agitated: "Guh-uh . . ."

"Fear not, we have prepared for you." A fireman's carry and a hike in the dark—then, if he survived the one kilometer haul, a stealthy transit back to the American side, land of neurological wards and intensive care facilities, where a private ambulance would be waiting to whisk him to a hospital bed. "The body of the force will return, taking the Pervert's army in the rear if he's still encamped. And should he occupy the palace, we have a warm welcome prepared for him."

Olga was of the opinion that it was better to beg forgiveness than to ask permission; and in any event, the warm welcome in question was one with a short expiry date—shorter than ever, now that she'd learned what that thrice-cursed bastard idiot Matthias had told the DEA, or whoever they were. And what Otto had been doing was the icing on a very unpalatable cake. To his credit, he'd actually *volunteered* the information. "Baron Henryk never put his faith in intangibles," he'd explained. "He wanted to *see* these mythical nuclear weapons. He wanted to *own* them. He argued about it with the duke, but then the duke changed his mind—one suspects Matthias forged his signature on the letter—and so the baron set me to oversee Matthias on organizing the theft. It was meant to be a harmless shell game, and additional leverage in council. Nobody had looked at them for more than eight years! How were we to know Matthias would sell his story to the outlanders?"

"Guh. Uh. Pa. Pat. Uh." He was clearly trying to say something. Alerted, Olga leaned closer.

"Please, I ask you, try to speak slowly. Is it a person?"

"Uh!"

"Patricia?" It was the obvious name: his half sister, mother of Helge, the wayward wildcat orphan and loose cannon who called herself Miriam.

"Yuh."

"Oh! Good. Do you want to see her?" *That could be difficult.* Like most of the Clan's elders who were familiar with American culture, she'd vanished into a deep cover identity when the shit hit the fan, and trying to bring her over could draw attention to her.

"Nuh."

"Alright." Olga racked her mind for options. "Do you have a message for her? Or about her? Hang on, if it's a message for her, blink once? About her, twice?"

One blink.

Olga sat up, heart hammering. *He's still inside there.* A hot flush of relief washed over her: The idea that Angbard, Duke Lofstrom, had lost his mind had been too terrible to voice, or even think. Paralyzed, deathly sick, but still the will to control went on. . . . "Can you spell it out? One for no, two for yes?"

Blink-blink.

"Milady, he looks very weak to me—" The first-aider sounded worried.

"He's the best judge of his condition," she said sharply. "And if he has a message of such import, he must give it. Have you pen and paper?"

"Uh, yes, milady."

"Then take a note."

It took half an hour, but they extracted two sentences from the duke before the corpsman's entreaties began to sway Olga. False starts and mistakes made it a frustrating process—but his words dispelled any remaining fear she had for his mind. Finally, she sighed and stood up. "I'll see it gets to her," she reassured the duke. "Tomorrow, we'll get you to a proper hospital bed. I must go now." She bowed and stepped back, then took the sheet of paper from the corpsman's pad. "You heard nothing," she warned him. "This must go no further. And the duke needs to rest now."

"Milady." He bowed as she left the room and hurried towards the improvised communications center downstairs.

Carl, Earl of Wu by Hjorth—and the commander of the small army currently encamped in the castle—looked up as she entered. By a miracle, Oliver, Earl Hjorth, was absent. "What news?"

"Nothing bad." She hurried to his side at the map table. "He's sleeping now," she continued quietly, "but he's very weak. The good news is, he has his senses. He gave me a message to relay to Patricia Thorold-Hjorth by any means necessary."

"He's talking? . . ." Carl's fist clenched.

"Do not hope for too much. It took much work to say this much." She passed him the note. "Please, send this by way of Earl Riordan. There is no way of knowing how long it will take to reach her, and I fear it may be urgent. I'd advise keeping it from Earl Oliver."

"Alright." Carl took the piece of paper and stared at it. "What does it mean?"

"You'll find out," Olga assured him. "In good time."

TELL PATRICIA GIVE CLINIC RECORDS TO HELGE. GET HELGE IN FRONT OF COUNCIL. MY WORD, HER PLAN B ONLY WAY FORWARD NOW.

3

WET WORK

❧

Owntown Boston, in summer: humid and warm and smelly with truck exhaust fumes, rumbling and roaring from the nearby turnpike. A well-dressed woman in late middle age driving an electric wheelchair along the sidewalk, chatting to a young woman walking beside her—a daughter, perhaps, or carer. The security guard glanced away from his screen, uninterested. He didn't notice them stop and turn abruptly to enter the lobby of the office suite he was supposed to be monitoring. Not that it would have made any difference. They didn't look like the sort of people he was supposed to keep out, and their faces didn't feature on any watch list of undesirables. Not that he'd have been able to keep them out, even if they did.

The woman in the wheelchair hummed towards the receptionist's station. "Iris Beckstein, to see Dr. Darling. He's expecting me." She smiled at the secretary: the self-assured smile of the financially secure.

"Sure, sign in here. . . ."

The receptionist's lack of interest was convenient, Iris noted; possibly the doctor had encouraged it, although if so, his overreliance on other security precautions was risky. Iris signed, and nodded, and waited while her companion signed. False names, one and all, but the false name she was using would be a red flag to the people who would, in due course, check the visitor book.

"This way, dear," Iris told her companion, then scooted towards the elevators. Mhara nodded and followed obediently, keeping her mouth shut. Despite having a good understanding of the tongue, she'd spent little enough time in America that her accent was still heavy. Most folks would mistake her for an Eastern European immigrant, but Iris didn't feel like taking risks around this office—especially in view of the contents of her bag. As the doors slid shut, Iris reached for the fourth floor button. "On my word—but not a moment sooner," she said in hochsprache, the underused words heavy in her mouth.

"Yes, milady."

"You are about to be exposed to some of our most perilous secrets. If they confuse or dismay you, you may speak to me about them in private—but they must go no further."

They ascended the rest of the way in silence. The lift was unusually slow, and Iris spent the time trying to relax. *Adrenaline makes fools of us all*, she reminded herself, then blinked irritably as the elevator doors opened. *Ah, well*.

The office suite was surprisingly quiet for this time of day, a few people moving between card-key-locked doors clutching mugs and papers. Iris rolled along the corridor, following memorized directions, until she found the correct door. She reached up with a card, swiped it, and pushed through as the lock clicked open.

"Hey, you can't come in—"

"Cover," she said in hochsprache. "Hello, Griben. Sit down, please." The door clicked shut behind Mhara as she felt the weight of an empty leather shoulder bag land on one of her chair's handles.

Griben ven Hjalmar, plump and goateed, in a brown three-piece suit, sat down slowly, keeping his hands clearly visible. His face was expressionless. The other man sitting in the swivel chair behind the desk was frozen in surprise. "And Dr. Darling. What a pleasant surprise."

"Mrs. Beckstein? What's the"—Darling swallowed convulsively—"what's going on?"

Iris smiled crookedly. "Griben, what a coincidence. I was just thinking about looking you up. What brings you here? Thinking about cleaning up some loose ends?"

Dr. Darling—lean, middle-aged, the picture of a successful gynecologist—was looking between ven Hjalmar, Iris, and the muzzle of Mhara's silenced Glock in slack-jawed surmise. "You—you—"

"I'd like to thank you both for the little number you played on my daughter. It wasn't *quite* what I had in mind when I suggested the arrangement."

Ven Hjalmar flushed beneath the force of her glare. "What did you *expect* us to do?" he demanded. "She was under house arrest! With an execution warrant on her head! You wanted the leverage—"

"Nevertheless." Iris shifted uncomfortably in her wheelchair. "This is neither the time nor the place for this discussion."

"Excuse me?" Three heads turned to stare at Dr. Darling. "What are you—"

"Griben, do you mind?" Iris asked casually, speaking hochsprache.

"If you absolutely must. I'd finished with him, anyway."

"Did you get the disks from him?" she added.

"Of course."

"What do you *want*?" demanded Darling.

In hochsprache: "Mhara, *now.*"

Outside the office, the two muffled shots would be mistaken for a door banging. Darling dropped forward across his desk, spilling blood and fatty tissue onto the keyboard of his PC.

Griben sighed. "Was that strictly necessary?"

"Yes," Iris said shortly. She glanced round. Mhara was standing, frozen, her pistol angled slightly upwards and a confused look in her eyes. "Mhara? Child?"

The young woman shook her head. "I'm sorry." She picked up the shoulder bag and carefully stowed her pistol inside, using hook-and-eye strips to secure it. "Never done that before."

"You've attended executions, surely. . . ."

"Yes, milady. But it's *different* when you do it yourself."

"You'll get used to it," Iris reassured her. "Griben, he knew too damned much. Family Trade are on our tail and he's not Outer Family or personal retainer. He had to go. You've got the disks. Mhara, the other device, please."

"Other—oh." Ven Hjalmar looked at the PC in distaste. "You don't expect me to"—

"I surely do." Iris held up a pair of latex gloves. "You'll want these."

None of them were particularly experienced at black-bag jobs; it took them nearly ten minutes to unscrew the casing of the PC and position the bulk eraser's electromagnet above the hard disk drive. Finally, Iris hit the power switch. "Ah, good," she said, as the disk error warning came up on the blood-specked screen. "Mhara, you see the filing cabinets yonder? You take the right one, Griben can take the middle, and I shall take the left. Start at the top and work down. You are looking for anything pertaining to Applied Genomics Corporation, the W-316 clinical trial, Angbard Lofstrom, Griben ven Hjalmar here, or adoption papers relating to children."

"*Adoption* papers?" Mhara sounded confused.

"Legal documents," Iris said blandly.

"Iris." Griben looked worried. "This is going to take some time. What if someone—"

Iris snorted. "You have your locket, yes? I had the site prepared."

"But we're on the fourth floor!"

"So there's a net. Try not to break your nose with your kneecaps. It'll be harder for me if we have to take it, so let us start searching right away, no?" She levered herself out of her wheelchair and shuffled cautiously towards the wall of cabinets.

The office was overheated, and the smells of burned powder and spilled blood hung over them as they pored over the file drawers. After ten minutes Griben finally hit pay dirt. "He had a file on Applied Genomics," he announced.

"Ah, excellent." Iris gestured at her wheelchair. "In there."

"Milady." Mhara gestured politely at another drawer. "Is this important?"

Iris leaned over to look. "Well, how interesting." She lifted the fat, spiral-bound document out of its hanger. "Names and addresses. It seems you're not the only doctor who doesn't trust computers to remember everything for you, Griben."

"Dash it! We specifically told him *not* to do that!"

Iris sighed. "I ordered someone to black-bag his house this morning. His divorce came through nine months ago, so I think there is no need to trouble his ex-wife and children." She frowned, pensive. "What have I forgotten?"

Griben nodded across the room. "I should check the bookcase. And the desk drawers. Just to be sure."

"An excellent idea. Perhaps you'd like to see me out, afterwards?"

Ven Hjalmar raised an eyebrow. "Why—"

Iris nodded at Mhara. "She has other tasks."

"Ah, jolly good." He nodded. Mhara picked up the files and waited attentively as he scoured the bookcases and finally the desk drawers—working carefully around Dr. Darling's body—then nodded again. "That's all," he announced. Darling's desk was mostly for show; beyond the usual collection of stationery items, the pedestal unit was empty.

Iris shuffled back to her wheelchair. "Good. Mhara?"

"Milady." She bobbed her head, holding the files two-handed.

"I want these files burned before we leave the building. Afterwards, make your way back to the house when you are ready."

"Yes, milady." Mhara smiled, a brief flash of expression crossing her face. Then she tilted her left wrist to expose the face of a wristwatch, and vanished.

"You're sure about the net," Griben said reflectively.

"*She's* sure about it, and that's what matters." Iris lowered herself carefully into the wheelchair. "Mind you, she was there when I ordered its construction."

A thoughtful pause, then: "I think I can see where your daughter gets it from."

"Oh dear." Iris whirred towards the door, then glanced over her shoulder with a fey expression. "Come *on*, Griben! We have a conspiracy to conceal and if you keep thinking about it we'll be here until suppertime."

They left the room with the conviction of a job well done, and no inkling of the significance of the encrypted memory stick attached to the key ring in the corpse's coat pocket.

In a muddy field outside Concord, behind a sign declaring it to be a HISTORY FAIRE, the circus-sized tent was swarming with spooks.

Colonel Smith's driver stopped outside the gate. A pair of police cars, their lights strobing, blocked the entrance; beyond the uniformed officers Smith could see parked buses and the tents of the forensic crews. Serious-looking officers in black windbreakers bearing the letters DEA paced around under the watchful eyes of guards in body armor and helmets. Casual rubberneckers might mistake them for a police SWAT team, but Smith was under no such illusion.

"Give me that badge." Smith waited as the cop checked his name against a clipboard, carefully compared his face to the photograph, then nodded. "Go ahead, sir. HQ is the third tent on the left."

"You heard him." Smith leaned back and closed his eyes for a minute as his driver crept across the rutted ground. Too many vehicles had come this way too recently. A familiar drumming noise prompted him to open his eyes. Sure enough, a big helicopter was thuttering across the sky, descending towards the field. *It's not black; just very, very, dark gray.* Smith suppressed a grin. What had happened at this site was no laughing matter. *How the* hell *did they manage it?* he asked himself as he opened the door and climbed out of the back of the car.

The mood in the headquarters tent was gray, too, as he discovered the moment he walked through the door. "Sir? How up to date are you?" Judith Herz, latterly of the FBI but currently answering to Smith, had been on-site when the shit hit the fan. Now she looked drained, hollows under her eyes from close to twenty-four hours supervising the site cleanup.

"I've been too busy fighting brushfires and keeping the press off your neck to track everything. Have you got time to give me a guided tour?"

Herz rubbed the side of her face then glanced at one of the men sitting in front of a rack of radios and laptop computers. "John, you want to take over for an hour? I need to bring the colonel up to speed."

"Okay, I'll do that." John—heavily built, wearing one of the ubiquitous DEA windbreakers, nodded briefly before turning back to his screen.

"This way, Colonel." Herz gestured back to the front awning of the tent. "Let me show you what we found."

Forensics had already finished with the big top before Herz beckoned Smith past the incident tape and into the open space within. Smith glanced around curiously. Like any big top, its roof was held up by a pair of huge posts. But the resemblance stopped at that point; there were no seats, no trapezes or safety nets, and nothing in this particular ring could be described as a laughing matter.

"It's a regular headquarters setup, we think," Herz commented as she walked towards a row of tables at one side of the huge tent. "Look." The tables showed every sign of having been abandoned in a hurry: folding chairs tipped over, equipment crates lying on their sides. One of the tables was covered completely by a large relief map, various implements strewn across it—notepads, pens, protractors, and folded pieces of card.

"Pay dirt," breathed Smith. He paused momentarily. "Has it been checked out?"

"Everything's been photographed in situ. I think they even dusted for fingerprints, just in case."

"Gotcha." Smith leaned over the map. It didn't take much to recognize the foothills, and the river valley forking downstream. But there was something odd about the map. He frowned. "Concord should be here, shouldn't it?"

Herz followed the direction of his finger. "I guess so."

"Hmm. Look." The moving finger trailed south. A much smaller clump of buildings perched beside the river, surrounded by a sharply incised wall. "This is printed. It's even got grid coordinates. Betcha they bought the map data from someone over here, in our world, then added their own survey points. Saves time, assuming the geography's the same, and I guess they would know about any major features like landslides."

Herz shook her head. "You mean this is a map of, of fairyland."

"It's not fairyland," Smith said sharply. "It's real enough that they can make a map of it like this, and plan . . ."

He paused, then peered back at the map. Hunting upstream of the small town, at the fork in the river, he found what he was looking for. "Go get one of our maps. I want to confirm that *this* is where we are," he said, moving one of the cardboard markers to sit atop the heptagonal feature he'd noticed. "They were here for a reason, and I want to know what they were doing that took nearly two hundred of the bastards."

He straightened up and looked around. There were more

tables dotted around, and a stack of empty kit bags, but the center of the tent was dominated by a two-story-high aluminum scaffold with ramps and ladders leading up to platforms on both upper floors. Surveyor's posts and reflector disks fastened to the uprights, and a pair of theodolites at opposite sides of the tent, made it clear that whoever had built the scaffold had taken pains over its exact location. Smith frowned, thoughtful. *Nearly two hundred of them and they vanished into thin air in less than three minutes. How did they avoid falling over each other?* A precision operation, like paratroops jumping in quick succession from the back of a plane. *And why did they do it out in public, risking detection?* It had to be something to do with this location, and whatever it was collocated with in the other time line.

Herz was muttering into a walkie-talkie. "I need geographic input. Is Amanda—yes, I'll hold, over."

Smith walked partway round the scaffold. A faint memory began to surface, grade school on an Air Force base somewhere in Germany: knights in armor, huge creaking wooden contraptions grinding their way across a field of battle towards a walled castle. The whole mediaeval thing. *It's a siege tower.* A siege tower without wheels, because you could build it in a parallel universe, butting right up against wherever you were going to go in. A siege tower without armor, and made of aluminum scaffolding components because they were cheap and easier to use than logs.

Voices pulled him back to the present. He glanced round, annoyed, then frowned. It was his political supervisor, Dr. James, with the cadaverous face and the connections to the current occupant of Number One Observatory Circle, plotting and scheming inside the beltway. A couple of flunkies—administrative assistants, pasty-skinned managerial types from Crypto city, even a discreet Secret Service bodyguard doing the men-in-black thing—followed him. "Ah, Eric! Excellent, Martin, you can stop trying to reach him now. What's your analysis?"

Smith took a deep breath, held it for a moment. The smells of crushed grass and gun oil and desperate men filled his nostrils. "It's a siege tower. They weren't running away from us, they were breaking *into* something." He gestured at the theodolites and the scaffolding. "That's positioned with extreme care. I think it's a siege tower—they had a target in their own world and this took them to a precise location. The map"—Herz was waving at him—"excuse me." He walked over to the table. "Yes?"

"You were right," she said. "We're here." Her finger stabbed at the heptagonal structure. "This thing is about five hundred feet across, look, concentric rings—does that remind you of anything?"

Smith nodded and turned to Dr. James. "If their map's telling the truth, that structure is some kind of fortification. And we already know from CLEANSWEEP that some kind of internal struggle was going down fourteen to sixteen days ago. We could do a lot worse than send a couple of scouts across in the next valley over." He cracked his knuckles, first the right hand then his left. "It's a shame we don't have anything that can touch them, because they're probably still there, in strength."

James grinned like a skull. "Well, I have an update for you. Let's take a walk."

BEGIN TELEPHONE TRANSCRIPT:

(A telephone buzzes for attention.)
"Hello?"
"Ah, is that the Lee residence?"
(Pause.) "Who is this?"
"I'd like to speak to James Lee, please. It is *dringen*—urgent."
(Pause.) "Please wait."
(Two minutes later.)
"Hello? Hello?"
"Who is this? Is—James? James, is that you?"

"Ah, yes— Who, um—"

"Poul, Poul ven Wu. You may remember me, from my cousin Raph's wedding to Kara ven—"

"Ah, yes! I remember now! Yes, indeed. How good to hear from you. But surely this isn't just a social call?"

"I wish it were. Unfortunately a somewhat delicate situation has arisen at short notice, and I hoped you might be able to advise me on how it might be resolved without undue difficulty."

(Pause.) "Ah. I see, I think." (Pause.) "Would this situation have anything to do with the events at the Thorold palace earlier this month?"

"Mm . . . in a manner of speaking, yes. It's a delicate matter, as I said, and we're anxious to resolve it without violating the terms of the settlement between our families, but it's quite urgent and it appears to be becoming time-critical."

"Hmm. Can you be more specific? I think I can safely say that we would also like to remain within the conditions of the truce, but I cannot commit to anything without my elders' approval, and I am quite anxious to know what I shall be putting before them."

(Pause.) "We would like to arrange for the safe passage of a substantial group of our people, from a location near Irongate—near Wergatsfurt—across a distance of some three miles, on foot, at night."

"Passage. You mean, from Wergatsfurt, in Gruinmarkt, to somewhere about three miles away, also in Gruinmarkt, but through our world, I take it?"

"Precisely." (Pause.) "In addition, the group is armed. Not civilian."

(Long pause.) "You're asking us to give safe passage to a small army."

(Hastily.) "Only for about three hours, at night! And there are only two hundred and eighteen of them. Eleven walking wounded, six stretcher cases. We don't want to attract attention—we want to keep it out of sight of the Polis, and everybody else. Can you—is it possible—to arrange this? I can supply details of the end-points of the sortie, and precise numbers—but what we would like, if it is possible, is not simply a dispensation within our agreement but active help. If you can organize covered trucks, and secure the destination, for example . . ."

"I can't agree to that, Poul. I don't have the authority to make agreements like that. I *can* tell you that my father can make a decision, but it would be better to petition him yourself—"

(Urgently) "It has to be done tonight!"

"I'm sure it does. And I can arrange for my father to see you within the hour—but the request must come directly from your lips to his ears." (Pause.) "You understand that he will expect some reward for this inconvenience."

"Of course." (Pause.) "We expect to pay for any assistance, and I am authorized to negotiate with you—or your father. Only understand that it is a matter of some urgency, and while we are prepared to be generous, we would take a very poor view of any attempt to exploit the situation to our detriment."

"Oh, that's understood. Give me an hour to prepare things and you will be welcome at my father's house. Do you need directions?"

END TRANSCRIPT

Erasmus Burgeson arrived in Fort Petrograd four days late, footsore and weary and out-of-pocket—but a free man, thanks to those extraordinary friends of Miriam Beckstein who had arrived just in time to stop the secret police from collaring the two of them.

After the shoot-out at the one-cow railroad station in the middle of nowhere, he'd taken up Miriam's invitation to help himself to the political officer's no-longer-needed steamer, and topped off both its tanks before cracking open the throttle and bumping across dirt tracks and paved military roads in the general direction of the southwest and the Bay Area. But the car had run out of steam ten miles before he reached Miwoc City, and he'd had second (and third) thoughts about the wisdom of paying a mechanic to come out and get her rolling again, in light of the car's blood-stained provenance. (Not to mention the bullet hole in the left, passenger side, door.)

So he'd walked into Miwoc, dusty and sore-footed, and taken a room in a working men's hostel, and spent the night lying awake listening to the fights and the begging and the runners clubbing indigents outside the thin wall of his dive—and set off for Fort Petrograd the next morning, whistling and doubtlessly mangling a ditty he'd picked up from Miriam, about a hotel in California.

It was a hundred miles to the big city, where the guns of Fort Petrograd loomed out across the headland of the bay, aiming south towards San Mateo. It shouldn't have taken three days, but Erasmus decided to avoid the railways—one close shave with the law was more than enough—and not risk buying an automobile: A solitary man driving alone was as good as a green flag to a certain kind of highwayman, and it would swallow all his remaining funds besides. The buses and streetcars that connected the grids of these western townships were more than adequate, if one made allowances for delayed connections . . . and the increasing number of checkpoints where nervous thief takers and magistrate's men stood guard with shotguns while the transport polis examined internal passports and work permits. These, at least, Erasmus was equipped to deceive, thanks to the package Edward had given him in New London.

Until, on the third day, the bus he was riding from Abadon reached Patwin (which Miriam would have pointed to on a map and called "Vallejo"), and ran into a general strike, and barricades, and grim-faced men beneath a blue flag slashed diagonally with a cross of St. Andrew beneath the glaring face of a wild turkey. "Ye can gae nae farthur," said the leader of the band blocking the high street, "wi'out an aye calling ye strikebreaker." He stood in front of the bus with arms crossed in front of him and the stolid self-confidence born of having two brothers-in-arms standing behind him with hunting rifles and an elderly and unreliable-looking carronade—probably looted from the town hall's front steps—to back *them* up.

"I'm no' arguing wi't'artillery," said the driver, turning to address his passengers. "End of t'road!"

An hour later, by means of various secret handshakes and circumlocutions, Erasmus was talking to the leader of the strike force, a lean, rat-faced man called Dunstable. "I was on my way to Fort Petrograd on Party business when I was forced off the train and only just escaped with my life. I need to get there immediately. Party business."

"Let me see what I can do," said Dunstable, then vanished into the back of the Town Aldermen's office, doubtless to cable for directions. The two hard-faced men with pistols sat with Erasmus in silence; he made himself comfortable until Dunstable returned. "Aye, well, your story checks out." Dunstable nodded at the two men. "Joe, go and get the mayor's runabout. Frank, you stay with Mister Burgeson here. You and Joe will drive Mister Burgeson straight to Fort Petrograd, to the Crimea Barracks—you know how to find it? Good. Our people hold it. When you get there, do as Mister Burgeson says."

Erasmus stood. "I'll send them back as soon as possible," he promised. "Good luck here."

"Luck?" Dunstable snorted. "Luck's got now't to do with it: People are starving and the frogs are trying to retake New France!"

"They're *what?*" Erasmus stared at him.

"Oh, the king's got it nailed down quiet like, but we know the score. Furrin troops in Red Club, a dauphin looking to set foot in New Orleans next week." Dunstable tapped the side of his nose. "Got to look fer our selves in times of unrest, 'aven't we?"

It took eight hours to drive the fifty miles from Patwin, overlooking the inner shore of the great bay, to Fort Petrograd and the downtown strip of barracks and museums and great houses that defined the core of western society, here on the edge of the Pacific. The roads were good, but the two ferries they required ran only infrequently at present, and they had to stop every five to ten miles to convince another roadblock, revolutionary caucus, civil defense brigade, emergency committee, republican guard, and ladies' union that they were not, in fact, agents of the secret political police, the French dauphin (who had simultaneously invaded New France, or Louisiana as the French called it, and Alaska, and the Brazilian Directorate, not to mention New London), or even the Black Fist Freedom Guard (which last was worryingly close to the truth). Luckily the situation was so confused, the news so hazy, that Erasmus discovered that sounding vague and asking lots of questions quickly convinced most of them that he was what he said he was—an innocent business traveler trapped on the road with his driver and bodyguard. A couple of the local militias made half-hearted attempts to shake him down, but his invincible self-righteousness, combined with a pious appeal to the forces of order and justice once the emergency resolved itself, scared them off. The British were, it seemed, still half-convinced that it was all a bad dream, and the breakdown of government—it seemed the exchequer had run out of money two days ago, and the king had told parliament to resign, and parliament had refused, and the unpaid dragoons had refused to clear the benches—was not quite real.

It was, in short, exactly the sort of confused pre-revolutionary situation that Erasmus had spent most of his life not praying, but hoping for. And he was in very nearly exactly the wrong place, if not for having the good luck to run into Dunstable and his fellow travelers.

The broad boulevards and steel-framed stone buildings of metropolitan Fort Petrograd were awash with excited strikers from the munitions factories and—not entirely to Erasmus's surprise—sailors from the vast naval base sprawling across the southwestern rim of the bay (which Miriam would have pointed to on a map and called "San Mateo"). Erasmus made a snap decision. "Forget the Crimea Barracks, take me to City Hall," he told Joe.

City Hall, a neoclassical lump of concrete reinforced with steel—and, curiously, featuring no windows less than eighteen feet above ground level, and clear lines of fire in all directions—was the logical place to go. And so, when they were stopped two blocks from the place by a barricade manned by marines who had torn their insignia of rank from their uniforms, Erasmus climbed out of the car. "I'm here to see Adam," he said openly. "Take me to him."

It took a while, but half an hour later Erasmus slid to the front of a queue of supplicants. They were queuing to see the man in the mayor's office, but the man behind the mayor's desk was not the mayor, and he wasn't doing ordinary civic business as usual. When Erasmus entered the room he was holding forth animatedly with a group of hard-looking types who he recognized instantly as party cadres. Sir Adam Burroughs had aged in the nearly twenty years since Erasmus had last seen him: His hair was thin and straggling, and his high forehead was deeply grooved with worry lines. But the magnetic charm and hyperactive temperament remained—

"Hello? Who's this?" Burroughs looked at him for a few seconds. Then his eyes widened. "Joshua? Is that you?"

"It is indeed." Erasmus bowed low—not a flourishing courtier's bow, but a salute born of deep respect. "Lady Margaret sends her regards, and her hopes for your success in this venture." He smiled. "Though it seems to me that you've made a good start already!"

"Joshua, man—" Burroughs stood up and flew from behind his desk, then gripped Erasmus by the shoulders. "It's been too long!" He turned to face his half-dozen assistants. "This man is Joshua Cooke! During the eighty-six he was my secretary and correspondent, he ran the *People's Voice* in New York. Since then he's been a mainstay of the movement out east." Eyes were staring, lips mumbling silently. "You've come to join us, I take it."

"Oh yes." Erasmus nodded. "But I go by the name of Erasmus Burgeson these days, and it's gotten to be something of a habit. And to plug you into what's been happening out east. I was delayed, I'm afraid, by the Polis—got away, but it was a near thing. And everywhere I went, rumor was chasing falsehood's tail for truth's bone. I take it loyalists are thin on the ground around here?"

"Vanished like rats from a sinking ship," grumped one of Burroughs's new assistants, a heavy-set fellow with a nautical beard. "We'll root 'em out."

"Organization first," Burroughs said mildly. "Josh—Erasmus, is it?—you've arrived at exactly the right time. We've got to get the word out, now that the Hanoverian has emptied his treasury, get control—I want you to take a flying picket down to the *Petrograd Times* and get the presses rolling again. And the telautograph senders on the east bay mount. You're going to be in charge of the propaganda ministry. Can you do that?"

Erasmus cracked his knuckles, grinning cadaverously. "It'll be a good start."

"An accident." Miriam stared at Brill across the width of the safe house's kitchen. *She looks like someone told her the family dog's got cancer.* "What kind of accident?"

"The duke—" Brill swallowed.

Huw sidestepped towards the sink, making an adroit grab for a water glass.

"Yes?" Miriam said encouragingly, her heart sinking.

"He's had a stroke, they say. World-walking."

"But why would he—" Huw fell silent, seeing Miriam's expression.

"The pretender's army took the Hjalmar Palace by treachery. His grace was organizing a force to take it back when . . . something happened, something bad. Near Concord. Everyone had to cross over in a hurry. They retook the fortifications, but the duke—"

Brilliana swallowed.

"Well *shit,*" Huw said angrily.

Miriam raised a finger. "Is he still alive?" she asked. "Is he conscious? Because—"

"Wait." Brill took the water glass from Huw's fingers. "Anything. To put in this?"

"There's a bottle of brandy in the luggage." Huw headed for the door. "Don't go away. Be right back."

Miriam pulled a stool out and steered it behind Brilliana, who sat, gratefully.

"He's in a bad way," she said eventually, visibly gathering her wits. "Paralyzed on one side. They need to get him to a neurology ward but they're trapped in the Hjalmar Palace—a big castle near Concord, in this world—by some Winter Crone-cursed police or paramilitary force that tried to raid them just as they were mounting the counterattack on the pretender's forces."

Huw reappeared with a dark green bottle. "Here." He splashed amber fluid into Brill's glass, then fetched down another and offered it to Miriam. "Yourself?"

"No thanks." She glanced at him dubiously as he poured two fingers for himself. "What if you need to drive somewhere?"

"Firstly, I delegate to Yul, and secondly, there's a difference between having a shot and getting drunk. Are you sure? . . ."

"Oh hell, go ahead." Miriam snorted. Sometimes it was the little things about her relatives who'd grown up in the Gruinmarkt that tripped her up the hardest, like their extremely un-American attitude to alcohol. "Can they get him to a hospital?"

Brill lowered her glass. "It's in train, I think. I mean, Olga's there, she's working something out with Earl Riordan. They couldn't tell me more—need to know. But—it's spooky. The feds swooped on ClanSec just as they concentrated to go across to relieve the Hjalmar Palace. It's almost as if someone told them exactly when—"

"Matthias is dead," Miriam interrupted.

"Matthias?" Huw looked fascinated. "Wasn't he the duke's personal secretary? I knew he disappeared, but—"

Miriam looked at Brill, who silently shook her head. "Later, Huw," she promised. "Brill, we need to get back to, to—" She stopped, the words *to wherever we need to be* piling up like a car crash on her tongue.

Brill took a sip of brandy. "By the time we could get back to the east coast it'll all be over," she said huskily. "The important thing is what happens after that."

I can't believe how fast it's all falling apart. Miriam shook her head. "Something about this doesn't make sense," she said slowly. "Things fell apart in Niejwein when Egon decided Henryk's little power play was a personal threat to him, that's clear. But this new stuff, the feds—it's one coincidence too many." She paused. "Could they be connected? Beyond the obvious, beyond Matthias defecting and spilling his guts?"

Brill gave her an odd look. "You might think that. I couldn't possibly comment."

"Oh for—" Miriam forced herself to stop. "Okay, let me tell you what I think is probably happening, Brill. *You're* in Angbard's chain of command, *you* deal with it."

"You'd better wait outside, Huw," Brill said sharply.

He shrugged and walked over to the door. "Call me when you've finished politicking," he called, then closed it.

Miriam took a deep breath and tried to gather the unraveling threads of her concentration. *Too much, too fast.* "I think that we figured out Matthias had defected seven, eight months ago, when it first happened. And what followed was a factional race to get into the best position to come out on top when the US government figured out what was going on and brought the hammer down on the trade network. I stood up and told them their business model was flawed, and they didn't do anything—but they weren't all ignoring me. The conservative faction, led by Baron Henryk, decided to shut me up, but they had to be subtle about it. Angbard didn't block him because he hoped they'd fail. Meanwhile, some other groups were looking into the possibilities dragged up by my stumbling over the hidden family and New Britain. That'd be where Huw comes in, yes? Angbard's sitting at the center of a web, like a spider, holding everything together— trying to keep business running as usual, but trying to hedge everybody's bets."

She swallowed, then took a sip of brandy. "Trouble is, everybody's doing different things. There have been sub rosa attempts to modernize the Clan going on for decades; I just didn't recognize them. That's what I got wrong—I took you all at face value, didn't look below the surface. Everyone pays lip service to the status quo, but not everyone goes along with it. There's the breeding program that was intended to rebuild the population base eroded by the civil war over the past fifty years, and crack the manpower monopoly effectively controlled by the marriage-brokering old grannies"—she watched Brilliana for signs of surprise, but didn't see any—"and that debating society and talking shop Huw's into. There's even Clan Security, for heaven's sake! Which is more like the, the Russian KGB, than something you'd expect in a post-feudal society like the Gruinmarkt. Am I right?"

She waited for Brill to say something, but the silence dragged out. After a few seconds, she cleared her throat and continued. "So, I upset a bunch of applecarts, and the fallout included Matthias going over the wall. I expect someone's been trying to negotiate with the feds, buying time, patching things up. And I expect everyone's been scrambling to secure a workable Plan B for their particular faction. I'm not going to ask what the hell ClanSec or the Council or whoever thought they were doing, messing around with stolen nukes, it's immaterial; I just want to note that it was a *really* bad idea, because from the feds' point of view it turned the Clan from a minor irritant into a serious menace. You can negotiate with a nuisance, but you shoot menaces—isn't that right?" She put her glass down and looked at Brill. After a minute, she asked: "Well?"

Brilliana looked uncomfortable. "I can't talk about . . . certain . . . matters without getting permission first. But broadly speaking"—she looked at Miriam appraisingly—"you are speculating along the right lines." She coughed. "But please, refrain from airing your speculation in public? Lest other factions conclude that you know more than you do, and attempt to silence you."

Miriam's left eyelid twitched. "I've had enough of that, thank you. Since even my dear mother is prone to, to . . ." It was too painful to continue. She rested one hand on her lap. "And what that bastard ven Hjalmar tried to do. Did." A long pause. "It's only been about six weeks. I could get an abortion. *If* I'm pregnant."

Brill looked at her oddly. "If you did that, you'd be throwing away your best leverage." She took another sip of brandy. "Because it's Creon's get, and you've got a fistful of witnesses to the betrothal, even—by implication—the pretender. That's the throne to the Gruinmarkt, Miriam."

"And it's my body." Miriam looked at her half-empty glass and twitched, then she picked it up again and swallowed it in a single mouthful. "Not that that seems to mean much to you people."

Brilliana reached out and grabbed her hand. "Helge!"

"What?" Miriam glared at her across the breakfast bar.

"This world is not fair or just. But I swore I would look after you—"

"—Who to?"

"To you, and to your uncle: but that is not important. I swore an oath to protect you. I must tell you that as long as you carry the heir to the throne of Niejwein, nobody in the six families will dare to lift a finger against you. And if, if we are still alive in eight months, things will be different. The pretender will be dead and Angbard will need a regent's council and at a minimum you will be on it. He told me, if necessary"—her voice cracked—"tell her that if she does this thing, all debts are canceled."

"And if I don't?" Miriam made as if to pull her arm back, but paused. "You know there are no guarantees. I'm old for this. Miscarriages aren't that unusual in older pregnancies. And there's only a fifty-fifty chance it's a boy, anyway. What if it doesn't work?"

"Then at least you tried." Brill moderated her voice. "You came back willingly: That weighs in your favor. The more you do for us, the harder it becomes for your enemies to belittle or ignore you. Thus has it ever been."

"You make it sound as if the Clan runs on honor."

"But it does!" Brill's expression of surprise took her aback. "How else do you control an aristocracy?"

"I don't think I'll ever understand you guys." Miriam watched while Brill refilled both their glasses. "Hey. Suppose I'm pregnant? You want to go easy with that."

"What's that got to do with it?" She looked perplexed.

"The Surgeon-General's—no, *fuck* it." Miriam picked up the glass. "Next time you send someone out for a pizza, try and get them to buy me a pregnancy test kit . . . hell, make that two of them, just in case." She sipped at her brandy defiantly. "So anyway, I kicked over an anthill. And Henryk's faction try to tie me down, to control the damage, and it backfires spectacularly and sets Egon off. Is that how I'm reading it? While at the same time, I set Matthias off, which set the feds on us. Right?"

"Wrong." Brill raised her glass and stared at it pensively. "It was a powder keg, Helge. Even before you returned, it was balanced on a sword's edge. You unleashed chaos, but without you—you strengthened Angbard's hand immensely, did you not notice that? And you have unleashed Huw. Don't underestimate him. He has connections. You can be at the center of things if you play the hand you have been dealt."

"There won't be any center to be at, if the feds figure out a way of getting over here in force," Miriam said darkly.

"They won't."

"Huh. But anyway. Is it alright to bring him back in?"

"What? You've finished spilling our innermost secrets?"

"Innermost secrets, feh: It's just uninformed speculation. No, I need to talk to Huw. *We* need to talk, that is."

"Oh. Alright." Brill stood up and walked to the door. "Huw!"

A moment's silence, then feet pounded down the staircase. "Yes? What's—oh."

"Come in, sit down," Miriam called over. "We've got to head back to Boston tomorrow, or as soon as possible."

"But—" Brill stopped. "Why?"

"No politics, remember?" Miriam twitched. "If Angbard's ill, we can't risk being too far away. But what's really important—Huw, I want you to tell me all about how you went about probing that new world. Because I think once everyone gets past running around and being worried about the pretender, we are really going to need to work out how to open up new worlds."

"Eh?" Brilliana stared at her. "I don't see why that's a priority right now."

Miriam sighed heavily and pushed her glass away. "It wouldn't be, if we were just up against another bunch of upstart aristocrats, or if the US government were entirely reliant on captured couriers. Huw, why don't you tell her about what we were discussing earlier?"

"The, uh, wild speculation?"

"Yes, that. I'm tired, I don't want to repeat myself, and I

think she needs to know." She stood up and stretched. "I'm going to catch a nap. Call me if anything happens."

Despite the summer heat, the sky was overcast and gray; it was threatening to rain as Dr. James led Colonel Smith around the side of the big top. Two minders followed at a discreet distance. "How certain are you that the bad guys are on the other side of that siege tower?"

Eric gave it scant seconds of consideration. "Very. They wouldn't have come out here and stuck a couple of hundred assets in a field for us to see without an extremely urgent motivation. These people aren't into cat and mouse games—they've been staying under cover very carefully until now. This has got all the signs of an emergency operation, and we disturbed them in the middle of it. That map alone, that's dynamite. And it checks out: The scaffolding is right in the middle of what looks like a major fortification in their world."

Dr. James halted—so fast that Eric nearly stumbled. "Good!" A curious half-smile played around his lips. "Then I've got a solution for you, son."

"A—" Eric did a double take. "Excuse me?"

"It's a political problem." James began walking again, more slowly this time. "We want to send them a *message*. They think they can play with us. They stole six nukes from the inactive inventory. The message we want to send is, 'if you play with us we will mess you up.' If I wasn't a man of faith I'd be using the f-word, Colonel. We want to send them a message and we want to underline *don't f– with us* in blood."

"In my experience," Eric commented, feeling light-headed, "messages signed in blood ought to be delivered in a way that ensures the recipients don't live long enough to read them. Anything else is asking for trouble."

"Spoken like a flyboy at heart. You're absolutely right. Nuke 'em 'til they glow, then shoot 'em in the dark." Eric stared at him until he nodded. "That's a direct quote from the vice president, son. Although *he* probably lifted it from someone else."

"That puts an interesting light on things," Eric agreed, slightly aghast. The Secret Service's code name for VPOTUS, DADDY WARBUCKS, was also a comment on his neo-conservative leanings, but such bloodthirsty words coming from the executive branch were somewhat surprising, even post-9/11.

"So he's getting you a piece of paper on the White House blotter," Dr. James continued blandly, "ordering you to take control of the gadget retrieved from Government Center and to, ah, *return* it to the person or persons who so carelessly left it under the Blue Line platform with *extreme* prejudice."

But! Smith's tongue froze. "But!" He tried again. It came out as almost a squeak. "We don't have nuclear release authority, we're not in the chain of command, you can't *do* that—"

"Son." James's smile turned icy. "They stole *six* of them. The United States does not give in to nuclear blackmail. Never mind that it would be *embarrassing* to return it to inventory, on the record that it went walkies on our watch; they stole it so you are going to shove it up their, their behind, so hard they can *taste* it. It's the perfect solution. It's completely deniable: They stole it, it went off in their hands. And it sends the right message. Mess with us and we will hurt you. And besides—" He slid his spectacles down his nose and pulled out a cleaning cloth. "Daddy Warbucks is *real keen* to make sure the FADMs work as designed. And Major Alvarez knows how to use them. He *is* part of the chain, and he's seconded to us. He knows what the score is. Why do you think we've been recruiting so widely . . . and selectively?"

"Okay," Eric said thoughtfully. "I follow the logic." He paused. "But how are we going to deliver it? We've only got two mules." He left unspoken the corollary: *Are you willing to let me strap an atomic device on a timer to a captured Clan courier who hates our guts?* It would violate so many protocols that the stack of charges would be higher than the Washington Monument.

"Well now." James stopped smiling. "You remember your little visit out west? They got Preparation Fifteen working. I'm having one of them flown out here right now—this will be its first deployment."

"Wait." Eric raised a hand. "Preparation Fifteen? I only saw number twelve. The, the disappearing tissue." Tissue harvested from the brain of a captured Clan member—God only knew what had happened to them because Eric certainly didn't want to. "Is Fifteen what I think it is?"

"Yes." Dr. James looked smug. "Push the button, watch the black box vanish. Along with whatever it's bolted to, as long as it's in a conductive sack and is isolated from earth. It's single-use, unfortunately; it has to be assembled by hand and lasts for about sixteen hours. But during that time—"

"Have you tried bolting one to an airframe?" Eric asked. "Sorry."

"Good question. We'd need two—one for the return trip—and they're not that reliable yet, but it's on the road map. You can test fly the helicopter if you want." James noticed Eric's expression. "That was a joke, son, you're not expendable."

"I'm not licensed for choppers," Smith muttered, under his breath. *Just in case you get any crazy ideas.* "So how are we going to deliver the, the physics package?"

"The usual way." James started walking again; they were almost round the circumference of the big top, the awning just in view around the curve of its flank. "Written orders are coming down from the White House; it's WARBUCK's toy, but he's gotten BOY WONDER to sign off on it, and we're—well, certain of the Joint Chiefs have been briefed about the PINNACLE BROKEN ARROW and it's been made clear to them that this is necessary. I gather they've even gotten Chief Justice Bork on board. You'll use your man Rand and his crew to prepare the gadget, they're already cleared. They'll hand it and the timer controller to Major Alvarez and Captain Hu, who have orders to put a timer controller on it, set to detonate sixty seconds after activation. It's tamperproof; any attempt to disarm it other than by using the code-wheel to enter the locking key will make it detonate, but they'll have the key to hand just in case. *You* will bolt the Preparation Fifteen unit to the detonation sequencer and put the gadget on top of the, the siege tower. You and the major will start the sequencer, push the button on the transport unit to send it across. If the transport unit fails, you can enter the disarm code and try again later. If it succeeds . . . it's *their* problem. May they burn in hell for making us do this," he added quietly.

4

COVERED WAGON

&

To a soldier in an army dependent on muscle power, there are few sights as grim as a fortress occupied by an enemy force standing directly in the line of advance.

The Hjalmar Palace was palatial only on the inside: Squatting behind ominous earthworks at the fork of a major river, the face it presented to the world at large was eyeless and intimidating, scarred by cannon and fire. The merchant clan barons who had reinforced and extended the revetments around the central keep over the past fifty years had not been as parochial as their backwoodsman cousins. They'd scoured the historical archives of the Boston Public Library, keeping a wary eye on the royal army's ironworks and the forging of their great siege bombards. Behind the outer wet moat and its fortified gatehouse, beyond the flat killing ground of the apron, the stone walls of the castle sank below ground level; backed by rammed earth to absorb the blows of any cannon balls that might make it over the rim, the walls rose harsh and steep before the deep dry moat.

It had taken treachery to get Otto's men into the palace the first time round, using a shortcut revealed under duress by one of the residents. He'd been in the process of preparing defenses against the inevitable attempt to retake the complex, but the Clan had struck back with astonishing speed and terrifying force—a far cry from their dilatory defensiveness when outlying estates and villages were picked off. *They weren't really exerting themselves until we threatened their fortresses instead of their farms,* Otto mused. It was an unpleasant realization. His defenses hadn't been ready; they'd driven him out and he still didn't know for sure precisely where they'd flooded back into the building from. But if nothing else, at least now he had a map of the internal layout. In principle that should make things easier. In practice—

He lowered his binoculars, then looked back. The fortress was still there, looming in the east, mocking him. *Your bones, at my feet,* it was saying. *Your blood: my mortar.*

A loud *crack!* caught his attention. Behind the line, the royal artillery's light cannon began to fire, deep-throated coughs that spat clouds of smoke and sparks as they threw cold iron at the gatehouse. Stone chips flew, but the gatehouse was, itself, a castle in miniature, and beyond it the drawbridge across the wet moat and the sunken road allowed the defenders to reinforce it at need. The range was almost half a mile: The bombardment wouldn't do much save to make the defenders keep their heads down. But that was better than nothing, Otto supposed. That, and the king's plan—if it worked—might get them close enough to the defenses to at least have a chance. And if the king's plan didn't work, *at least we've got an entire army,* he told himself. Scant comfort, looking up at those ramparts.

Otto turned back to the clump of men waiting behind him. "Tomorrow the king's going to reduce the gatehouse," he announced. "Then it's right on to the castle. But we've got an easy job to do. Once Raeder's men finish moving the ammunition up, we're to advance behind the vanguard and keep the witches' heads down." He looked his men in their eyes. "There will be *no* indiscriminate firing." *Not like the day before yesterday,* when his undertrained men had burned through crates of priceless ammunition and wrecked a pair of irreplaceable M60 barrels. "There will be no damaged guns. If any man wrecks a witch-gun barrel by firing too fast, I'll forge it to red-heat and beat him to death with it. And there will be no casualties, if I have any say in the matter." He assayed a thin smile. His hetmen had been quietly gloomy, a minute ago; now they visibly cheered up. "The other side's to do the dying today, and for our side, the fresh troops are to be the making of them. We'll just stay nice and safe in the rear, and rain on the enemy battlements with lead."

"Aye!" Shutz knew his cue, and put his leathery lungs into it. The sergeants and hetmen, not to mention the sprinkling of hedge-knights who'd joined his banner out of hope of self-enrichment, joined in enthusiastically.

"To your men, then, and let them know," Otto said, allowing himself to relax slightly. "I will make an inspection round in the next hour, and give you your disposition before we advance, an hour before sunset."

Night fell heavy on the castle walls, illuminated by the slow lightning of the field cannon and the echoing thunder, and the moans of the victims, growing weaker now. Olga stared from a darkened window casement, following the action around the base of the gatehouse, picked out in the livid green of night vision goggles. "The stupid, *stupid* bastards," she hissed.

Behind her, Earl Oliver cleared his throat. The distant sounds of preparations, banging and scraping and swearing, carried through the door from the grand hall. "As long as the Pervert's troops think we're heavily invested, and unable to move . . ."

"But the waste! Lightning Child strike him blind." Olga was not prone to fits of unreasoning rage. Bright, hot, anger was no stranger; but it passed rapidly, and she knew better than to let it rule her. But what the king had done outside the barred gate of the moat house was something else. *It's a deliberate provocation,* she told herself. *He doesn't want or expect our surrender, so he thinks to unhinge us.* And he was certainly trying hard. No one sane would have used noble prisoners as he had done outside the gatehouse, forgoing all hope of ransom and calling down eternal blood feud from their surviving relatives.

"Carl will deal with him tomorrow, I am sure," Oliver declared, although whether he was being patronizing towards her age and status, or merely ironically detached, Olga was unsure. "Tonight we have other work."

"Indeed." Olga lowered her goggles and switched them off, blinking at the twilight.

"Meanwhile, Earl Riordan sent his compliments, and would like to know what additional resources you need to move the duke, and when you'll be ready."

Since when is he employing you *as a messenger boy?* Olga stepped aside from the window and turned to face him. "I've got a corpsman and two soldiers, one to do the portage and one secondary bodyguard; between them they're a stretcher team. That's plenty until we get to the crossover point. What I then need is for Grieffen or whoever's in Central Ops to arrange to have a secure ambulance waiting for us in Concord at zero four hundred hours, and I need their mobile number so I can guide them in when we cross over." She patted her belt. "I've got a GPS unit and a phone. We'll travel with everyone else as far as the drop zone then continue on a little further before we go back to the United States." It wasn't the entire truth—and not just because she didn't trust the Baron. Oliver was trustworthy after his own fashion; but his loyalty was to his conception of the Clan, not to Olga's faction. He didn't have any need to know the details, and Olga wasn't inclined to take even the remotest of risks with the duke's personal security.

"Do you want me to arrange the ambulance?" he asked attentively.

That did it: He *was* questioning her competence. "No!" she snapped. "I'll do it myself. The sooner I see him in a hospital bed the happier I'll be." Moving an acute stroke patient was risky enough without trying to do it in the dark, possibly under fire, and without benefit of any specialized medication more sophisticated than a couple of aspirin; the only reason even to consider it was out there in the dark and the chaos before the gatehouse, broken on the wheel.

"So will we all," he said piously, turning to leave.

The hours passed quickly, in a frenzy of preparations for the evacuation. Not everyone was to leave; someone had to light the keep, fill the helmets visibly watching over it, and fire the occasional volley to convince the besieging forces that the palace wasn't an empty prize. But eight in every ten men and women would be world-walking out of the Hjalmar Palace before dawn, stealing away like thieves in the night once the hastily printed and laminated knotwork cards arrived. Almost everyone—Olga, the duke, and the wounded excepted—would return, with the early morning sun at their backs, half a mile behind the pretender's encampment. Trapped between the machine guns on the battlements and the rifles and recoilless rockets of the mobile force, the royalists would have scant time to regret their misplaced allegiance; their best strategy ought to be to melt back into the trees again. But from the lack of movement in the enemy camp it looked as if they'd swallowed the bait: While they clearly knew of the world-walker's ability, it seemed that they had not fully understood its tactical significance. That, or their commander was getting greedy.

Olga took a couple of hours to catch a nap, on a cot at the end of Angbard's bed. She awakened in near-darkness as a hand touched her shoulder. She grasped a wrist almost before she opened her eyes. "What time? . . ."

"Midnight plus four minutes, milady." The soldier—a stocky woman called Irma, one of Helmut's lance and the daughter of an earl, if Olga remembered her rightly—straightened up. "Martyn and I are your detail, along with Gerd"—the corpsman—"to take his grace to safety, is that right?"

"Yes," Olga said tersely. She rubbed her eyes and sat up, shook her head to clear the cobwebs, and yawned. "You have a stretcher, yes? And suitable clothes."

"A stretcher, aye," Gerd called softly from the far side of the four-poster bed. "He still sleeps, milady," he added, forestalling her next question.

Irma grimaced. "I hate stretchers." She stepped back, to leave Olga some space. "On the subject of suitable clothes—we are going to America, to meet an ambulance, at dead of night, I was told? But this other world, I've never been there before. So I don't know what's a suitable disguise for sneaking around there. . . ."

"Don't worry about that aspect of things, we've got transport." *I hope.* Olga sat up creakily. "Here's the plan. We're going to cross over with everyone else. Have the cards arrived yet?" Irma shook her head. "Well. When they arrive—it's a new world. This site is undeveloped farmland. Our agents have laid on trucks, and they'll drive Captain Hjorth and his force to the drop-off point for the counterattack. We'll be taking a car into Irongate, which is near as makes no difference sitting on the south side of Concord, and where there's a doppelgangered building in this world. Then we make two more transfers, crossing back at zero five hundred, and I'll phone for an ambulance. I've got GPS, so we should be picked up within half an hour. Our main challenges are: keeping his grace comfortable, avoiding attention from the locals, and not killing ourselves by world-walking too much. Is that clear?"

"Yes, milady. Makes things easier." Irma shook her head. "Four crossings in four hours—that's harsh."

"Yes. That's why for the first crossing we'll all be going piggyback on whichever members of your lance draw the short straws. And for the second crossing, Gerd will carry his grace and Martyn will carry you. On the third crossing, you can take the duke. The fourth will be the hardest, but that way, only one of us risks breaking our head."

"Do you think we should ditch our field gear?"

Olga thought for a moment. "If it's not too much to carry, I think we should hang onto it until we're ready to make the final transit. But once we hit Concord"—she paused—"we can't be wearing armor or carrying long arms. What clothing did you find for us?"

"Nothing for sure, milady, we must see if it fits—but the baron's family maintained a wardrobe with some American clothing, and it has not been looted yet. I hope," she added under her breath.

"Let's go see, shall we," Olga suggested, stretching as she stood up. Her own state she passed over: She and Angbard had never expected to wind up here, and her neat trouser suit would be fine. "We need clothing that will pass at a distance for Gerd, Martyn, and you."

"This way, then." Irma led her from the master bedroom into an adjacent room, its rich paneling splintered and holed by small arms fire. Chests of drawers and a huge wooden chest dominated half a wall. "I think this is what you're looking for."

Late afternoon.

Miriam segued into wakefulness to the rattle and jabber of daytime television fuzzed into incoherence through a thin stud wall. Gathering her wits, she rolled over. *The bed isn't moving,* she realized. She'd found it difficult to rest, her worries chasing their tails through her mind, but she'd spent the last few nights on a transcontinental express train and the novelty of a bed that didn't sway side-to-side and periodically bump across railroad points had eventually drawn her down into a deep abyss of dreamless sleep. Yawning, she sat up and rolled off the comforter. *What time is it?* . . . She glanced at the dressing table. Her notebook PC sat there, its LEDs winking as it charged. Whether it would start up was a moot point—it had spent six months in a hidden compartment in a disused office—but it had a clock; maybe it would still be working. She reached over and pressed the power button, then started gathering her clothes.

The regular startup chord and busy clicking of a hard disk provided welcome background noise as she dressed; but as the computer seemed to want to twiddle its thumbs instead of talking to her, she locked the screen and headed for the bathroom, and then the stairs, rather than waiting. To think that only four days ago she'd risked arrest and imprisonment to retake the thing, seeing it as central to her hopes for survival and prosperity! . . . Her understanding of her circumstances was changing almost from hour to hour, leaving her adrift and unable to rely on plans she'd made only the day before. It gave her an anxious sense of insecurity, rising to the level of nervous dread whenever her thoughts circled back to the pregnancy question.

The television noise was coming from the living room, along with other sounds. As Miriam pushed the door open she caught a burst of conversation: "She's right, then what are we going to do? We won't be able to go back! Had you thought of"—A blond head turned—"Oh, hi!"

Miriam paused. "I hope I'm not interrupting anything. . . ."

"Not really." Huw was slouched in a recliner, propping up a laptop, while the two younger ones, Yul and Elena, had been either watching TV or arguing about something while sharing a large pizza of uncertain parentage. "Feel free to join us."

"Yah," agreed Yul, chewing rhythmically.

Elena thumped him. "Don't talk with your mouth full!"

"Yuh." He took her punch on one shoulder, looking amused rather than hurt.

Miriam turned to address Huw. "Where's Brill?"

"Oh, she went out." He sounded disinterested. "Hmm, that's interesting."

Miriam glanced at the window. It was clearly getting late, and the shadows of the trees out front were lengthening. "Is there anything to eat around here?" Her gaze was drawn to Elena and Yul's pizza, almost against her will.

"Uh?" Huw looked up at her, and visibly did a double take. "Food? Um . . . yeah, food! Just a minute." A rattle of hastily struck keys later, he closed the laptop's lid and stood up. "Let's see what's in the kitchen?"

The kitchen was as sparsely equipped as it had been earlier in the afternoon. Huw headed straight for the freezer and the microwave, but Miriam stopped him. "Let me." While she rooted around in the cupboards, she asked, "Any idea where Brill went? Did she ask you to get me a pregnancy test kit?"

"A what?" He walked over to the kitchen door and closed it carefully. "No, that's women's stuff. If you asked for such a thing, she wouldn't trust a man to procure it."

"Oh." Miriam froze for a couple of seconds, disappointed. Then she sighed and opened the next cupboard. "So where did she go?"

"If not to attend to your request, I'd guess she has a private call to make. She was getting extremely itchy about being on the wrong coast, and even itchier about how we're going to get back out east without attracting attention."

"Attention"—Miriam paused to pull out a can of tomatoes and a bag of pasta—"what kind of attention?"

"She came out here in the company biz-jet, but . . . someone tipped the feds off about where ClanSec were concentrating? Somewhere near Concord, apparently. We've had hints"—Miriam rattled past him, rifling a drawer in search of utensils—"they're getting serious about tracking us down.

So I don't think there's a biz-jet ride home in our immediate future." Miriam slammed the cupboard door. "What?"

"This is useless!" She pointed at her haul. "What did they think we were going to do, eat at Mickey D's every day?"

"Freezer. Microwave." Huw pulled a face. "If you were stocking a house for a bunch of kids who're not used to living away from home without servants, what would you do?"

"Leave a cookbook!"

"We-ell, okay." Huw made for the freezer again. "Memo to Duke Angbard Lofstrom, Office of Clan Security. Re: training program for armed couriers. Classification: Clan Confidential. All couriers must attend mandatory *Cooking with Rachael Ray* video screening and Culinary Skills 101 course prior to commencing overnight missions. Malnutrition a threat to morale, combat-readiness, and operational security." He straightened up, a pizza box in each hand. "Meat lover's feast or four cheese, my lady?"

"Oh hell, I'll take the cheese." She forced a smile to take the sting out of her words. "Sorry. It just bugs me."

"It'd be good to have a staff, or use a hotel or something," Huw agreed. "But this is less conspicuous, and less conspicuous is good right now." He pulled a face.

"What do you mean?" She pulled out a chair and sat down.

"Well." He slid the first pizza onto a plate and put it in the microwave. "I have a nasty suspicion that in the interests of looking inconspicuous we're going to end up driving back to Massachusetts. Or driving part of the way, to avoid tracking. If we just fly point-to-point and they're paying attention we'd show up. And then there's the communication discipline. All Internet traffic is monitored by the NSA. *All* of it. So we fall back on 1930's tech—old-fashioned letters written in runic hochsprache, flash memory cards sealed under postage stamps instead of microdots, that kind of thing. It's probably why my lady Brilliana is taking so long."

"Oh." Miriam stared at the second pizza, feeling a stab of acute déjà vu. It was just like Erasmus's problems in New

Britain, seen through a high tech looking glass. "I think I'm getting a headache."

The oven pinged for attention. Huw opened it, sniffed, then slid the steaming microwave-limp pizza in front of her. "Sorry—"

"Don't be, it's not your fault." She picked up a knife and began to cut as he put the second pizza in. "What do you want, Huw?"

"Huh?"

"What do you *want?*" She put down her knife. "Here, help yourself to a slice."

"Uh, you mean, what do I want, as in, what is my heart's desire, or what do I want, as in, what am I trying to achieve right now?" He reached over and took a piece, holding it twitchily on his fingertips.

"The former." Miriam picked up a wedge of hot pizza and nibbled at it. "Because I'd say, right now you're trying not to burn your fingers."

"Ouch, yes! Um, life's little ambitions. I want to finish my masters, and I wanted to do a Ph.D., obviously. Only the duke more or less handed me a doctoral subject a couple of weeks ago! Hell, not a doctorate: a life's work. The implications are *enormous.* As for the other stuff . . . I'm a younger son. Clan shareholder, but at least I'm not going to get roped in and tied down into running a backwoods estate. There's more to life than the Gruinmarkt and if I must do the getting married and raising a family thing I want to do it somewhere civilized, with electricity and running water, and a partner of my own choosing."

"Got anyone in mind?"

"Oh, I think so." His expression turned inward for a moment. "Although it's too early to ask. . . ." He shook his head. The microwave dinged again. "Is that what you wanted to know?"

"It'll do for a start." Miriam watched as he stood up and pulled the second pizza out of the oven. "How many—of your generation—do you think see eye-to-eye with you on the last bit? Electricity and running water and marrying for love rather than because your parents say so?"

Huw reached for the knife. "It's funny . . . there are a bunch of foreign students at MIT? You can't go there and not know a couple of them. We had a lot in common. It's like, we all got used to the amenities and advantages of living over here, but it's not *home*. The Chinese and Middle-Eastern and developing-nation students all wanted to spend time over here, earning a stake, maybe settle down. It's a deprivation thing. I didn't see that with the European students—there weren't as many of them, either—but then, you wouldn't. The difference in standards of living isn't so pronounced. But you want to know about my generation? There are those who've never spent much time over here—a minority, these days—and they don't know any better, but there's an outright majority who'd be over the wall in an instant if they could keep visitation rights. And if you promised to install electricity and running water and start Niejwein developing, they'd elect you pope-emperor. Shame that's not going to happen, of course. I'd have liked to see you on the throne in the Summer Palace, taking names and kicking butt. I think you'd have been good at it."

"You think." Miriam gnawed at a fresh chunk of pizza. "Well, we've got a bigger problem now."

"Yes, I was just thinking that. . . ." Huw slid another portion onto her plate. "Here, have a chunk of mine. Um. So what's *your* life's ambition?"

"Uh?" Miriam stared at him, a chunk of pizza crust held in one hand. "Excuse me?"

"Go on." Huw grinned. "There must be something, right? Or someone?"

"I—uh." She lowered the piece of crust very carefully, as if it had suddenly been replaced by high explosive. "You know," she continued, in a thoughtful tone of voice, "I really have absolutely no idea." She cleared her throat. "Is there anything to drink?"

"Wine, or Diet Coke?"

"Ugh. Wine, I think, just not too much of it. . . ."

"Okay." Huw fetched a pair of glasses and a bottle.

"I used to think I had the normal kinds of ambition," she said thoughtfully. "Married, kids, the family thing. Finish college, get a job. Except it didn't quite work out right, whatever I did. I did everything the wrong way round, the kid came too soon and I gave her up for adoption because things were . . . fucked up right then? Yes, that's about the size of it. Mom suggested it, I think." Her face froze for a moment. "I wonder why," she said softly.

Huw slid a glass in front of her. "I didn't know you had a child?"

"Most people don't." She sipped briefly, then took a mouthful of wine. "I married him. The father. Afterwards, I mean. And it didn't work out and we got divorced." She stifled an unhappy laugh. That's what I mean about doing things in the wrong order. And before you ask, no, I'm not in contact with the adoptive parents. Mom might know how to trace them, but I bet"—she looked thoughtful—"she won't have made it easy. For blackmail, you see. So anyway, after my marriage fell apart I had a career for a decade until some slime in a vice president's office flushed it down the toilet. And I'd still *have* a career, a freelance one, except I discovered I had a family, and they wanted me to get married and have a baby, preferably in the right order, thanks, electricity and running water strictly optional. Oh, and my mother is an alien in both senses of the word; the first man I met in ten years who I thought I'd be willing to risk the marriage thing with was shot dead in front of me; the boyfriend before *that,* who I dropped because of the thousand-yard stare, turns out to be a government spy who's got my number; I'm probably pregnant with a different dead man's baby; and the whole world's turned to shit." She was gripping the glass much too tightly, she realized. "I just want it to *stop.*"

Huw was staring at her as if she'd grown a second head.

Poor kid, she thought. *Still at the mooning after girlfriends stage, not sure what he wants—why did I dump all that on him?* Now she knew what to look for—now she knew the pressure that had broken Roland—she could see what was looming in his future, the inevitable collision between youthful optimism and brutal realpolitik. *Did I really just say all that?*

While she was trying to work it out, Huw reached across the breakfast bar and laid a finger on the back of her hand. "You've been bottling that up for a long time, haven't you?"

"How old are you?" she asked.

"I'm twenty-seven," he said calmly, taking her by surprise: He had five years on her estimate. "And I hear what you're not saying. You're what, thirty? Thirty-one? And—"

"Thirty-four," she heard herself saying.

"—Thirty-four is a hard age to be finding out about the Clan for the first time, and even harder if you're a woman. It's a shame you're not ten or fifteen years older," he continued, tilting his head to one side as he stared at her, "because they understand old maids; they wouldn't bother trying to marry you off." He shook his head abruptly. "I'm sorry, I'm treating your life like a puzzle, but it's . . ."

"No, that's okay."

"Ah, thank you." He paused for a few seconds. "I shall forget whatever you wish me to, of course."

"Um?" Miriam blinked.

"I assume you don't want your confidences written up and mailed to every gossip and scandalmonger in the Gruinmarkt?" He raised a wicked eyebrow.

"Of course not!" Catching the gleam in his eye: "You wouldn't. Right?"

"I'm not suicidal." He calmly reached out and took the final wedge of her pizza. "I bribe easily."

"Here's to wine and pizza!" She raised her glass, trying to cover her rattled nerves with a veneer of flippancy. *Damn, he's not that unsophisticated at all. Why do I keep getting these people wrong?*

"Wine and pizza." Huw let her off the hook gracefully.

"You wanted to know what my life's ambitions were," she said slowly. "May I ask why?"

Huw stopped chewing, then swallowed. "I'd like to know what motivates the leader I'm betting my life on." He looked at her quizzically. "That heavy enough for you?"

"Whoa!" She put her glass down slightly too hard. "I'm not leading anyone!" But Brill's words, earlier, returned to her memory. *Your mother intends to put you on the throne; and we intend to make sure you're not just there for show.* "I'm—" She stopped, at a loss for words.

"You're going to end up leading us whether you like it or not," Huw said mildly. "I'm not going to shove you into it, or anything like that. You're just in the right position at the right time, and if you *don't,* we'll all hang. Or worse."

"What do you mean?" She leaned forward.

Huw turned his head and looked at the window, his expression shuttered. "The duke has been holding the Clan together, through ClanSec, for a generation. He's, he's a modernizer, in his own way. But there aren't enough of us, and he's aging. He's also a fascist." Huw held up a finger: "I say that in the strict technical sense of the word—he's what you get when you take the principle of aristocratic exceptionalism and push it down a level onto the bourgeoisie, and throw in a big dose of the subordination of the will of the individual to the needs of the collective. Ahem."

He took a sip of wine. "Sorry, Political Econ 301, back before I ended up in MIT. The Clan—we're only five generations removed from folks who remember being itinerant tinkers. We are the nearest thing that the Gruinmarkt has thrown up to a middle class, and it's the lack of any effective alternative that had our great-grandparents buying titles of nobility and living it up. Anyway, the duke has taken a bunch of warring, feuding extended families and given them a security organization that guards them all. He's kicked butt and taken names, and secured a truce, and virtually everyone now agrees it's a good thing. But he's a single point of failure. When he goes, who's going to be the next generalissimo? *Your* trouble is that you're his niece, by his red-headed wildcat stepsister. More importantly, you're the only surviving one in the direct line of succession—the attrition rate forty years ago was fearsome. So if you decide not to play your cards you'd better be ready to run like hell. Whichever of the conservative hard-liners comes out on top will figure you're a mortal threat."

"Hang on, whichever? Conservatives? Aren't you jumping the gun—"

"No, because *we're not ready.* Give us another few years and maybe Earl Riordan could do it. Or Olga, Baroness Thorold, although she's even younger. There are others: Kennard Heilbrunner ven Arnesen, Albericht Hjalmar-Hjorth. But they're not in position. You're in an unusual spot: You're young but not too young, you've got *different* experience, you demonstrated a remarkable ability to innovate under pressure, and—the icing on the cake—assuming you're pregnant, you're carrying a legitimate heir to the throne. Or at least one who everyone who survived the betrothal will swear is legitimate, and that's what counts. And they'll swear to it because, while the old nobility wouldn't know a DNA paternity test from a hole in the ground, the *Clan* nobility have heard of it, and even the old folks have a near-superstitious respect for the products of science."

"But I'm not"—Miriam stopped. She picked up her glass again, rolling it between her palms. "Did Brill tell you the details of Dr. ven Hjalmar's creepy plan?" Huw nodded. "Good. But you know something? I'm old, and not all pregnancies come to term, and I am really *not fucking happy* about being turned into a brood mare. And I completed enough of pre-med that if—that's an *if*—I decide to lose it, you—that's a collective *you*—are going to have to keep me in a straitjacket for the next nine months if you want your precious heir. Assuming it exists and it's a boy. And I haven't made my mind up yet. And as for what ven Hjalmar's got coming, if he isn't dead, if I ever see him again . . ."

Silence. Then Huw spoke, in a low voice, as if talking to himself: "Miriam, if you are pregnant and you decide you don't want to go through with it, I would consider it a matter of my *personal* honor to help you end it. Just as long as you keep it quiet . . . the old folks, they wouldn't understand. But I won't be party to keeping you in a straitjacket."

"Uh. I. Er." Miriam drained her wineglass, trying to cover her confusion. "What you just offered. You know what you just said?"

"Yes." Huw nodded. "I will either get you the appropriate medication, or, if it's too late for that, help you get to an abortion clinic." He paused. "It wouldn't be the first time I've helped a girl out that way."

"Uh." Miriam stared at him. *Just when I think I'm getting to understand them* . . . "No offense, but you made it sound like organizing a shopping trip. . . ."

"I may be an MIT graduate student, but I'm from *the Gruinmarkt.*" Huw visibly searched for words. "We don't place much stock in a babe 'til it's born, usually. Which is perhaps a good thing. You wouldn't want it to be born if it would trigger a blood feud that would claim its own—and its parents'—lives, would you?"

"But—you said it was leverage—"

"Yes, I did." He looked back at her. "But it's not the only lever you've got. The duke's accident elevates your rank in the game. You might still have a chance, even if you throw it away." He slid off his bar stool and picked up the dirty plates. "Just try to give the rest of us some warning when you make your mind up, huh?"

"I know what this looks like." She was still gripping the wineglass tightly, she realized, tightly enough to stop her hands shaking. "I am not going to flip. I've been here before, a long time ago."

"But"—Huw peered at her—"you're doing fine, so far."

"It's a control thing." Miriam forced herself to let go of the glass. "You never know, I might *not* be pregnant. I need a test kit. And then I need some space to think, to get my head around this." She paused. "Were you serious about that offer?"

Huw hesitated for a few seconds before answering. "All the plans anyone's making—they all rely on your active participation. We need you to trust us. Therefore"—he shrugged uncomfortably—"having made that offer I'm bound by it; if I forswear myself you'll never trust me, or any of us, ever again. And we, my faction, need you to show us what to do. That's more important than any crazy plan Henryk hatched to manipulate the succession. We need your trust. And that's something that can only be bought with our own."

Three o'clock in the morning.

The occasional crack of heavy-caliber gunfire, punctuated by the boom of a black-powder cannon, split the night-time quiet outside the castle walls. Nobody was getting much sleep, least of all the guards who hunkered down in the courtyard around the central keep, night-vision goggles active, waiting for a sign.

The sign, when it came, was a mere flickering in the shadows near the dynamited well house. Two of the guards spotted it at once, lowered their guns, and darted out across the open ground towards it. Their target bent over, emptying his stomach on the hard-packed cobblestones. "This way, sir! We need to get under cover."

The traveler nodded weakly, straightening up. "Take. This." He held out a shoulder bag. "I'll mark the spot. It's crowded around there." His clothing was unfamiliar, but not his face; the sergeant nodded and took his bag.

"You sit down and wait, then. We'll be along presently." He glanced at the sky: So far the enemy forces hadn't tried lobbing shells into the courtyard at random, but it was only a matter of time before they got bored with sniping at window casements. "Try to stay close to the wall."

He dashed back towards the keep, not bothering to jink—

they held the walls so far, Lightning Child be praised—
going flat-out with the shoulder bag clenched in both hands.

Carl was waiting in the grand hall with his staff. By lamp-
light, his face was heavily lined. He seemed, to the sergeant's
eye, to have aged a decade in the past two days. "Let's see
that," he suggested.

"Sir."

The guard up-ended the bag's contents in the middle of
the table with a thin clatter of plastic. Carl picked one of the
cards up and carefully angled it for a glance. He drew
breath sharply. "What do you think?"

Oliver Hjorth took the card and squinted at it. "Yes, this
looks like the right thing." He glanced at the guard. "You
recognized the courier."

"It's Morgan du Hjalmar, somewhat the worse for wear."

The baron thought for a moment. "He'll be wanting a
ride back over, won't he."

Carl nodded. "See to it," he told the sergeant, then glanced
sideways at Helmut Anders, his lieutenant. "Get everyone
moving out. The recon lance first, as planned, then if the insertion is cold the, the casualty and his party"—he couldn't
bring himself to refer to the duke by name—"followed by
everyone else. My lord Hjorth, if you'd care to accompany
my headquarters staff . . . Let's get a move on, people!"

The crowd gathered around the table scattered, except
for the core of officers and Helmut, who carefully removed
his helmet and scooped the laminated plastic cards into it,
being careful to avert his eyes. He moved to stand by the
door, waiting for the clatter and clump of boots as the recon
lance descended the grand staircase, weapons ready.

"Take a card, move on out, Morgan over by the well
house will show you the transit spot," he told them, holding
the helmet before him. "You know what to do."

"Secure the area!" Erik grinned at Helmut, his enthusiasm evidently barely dampened by the disaster on the roof-
top two days ago.

"They're supposed to be friendly," Helmut chided him. "So use your discretion."

"Aye!" Erik took a card and stepped forward. "Come on, you guys. Party's this way."

Olga watched from the back of the hall as the recon lance marched towards the well house and an appointment with an uncertain world. *Better them than me,* she told herself. There were any number of things that could go wrong. They might have the wrong knotwork, a subtle flaw in the design, and go . . . somewhere. Or the long-lost cousins of the hidden family might decide to use this opportunity to settle their old score against the eastern families. Any number of nasty little possibilities lay in that particular direction. Morgan's appearance suggested otherwise, but Olga had no great faith in his abilities, especially after what Helge— Miriam—had told her about the way he'd run her works in New Britain into the ground. *Whatever can go wrong, probably has* already *gone wrong, and there's no point worrying about it.* She tried the thought for size and decided it was an ill-fit for her anxiety. There's nothing to be done but wait and see. . . .

Minutes passed, then there was another flicker in the shadows, out in the courtyard. A brief pause, then a figure trotted back towards the great hall.

"Sir! The area was as described, and Cornet du Thorold sends word that he has secured the perimeter." The soldier looked slightly pale, but otherwise in good shape—he'd made his first transit on a comrade's back, specifically so he'd be able to make a quick return dash. "To my eye it's looking good. There are four covered trucks waiting, and eight men, not obviously armed, with your cousin Leonhard."

"Good." Captain Wu nodded. Then he glanced Olga's way. "Your cue, milady."

"Indeed." Olga turned back to the side chamber where her small team was waiting. They'd brought the duke downstairs earlier. Now he lay on a stretcher, eyes closed, breathing so slowly that she had to watch him closely to be sure he was still alive. "Come on," she told Irma, Gerd, Martyn, and the four soldiers she'd roped in. "Let's get him to safety."

The slow march out to the moonlit well house, matching her pace to the stretcher beside her, the smooth touch of the laminated card between her fingers: Olga felt herself winding tight as a watch spring. The gun slung across her shoulder was a familiar presence, but for once it was oppressive: If she found herself using it in the next few minutes, then the duke's life—and by extension, the stable governance of the Clan—would be in mortal jeopardy. This has to work. *Because if it doesn't . . .*

Seconds spun down into focused moments. Olga found herself crouching astride a heavily built trooper. "Are we ready?" she asked, as the soldiers raised their cards and shone pocket flashlights on them. "Because—"

The world lurched—

"Oh," she said, and slid down her porter's back as he staggered.

There were *floodlights.* And walls of wood, and between the walls, four large trucks of unfamiliar design, and soldiers. *Familiar* soldiers, thank Sky Father, in defensive positions near the gates to the compound. "What *is* this place?" she demanded.

"Lumberyard," said Leonhard Wu, beside her shoulder.

Olga suppressed an unladylike urge to punch him. Leonhard always left her feeling slightly dirty: something about the way his gaze always lingered for just a few seconds too long. "Nice to see you, too," she replied. *Whose lumberyard,* she left unasked. The security implications were likely to prove disquieting, and right now she had a single task to focus on—

"How is he?" she asked Gerd, who crouched beside the duke, holding his wrist.

"As good as can—"

"—Is that the *duke?*" Leonhard's voice cracked into a squawk.

"Hsst." Olga leaned towards him. "This is not Angbard Lofstrom, he wasn't here, and you haven't seen him. Not now, not here, not in this state. Do you understand?" She smiled coldly.

"No need for that!" He nearly collapsed in his haste to back away. "Ah, no, I haven't seen anything. But, uh, don't you think you ought to get your nothing-to-see-here out of sight, Olga? Before the cousins—"

"That's the idea." She nodded at the trucks. "Which of them is designated for officers?"

"That one—"

"Good. You can help Gerd here carry John Doe over to the load bed and make him comfortable. Hmm. Irma, why don't you go with Leonhard here and make sure everyone works together splendidly? I have another job to do before we leave."

She left Leonhard looking over his shoulder at her in fear and strode towards the gate, where Erik, the cornet in charge of the recon lance, stood with a couple of unfamiliar men in strange, drab clothing.

"Cornet, gentlemen." She nodded. "I believe you have a tactical plan."

One of the men looked vaguely familiar. "Lady, ah, Thorold-Hjorth? You are a friend of, of Helge?"

She blinked. "Yes. You are . . . ah, Sir James." She bobbed her head. "I see you made it back home."

"Indeed." He smiled faintly. "And how may I serve you?"

"Let's walk."

"Certainly."

James Lee had been dangerously smooth, she remembered, so smooth you could almost forget that his uncle and ancestors had waged a quiet war of assassination against her parents and grandparents, almost as soon as they'd concluded—erroneously—that their patriarch had been abandoned by his eastern brothers. James was friendly, affable, polished, and a much better diplomat than anyone had expected when, as part of the settlement between the families, he'd been sent to stay in Niejwein as a guest—or hostage. *Which makes him dangerous,* she reminded herself. "I have a little problem," she said quietly.

"A problem?" He raised an eyebrow as they neared the rear of the truck where Irma and Gerd, with Leonhard's unwilling help, were lifting the duke into the covered load bed.

"A passenger who is somewhat . . . sick. We need dropping off elsewhere from the rest of Carl's men, to make a crossing to the United States where he can receive urgent medical care."

"If he's so sick, why—" James paused. "Oh. Who is he?"

"I don't think you want to know. Officially."

James paused in midstride. "There have been signals," he said. "Huge disturbances, civil strife in Gruinmarkt. We have eyes and ears; we cannot help but notice that things are not going according to your plans."

Olga nodded politely, trying not to give anything away. "Your point, sir?"

"You are imposing on us for a big favor," he pointed out. "Six months ago our elders were at daggers' drawn. Some of them are still not sure that sheathing them was a good idea. We have our own external security problems, especially here, and escorting your soldiers through our territory is bound to attract unwanted attention. I'm sorry to have to say this so bluntly, but I need something to give my elders, lest they conclude that you have nothing to offer them."

"I see." Olga kept her smile bland as she frantically considered and discarded options. *Shoot his men and steal their vehicles* was, regrettably, not viable; without native guides to the roads of Irongate they'd risk getting hopelessly lost, and in any case the hidden family's elders wouldn't have sent James without an insurance policy. *Offer him something later* would send entirely the wrong signal, make her look as weak as the debtor turning out his purse before a loan shark's collection agents. Her every instinct screamed *no* at the idea of showing him the duke in his current state, but on the other hand . . .

"Let me put it to you that your elders' interests are served by the continued stability of our existing leadership," she pointed out. "If one of our . . . leaders . . . had experienced an unfortunate mishap, perhaps in the course of world-walking, it would hardly enhance your security to keep him from reaching medical treatment."

"Of course not." James nodded. "And if I thought for a second that one of your leaders was so stricken, I would of course offer them the hospitality of our house—at least, for as long as they lingered." He raised an eyebrow quizzically.

Olga sighed. "You know we travel to another world, not like New Britain." Well, of course he did. "Their doctors can work miracles, often—at least, they are better than anything I've ever seen here, or anything available back home. It does not reflect on your honor that I must decline your offer of hospitality; it is merely the fact that the casualty might survive if we can get him into the hospital that is waiting for him, but he will probably die if we linger here." She looked James Lee in the eye. "And if he dies without a designated successor, all hell will break loose."

James swallowed. The violent amber flare of the floodlights made it hard to be sure, but it seemed to her that he looked paler than normal. "If it's the duke—" He began to turn towards the truck, and Olga grabbed him by one elbow.

"Don't!" she said urgently. "Don't get involved. Forget your speculation. It's not the duke; the duke cannot possibly be allowed to be less than hale, lest a struggle to inherit his seat break out in the middle of a civil war with the Pervert's faction. Let Ang— Let our sick officer pass, and if he recovers he will remember; and if he dies, you can remind his successors that you acted in good faith. But if you delay us and he dies . . . you wouldn't want that to happen."

She felt him tense under her hand, and clenched her teeth. James was taller than she, and significantly stronger: If he chose not to be restrained, if he insisted on looking in the truck—

He relaxed infinitesimally, and nodded. "You'd better go, my lady." Shadows flickered behind them—another lance of Wu's soldiers coming through. "Right now. Your men Leonhard or Morgan, one of them can guide you. Take this truck; I will arrange a replacement for your comrades." Olga released his elbow. He rubbed it with his other hand. "I hope you are right about your dream-world's doctors. Losing the thin white duke at this point would indeed not be in our interests."

"I'm pleased you agree." Olga glanced round, spotted Leonhard walking towards the driver's cabin. "I'd better go."

"One thing," James said hastily. "Is there any news of the lady Helge?"

"Helge?" Olga looked back at him. "She passed through New London a week ago. One of my peers is following her."

"Oh," James said quietly. "Well, good luck to her." He turned and walked back towards the gate.

Olga watched him speculatively for a few seconds. *Now what was that about?* she wondered. But there was no time to be lost, not with the duke stricken and semiconscious on the back. She climbed into the cab of the truck behind Leonhard and a close-lipped driver. "Let's go," she told them. "There's no time to lose."

5

THE EXECUTION PROTOCOL

❦

Governments run on order and process. There was probably a protocol for everything, thought agent Judith Herz—formerly of the FBI, now attached semipermanently to the Family Trade Organization—short of launching a nuclear attack on your own territory. Unfortunately that was exactly what she'd been tasked with doing, and probably nobody since the more psychotic members of the Joint Chiefs of Staff tasked with planning Operation Northwood during the 1960s had even imagined it. And even though a checklist had come down from on high and the colonel and Major Alvarez had confirmed it looked good, just thinking about it gave her a headache.

(1) Secure the package at all times. She glanced up from her clipboard, across the muddy field, at the white armored truck with the rectangular box body. The floodlights they'd hastily rigged that afternoon showed that it was having some difficulty reversing towards the big top; the rear axle would periodically spin, the engine roaring like an angry tiger as the driver grappled with its overweight carcass. *Maybe we*

ought to have just used a minivan, she thought. *With a suitable escort, it would have been less conspicuous. . . .* On the other hand, the armed guards in the back, watching each other as well as the physics package, would probably disagree.

(2) *Do not deploy the package until arrival of ARM-BAND.* Armband, whatever it was—some kind of magic box that did whatever it was the world-walking freaks from fairyland did in their heads—had landed at MacArthur Airport; she'd sent Rich Hall and Amanda Cruz to pick it up. *Check.*

(3) *PAL codes—call WARBUCKS for release authorization.* That was the bit that brought her out in a cold sweat, because along with the half-dozen unsmiling federal agents from the NNSA, call sign *WARBUCKS* meant that this was the real deal, that the permissive action lock code to activate the nuclear device would be issued by the vice president himself, as explained in the signed Presidential Order she'd been allowed to read—but not to hold—by the corpse-faced bastard from the West Wing who Colonel Smith answered to. *Since when does the President give WARBUCKS backpack nukes to play with, anyway?* she asked herself; but it *looked* official enough, and the folder full of top secret code words that had landed on her desk with a palpable thud yesterday suggested that this might be a cowboy operation, but if so, it was being led by the number one rancher himself. At least, that was what the signatures of half the National Command Authority and a couple of Supreme Court justices implied.

(4) *FADM/ARMBAND final assembly and PAL programming to be carried out on launch scaffold.* The thing in the tent gave her the creeps; Smith called it a transdimensional siege tower, but it looked too close to a field-expedient gallows for her liking. She was going to go up there with Dr. Rand and a posse of inspectors from NNSA and a couple of army officers and when they came down from the platform some person or persons unknown would be dead.

Not that she was anti-death-penalty or anything, but she'd started out as an FBI agent: The anonymous military way of killing felt profoundly wrong, like a gap in a row of teeth, or a death in the family.

(5) *ARMBAND failure contingency plan. That* was the worst bit of all, because if ARMBAND failed to work as advertised, she and Lucius Rand and everyone else would be standing on a scaffold with a ticking bomb on a sixty-second countdown, and they'd get precisely two chances to enter the eight-digit abort code.

It was a good thing that she'd taken the time for holy communion and attended confession that morning, she thought, as she walked towards the tent. It had been a long day, and she had a feeling that the night was going to be even longer.

Her earbud crackled: "Herz, speak to me." It was the colonel.

"Stage one is in hand, I'm waiting on news of ARMBAND." Out of one corner of her eye she saw moving headlights, another of the undercover patrol cars circling the block slowly, looking for rubberneckers. "Everything seems to be on track so far."

"Please hold." She walked on, briefly looking round to check on the armored car. (It was reversing again, pulling free of the patch of soft ground that had stymied it.) "Okay, that's good. Update me if there are any developments."

So the colonel is jittery? Good. A uniform over near the support truck from the NNSA was waving to her; local cops drafted in for crowd control and vehicle marshaling. She changed course towards him. *So he should be.* "What's up?" she demanded.

"Uh, agent—" He was nervous; not used to dealing with FBI.

"Herz." She nodded. "You have something."

"Yeah, there's a car at the north quadrant entrance, driver says it's for you. Name of Hall."

"Oh."—*what's Rich doing up* there?—"If that's Rich

Hall and Amanda Cruz, we're expecting them." She kicked herself mentally: *Should have told them which gate to use.* "Let them in. They've got a package we're expecting."

"Sure thing, ma'am." He leaned over towards the driver's window of the patrol car, talking to his partner. Herz walked on, jittery with too much poor-quality caffeine and a rising sense of tension. *We're about to fire the opening shot in a war,* she thought. *I wonder where it's going to end. . . .*

It was dark, and the moon already riding low in the sky outside the kitchen window, when Huw yawned and conceded defeat. He saved the draft of his report, closed the lid of his laptop, picked up two glasses and a bottle of zinfandel, and went upstairs to bed.

As he closed the door and turned on the light, the bedding moved. A tousled head appeared: "What kept you?"

"I have a report to write, in case you'd forgotten." He put the glasses and the bottle down on the dressing table and began to unbutton his shirt. "I hope you had a better day than I did, my lady."

"I very much doubt it." She sat up and plumped up the pillows. As the comforter dropped, he saw that she was naked. Catching his gaze, she smiled. "Lock the door?"

"Sure." He dropped his shirt on the carpet, let his jeans fall, then went to the door and shot the dead bolt. Then he picked up the wine bottle and twisted the screw cap. "What happened?"

"Head office are going mad." She screwed up her face. "It's *unreal.* The council are running around like half-headed turkey fowl, the whole flock of them."

"Well, that's a surprise." He filled a glass, sniffed it, then held it out to her. She took it. "Any word? . . ."

"Olga's bringing him out within the next hour. Assuming nobody attacks the ambulance, he'll be in a hospital bed by dawn. The last word from that quarter is that he's tried to talk, since the incident."

Huw filled his own wineglass, then sat down on the edge of the bed. "Can we forget about politics for a few hours? I know you want me to bring you up to date on what I was doing back in New York, and I'm sure you've got a lot of stuff to tell me about what's been going on since the last time we were together, but I would like, for once, to take some time out with you. Just you and me alone, with no unquiet ghosts."

Her frown faded slightly. "I wish we could." She sighed. "But there's so much riding on this. We'll have time later, if we succeed, but"—she glanced at the door anxiously—" there's so much that can still go wrong. If Miriam has any mad ideas about running away . . ."

"Well, that's an interesting question. While you were away, we had a talk. She seemed to need it."

"Oh?" Brilliana drank down a mouthful of wine. "How is she doing?"

"Not well, but I don't *think* she's going to run out on us, as long as she feels we're standing alongside her."

"It's *that* bad? I've known her for, ah, nearly a year, and her highness does not strike me as disloyal to her friends."

Huw did not miss the significance of the honorific. "She hasn't acceded to that rank yet. Has she?"

"No." Brill's expression was bleak. "I don't think she's even realized, yet, what it means—she was having a difficult time understanding that vile business of Henryk's, much less thinking about what is going to happen . . ."

"Er, I think you're wrong." Huw emptied his glass in one long swallow. "Needed that. Excuse me. Did you buy her a pregnancy test kit?" He refilled her glass, then topped up his own.

"I—yes, but I haven't given it to her yet. She asked you about that?"

"She is remarkably open, but her ability to trust— anyone, I think—is badly damaged by the whole business of the succession. I . . . I offered to help her obtain an abortion if she thought she needed one."

"Huw!" Brill clapped one hand to her mouth. Then: "Why?"

"She raised the subject." Huw hunched his shoulders. "I don't think she will, but . . . if she feels pressured, what will she do?"

"React," Brill said automatically. "Oh. Yes, that was cleverly played, my love. But you should have warned me. That's too clever by half. What if she'd called your bluff?"

"What if it wasn't a bluff?" He shrugged. "She's no use to our cause if she doesn't trust us. No use to anyone *at all*. That is true whether or not she has a royal bun in the oven. We're trying to break the pattern, not reinforce it."

"Uh-huh. Winning her trust is one thing." She leaned towards him. "But you'd help her shoot herself in the head?"

"If I was convinced that she wanted to, and knew what she was asking for . . . yes." He looked at Brilliana with a bleakness that sat badly with his age. "I'd try to save her first, mind you."

"Would you try to save *me* from my worst urges?" she asked sharply.

Huw put his glass down. "That's one of those questions to which there's no safe answer, isn't it?"

"Yes." She drained her own glass and reached across him, to put it down beside his. He shivered as she pushed her breasts against his side; her nipples were stiff. "My worst urge right now says I want you to fuck me like there's no tomorrow. Because tomorrow"—she ran her hand down his chest—"we might both be dead."

Erasmus was going over the next morning's news with John Winstanley and Oliver Smith, the party commissioners for truth and justice, when word of the abdication came in.

Smith was reading down a plate, his lips moving silently as he read the raised bright mirror-text of the lead: ". . . and we call upon all right minded men to, hang on, here's a dropped—"

"Yes, *yes,*" Erasmus said acidly. "No need for *that,* leave it to the subs. What I need to know is, do you think it's sound?"

"Is it *sound?*" Winstanley nodded lugubriously. "Well, that's the—"

The door rattled open. Burgeson looked up sharply. "What is it?" he demanded.

The messenger boy—or youth—looked unabashed: "It's Mr. Burroughs, sir! He wants you to come, quick like! 'E says it's important!"

Erasmus stared at him. "Where is he?" he demanded.

"'E's in the mayor's mansion, sir! There's news from out east—a train just came in, and there was folks on it who said the king's abdicated!"

Erasmus glanced at Smith. "I think you'd better hold the front page," he said mildly, "I'm going to go see what this is all about."

It was an overcast, gray summer's day outside, with a thin fog from the bay pumped up to a malignant brown haze by the smoke from a hundred thousand stoves and steam cars on this side of the bay. Fishing boats were maneuvering around the wharves, working their way in and out of the harbor as if the crisis of the past weeks was just a distant rumor. From the front steps, waiting as his men brought the car round to him, Erasmus could just make out the dots of the picket fleet in the distance, military yachts and korfes riding at anchor to defend the coast against the approach of French bombardiers or submarines. He eyed them warily every morning, half afraid they would finally make their move, choosing sides in the coming struggle. Word from the cadres aboard the ships was that the sailors were restive, unpaid for months now, but that the officers remained crown loyalists for the most part. Should putsch come to shove, it would be an ugly affair—and one that the realm's foreign

enemies would be keen to exploit. Which was probably why
John Frederick had not tried his luck by ordering the picket
into the bay to put down the provisional government forces.
It was a card he could only play once, and if it failed, he
might as well dust off Cromwell's block. Although if the
messenger lad was right . . .

By the time he arrived at the mayoral mansion, a light rain
was falling and the onshore breeze was stiffening, blowing
the smog apart. Erasmus paused for a deep breath as he
stepped out of the back of the car, relishing the feel of air in
lungs he'd almost despaired of a year ago. *Where are you
now, Miriam?* he wondered briefly. It was her medication
that had cured him, of that he was certain, even though the
weird pills had turned his urine blue and disrupted his
digestion. *What other magic tricks do you have up your
sleeve?* It was something he'd have to explain to the chairman, sooner or later—if he could work out how to broach
the subject without sounding as if he'd taken leave of his
senses. "Follow," he said over his shoulder. The two bodyguards and the woman from the stenography pool moved
hastily into position.

The committee offices on the first floor were seething—
nobody was at their posts except for the militia guards,
their rifles clenched in nervous hands. "Where's the chairman?" Erasmus demanded when they came to the first checkpoint.

"He's in the committee room, sir," said the senior man—
Erasmus, being a regular enough visitor (and a member of
the committee to boot), ranked above the regular interrogation such a question might have drawn from a stranger.
"Can you tell us what's going on?"

"That's why I'm here." Erasmus grimaced. "There'll be a
statement later." He glanced at his stenographer. "Minute
that for me." He swept through the corridors towards the
former dining room that Sir Adam had requisitioned as a
meeting place for the committee, only pausing at the door

where two heavies in the red, white, and blue armbands of internal security waited with shotguns. "Erasmus Burgeson, commissioner for information, here to see the chairman," announced one of his guards.

"Aye, right." *These* guards were going by the book. Erasmus waited patiently as the senior one uncapped a speaking tube and announced him, then listened for instructions. "You're to go in, sir. Your party"—a thumb gesture—"can wait in the guardroom."

Burgeson nodded at them. "You heard him." And then he opened the door.

The Committee for Democratic Accountability was neither accountable, nor democratic, nor even much of a committee—these words were all statements of aspiration, as much as anything else, for in the early days of building a better nation these words held power, and it was Sir Adam's hope that his institutions would grow into their names. Personally, Erasmus thought this was dangerously naïve— he'd read a number of books that Miriam had loaned him, strange books describing the historical processes of her even stranger world—but it was at least worth a try. Not *all* revolutions ended up eating their young, and heaven knew it was an opportunity to break with the dead hand of the oppressive past, but the thought that *this* revolution might go the way of some of those in Miriam's books had kept him awake into the small hours on more nights than he cared to think about.

Inside the committee room, there was an atmosphere of euphoria. Sir Adam was standing behind the lectern, and about half the delegates from the district councils seemed to have packed themselves in. Someone had opened a crate of cava and orange farmers from down south were toasting shipyard workers from the east bay with foam sparkling from their chipped tea mugs. Erasmus grabbed the first shoulder he could catch inside the doorway. "What's going on?" he demanded.

"It's the king!" The man grinned broadly. "He's gone! Packed up his bags in New London and ran. The garrison in Montreal picked him up!"

A sharp stab of anxiety gnawed at Erasmus. "Are they ours?"

"They mutinied three weeks ago and elected a workers' and soldiers' council! They're with the white guards!"

Erasmus blinked. "Excuse me." He began to elbow his way through the crush towards the lectern where Sir Adam was earnestly holding forth to a gaggle of inner party gray-beards who remained obdurately sober in the face of the collective derangement.

"Ah, Erasmus." Sir Adam smiled. "I gather the good news has reached you."

"I need to know where it came from"—Erasmus pointed a thumb over his shoulder—"if we're to get the word out where it's needed. I've got a stenographer waiting in the guardroom, and a front page to fill by three."

"That's easy enough." Burroughs gestured. "You know Edward MacDonald, I take it."

Erasmus nodded. "We've met." Ed, Lady Bishop's right hand man, nodded back, cautiously.

"He brought certain other news of your activities out east, news that I personally consider would stretch the bounds of credibility—if anyone less than Lady Bishop vouched for their truth." Burroughs contemplated Erasmus, an expression of perplexity on his face that reminded Burgeson of a school-teacher examining a pupil who had just done something that, while not actually deserving of punishment, was inex-plicably wrong. "We'll need to talk about it in due course."

"Yes, we will." Erasmus surprised himself with the assur-ance of his answer. "But this isn't the time for addressing long-term problems. We've got to get the word of these mo-mentous events out first. Once the loyalists realize they have been abandoned by their false monarch, that will change the entire situation!" He nodded at Edward. "What's happened out east? What can you tell me that I can print? I need pictures, damn it! Who witnessed the events?"

The attack began an hour before dawn. Otto ven Neuhalle watched from a discreet distance as his men walked their precious M60s onto the front of the gatehouse from long range, firing parsimonious bursts—wary of his threats to damage any man who damaged his precious guns. The defenders declined to fire randomly into the dark, although a ghastly white glare opened its unblinking eye above the barred front gate, casting long shadows across the beaten ground before it—shadows that promised pain and death to anyone who ventured into view of the firing slits in the walls.

"Keep their heads down!" he shouted at Shutz and his men. "But watch for our own!"

They didn't have many minutes to wait. Creaking and squealing with an ominous rumble, two large wagons rolled round the shoulder of the hill, following the road that led to the gate. The bullocks that pulled them didn't sound too happy, roaring and lowing beneath their heavy burden. Otto bared his teeth as he heard the voice of their driver and the crack of his whip.

"This should be fun," a familiar voice commented from behind him.

Otto shivered as a chilly sweat broke out across the nape of his neck. "Your Majesty has the better of me." He turned around slowly—it was a faux pas to turn one's back on the monarch, and he had no desire to draw attention to it—and bowed deeply.

"Rise." The king gestured impatiently. The lance of royal bodyguards around him faced outward; the armor and colors he wore were indistinguishable from their uniform, but for the lack of an armband of rank. "Two minutes, no more. They should be shooting by now."

Otto found his tongue. "May I ask if the carts are for men or explosives, my liege? I need to prepare my men. . . ."

"Explosives." Egon nodded towards them. "The driver will take them up to the gate then set them off."

"The—oh." Otto nodded. The driver would do what he was told, or his family would be done by as the king had decreed: probably something creatively horrible, to reinforce his reputation as a strong and ruthless monarch. "By your leave, I shall order my men to take cover just before the blast."

"We wish them to advance and provide covering fire for the cavalry immediately afterwards," Egon added offhand.

"Cavalry?" Otto bit his tongue, but even so the word slipped out first. Beyond the gatehouse was a wet moat, and then a steep descent into a dry moat before the gate into the castle's outer battlements. Nobody in their right mind would use cavalry against the layered defenses of a castle!

"Cavalry." The royal grin was almost impish. "I hope you find it educational."

"My lord—" One of the guards cleared his throat.

"Momentarily." Egon stared at Otto. "I intend to surprise *everyone,* Baron. This is just the start."

Otto bowed his neck jerkily. "Yes, Your Majesty."

"Go." Dismissed, Otto turned to warn Shutz and his gunners about the wagons—and to leave the king's disturbing presence. Behind him, Egon was mounting the saddle of a stallion from the royal stable. A pair of irreplaceable witch-clan night vision glasses hung from his pommel.

The defenders were asleep, dead, or incompetent, Otto decided as he watched the wagons roll along the road towards the gatehouse. Or they'd been struck blind by Sky Father. The glaring hell-light cast a lurid glow across the ground before the gatehouse, but there was no shouted challenge, no crack of gunfire. *What are they* doing? He wondered. A horrid surmise began to gnaw at his imagination. *They're dead, or gone, and we're advancing into their ground while they sneak through the land of the dead, to ambush us from behind—*

Rapid fire crackled from the gatehouse, followed by a

squealing roar of bovine distress: Otto breathed again. *Not dead or gone, just incompetent.* They'd shown little sign of movement earlier in the campaign, and despite their lightning-fast assault on the castle when he'd taken it, they'd failed to follow through. The witch-clan were traders, after all, lowborn tinkers, not knights and soldiers. He grinned as the wagon ground forward faster, the uninjured oxen panicked halfway to a stampede by the gunfire and the smell of blood. It had fifty yards to go, then forty—*why aren't they firing? Are they low on ammunition?*—then twenty, then—

Otto knelt close to the ground, bracing himself, mouth open to keep his ears from hurting. The moments stretched on, as he counted up to twenty heartbeats.

"Is he dead?" called one of his gunners.

"I think—" someone began to reply, but the rest of his comment was forestalled by a searing flash. A second later the sound reached Otto, a door the size of a mountainside slamming shut beside his head. The ground shook. A couple of seconds later still, the gravel and fragments rained down around the smoke-filled hole. "What was *that?*" Otto shouted, barely able to hear himself. It wasn't like any powder explosion he'd ever heard, and he'd heard enough in his time. *What's the Pervert got his hands on now?* he added silently, straightening up.

The hell-light had gone out, along with the front of the gatehouse. The wagon hadn't been small—there could have been half a ton, or even a ton, of explosives in it; whatever kind of explosives the king's alchemists had cooked up, using lore stolen from the witches.

Otto cleared his dry throat, spat experimentally. "Break them down, get ready to move out," he shouted at Shutz. "The cavalry will be through here next."

Shutz looked baffled, then pointed to his ears. Otto nodded. *"Scheisse."* He gestured at the now-silent machine guns, miming packing them and moving forward. Shutz nodded, then opened his mouth and began shouting orders. Or at least he appeared to be telling troopers what to do: Otto found to his bemusement that he couldn't hear them.

The ground was still shaking. Peering back up the road, it wasn't hard for Otto to see why. Two more wagons were plodding grimly towards the pile of dust and smoke that had been the gatehouse—and behind them, what looked like a battalion of royal dragoons. In the predawn twilight they rode at no more than a slow walking pace. Otto shook his head; the ringing in his ears went on, but he was beginning to hear other sounds now. He raised his glasses, fumbled with the power button, and peered at the wagon. *This* one carried soldiers in helmets and half-armor, and a complicated mess of stuff, not the barrels of explosives he'd half-expected to see. "Interesting," he murmured, looking round for a messenger. "You!"

"My lord!" The man shouted.

"Tell Anders to get his guns ready to move. We're to cover this force." He pointed at the approaching dragoons. "They're going to break in. Go!" *How* they were going to break into the castle he had no idea, but Egon clearly expected them to do so, and Otto had more than a slight suspicion that the new explosives in the oxcart weren't Egon's only surprise.

Strung out on caffeine and fatigue, Judith Herz suppressed a yawn as she watched the technicians with the handcart maneuver the device into position on the scaffold. There was a big cross spray-painted in the middle of the top level, and they were taking pains to move it so that it was centered perfectly. The size of a beer keg, with a briefcase-sized detonation controller strapped to it with duct tape, the FADM didn't look particularly menacing. She glanced over at Rich Hall, who was sitting patiently in a director's chair, the Pelikan case containing ARMBAND between his feet. Cruz was about, somewhere, of course: They were taking pains to keep it within arm's reach at all times. *Good,* Judith thought tiredly. *Everything's ready, except for the PAL codes.* And head office, of course, but they'd be on-site shortly. The sooner they could get everything hooked up, the sooner they could all go and get some well-earned sleep.

A flicker of motion near the entrance to the tent caught her eye and she looked round. The new arrivals seemed tired: the colonel, talking animatedly to the man-in-black from the West Wing, a couple of aides following in their wake. *Oh great,* she thought: *rubberneckers.* "Wait here," she hold the technicians, then walked down the ramp to meet the newcomers.

"Colonel." She smiled. "And, uh, Dr. James."

Smith glanced sidelong at him. "He's our vertical liaison. With WARBUCKS."

"Dead straight." Dr. James looked tired, too: The bags under his eyes suggested the lights had been burning late in the Naval Observatory grounds. "Let's take a look at the package."

"We haven't attached ARMBAND yet," Judith began to say as Dr. James marched straight towards the scaffold.

"Then do it, right now. We need to get this thing done."

What's the sudden hurry? she wondered. "Yes. Sir." She waved at Rich, who sat up sharply and mimed a query until she beckoned. "What's up?"

"Change of situation." James was terse. "I have the PAL codes." He tapped his breast pocket. "Colonel?"

"Dr. James is here as an official observer for the White House," Smith reassured her. "Also, we have Donald Reckitt from NNSA, Mary Kay Kare from, from the people who made ARMBAND, Richard Tracy from the Office of Special Plans—"

The introductions went on until the scaffolding began to creak under their weight. Finally they worked their way down through the layers of observers and their credentials to the technical staff. "And Dr. Rand, who will confirm that the munition is release ready, check the connections to the detonation controller, and hand over to Major Alvarez and Captain Hu for deployment."

"Certainly. If you folks wouldn't mind giving me some elbow room? . . ." Rand, fiftyish and somewhat bohemian in appearance, looked as irritated by the institutional rubbernecking as Herz felt. As FTO's tame expert on these gadgets—indeed, as one of the nation's leading experts—he'd studied under Teddy Taylor, although the Comprehensive Test Ban Treaty meant that his expertise was somewhat abstract—he understood the FADMs as well as anyone else. And he ran through his checklist surprisingly rapidly. "All looking good," he announced, finally. "Considering where it's been."

"That's enough about that." Dr. James spoke sharply: "Not everyone here is briefed."

"Oh? Really." Rand smiled lopsidedly as he straightened up. "Well that makes it alright then." He patted the bomb, almost affectionately. "For what it's worth, this one's ready to go. Excuse me, ladies, gentlemen . . ."

As Rand left the platform, the colonel glanced at Herz. "If you want to call the items? . . ."

"Uh, yes, sir . . ." She stared at her clipboard and blinked a few times, wishing the tension between her brows would go away. Focusing was hard. "PAL Codes. I need to contact WAR— the designated release authority," she corrected. She looked at Dr. James.

He nodded. "This is what you want," he said, handing her a manilla envelope from his jacket pocket.

Judith slit it open with a fingernail. There was a single sheet of paper, on White House stationery, with a brief note, a pair of eight-digit numbers, and a famous signature. "Well." She breathed out. "This looks to be in order, so"—she clipped it behind her checklist—"we move on to ARMBAND. Rich, this is your curtain call. Major? We're ready to attach ARMBAND."

Alvarez waved Rich Hall through to the front of the

platform. "Okay, here it is," he said. He cleared his throat. "I've only done this a couple of times before."

He opened the shockproof case and pulled out four black rubber feet. "Shoes." Rocking the bomb carefully side to side, he wedged the feet underneath it. "The payload needs to be electrostatically isolated from ground, or this won't work." Next, he picked up a drab plastic box, its upper face broken only by a winking red LED, a button, and a key slot. "Okay, now for the duct tape." With that, he pulled out a reel of duct tape and a box cutter, and taped the box to the top of the bomb. Finally, he held up a key: "arming key." He inserted it in the slot and gave it a half turn, and addressed Alvarez: "ARMBAND is not yet armed. To activate it, it's necessary to give the key another half turn, then push the button. Five seconds later, it does its stuff. You do *not* want to be touching it when that happens." He picked up his case and stepped back. "You have control now."

"I have control," Alvarez echoed. He nodded at Wall: "You'd better leave the platform now, sir."

Is that all? Judith blinked again, feeling obscurely cheated. It was like black magic—a device that could transport a payload into another universe?—and yet it seemed so mundane.

"Agent Herz?" Colonel Smith prodded her.

"Oh? I'm sorry." She nodded. "Major Alvarez?" she called.

"Ma'am." Alvarez and Hu were out of uniform—nobody wanted inconvenient questions about what army officers were doing in a field outside Concord—but nobody would mistake them for civilians, not with that crew cut and attitude. "I have the checklist."

He knelt down beside the package and unclipped a panel on the detonation controller strapped to the side of the bomb. Pulling open a laminated ring-bound checklist, he began to flip through pages, periodically double-checking a switch position. "Check, please," he told Hu.

"Check."

"I need the PAL code now."

"Here are your numbers." Herz read out the eight-digit sequence from the letter. The audience fell silent, like witnesses at an execution. As, in a manner of speaking, they were: Alvarez and Hu the hangmen, adjusting the noose; Herz the prison governor, handing over the death warrant; and parties unknown standing on the trapdoor . . . *well, at least they won't feel a thing,* she told herself. *More than you can say for their victims, over the years.* "Remember, we want a sixty-second delay. If the package doesn't disappear in front of your eyes within ten seconds, then turn the key to safe ARMBAND and enter the abort code. Are you ready?"

"We're ready," Alvarez called.

"Ready!" Hu echoed.

Alvarez carefully closed the cover on the detonation controller, but—Herz noted—neglected to latch it shut. *That* wasn't in the checklist, at a guess.

The silence was oppressive. Finally, Dr. James cleared his throat. "Major Alvarez, with the authority vested in me by the executive order you have received, I order you to proceed."

Three days ago, the bulk of the Clan's mobile security force had concentrated in a field near Concord, arriving in buses disguised as costumed medievalists. Now, in the predawn light, they'd made it three miles down the road—riding in the backs of steam-powered livestock trucks, disguised as filthy, fight-worn anachronists. Their leader, the duke, and his paramedic and bodyguards, led by the lady Olga, had split off ten minutes ago, heading for an uncertain rendezvous and a waiting ambulance. That left Carl, captain of Security, with a reduced command and a monstrous headache; but at least it was better than being bottled up in that stone death trap.

"You're sure this is the spot." He fixed Morgan with a well-practiced stare.

"Yuh-ess." Morgan yawned hugely. "My apologies, sir Captain. We are two miles southwest of the gates of the

Hjalmar Palace, fifty yards north of the milestone, and the cross yonder"—he gestured—"marks the center of the road." The road was little more than a dirt track, but had the singular advantage of being a known quantity. "Last night the pretender's forces were encamped a mile down the road from the gatehouse, dispersed in tents through the woods to either side. Watchers on the hill slope, of course. I cannot be sure—we have no recent intelligence—but I don't believe the camp extended more than two miles down the road to Wergatsfurt. So we *should* be a few hundred yards beyond their rear perimeter, as of last night."

"Right." Carl turned to Helmut. "Are the men ready?"

"As ready as we can be." Helmut's normally taciturn demeanor was positively stony. Which wasn't good.

"How much ammunition did we end up leaving behind?"

"For the Dragons? Most of it. Stefan's got just eight rounds. The SAWs are better—we divided up the belts. I'd say, three thousand rounds per gun. And of course the light arms, we're fully equipped from the castle's armory. But food and water—it's not good."

"Well, we'll just have to do the job before that becomes an issue." Carl paused in thought. "Have the men dose up with prophylactics before we cross over. We need a marker for the crossover point on the other side"—he pointed at the rough wooden crucifix that marked Morgan's survey point— "and make sure everyone knows that if we move to retreat, that's the rendezvous point. Have Olaf's section position their M47 fifty yards forward of that marker, with one of the SAWs for covering fire"—Carl paced towards the perimeter of the fenced-in field to which the Lee's trucks had brought them—"and get Erik's people to cross over here. Hmm. If there's any sign of the Pervert's bodyguard, Little Dimmir's lance can concentrate on nailing them with support from Erik's people, and Arthur's SAW section if they're dug in *there*." He continued laying out the deployment as Helmut and two sergeants followed him around the perimeter, making notes. It was all ad hoc, dangerously under-planned and hasty, but if there was one thing they didn't have, it was time for a careful setup. Finally, he finished: "That's it. Brief your men and get them into position. We go in, hmm, zero-six-hundred, that's just under half an hour. Get moving!"

Otto's itchy sense of unease grew stronger with every step he took towards the moat. Ahead of him, the roar of the royal cannon provided a drumbeat punctuation to the sounds of advance: men shouting, chanting the king's name; boots tramping out the rhythm of the march in time to the beat of their drummers; horses clattering on the cobbled roadbed, neighing, jingling kit; and periodically a spastic belch of machine-gun fire arcing overhead, crackling and whining off the stony roofline of the walls.

They're not shooting back, he realized, a hundred yards past the gatehouse, as he paused in a dip in the ground. Sometime in the past couple of hours the witches had cleared out. *Which means—*

"Forward for the Gruinmarkt!" The voice behind the cry was half-hoarse, but instantly recognizable as the royal life guards took up the call. "The witches have fled before us!" The life guards flooded forward like a pack of hounds following an injured deer.

"Well, fuck it," Otto grunted. "Jorg!"

"Sir."

"Tell Heidlor to set his guns up here and range in on the keep's door. Indirect fire."

"Sir!" Jorg paused. "But aren't we—"

"Do it!"

Otto raised his glasses and studied the near horizon, shockingly close. In the predawn gloom the castle was a brooding presence up ahead, its upper ramparts topping the huge dry moat beyond the rise. *They've had two days to prepare for this, and they like blowing things up. What would I do in their shoes?* "Jorg!"

Jorg, panting, hurried back towards him. "Sir?"

"Tell Heidlor to range in on the keep's door *and* to keep a watch out behind us, ranged in on the road past the gatehouse."

"The gatehouse, sir? But we came that way—"

"Exactly." Otto bared his teeth at the man; Jorg ducked his head hastily and ran back towards the gunners and their overloaded mules.

Otto settled down, kneeling, to watch the lines of advance. The lack of fire from the castle worried him, but he had scarcely raised his glasses again when a loud and hearty hail demanded his attention. "Ahem, my lord Neuhalle!" The interruption leaned over the pommel of his horse to look down at Otto. It was Geraunt, Earl Marlburg, one of the king's younger and more enthusiastic vassals.

"Yes, Sir Geraunt?" Otto stared up at him, annoyed.

"His majesty sends word!" Geraunt was obviously excited. He drew a message tube out of his sleeve and extended it towards Otto. "A change to your disposition. You are to turn around and withdraw to the gatehouse, there to cover the approaches to the castle, he says."

"Right." Otto took the tube. A wave of palpable relief washed through him. Not that he was a coward—certainly the past month of campaigning had given the lie to that—but the idea of advancing into a booby-trapped castle did not fill him with joy. If the king wanted him to stake out the approaches to the castle, against the stab in the back with a witch's knife that Otto himself half-expected, then that was a reassuringly known quantity. More importantly it suggested that his majesty was, if not exactly sane, then no crazier than any other fox. "Can you tell me what his majesty intends?"

Sir Geraunt hunkered down, putting his horse between Otto and the keep. Otto looked up at him: "His majesty is most exercised; he says the witches have fled before him, and probably laid mines to bring down the keep, so he intends to secure the inner walls, then bring in sappers to find the—"

The world flashed white, twice, in a tenth of the beat of a heart. Everything was white as the face of the noonday sun, except for the knife-edge shadow of Sir Geraunt, freakishly cast across Otto's upper body and head.

Otto blinked as a wave of heat washed across his skin. A giant the size of a mountain had opened the door of a kiln full of molten iron big enough to forge the hammer of the gods, and the glare surged overhead, stifling and oppressive. The sensation of heat faded over the duration of two heartbeats and he opened his eyes, but everything was blotchy and purple-white with afterimages. *Was that an explosion?* he thought numbly, as reflex or shock made him collapse back into the ground cover. What was left of Sir Geraunt's mount, with what was left of Sir Geraunt still astride it, began to fall sideways into his depression. Neither of them lived, which was perhaps a mercy, because while Sir Geraunt and his horse were intact and unblemished on the side that fell towards Otto, their opposite side—that had faced the castle—was scorched to charcoal around a delicate intaglio of bone.

The castle was no longer there. Where the keep had crouched within its courtyard, shielded by the outer walls and their rammed-earth revetments, a skull-shape of dust and fire was rising, its cap looming over the ramparts like a curious salamander crawling from its volcanic home to survey its surroundings.

As Otto fell, a blast of fiery wind pulsed across the burning grass that covered the approaches to the castle, casting aloft the calcined bodies of the men and animals who had been caught in the open at the moment of the heat flash. Burning sticks and a shotgun blast of fractured gravel caromed off the ground. A scant second later the shock front reversed, sucking back towards the roiling bubble of flames as it rose from the center of the fortification on a stem of dirt and debris.

Otto inhaled a mouth-watering stench of cooking meat and hot air and tried to collect his scattered wits. Something was holding his legs down. He couldn't see anything—just violet afterimages stubbornly refusing to fade when he screwed his eyes shut. Panicking, he tried to kick, but without vision he couldn't see the dead horse lying atop him. His back was a dull mass of pain where he'd fallen, and the *smell—have they taken me down to Hel, the choosers of the slain?* he wondered dizzily as he turned his damaged eyes towards the furious underside of the mushroom cloud.

Carl stared at the turbulent caul of smoke rising above the ridgeline and swallowed, forcing back the sharp taste of stomach acid at the back of his tongue. His head pounded, but his eyes were clear. Around him, soldiers stared slack-jawed at the ominous thunderhead. The predawn sky was just turning dark blue, but the fires ignited by the bomb brought their own light to the scene, so for the moment their faces were stained ruddy with a mixture of awe and fear.

"Is that what I think it is?" asked Helmut.

Baron Hjorth cleared his throat. "It can't be," he said confidently. "They're all supposed to be under lock . . . and key. . . ." He trailed off into an uncertain silence.

Carl took him by the elbow. More soldiers were spilling in out of the air, staggering or bending over in some cases—two world-walks in three hours was a brutal pace, even for the young and fit—and Carl had to step around them as he steered Oliver a hundred meters up the road in the direction of the castle. "That." He gestured. "Is. A mushroom cloud. Yes?"

Oliver blinked rapidly. "I think so." He swallowed. "I've never seen one before."

"Well. *Where the fuck did it come from?*"

"Don't ask me!" Oliver snarled. "*I* didn't do it! God-on-a-stick, what do you take me for? All our bombs are accounted for as of last Tuesday except for the one Matthias"—he stopped dead for a moment—"Oh dear."

"If that *bastard* Matthias—"

Oliver cut him off with a slashing gesture. "Trust me, Matthias is dead." He closed his eyes, composing himself. "This is someone else. Sending us a message." He opened his eyes. "How old is that . . . thing?"

Carl glanced up, uneasily sniffing the air: The tang of wood smoke spoke of pine trees on the reverse slope ignited by the heat flash. "I don't know. Not old—see the stem? It hasn't drifted." His guts loosened as he realized, *if I'd timed this just a little later we'd still have been there.* He licked his thumb and held it up. There was a faint breeze from the south, blowing towards the castle. "Um. What, if anything, do you know about fallout?"

"The poison rain these things shed? I think we should forget the Pervert and get your men out of here. Forced march. If you want to set up guns south of Wergatsfurt and catch any stragglers you're welcome to them, but if they were camped a mile yonder"—he gestured towards the cloud—"I don't know. They *might* have survived, if they dug in for the night. Although I don't give much for their chances if that fire starts to spread."

Carl grinned humorlessly. "Have you ever known the Pervert to refuse a chance to stab us in the back, my lord? Dawn attacks a speciality, remember?"

Oliver shook his head.

"Come." Carl turned his back on the cloud. "I'll leave two men to scout the area in an hour's time. The rest—let's hit the road. I'll have time to worry about whoever's sending us *messages* when I've hunted down and killed the last of the pretender's men."

Behind them a dark rain began to fall on the battlefield, fat drops turbid with radioactive dust scorched from the stones of the castle and the bones of the men who had followed their usurper-king into the radius of the fireball. The survivors, burned and broken—those that could move—cupped their hands to catch the rain and drank greedily.

Otto Neuhalle, and the ten survivors of his company, were among them. They did not know—nor could they—that the man-portable nuclear weapon responsible for the fireball had a maximum yield of only one kiloton, and that such bombs are inherently dirty, and that this blast had been, by nuclear standards, absolutely filthy; that it had failed to consume even a tenth of its plutonium core, and had scooped up huge masses of debris and irradiated it before scattering it tightly around ground zero.

Dead men, drinking bitter rain.

6

REALIGNMENTS

☙

I f he's dead, we're so screwed."

Brill's fingers whitened on the steering wheel, but Miriam took Huw's gloomy appraisal as a conversational opportunity. They were coming less frequently today, as the reality of driving across a continent took hold. "Isn't that a little pessimistic?"

Huw closed the lid of his laptop and carefully unplugged the cable from the satphone. He slid them both into their pockets in the flight case before he replied. "It's not sounding good. They got him into the high dependency unit more than seventy-two hours after the initial intracerebral hemorrhage. He's still alive, but he's confused and only semiconscious and, uh, I've done some reading. More than forty percent of patients with that kind of hemorrhage die within a month."

Yul, sprawled across the van's third bench seat, chose that moment to emit a thunderous snore. Elena, who'd been lying asleep with her head in his lap, shuddered and opened her eyes, then yawned. "What?"

"He's not dead yet," Miriam observed tiredly. "He's not going to die of anything nonmedical, not with Olga looking out for him. And he's got the best treatment money can buy."

"Which is not saying a lot."

Brill hunched her shoulders behind the wheel, pulling out to inch past a big rig. "Listen, Huw, why don't you just shut up?" she snapped.

"Wha? . . ." Huw gaped.

"Hush, Brill, he doesn't know my uncle—his grace—like you do." Miriam glanced in her sunshade mirror and spotted Elena sitting up, clearly fascinated. "Sorry, but he's right. I hope he *does* pull through, but the odds aren't much better than fifty-fifty. And we ought to have some idea about what to do if we get there and . . ." She trailed off, diving back into her thoughts.

"I don't want to think about it," said Brill. "I'm sorry, Huw. I should not exercise myself over your words. Many will be thinking them. But I feel so helpless." She thumped the steering column. "I wish I could drive faster!"

"If you get pulled for speeding, and he *does* recover—" Elena began.

Miriam snorted. "Enough of that, kid. What's more important to you, Brill: getting there, or going fast? You don't want to get a traffic stop. Think of the poor cop's widow and orphans, if it helps."

"You are perfectly correct, as usual, milady." Brill sighed. "What other news, Sir Huw?"

"Um." Huw stretched, extending his legs under Miriam's seat and his arms backwards to touch the ceiling above his brother's head. "There's a condition red lockdown. Avoid commercial flights, avoid all contact with the authorities, avoid unnecessary travel, lock the doors and bar the windows. Something about a major battle near Wergatsfurt, and something really bad happening to the Pervert's army. Sounds like my Lord Riordan opened a can of whoop-ass or something.

But you'd expect them to sound a little less tense if they'd nailed the bad guys properly, wouldn't you?"

"Not necessarily." Miriam sounded thoughtful. "If there's been an army running wild through the countryside in a civil war, it could take a long time for things to get back to normal. Look at Iraq: They went in *weeks* ago and it's still a mess, whether or not the President declared 'Mission Accomplished.'" She paused. "Egon could be down, but what about the rest of his vassals? The Duke of Niejwein, this that and the other baron or earl or whatever. It's not over until the council hammers out a settlement that ends the fighting." She rubbed her belly thoughtfully, then paused. "And I need to see a doctor." The test kit had been unequivocal, but the uncertainty over the sex of the fetus remained. "Then get a seat at the table before they decide I'm just one of the chess pieces."

"A chess piece with a posse!" Elena giggled.

"*Not* funny," Huw chided her.

Her moué mirrored Brill's, for an entirely different reason. "I suppose not," she said. "I was just joking."

"Bored now," Yul mocked, having woken up in the preceding minute or two. "Are we there yet?" he squeaked in a falsetto imitation.

"Bastard!" Elena thumped him over the head with a travel pillow.

"Children! . . ." Huw shook his head. "I'm sorry," he mouthed at Miriam by way of the mirror.

Miriam glanced sidelong at Brill. "How long have you known these reprobates?"

"Long enough to know they're just acting out because they're over here for the first time." She braced her arms across the steering wheel, slumping forward in evident boredom. "They get dizzy."

"Don't tell me you weren't like this on your first time out?" Miriam thought back to the first time she'd brought Brill over to Boston (her version of Boston—not the curious

retarded twin in New Britain). She'd thought Brill was a
naïve ingénue and a scion of the outer families, not able to
world-walk for herself, not realizing Angbard would never
have turned her loose in Niejwein without planting one or
more of his valkyries on her as spy and bodyguard.

"My first time out was"—Brill looked pensive—"I was
twelve, I think. But I had a false identity in my own name
by the time I was fourteen. Thanks to the duke. He believed
in starting them early."

"Lucky cow." Elena giggled again.

*I am trapped on a school bus in the middle of flyover
country with a bunch of overarmed and undersocialized
postadolescents*, Miriam realized, *and there's no way out.*
She sighed. "Starting what early?"

"Starting the doppelganger identities. It's only sensible,
you know. He wanted to put as many of us as possible
through the right kind of finishing school—Harvard, Yale,
the Marine Corps—in case we ever have to evacuate."

"Evacuate." The gears whirred in Miriam's head. "Evacuate the Gruinmarkt?" If that was even on the menu—"Why
hasn't it already happened?"

"Would you voluntarily abandon your home? Your
world?" Brill looked at her oddly.

"Um. It's home, right?" The idea resonated with her own
experience. "But there are no decent roads, no indoor plumb-
ing, hedge-lords with pigs in their halls, a social setup out of
the dark ages—why would you stay?"

"Home is where everyone you know is," said Brill. "That
doesn't mean you've got to love it—you know my thoughts,
my lady! What you *can't* do is ignore it."

Miriam fell silent for a couple of minutes, thinking. She'd
had a taste of living another life in another world—but it
had strings attached, and not ones to her liking, in Baron
Henryk's captivity. Then she'd escaped during the debacle
at the betrothal, and considered making a run for it when
she was in New Britain; thought hard about going native,
dropping out, leaving everything behind for a false identity.

New Britain had big drawbacks, especially compared to home, but at least it was free of reactionary aristocrats who wanted to turn her into a dynastic slave. And if she'd done it, it would have been through her own choice. *But I decided to come back,* she realized. *I've got a family and while I was busy being independent they got their claws into me.*

"What do you need a doppelganger identity for, then?" She paused. "I mean, if all it's for is to maintain a toehold identity in this world . . ."

"Identity is a lever," Huw said gnomically. "The fulcrum is world-walking."

"But what do you want a lever *for?*" Miriam persisted.

"So we can move the world!" Brill straightened her back, looking straight ahead.

Then Elena chirped up again: "Are we nearly there, yet?"

In the end, it took them eighty-five hours to make a journey that would have taken a day if they'd been able to fly direct. Eighty-five hours and two changes of vehicle and three changes of plates, driving licenses, and other ID documents—care of certain arrangements the Clan maintained with local contractors.

With five drivers available they could have shaved a couple of hours off if they hadn't changed vehicles and taken certain other precautions, and a whole eight hours if Miriam hadn't insisted on stopping for the night at a motel outside Syracuse. "I am going to visit the duke tomorrow," she pointed out. "I need to sleep properly, I need a shower, and I need to not look like I've been sleeping in a van for a week, because I don't know *who else* will be visiting the duke. This is politics. Do you have a problem with that?"

"No," Brill agreed meekly—and the morning after the motel stop they lost another two hours in a strip mall, hunting suitable shoes, a business suit, and some spray to keep Miriam's bleached hair from going in all directions.

"How do I look?" asked Miriam.

"Scary," Brill admitted after a pause. "But it'll do."

"You think so?"

"Stop worrying. If any knave denigrates your topiary, I'll shoot him."

Miriam gave her an old-fashioned look as she climbed in the cab of the new van, but Brilliana was obviously in high spirits—probably in anticipation of their arrival. *It's alright for her, she's not the one who has to confront them,* Miriam reminded herself. *She's not the one with the unwanted pregnancy.* Her stomach burned with acid indigestion, product of stress and too much Diet Pepsi. "Let's go," she told Huw (for it was his turn behind the wheel). "I want to get this over with."

Cerebrovascular incidents were a familiar and unpleasant problem for the Clan: World-walking induced abrupt blood-pressure spikes, and far too many of their number died of strokes. But Miriam still had to grapple with her disbelief as Huw pulled up outside a discreet, shrub-fronted clinic in the outskirts of Springfield. "Forty beds? *All* of them?"

"Yes, milady." Huw reached for the parking brake. "It's the price of doing business."

She glanced at him sharply, but his expression was deadly serious. "Nobody knows why, I suppose?"

"Indeed." The engine stopped. "It's on my research list. A way down." He swallowed. "I suppose you're going to say, because I'm young."

"No, it's more like I was thinking, it might tell us something about the family talent," Miriam replied. She dabbed at a stray wisp of hair in the mirror, split ends mocking her. "I knew it was a problem. I didn't realize it was this big a problem, though. There's too much to do, isn't there?"

"I'm working on it," Huw said soberly. "It's just that my to-do list is eight years long."

"I beg your pardon, Miriam." Brill sounded as tense as she felt. "Visitors hours . . ."

"Alright." Miriam opened her door and carefully climbed

down from the van. She pulled a face as she caught her re-
flection in the mirror: Appearances counted for a lot when
dealing with the elders and the formal Clan hierarchy. "I
look a mess. Let's get on with this."

Behind her, Yul and Elena were dismounting. "With
your permission, I'll take point, my lady." Elena winked at
her as she swung a sports bag over her shoulder. "*I* think
you look just fine."

Miriam looked at Brill in mute appeal. "Let her do it, it's
what she does best," Brill replied. "Yul, rear guard. Huw?
Lock up and let's go." All of them, Miriam realized, were
armed—but Elena was the one with the serious firepower
in her bag. *What am I doing here?* she asked herself as they
crossed the car park towards the doors to reception: *How
did I get into this mess?* Unfortunately, that question was
easy enough to answer: *Mom dumped me in at the deep end,
sink or swim.* Iris had raised her in the United States in ignorance of the Clan families, for her own reasons—reasons
that could be viewed as cold-bloodedly calculating rather
than compassionate, depending on whether Iris thought
of herself as a player or a fugitive. Not that she could hate
Iris—or Patricia, to her extended family—either way; her
mother had been under enormous pressure at the time. *But
I wish she'd prepared me better.*

Getting into the small and very exclusive hospital that
the Clan maintained for their brainstruck was not a simple
matter of walking up to the reception desk and saying,
"Hello, I've come to visit Angbard Lofstrom." Even leaving
aside the small matter of the DEA's most wanted list and
the question of his place on it, Angbard had enemies, many
of whom might well consider hospital visiting hours to be
the perfect time to even up old scores. So Miriam was un-
surprised when her introductory statement of intent, "Hello,
I've come to visit Angbard Lofstrom," resulted in the orna-
mental receptionist staring vacuously up at her as if she'd
demanded money with threats. A serious-faced young man

whose dark suit was cut to conceal his sidearm bounced out
from behind a glass screen off to one side, sized them up,
then relaxed momentarily. "Wer' isht?" he demanded.

Brill replied in machine-gun hochsprache, too fast for
Miriam to catch. The young man looked surprised, but
mildly relieved as he replied. Then he turned to Miriam.
"My lady, if you please"—he pointed at a seating area off
to one side—"to wait there in?" His English was heavily
accented.

"Ja—" Brill replied at length. "Bertil says he needs to
check our identities before he can let us in," she explained
to Miriam. "He knows who we are."

"Good." Miriam allowed herself to be led to the waiting
area. "Any idea how long? . . ."

"Not long." Brill didn't bother sitting down. "They'll just
need time to make sure we didn't bring any unwanted company." Her posture was relaxed, but Miriam couldn't help
noticing the way her eyeballs flickered from doors to windows.

A minute passed before another of the dark-suited security guards came in through a door behind the receptionist's desk. *They always look like Mormon missionaries,*
Miriam noted, *or Secret Service agents. That's a* weakness,
isn't it? Angbard's guidelines for looking inconspicuous
had evolved decades earlier; after her weeks on the run and
the tutorial in escape and evasion she'd received from the
Leveler underground, their uniform consistency now struck
her as a weakness, like wearing a flashing neon sign adver-
tising *Clan operation here.*

"My lady?" The new guy walked straight over to Miriam
and half bowed to her. "If you would come this way,
please?"

"I'm bringing my companions," she said.

"Ah." His eyes focused on Elena's shoulder bag. "I would
like to see that, please."

Elena looked as if she was about to object. Miriam shook
her head. "Show him."

Elena opened her bag reluctantly and the guard looked inside. He blinked. "Hmm. You may come, but please unload and safe your arm." He shrugged at Miriam apologetically. "I am sorry but it is a matter of policy—no armor-piercing loads are allowed. The rest of you, pistols only? No concealed shotguns?" His lips quirked. "Good. If you would follow me . . ."

Elena trailed behind them, her hands buried in her bag, from which muffled clicking noises were emerging.

Another hospital corridor leading to another hospital room, like a hotel with oxygen lines and diagnostic machines in place of the Internet hub and minibar. *I'm getting to hate these places,* she realized, as she followed the broad shoulders and buzz cut of her guide. "Have you been here before?" she asked Brill.

"Yes." Brilliana seemed reluctant to say more, so she dropped the topic.

They passed a set of fire doors, then a nursing station, and finally came to a door where a pair of machine-gun missionaries were standing easy. Their guide knocked twice, then opened the door. "More visitors," he said quietly.

The first thing Miriam saw in the small hospital room was a bed with a body in it and people gathered around, their backs turned to her. Then one of them looked round: "Olga!"

Olga's expression of startled relief emboldened Miriam to take a step forward.

"Miriam—"

Then the woman beside Olga looked up. "Miriam?" And her heart fluttered and skipped a beat.

"Mom?"

"Ach, *scheisse.* You didn't need to see him like this."

Iris stared up at her. She looked tired, and apprehensive—guilty, perhaps—and worried. Miriam looked past her at the figure in the bed. "Maybe not, Mom, but let me be the judge of that." There was an ache in her throat as she looked at Olga. "How is he?"

Olga shook her head. "He is not good," she said. "Earlier, he could speak, he spoke of you—but not since we moved him. He is barely conscious."

"Then why *did* you move—"

Iris cut in. "They were under siege, kid. You know, bad guys with machine guns shooting at them? They wouldn't have relocated him if staying was an option. You can ask Dr. MacDonald later if you want to know more." She nodded at Brilliana. "Who are your companions?"

Brill gestured. "They're mine. *Ours.*" She put an odd emphasis on the words. "Who's seen his grace in this condition?"

"Everyone and their dog." Iris addressed Miriam: "I'm expecting that little shitweasel Julius Arnesen to turn up any minute now. Oliver Hjorth is making himself surprisingly useful, all things considered—I think he finally worked out how unreliable mother-dearest is"—the dowager Hildegarde, who seemed to take Miriam's mere existence as a personal insult—"and Mors Hjalmar is running interference for me. The silver lining on this particular shit sandwich is that most of the conservative tribal elders attended your betrothal, Miriam. They were in the Summer Palace when Egon staged his little divertissement—we came out much better. Also, they're on the back foot now because of the troubles at home. But once they get a grip on how ill my half brother is, they're going to jump us. You can be sure of it."

"Good!" said Miriam, surprising herself—and, from their reactions, everybody else. "Let them." She sidestepped around Brill and got her first good look at the duke.

Last time she'd seen him, months ago, Angbard had seemed implacable and unstoppable: a mafia don at the height of his power, self-assured and calculating, a healthy sixty-something executive whose polished exterior masked the ruthless drive and cynical outlook within. Lying half-asleep in a hospital bed, an intravenous drip in his left arm and the cables of an EEG taped to his patchily shaved head, he looked pathetic and broken. His skin was translucent, stretched thin across ancient muscles, the outline of bones showing through at elbows and shoulders; his closed eyes were half-sunk in their sockets. His breathing was shallow and slow.

Iris cleared her throat. "Are you sure you don't want to reconsider that?"

Miriam looked her mother in the eye. "Can you think of a better time?"

"Ladies—" Heads turned. The Clan security officer who'd brought them here paused. "Perhaps you would like to move to the conference room? He is not well, and the doctor said not to disturb him overly. They will try to feed him in half an hour, and need space. . . ."

"That sounds like a good idea," said Brilliana. "Will you call us if any other visitors arrive, Carlos?"

"I'll do that." He nodded. "This way, please."

Over peppermint tea and refreshments in the conference room, Miriam eyed Iris warily. "You're looking healthy."

Iris nodded. "Over here, treatment is easier to come by." She was making do with a single cane, moving without any obvious signs of the multiple sclerosis that periodically confined her to a wheelchair. "And certain bottlenecks are . . . no longer present." Months ago, she'd as good as told Miriam that she was on her own: that Hildegarde—or other members of the conservative faction—had a death grip on the supply of medicines she needed, and if Iris went against their will she'd stay in a wheelchair in the near-medieval conditions of the Gruinmarkt until she rotted.

"How nice." Miriam managed an acidic smile. "So what happens now?"

Iris looked at her sharply. "That depends on you, kid. Depends on whether you're willing to play ball."

"That depends on what rules the ball game is played by."

Her mother nodded. "Yes, well; the rules are changing." She glanced at the young people gathered at the other end of the room, chatting over drinks and snacks. "There's a garden here. Are you up to pushing a wheelchair?"

"I think I can trust them, Mom." Miriam let a note of exasperation into her voice.

"More fool you, then," Iris said tartly. "Your uncle trusted me, and look where it got him. . . ." She trailed off thoughtfully, then shrugged. "You may be right about them. I'm not saying you're not. Just . . . don't be so certain of people. You can never tell in advance who's going to betray you. And we need to talk in private, just you and me. So let's get a wheelchair and go look at the flowers."

"What's to talk about that needs so much secrecy?" Miriam asked.

Iris smiled crookedly. "Oh, you'd be surprised, kid. I've got a plan. And I figure *you've* got a plan, too. So, let's walk, and I'll tell you mine if you tell me yours."

"After the last plan you hatched that got me sucked in . . ." Miriam followed Iris slowly into the corridor, shaking her head. "But it got worse. You know what those bastards have done to me?"

"Yes." A moment's pause, then: "Mother-dearest told me, right before the betrothal. She was very proud of it." Miriam quailed at the tone in Iris's—her own mother's—voice. A stranger might not have recognized it, but Miriam had grown up knowing what it signified: the unnatural calm before a storm of coldly righteous anger. "I'm appalled, but not surprised. That's how they play the game, after all. They were raised to only value us for one thing." They reached the nursing station; an empty wheelchair waited beside it. "If you could push? . . ." Iris asked.

The garden was bright and empty, neatly manicured lawns bordered by magnolia hedges. "You said the rules had changed," Miriam said quietly. "But I don't see much sign of them changing."

"As I said, I've been developing a plan. It's a long-term project—you don't get an entrenched aristocracy to change how they do things overnight—and it relies on an indirect approach; the first step is to build a coalition and the second is to steer it. So I've been cutting deals, finding out what it'll take to get various parties to sign on. For it to succeed, we've got to work together, but everyone I've spoken to so far seems to be willing to do that—for their own reasons, if not for mine. Now . . . the one thing the Conservatives will rely on is the sure knowledge that mothers and daughters always work at cross-purposes. They *always* stab each other in the back, because the way the Clan is set up to encourage arranged first-cousin marriages puts them in conflict. But . . . our rules are different. That's a big part of why I raised you in the United States, by the way. I wanted a daughter I could trust, a daughter who'd trust *me*. A daughter I could work with rather than against."

Miriam stared at the backs of her hands on the handles of the wheelchair. A daughter's hands. Trusting, maybe too trusting. "What do you want?" she asked.

Iris chuckled quietly. "Well, let me see . . . knowing you, you're planning something to do with business models and new worlds. Am I right? You're plotting a business revolution." Without waiting for Miriam's assent she continued: "*My* plan is a bit different. I just want to make sure that no daughter of the families ever goes through what you've been put through ever again, for dynastic reasons. Or what I went through. That's all; nothing huge."

Miriam cleared her throat. "But. You'd need to break the Clan's entire structure to do that," she said conversationally. She could hear the blood throbbing in her ears.

"Yes," said Iris. "You see? You're not the only one of us who wants a revolution." Her voice dropped a notch. "The trouble is, like I said: I can't make it work without your help. You're in a powerful position, and better still, you've got a perfect excuse for moving across social boundaries rather than obeying convention. It's not going to be obvious to onlookers whether you're doing stuff deliberately or because you don't know better. Which gives you a certain freedom of action. . . . Meanwhile, my plan depends on us agreeing to cooperate, and that's something the braid system tends to discourage. See? A year ago you wouldn't have been this suspicious of my motives. That's part of the problem. I know it's a lot to ask of you—but I want you to trust me to help you."

Miriam stared at the back of her mother's head, her mind a whirl of emotions. Once, a year ago, she'd have trusted Iris implicitly, but now that she knew the forge her mother had been tempered in, a tiny voice urged caution. "Tell me exactly what you're planning," she said slowly, "then I'll tell you what *I'm* planning."

"And then?"

"Then perhaps we can do a deal."

Working in the belly of the beast, supervising the electrically-driven presses of the *Petrograd Times* and minding the telautograph senders that broadcast the message of the Committee for Democratic Accountability up and down the western seaboard, Erasmus had little time to spare for mundane tasks—he slept under his desk, having not had time even to requisition a room in a miner's flophouse—but a superb perspective on the revolution. "We're going to succeed," he told John Winstanley one morning, over tea. "I think this time it's actually going to *work.*"

Winstanley had stared at him. "You thought it might not? Careful, citizen!"

"Feh." Burgeson snorted. "I've spent half my life in exile, *citizen,* working underground for a second chance. Ask Sir Adam, or Lady Bishop, if you doubt my commitment. And I'll willingly do it all over again and go for third time lucky, and even a fourth, if this one doesn't succeed. I'm just pleased to note that it probably won't be necessary and taking advantage of your discretion to vent a little steam in company where it won't fog the minds of the new fish."

"Ahem. Well, then, I certainly can't find fault with *that.*

I'm sorry, Erasmus. Sometimes it's hard to be sure who's reliable and who isn't."

Burgeson turned his attention back to the pile of communiques on the table, studiously ignoring the Truth Commissioner. He was rapidly developing a jaundiced view of many of his fellow revolutionaries, now that the time to come out of the shadows and march for freedom and democracy had arrived; too many of them stood revealed as time-servers and insidious busybodies, who glowingly talked up their activities in the underground struggle with scant evidence of actually having done anything. *I didn't spend twenty years as a fugitive just so the likes of you could criticize me for pessimism,* citizen. The New Men seemed to be more preoccupied with rooting out dissenters and those lacking in ideological zeal than in actually building a better nation, but Erasmus wasn't yet sure enough of his footing to speak out against them. The rot had spread surprisingly far in a matter of weeks. *Not so surprising, if what the membership subcommittee reports is right,* he reminded himself; the council's declared members—whose number could all count on a short drop to the end of a rope if the revolution failed—had quadrupled in the past two weeks, and just keeping Polis informers out of the rank and file was proving a challenge.

"Let's see," he said. "Jim, if you'd be so good? . . ."

"Ayup." Jim, who Erasmus had drafted as a sub-editor as soon as he'd ascertained his literacy, picked up the top of the pile. "Lessee now. Yesterday, Telegraph Street, Cyprus Hill: A people's collective has seized control of the Jevons Ironworks and Steam Corporation factory and is restarting the manufacturing of parts for the war effort, with the arming of the Cyprus Hill militia as a first priority. The first four armored steamers have been delivered and are patrolling the Hispaniola Reaches already."

"Bottom drawer," Erasmus said instantly. "Next."

"Yesterday, Dunedin: The ships of the Ontario patrol

have put into harbor and their officers and men have raised the people's flag. That's the last of the undeclared territorial and riverine patrols—"

"Get that on the wire. Hold page three, this sounds promising."

"A moment." Winstanley leaned forward. "Are those ships under control of people's commissioners? Because if not, how do we know they're not planning—"

Burgeson glared at him. "That's not your department," he said, "nor mine. If you want to waste your time, make inquiries; my job is to get the news out, and this is news." He turned back to Jim. "Get someone to look for some stock pictures of the Ontario patrol. I know: you, Bill. Go now, find pictures."

Bill, the put-upon trainee sub, darted off through the news room towards the stairs down to the library. "Next story," Erasmus said wearily.

"Yesterday. People's courts in Santiago have arrested and tried sixteen Polis commissars and eleven informers for crimes against the people: Three have been executed for ordering the arrest and torture of patriots during the Andean campaign last fall. More details . . ."

"Run it. Paper only, inside pages." Erasmus jotted down a quick note on his pad. "Next."

"Today. Communique from the New London people's committee: A people's provisional council will be voted in, by open polling next Tuesday, to form a constitutional convention that will determine the structure of the people's congress and establish a timetable for its election. Lots of details here. Um, delegates from the provinces are to attend, as are members of the inner council—"

"Stop." Erasmus stood. "That's the front page for you, right there, and get it on the wire. I'll need a copy for reference while I write the editorial. Go get it now." He glanced at Winstanley, who was examining his fingernails. "Coming?"

"What? Where?"

Erasmus closed his eyes for a few seconds, feeling every second of his years. *Give me strength.* When he opened them again, he spoke evenly. "I don't know about you, but *I* am going to see Sir Adam, who will surely be preparing to depart *very shortly,* in order to learn what he expects of me in his absence." He paused. Winstanley was looking at him dumbly. "I expect he'll have some errands for you to run," he added, not unkindly.

"What—oh? But. Surely? . . ." Winstanley looked confused.

"You weren't listening, were you? Or rather, you were listening to the *voice,* not to the *words.*"

Winstanley flinched. "I say, there's no need for—"

"Negativism?" Erasmus smiled humorlessly. "Get your jacket, man. We have to see the chief right away."

"The correct salutation is 'citizen.'" Winstanley levered himself out of his chair with a glare.

"Certainly, *citizen.*" Erasmus headed for the door.

Over in the Committee Palace (its new name hastily hacked into a layer of fresh cement that covered the carved lintel of the former mayoral mansion), Erasmus found the usual ant-heap a-buzzing with petitioners, delegates from regional committees from places as far afield as Chihuahua and North Cascadia, guards drawn from the local militia, and the anxious families of arrested king's men. "Commissioner Burgeson, to see Sir Adam," he told the harried page waiting in the Hall of People's Justice (formerly the western state dining room).

"This way, sir. You're just in time."

Am I, now? He stifled a wince as the door opened. "Ah! Erasmus." Sir Adam grinned impishly and stood up, cutting off the manager or committee member who had been talking to him. "I'd just sent a courier for you. Did he arrive?"

"A courier? No, we must have passed in the street."

Burgeson glanced round. The manager or committee member was an unfamiliar face; Burgeson's secretary Joseph MacDonald, though . . . "I take it you're going east?"

"*We're* going, Erasmus." Sir Adam inspected him curiously. "Unless you have more pressing concerns to keep you in this provincial capital than the business of keeping the people appraised of the progress of the new constitutional convention?"

"I'm sure Jim and Judas between them can keep the press and the wire running, just as long as you leave orders to keep that sheep Winstanley away from the hay. But I assumed we'd be here a bit longer. . . . Do you really need me merely as a stenographer or ordinary correspondent?"

"God, no!" Sir Adam looked him in the eye. "I need you in the capital, doing what you've started here, only on a larger scale. *You* pick the correspondents—and the editors—then leave them to it unless they go off course. But we're about to up our game, man, and I want someone riding herd on the gossipmongers who knows what he's doing."

Erasmus's cheek twitched. "The correct salutation is 'citizen,' or so Citizen Winstanley keeps reminding me, but aside from that I take your point." He grinned. "So what's the plan?"

"The militia—rather, an army air wing who have signed to us—are arranging for a mail packet to fly from Prussian Ridge encampment tonight. You and I will be on it, along with a dozen trusted cadre—Haynes, Smith, Joe, Miss Rutherford, a few others, I've written a memo—your copy is on its way to the wrong place—and we shall arrive in New London the day after tomorrow. Andrew White is collating the lists of longtime party members for us to review when we arrive. You will take your pick of staff for a new Communications Committee, which will take over from the Truth and Justice commissioners when the congressional committee sits. Edicts are being drafted to nationalize all the telautographs and printing presses and place them under your ministry. Are you for it?"

"*All* of them?" Erasmus raised an eyebrow; Sir Adam nodded. "Well, that's reassuring—nothing like half measures to short the stew pot." He rubbed his hands together. "Yes, I'm up for it. But, one question—"

"Yes? Spit it out, man!"

Erasmus grimaced. "Is there somewhere in this place where I can catch a bath and some fresh clothes? I've been living in my office for the past week—I'd rather not stand up in front of a room full of newspaper owners and tell them I'm holding their front pages to ransom smelling like a tramp. . . ."

The next day, Miriam visited the clinic again—this time, for her own appointment.

Brill had found her an anonymous motel suite near the interstate, along with a survival kit. "Here's your driving license, credit card, and phone. Want to do dinner?"

"Sounds like a plan. Uh, what about you guys?"

"Oh, we'll be around." Brill looked amused. "I thought you'd appreciate some privacy. Tomorrow . . ."

"Yeah, that."

Tomorrow dawned hot and early through the picture window in the suite's lounge; Miriam rolled over and buried her face in the pillow until the bedside alarm radio cut in, reminding her that she really needed to get up. She sat up slowly, fuzzy-headed and confused: *Where am I?* A concatenation of hotel bedrooms seemed to blur behind her. *What am I—oh.* And so it began—the first day of Iris's, of her own, little conspiracy.

She swallowed, feeling a mild sense of nauseous dread. *You can't avoid this step,* a little voice reminded her. *But it's too much like admitting it's real.* The result of the cheap pregnancy test kit on the road had left her feeling numb but clearheaded. Going to see an OB/GYN and finding out whether it was a boy was the inexorable next step down the road, but she wasn't ready to face up to her destination yet, or to decide whether she was going to go there or stamp on the brake pedal. As she brushed her teeth, combed out her hair—which was darkening at the roots again, after its brutal treatment in New London—and pulled on her clothes, she found herself treasuring every remaining second of her indecision.

Brill was waiting for her downstairs in the lobby, concealed behind a newspaper. She rustled it as she rose, to signal her presence. "Ready?" she asked.

"Let's get this over with." Miriam managed a brittle smile.

"As my lady wishes."

While Miriam had been held prisoner for a couple of months by Baron Henryk—held in the conditions of a most privileged prisoner, the troublesome heiress of a noble family who must needs be mewed up and married off before she embarrassed the elders enough to warrant strangling— the baron had arranged a most unpleasant medical examination for her by a doctor who specialized in making sure that the family tree always bore fruit in the right places. And seven weeks later, give or take a couple of days, her period was *still* late, and she was regularly skipping breakfast. Not to mention the other, terrifying symptom: the loss of her ability to world-walk. There was no room for doubt in her mind, even before the test stick had shown her the treacherous blue label. *It's not like I haven't been pregnant before,* she'd told herself. But dealing with it was another matter entirely, and if it was male, potentially heir to an explosive situation . . . this wasn't about *her* doubts and fears. It was about everybody else's. *And Mom. Mustn't forget Mom.*

"Your pardon, Miriam—aren't you a bit tense?"

"Put yourself in my shoes. How would *you* feel?"

"I'd be petrified! If it's a boy it's the heir—" Brill stopped, her hands gripping the steering wheel.

"That's what we're going to find out," Miriam agreed. With the free run of a fertility clinic, ven Hjalmar would have been able to put his sperm samples through a sex sorting protocol, and while that wasn't a surefire guarantee, she wasn't inclined to bet against it. "But what about me?"

Brill paused for a few seconds. "I'm sorry."

Miriam took a deep breath, then let it out slowly. "Don't be. What's done is not your fault." *What happens next, though* . . . "Just get me there and back. Then we'll talk."

This time there was no security cordon of bible-scholar bandits to penetrate, just a brilliant and vacuous smile from the receptionist followed by directions to a waiting room. "Dr. Price is waiting for you," she added as Miriam put one foot in front of the other and forced herself along the corridor. Brilliana, behind her, felt like the shadow of all her fears, come to escort her to the examination room. *I've done this before,* she reminded herself. *Yes, but you were twenty-one and indecisive and Mom guilt-tripped you* out of *having an abortion*—and *there* was a nasty thought, because how certain was she that Mom wasn't playing a riff on that same head game all over again?

Seven weeks along. All I have to do is ask. Huw said he'd sort everything out. She held the thought like the key to a prison cell as she paused on the threshold of the examination room, and the guy with curly brown hair sitting at the desk turned to look at her and then rose to greet her. "Hello? Are you Miriam? I'm Dr. Price, Alan Price." His eyes tracked past her. "And this is . . ."

"A friend." She practiced her smile again; she had a feeling that if she was going to go through with this she'd be needing it a lot over the next weeks and months. "Hi. I understand you're an OB/GYN." She shuffled sideways as he gestured towards a chair. "Have you ever worked with Dr. ven Hjalmar?"

Price frowned. "Van Hjelmar . . . no, doesn't ring a bell." He shook his head. "Were you seeing him?"

"A different practice." Miriam sat down heavily, as if her strings had been cut; a vast weight of dread that she hadn't even been aware of disappeared. "I really didn't like him. Hence this, uh . . ."

"I understand." Price leaned over and dragged a third chair into position, then waved Brilliana towards it. His face assumed an expression of professional interest. "And your mother, I gather, suggested? . . ."

"Yes." Miriam took another deep breath. "My fiancé is, uh—"

"—He died last month," Brill picked up without a pause.

"Oh, I'm sorry!" Price sat up. "Well, that probably explains it."

"It was a shooting accident," Miriam said tonelessly, earning her a sharp look from Brill.

"Eh." Price glanced back at his computer screen. "Alright. So you were on his HMO plan, but now you've moved to—oh, I see. Well. I think my receptionist's got the new release forms through—if you can sign one and get your old practitioner's details to us we can take it from there."

"Okay." Miriam nodded.

"Meanwhile? . . ." Price raised an eyebrow.

"Well." Miriam managed to get a grip on her breathing: *mustn't start hyperventilating.* "I'm pregnant." It was funny how you could change your script and the person who you were talking to would fall into a new pattern of their own, she thought as she watched Price visibly tense as he tried to keep up with the conversation: from polite sympathy through to curiosity to a quickly suppressed wince. Brill glanced sidelong at her again: *You're laying it on too thick, back off!* "It wasn't planned," she added, not backpedaling exactly but trying to fill in enough details to put Price back on ground he was comfortable with, that wouldn't raise any questions. "We were going to wait until after the wedding. But . . ." She shrugged helplessly.

"I see." Price was visibly trying to get a grip on the situation. "Well, then." He cleared his throat. "Have you used a pregnancy test kit?"

"Yes. I assume you'll want a urine sample so you can verify? . . ."

"Yes." Price opened his desk drawer and removed a collection jar. "If you wouldn't mind? The rest room is through there."

When Miriam returned she placed the collection jar on the desk as carefully as if it were full of nitroglycerin. "Here it is."

"Right." Price looked as if he was about to say something else, then changed his mind at the last moment. "I'll run it right now and then we can take it from there. Is that okay?"

Miriam didn't trust herself to reply. She nodded jerkily.

"Okay. I'll be right back." Price pulled on a blue disposable glove, then stood up and carried the sample jar out through a side door.

Miriam looked at Brill. "How discreet is he going to be?"

"Very. He's on salary. Our dime."

"Ah."

They sat in silence for five minutes; then, as Miriam was considering her conversational options, Dr. Price opened the door again. He was, she noticed, no longer wearing the glove. There was a brief, awkward silence as he sat down again, then: "It's positive," he confirmed. Then he picked up his pen and a notepad. "How long ago did you last have sex?"

The question threw Miriam for a moment, bringing back unwelcome memories of Roland. She was about to say "at least eight months ago," when suddenly she realized, *that's not what he's asking.* "Seven weeks," she said. A little white lie; sex had nothing to do with her current situation, except in the most abstract imaginable sense.

"Well. You've made it through the riskiest period—most spontaneous miscarriages occur in the first eight weeks. So the next question is—I'm assuming you're here because you want to continue with it?" He paused, prompting.

Miriam could feel the blood pounding in her ears. No matter how she unpacked the question it didn't quite make sense to her: It felt like the introduction to a much larger question, monstrously large, an iceberg of possibilities. *I could say no,* she thought. *Get this over with right now. Quit the game.* Mom might disapprove, the duke might object when he recovered, but they couldn't stop her if . . . Miriam opened her mouth. "Yes," she heard herself whisper hoarsely. She swallowed. "Yes," she said again, louder; thinking, *I can change my mind later. There's still time.* "I'm assuming you're going to want to schedule an amniocentesis appointment, for," she swallowed, "things like Down's syndrome and hydrocephalus? Will you be able to check on the—my baby's—sex?"

"Eh, we can do that. It's a bit early for amniocentesis right now, though, if it's only been seven weeks. I'd like to start by asking some questions about your family and medical history. Then I'm going to take a blood sample to get started with, while we're waiting for your old records to arrive. Shall we begin?"

7

OATH OF FEALTY

❦

After they left the clinic, Brill drove Miriam back to the motel. Miriam could hear the questions tumbling over and over in her head: The silence was so loud that it roared. *And now, the talk,* Miriam thought, keyed up and tense. It had to come to this sooner or later. . . .

"You said you wanted to talk," Brill said into the abrupt emptiness that flooded the car's interior as she turned off the ignition. She studied Miriam in her mirror, carefully avoiding eye contact.

"Yes, yes I did." Miriam opened her door. "Do you have time to come in?"

"Of course." Brilliana looked as if she were walking on eggshells. "I imagine this must be hard to adjust to."

"That's the least of it." Miriam held her tongue as they entered the lobby and walked to her door. "Come in."

Brill had rented a suite for her; Miriam took the sofa, and the younger woman perched on the armchair opposite. For a few seconds they stared at each other in silence. Finally, Brill cracked. "It's hard, isn't it?"

"Yes." Miriam kept her eyes on her. "I have three questions, Brill."

"Three? Is that all?"

"I think so." *Because if you can't convince me I can trust you, then* . . . well, *that* was an interesting question, and not one Miriam wanted to consider just yet. "You work directly for Angbard, don't you? Tell me, are you sworn to him personally? A vassal under his patronage?"

Brilliana looked at her warily. "You never asked before." She rubbed her cheek thoughtfully. "What makes you ask?"

Miriam licked her lips. "I'd like a straight answer. Please."

Suddenly Brill's expression cleared. "Oh!" The penny had clearly dropped. "I am ranked as a sergeant in the Clan's Security, that is clear enough. But you have the rest of it, too: His grace swore me to his personal service." She looked Miriam in the eye. "To be discharged by death, or his word."

"Ah." Miriam nodded, very slightly. *So Mom was telling the truth.* A tension in her chest began to unclench.

"Why do you ask?" Brill repeated.

Miriam took a deep breath. "You—you, and Huw, and my mother, and the tooth fairy, for all I know—say you want me to trust you. Well, right now I find I'm very short on trust. I've been locked up, beaten, I've been *impregnated*"— she paused to breathe again—"then suddenly a couple of weeks later it's all 'trust us, we want you to lead us'! And— factional differences or not—I'm having a hard time buying it. So. Second question. Why did Angbard sic you onto me?"

Brill closed her eyes, startling Miriam. "Crone give me patience"—she opened her eyes again—"Helge, he's your *uncle*. He married but his wife died years ago and they produced no offspring—don't you get it?"

"But surely—"

"Surely *nothing!* Have you no idea how violent the civil war was? His line were targets! Your mother was targeted, her husband killed! The whole reason for Clan Security is to prevent anything like that happening ever again! Meanwhile, you, you—" Brill's shoulders were shaking. "Please!"

"Please, what?" Miriam stared, bewildered. "It's this social thing again, isn't it? What am I doing wrong *this* time?"

With a visible effort, Brilliana collected herself. "You're your mother's heir," she said quietly. "How hard is it to see that you're also your *uncle's* heir? Or at least his closest surviving descendant by distaff—you're a woman, so you won't inherit everything, but you're attached to the title to a whole damned *duchy.* God-on-a-stick, Helge, don't you get it? Henryk wanted you under his thumb because it gave him a weapon against his grace! And it shut you up, but they've always had a casual way with their women," she added with offhand venom. Then she looked back at Miriam. "I am a sworn vassal of your uncle, Helge. Sworn to protect his interests. You are his next of kin. Need I to draw you a diagram?"

"Uh." *Oh boy.* Miriam turned it all over in her mind. *Damn, I'm really going to have to work on figuring out how these extended family links work!* "But your direct loyalty is to him, not to me. Right?"

"That's the picture," Brilliana said sharply. "I love you like a sister, but you can be so slow at times!"

"Well, then." Miriam glanced at the window. "Maybe it's because I've been playing the wrong card game all along," she said slowly. Then she looked back at Brill. "I've been here a year and I haven't so much as sworn a swineherd to my service. Right?"

Brill's eyes widened. "You can't. I'm sworn to his grace, unto the death—his or mine."

Miriam nodded, satisfied. *Thanks, Mom.* "I understand. But his grace is clearly ill—possibly on his deathbed?"

Brill nodded jerkily.

"Well, then. I believe there is a thing called an oath contingent, yes?"

"Who told you about *that?*"

"Look." Miriam leaned forward. "What are you going to do if—when—my uncle dies?"

"But that's different!" It came out almost as a wail.

"Not according to my mother." Miriam pinned her in place with a stare. "In the old days, oaths contingent were quite common—to ensure a secure succession in event of an assassination. The contingent liege's orders are overridden by those of the first lord living. Yes?"

"I suppose so. But—"

"Brill." Miriam paused. "This is my third question. Did his grace give you any orders that would bring you into a conflict of loyalty if you were sworn to me by an oath contingent?"

The younger woman looked at her, wide-eyed as a doe in the headlights of a truck. "Yes," she whispered.

"Uh-oh." Miriam flopped back on the sofa. She rubbed her forehead. "Well, there goes *that* good—"

"Wait." Brill raised a hand. "You would not have raised the oath contingent unless you planned to live among us, would you?"

Miriam steeled herself. "I need sworn vassals to defend me if I'm going to live in the Gruinmarkt. I was hoping—"

"Well." Brill took a deep breath. "Then the conflict of interests does not arise." She grimaced. "His grace directed me—while you were in New Britain—to bring you back, alive or dead. Preferably alive, but—"

"Whoa." Miriam stared at her. "Do I want to hear this?"

Brill shuffled, uncomfortable. "You are not planning to offer your services to the American government. Are you?"

"I—" Miriam flashed back to what Mike had told her in the walls of a smoldering palace. "No. No way."

"Well." Brill held out her hands across the coffee table. "In that case, I can swear to you. If"—she made eye contact—"you still want me?"

Miriam swallowed. ("It's a bit like a marriage," Iris had told her. "A big, rowdy, polygamous one, arguments and all. Minus the sex.") "This means you're going to be part of my household and responsibilities for life, doesn't it?"

"Once his grace dies or otherwise discharges me." Brill ducked her head.

"Then"—Miriam reached out and caught her hands—"I accept. Your oath of loyalty, contingent on the word of your first liege." She stood, slowly, pulling Brill with her. "We can swear to each other in front of witnesses later, can't we?"

"Whenever you ask, milady." Brilliana bowed low and kissed the backs of both her hands. "There, that is the minimal form. It is done." Then she smiled happily.

"Tell me," said Miriam. "I was a real idiot not to do this when I first arrived, wasn't I? There are other people I should be swearing, aren't there?"

"Yes, milady." Brill straightened up, her eyes glistening. Then she leaned forward and, surprising Miriam, kissed her on the mouth. Before Miriam could recoil or respond she took a step away. "It's going to be so much *fun* working for you! I can tell."

Barely a week had passed, but the atmosphere in this meeting was darker by far than its predecessor. The venue was the same—an air-conditioned conference room in a Sheraton hotel adjoining a conference center in the middle of downtown Boston, with heavily padded leather chairs arranged around a boardroom table. And now as then, the attendees were dressed as conservatively as a party of merchant bankers. But there were fewer of them today, barely a round dozen; some of the faces had changed, and two of the newcomers were women. It was, however, none of his business, decided the hotel facilities manager who was seeing to their needs; they were good customers—quiet, serious, utterly unlikely to start shooting each other or snorting crank in the rest room.

Which just went to show how misleading appearances could be.

There were thirteen seats at the table today, but one of them—at its head—was vacant. The broad-shouldered man sitting to its left nodded to a younger fellow at the far end. "Rudi, please shut the door. If you would pay attention, please?"

The quiet conversation ebbed as Rudi sat down again, the door securely locked behind him. "I think we'll begin with a situation report," Riordan said quietly. "Lady Thorold, if you wouldn't mind?"

"Of course." Olga opened the leather conference folder she'd brought to the meeting; in a severe black suit, with her long blond hair tied back, she resembled a trial lawyer rather than an intelligence officer. "The duke's medical condition is stable. That's the good news."

Olga read from her notes: "The average thirty-day survival figures for subarachnoid hemorrhage are around six-tenths. His grace has already come through the main danger period, but the doctors agree his chances of full recovery are slight. He's paralyzed on the left side, and his speech is impaired. They can't evaluate his mental functioning yet. He may recover some of his faculties, but he's likely to be mobility-challenged—probably wheelchair-bound, possibly bedridden—for life. They've scheduled a second MRI for him tomorrow to track the reduction of the thrombosis, and they should have more to report on Friday." She managed the medical terms with an ease that might have surprised Miriam, had she been present; but then, she'd checked her carefully cultivated airhead persona at the door. "The balance of medical opinion is that his grace will definitely not be able to resume even light duties for at least thirty days. Even if he makes a significant recovery, he is unlikely to be back in the chair"—her eyes tracked to the empty seat at the head of the table—"for half a year."

The attentive silence she'd been speaking into dissolved in a buzz of expressions of shock and sharply indrawn breath. Earl Riordan brought his hand down on the edge of the table. "Silence!" he barked. "We knew it was going to be bad. Thank you, milady." He grimaced. "We have a chain of command here. I recognize that I am not equipped to replace his grace in his capacity of director of security policy, or in his management of the intelligence apparatus, but for the former we have the Council of Lords, and for the latter"—he glanced sideways: Olga inclined her head—"there is a parallel line of authority. For the time being I will assume operational command, until his grace resumes his duties or I am removed by order of the Council. Is that clear?"

There was a vigorous outbreak of nodding. "Have you met with the Council yet?" asked Carl, with uncharacteristic hesitancy.

"That's where I'm going as soon as we conclude this meeting." Riordan leaned back. "Does anyone else wish to comment? On the record?"

"You're going to find it hard to convince the stick-in-the-muds to accept Lady Thorold as acting director of intelligence," remarked Carl, his arms crossed.

"They'll like my second-choice candidate even less." Riordan bared his teeth. "Are you questioning her fitness for the role, or merely her sex?"

Carl shook his head, his expression shuttered. "Just saying," he muttered.

Riordan glanced round the table as Olga closed her file and leaned back, trying to keep all expression off her face.

"I've worked with her for the past six years and I would not propose her for this position if I doubted her capability," Riordan said sharply. "The empty pots in the conservative club can rattle as much as they please; it's as good an issue as any to remind them that this is not business as usual."

There was a general rumble of agreement. "You're in the saddle now," Olga murmured in Riordan's ear. "Just try not to fall off."

Riordan flushed slightly. "Right. Next item." He glanced

up. "Rudi. Your flying machine. You are hereby ordered to prepare a report on the feasibility of equipping, supplying, training, and operating a squadron of no fewer than six and no more than twelve aircraft, within the Gruinmarkt. Tasks will be scouting and surveillance, and—if you can work out how to do it—medical evacuation. Your initial corvée budget is twelve tons. I want it on my desk, with costing, in three days' time. I understand that training pilots and observers takes time, so I want a list of candidate names—outer families for preference, we can't routinely divert world-walkers to a hazardous auxiliary duty. Any problems?"

Rudi looked awestruck. "I can do it! Sir."

"That's what I like to hear." Riordan didn't smile. "Kiril, Rudi's got priority over *everything* except first-class post; even ammunition resupply. We need an airborne capability; I've discussed it with Count Julius already, and it's going to happen. So. Next item, the Hjalmar Palace. Carl. What can you tell us?"

The heavyset man shrugged lazily, almost indolently. Riordan took no offense; he'd worked with him long enough to know better than to think it an insult. "The palace is gone. Sorry, but that's all there is to say about it. Snurri and Ray took samples and we had them analyzed, and they found fallout. Cesium-131, strontium-90, lots of carbon-14. Snurri and Ray indented for new boots and fatigues and I've sent them to the clinic, just in case."

"Scheisse." Nobody but Olga really noticed Riordan's one-word curse, because nobody but Olga was listening to anything but the sound of their own voices. Clan Security, though a highly disciplined organization in the field, tended to operate more like a bickering extended family behind closed doors. "Silence!" Riordan whacked the tabletop. "Let him finish, damn you!"

"Thank you, cuz." Carl's face twisted in something horribly close to a smile. "They couldn't measure the crater because there isn't one. The keep was blown out, completely shattered, but the inner walls of the sunken moat caught the blast, and the foundations are solid stone, all the way down. But we got a good estimate of how big it was from the remains the pretender's men left on the field. Half a kiloton, and it probably went off in the vicinity of the treason room we used for the assault. Sir, do you know what's going on? Because if so, an announcement might quell some of the crazier rumors that are floating around. . . ."

Riordan sighed. "Unfortunately, the rumors hold more than a grain of truth." This time around he didn't try to maintain order. Instead, he leaned back and waited, arms crossed, for the inevitable flood of questions to die down to a trickle. "Are we ready now?" His cheek twitched. "Milady, I believe you have a summary."

Olga glanced around the table. Twelve pairs of eyes looked back at her with expressions ranging from disbelief to disgust. "Eighteen years ago the Council, sitting in camera with the duke present, discussed the question of our long-term relationship with the United States. Of particular concern was the matter of leverage, if and when the American rulers discovered us."

She picked up a glass and filled it from the jug on the table. Nobody spoke; curiosity was, it seemed, a more valuable currency than outrage. "A variety of strategies were discussed. Our predecessors' reliance on access to the special files of the American investigator Hoover was clearly coming to an end—Hoover's death, and the subsequent reorganization of the American secret police, along with their adoption of computerized files, rendered that particular channel obsolete. Computers in general have proven to be a major obstacle: We can't just raid the locked filing cabinets at night. So a couple of new plans were set up."

She saw a couple of heads nodding along at the far end of the table and tried to suppress a smile. "I believe Piotr has just put two and two together and worked out why the duke took it upon himself to issue certain career advice. Piotr spent six years in the USAF, not as an aerial knight but as a black-handed munitions officer. Unfortunately he did not enter precisely the speciality the duke had in mind . . . but others did." More of her audience were clearly putting two and two together. Finally, Rudi raised a hand. "Yes?"

"I looked into this. Nukes—they're not light! You couldn't world-walk one across. At the least, you'd have to disassemble it first, wouldn't you?"

"Normally, yes." She nodded. "But. Back in the sixties, the Americans developed small demolition devices, the SADM, for engineers to use in demolishing bridges in enemy territory. Small is a figure of speech—a strong man could carry one on his back for short distances—but it was ideal for our purposes. Then, in the seventies, they created a storable type, the FADM, to leave in the custody of their allies, to use in resistance operations. The friends they picked were not trustworthy"—an understatement: The Italian fascists who'd blown up the Bologna railway station in the 1970s had nearly sparked a civil war—"and the FADMs were returned to their stores, but they weren't all scrapped. A decade ago we finally placed a man in the nuclear inspectorate, with access. He surveyed the storage site, organized the doppelganger revetment, and we were in. Reverse-engineering the permissive action locks took less than two years. Then we had our own nuclear stockpile."

She raised her glass, drank deeply. "The matter rested with his grace until the last year. It appears that the traitor Matthias had access to the procedures, and to his grace's seal. He ordered one of the devices removed from storage and transported to Boston." She waited as the shocked muttering subsided. "More recently, we learned that the Americans had learned of this weapon. Our traitor had apparently threatened them with it. They indicated their displeasure and demanded our cooperation in retrieving it. I think"—her gaze flickered towards Carl—"that most likely they found it and, by doing so, decided to send us a message. Either that, or our traitor has struck at us—but he is no world-walker. Meanwhile, we know the American secret police hold some of ours prisoner."

"But how—"

"What are we going to—"

"Silence!" The word having had its desired effect, Riordan continued, quietly. "They can hurt us, as they've demonstrated. They could have picked the Summer Palace in Niejwein. They could have picked the Thorold castle. We know they've captured couriers and forced them to carry spies over, but this is a new threat. We don't know *what* they can do. All we know for certain is that our strongholds are not only undoppelgangered, they may very well be traps."

He fell silent. Carl cleared his throat. Deceptively mildly, he asked, "Can we get our hands on some more?"

Olga, who had been rolling the empty water glass between her hands, put it down. "That's already taken care of," she said.

"In any event, it's not a solution," Riordan said dismissively. "At best it's a minimal deterrent. We can hurt them—we can kill tens of thousands—but you know how the Americans respond to an attack. They are relentless, and they will slaughter millions without remorse to avenge a pinprick, should it embarrass them. Worse, their councils and congresses are so contrived that *they cannot surrender.* Any leader who advocates surrender is ridiculed and risks removal from office. And *this* leader—" He shook his head. "They haven't felt the tread of conquering boots on their land in more than a lifetime, and for most of a lifetime they have been an empire, mighty and powerful; there is a level at which they do not believe it is possible for them to be beaten. So if we're going to confront them, the last thing we should do is fight them openly, on ground of their own choosing."

"Such as the Gruinmarkt," said one of the new faces at the table, who had been sitting quietly at the back of the room until now. Heads turned towards him. "My apologies, mi-lady. But . . ." He shrugged, impatiently. "Someone needs to get to the *point*."

"Quite right," muttered Carl.

"Earl Wu." Riordan looked at him. "You spoke out of turn."

"Then I apologize." Wu looked unrepentant.

The staring match threatened to escalate into outright acrimony. Olga took a deep breath. "I believe his lordship is referring to certain informed speculation circulating in the intelligence committee over the past couple of days," she said. "Rumors."

"What rumors?" Riordan looked at her.

"We take our ability for granted." Olga raised a hand to her throat, to the thin gold chain from which hung a locket containing the Clan sigil. "And for a long time we've as-sumed that we were limited to the two worlds, to *home* and to *here*. But now we know there are at least two more worlds. How many more could there be? We didn't know as much as we thought we did. Or rather, much of what we thought we knew of our own limits was a consequence of timidity and custom." The muttering began again. "The Americans have told their scientists to find out how our talent works. They've actually told us this. *Threatening* us with it. They don't believe in magic: If they can see something in front of their eyes, then they can work out how it happens. They've demanded our surrender." She licked her lips. "We need contingency plans. Because they might be bluffing—but if they're not, if they *have* found a way to send weapons and people between worlds by science, then we're in horrible danger. The Council needs to answer the question, what is to be done? And if they won't, *someone's* going to have to do it for them. That *someone* being us."

Getting to see the colonel was a nontrivial problem; he was a busy man, and Mike was on medical leave with a leg that wasn't going to bear his weight any time soon and a wiretap on his phone line. But he needed to talk to the colonel. Colonel Smith was, if not a friend, then at least the kind of boss who gave a shit what happened to his subordinates. The kind who figured a chain of command ran in two directions, not one. Unlike Dr. James and his shadowy sponsors.

After James's false flag ambulance had dropped him off at the hospital to be poked and prodded, Mike had caught a taxi home, lost in thought. A bomb in a mobile phone, to be handed out like candy and detonated at will, was a scary kind of message to send. It said, *we have nothing to talk about.* It said, *we want you dead, and we don't care how. We don't even care much who you are.* Mike shuddered slightly as he recalled how Olga's cynicism had startled him: "How do we know there isn't a bomb in the earpiece?" she'd asked. Well, he'd denied it indignantly enough—and now she'd think he was a liar. More importantly, Miriam's Machiavellian mother, and whoever she was working with— would also be convinced that the diplomatic dickering the colonel had supposedly been trying to get off the ground was a sting. *Dr. James has deliberately killed any chance we've got of negotiating a peaceful settlement,* he realized. *He's burned any chance of me ever being seen as a trustworthy—honorable—negotiator. And he's playing some kind of double game and going behind Smith's back. What the hell is going on?*

Mike's total exposure on the other side of the wall of worlds was measured in days, but he'd seen enough (hell, he'd smelled, heard, and tasted enough) to suspect that Dr. James was working on very incomplete information—or his plans had very little to do with the reality on the ground of the Gruinmarkt. Worse, he seemed to be just about ignoring the Clan, the enigmatic world-walkers who'd been a huge thorn in the DEA's collective ass for the past thirty years or more; it was almost as if he figured that a sufficient display of shock and awe would make them fold without a fight. But in Mike's experience, beating on somebody without giving them any way out was a great way to make them do their damnedest to kill you. Mike's instinct for self-preservation told him that pursuing the matter was a bad idea, and normally he'd have listened to it, but he had an uneasy feeling that this situation broke all the rules. If Dr. James was really off the rails someone needed to call him on it—and the logical person wasn't Mike but his boss.

It took Mike a day to nerve himself to make his move. He spent it at home, planning, running through all the outcomes he could imagine. "What can possibly go wrong?" he asked Oscar, while making a list of bullet points on a legal pad. The elderly tomcat paused from washing his paw to give him such a look of bleak suspicion that Mike had to smile. "It's like that, huh?"

The next morning, he shoehorned himself into his car and drove carefully to a nearby strip mall, which had seen better days, and where, if he remembered correctly, there might still be some beaten-up pay phones tucked away in a corner. His memory turned out to be correct. Staking out a booth and using his mobile as an address book, he dialed a certain exdirectory number. *Seven minutes,* he told himself. *Ten, max.*

"Hello?" It wasn't Colonel Smith, but the voice was familiar.

"Janice? It's Mike Fleming here. Can I please have a word with the colonel?"

There was a pause. "Mike? You're on an unsecured line, you know that?"

"I have a problem with my home phone. Can you put me through?"

A longer pause. "I—see. Please hold." The hold music cut off after half a minute. "Okay, I'm transferring you now."

"Mike?" It was Colonel Smith. He tensed. Until now, he hadn't been entirely sure it was going to work, but now he was committed, upcoming security vetting or no. *I could be throwing my career away,* he thought, feeling mildly nauseous.

"Hi, boss."

"Mike, you're still signed off sick. What's up?" Smith sounded concerned.

"Oh, nothing much. I was wondering, though, if you'd be free to do lunch sometime?"

"If I'd be—" There was a muffled sound, as of a hand covering a mic. "Lunch? Oh, right. Look, I'm tied up right now, but how about we brown bag it some time soon?"

Mike nodded to himself. Message received: The last time the colonel had dropped round with a brown bag there'd been a bomb and a gun in it. "Sure. It's not urgent, I don't want to drag you out of the office—how about next Wednesday?" It was one of the older field-expedient codes: ignore negatives, treat them as emphasis. Mike just hoped the colonel had been to the same school.

"Maybe sooner," Smith reassured him. "I'll see you around."

When he hung up, Mike almost collapsed on the spot. He'd been on the phone for two minutes. His arms were aching and he could feel the sweat in the small of his back. *Shit.* He pulled out the antibacterial gel wipes and applied them vigorously to the mouthpiece of the phone—he'd held the receiver and dialed the numbers with a gloved hand, but there were bound to be residues, DNA sequences, whatever— then mentally crossed it off his list of untapped numbers, for good. That left the polygraph, *but,* he figured, *raising chain-of-command concerns with one's immediate superior isn't normally a sacking offense.* And Dr. James hadn't told him *not* to, either.

He'd hoped the colonel would deduce the urgency in his invitation and he was right. Barely half an hour after he arrived home the doorbell rang. *Too soon,* way *too soon!* his nerves gibbered at him as he hobbled towards the entryphone, but the small monitor showed him a single figure on the front step. "Come on up," he said, eyeballing the top of his boss's head with trepidation. A moment later, he opened the door.

"This had better be good," said Smith, standing on the front step with a bag that contained—if Mike was any kind of judge—something from Burger King.

Mike hung back. "To your knowledge, is this apartment bugged?"

"Is—" Smith raised an eyebrow, an expression of deep concern on his face: concern for Mike's sanity, in all probability. "If I thought it was bugged, I wouldn't be here. What's up?"

"Maybe nothing. To your knowledge, was there anything hinky about the mobile phone you dropped off with me last time you visited."

"Was there"—Mike had never really seen a man's pupils dilate like that, up close—"what?" He could see irritation and curiosity fighting out in Smith's face.

"Let me get my coat. You're driving."

"You bet." Smith shook his head. "This had better be good."

The colonel drove a Town Car—anonymous, not obviously government issue. He didn't say a word until they were a mile down the road. "This car is not bugged. I swept it myself. Talk."

Mike swallowed. "You're my boss. In my chain of command. I'm talking to you because I'm not from the other side of the fence—Is it normal for someone higher up the chain of command to do a false-flag pickup and brief a subordinate against their line officer?"

Smith didn't say anything, but Mike noticed his knuckles whiten against the leather steering wheel.

"Because if so," Mike continued, "I'd really like to know, so I can claim my pension and get the hell out."

Smith whistled tunelessly between his teeth. "You're telling me someone's been messing with you—Dr. James. Right?"

"That's the one."

"Shit!" Smith thumped the center of the steering wheel so hard Mike twitched. "Sorry. I thought I'd cured him of that." He flicked a turn signal on, then peeled over onto an exit ramp. "What did he want you to do?"

"It's what I've already done, as much as anything else—the mobile phone you gave me, to pass on to the other side? Did you know it had a bomb in the earpiece? At least, that's what Dr. James told me. He also told me he was reassigning me to some kind of expeditionary force. Do you know anything about that?"

"You sure about the phone?" Smith sounded troubled.

"That's what he said. It gets worse. When I handed the thing over, my contact actually came out and asked me to my face whether there was a bomb in it. I said no, of course, but it sounds like they're about as paranoid as the doctor. If they check it and find there *is* a bomb in it . . ."

"That's a matter for the policy folks to deliberate on," Smith said as he changed lanes. "Mike, I know what you're asking and why, and I've got to say, that's not your question—or mine—to ask. Incidentally, you don't need to worry about any fallout; we've got a signed executive order waiting to cover our asses. But let me spin you a scenario? Put yourself in the doctor's shoes. He knew they had a stolen FADM and he wanted it back, and he had to send them a message that he meant business. You were talking to their, their liberals. But we don't *want* to talk to their liberals. Liberals are predisposed to talk; the doctor wants to get the attention of their hard-liners, get *them* to fold. We'd already told them that we wanted the weapon back. Negotiation beyond that point was useless: They could hand it over and we'd think about talking, but if not, no deal. So . . . if you look at it from his angle, a phone bomb would underline the message that we were pissed and we wanted our toy back. To the doctor's way of thinking, if they found it, no big deal: It underlines the message. If it worked, waxing one weak sister would send a message to their *other* faction that we mean business. At least, that's how he works." He tapped his fingers on the steering wheel air bag cover.

"With respect, sir, that's crazy. The Clan doesn't work that way; what might work with a criminal enterprise or a dictatorship is the wrong way to go about nudging a hereditary aristocracy. He's talking about assassinating someone's mother or brother. They'll see it as cause for a blood feud!"

"Hmm. That's another way of looking at things. Only it's already out of date. Mike, you swore an oath. Can I rely on you to keep this to yourself?"

Fleming nodded, uncertain. "I guess so." Part of him wanted to interrupt: *But you're wrong!* He'd spent two stinking days running a fever in a horse-drawn carriage with Miriam's mother and the Russian ice princess with the sniper's rifle, and every instinct screamed that the colonel's scenario setup was glaringly wrong—that to those folks, the political was personal, very personal indeed, and a phone bomb in the wrong ear wouldn't be treated as a message but as grounds for a bloody feud played out by the assassination of public figures—but at the same time, the colonel obviously had something else on his mind. And he had a sick, sinking feeling that trying to bring conflicting facts to the colonel's attention, much less Dr. James's, would lead to dismissal of his concerns at best. At worst—*don't go there,* he told himself.

"You didn't hear this from me, and you will *not* repeat it, but a few days ago we did an audit. The bad guys didn't stop at just one nuke. We're fairly certain our quiver is missing six arrows—that's how many are missing, including the one we recovered, and the MO was the same for each theft."

"Six—shit! What happened?"

"Too much." Smith paused for a few seconds, cutting in behind a tractor-trailer. "The doctor sent the one we found back to them: Another of his little messages. He has, it seems, got some special friends in Special Forces, and contacts all the way up to the National Command Authority. He's gotten the right help to build his own stovepiped parallel command and control chain for these gadgets, and he's gotten VPOTUS's ear, and VPOTUS got the president to sign off on it. . . . Hopefully it killed a bunch of their troops. There's been a determination that we are at war; this isn't a counter-terrorism op anymore, nor a smuggling interdiction. They've even gone to the Supremes to get a secret ruling that *Posse Comitatus* doesn't apply to parallel universes.

"To VPOTUS's way of thinking, these guys are as much a threat to us as Chemical Ali was—hell, even more of a threat. The closest thing to a weapon of mass destruction *he* had was Saddam's head on a stick, but he had to go, visibly and publicly, and these guys have to go, too. Even when it was just one nuke, if they'd given it back to us when we asked nicely, and sued for terms . . . it was going to be difficult. Anyway, there's no use crying over spilt milk. The five remaining bombs aren't enough to hurt us significantly— but they're more than enough justification for what's coming next. There's a lab out west that's been making progress on a gizmo for moving stuff between, uh, parallel universes. And you know what the price of gas is. If we can make it work, it'll be a lot easier to get at the oil under their version of Texas than to deal with the Saudis. That'll be what WAR-BUCKS is thinking, and it's going to be what he's telling James to expedite. When Wolfowitz gets through fixing up Iraq . . . do I need to draw you a diagram?"

At war. Mike shook his head. "So you're telling me this is just another oil war? Has anyone told Congress that they're supposed to have authorized this?"

"You know as well as I do that that's not how things happen in this administration. They're looking to our national security in the broadest terms, and when they've got their ducks lined up in a row, well: They've got a majority in Congress, they're even in the Senate, and the other side have given them the most pliable minority leader in decades. Lie-berman's terrified of not looking tough on security issues, and lets WARBUCKS play him like a piano. That's why the president's style of leadership works: He decides, and then WARBUCKS gives him the leverage."

"Not, he decides whatever WARBUCKS wants him to?"

Smith gave him an old-fashioned look. "That's not for you or me to comment on, Mister Fleming. Either way, though, the narcoterrorism angle and the stolen nukes will make great headline copy if—when—it leaks out in public. We can call them Taliban 2.0, now with nukes: It'll play well in Peoria, and the paranoia aspect—bad guys who can click their heels and vanish into thin air—is going to keep everyone on their toes. Bottom line is, those guys picked the wrong administration to mess with." Smith glanced sidelong at Mike. "But I'm a lot less happy about Dr. James's habit of going outside the chain of command."

Mike nerved himself. "Aren't you a bit worried that the doctor may be completely misreading how these people will react? They're not narcoterrorists and they're not hicks, they've got their own way of doing things—"

"It doesn't matter *how* they respond," said the colonel. "They're roadkill, son. A decision has been made, at the highest level. We don't negotiate in good faith with nuclear terrorists: We lie to them and then we kill them. The oil is a side issue. If you've got a problem with that, tell me now; I'll find you a desk to fly where I can keep an eye on you and you don't have to do anything *objectionable*." The final word came out with an ironic drawl and a raised eyebrow.

For a bleak, clear moment Mike could see it all bearing down on him: a continent of lies and weasel-worded justifications, lies on both sides—Olga couldn't have been as ignorant as she'd professed, not if six of the things were missing—and onrushing bloody-handed strife. From the administration on down, policy set by the realpolitik dictates of securing the nation's borders and energy supplies . . . up against an adversary who had stolen nuclear weapons and dealt with enemies by tit-for-tat revenge slaying.

"I'm on board," he said, holding his misgivings close to his chest. "I just hope those missing nukes show up."

"So do I." The colonel grimaced. "And so do the people we've got looking for them."

BEGIN RECORDING:

"My lord Gruen, his lordship Oliver, Earl Hjorth."
    (Sound of door closing.)
    "Ah, Oliver."
    My lord Baron! If you would care to take a seat? . . . We are awaiting her grace, and Baron Schwartzwasser. I think then we may proceed. . . ."
    (Eighteen minutes pass. More people arrive.)
    ". . . Let us begin." (Clears throat.) "I declare this session open. My lord Gruen, you requested this meeting, I believe to discuss the recent incident in the northwest?"
    "Yes, yes I did! Thank you, my lord. I have reports—"
    "—It's insupportable!"
    "My lady? Do you have something you feel you must contribute, or can we hear Lord Gruen's report first?"
    "It's insupportable!" (Vile muttered imprecations.) "Ignore me. I am just an old grandmother. . . ."
    "Hardly that, my lady. Lord Gruen?"
    "I am inclined to agree with her grace, as it happens: Her description of it is succinct. Here are the facts of the matter. The Pervert's army split into three columns, which dispersed and harried our estates grievously. His grace Duke Lofstrom responded by dispersing small defensive forces among the noble households, but concentrating the main body of our Security corvée in the Anglische world as a flying column. He was most insistent that at some point the Pervert would bring his arms together to invest one of our great estates, in the hope of drawing us into a battle in which, outnumbered, we would fall.
    "Despite our entreaties to defend our estates adequately and wipe out the attacking columns, he deliberately starved us of troops, claiming that he must needs give the Pervert a false, weak, picture of our strength of arms, and that in

any case there were insufficient soldiers to defend all our households."

(Sound of paper shuffling.)

"Despite one's worst fears as to his motivation, I must concede that Isjlmeer and Nordtsman received no more succor than did Giraunt Dire and Hjalmar; the duke applied his neglect evenhandedly, failing to relieve his own party inasmuch as he also neglected our own. I do not, therefore, believe that there would be support for a move to relieve him in Committee, especially in view of the accuracy of his prediction. The Pervert *did* concentrate his forces to attack the Hjalmar Palace, evidently with treachery in mind, and in doing so he placed his army within reach of the duke's flying column. Unimpeachable sources tell me that the Pervert's forces had stolen machine guns, but were inadequately supplied and poorly deployed to resist the attack that Earl Riordan was preparing."

(Throat clearing.)

"Yes, my lord?"

"Are you then confirming that, that Angbard's strategy was *sound?*"

(Pause.)

"I would prefer to say that it wasn't obviously *un*sound, my lord. Clearly, his parsimony in the defense of our estates bled us grievously. But equally clearly, if he *had* committed troops to our defense, he would have been unable to concentrate the forces he needed for a counterattack, and he would have ceded the initiative to the Pervert. It is possible that a more aggressive strategy of engagement would have borne fruit earlier, but one cannot be certain."

"Oh." (Disappointed.)

"Indeed." (Drily.) "I am much more concerned by the unexpected outcome of the events at the fork in the Wergat. There is considerable confusion—the Anglischprache attack on the duke's forces, the duke's ictus, the exfiltra-

tion through the *other* Anglische realm with the conniv-
ance of the traitor family—and lastly, the, the *atomic
bomb*. I was hoping my lord Hjorth might shed some light
on that latter."

(Muttering.) "My lords, my lady. If I may speak?"

Her grace: "You may speak until the cows come home,
and convince no one."

"Nevertheless, if I may speak? . . ."

(Conversation dies down.)

"Thank you. Of the duke's condition, I shall speak later:
As your representative on the security committee I believe
I may brief you on the subject. But to get back to the matter
in hand, my sources tell me that when the traitor Matthias
fled to the Anglischprache king-president's party nine
months ago, he clearly gave them much more than anyone
anticipated. Previous fugitives have been taken for mad-
men and incarcerated, or we have been able to hunt them
down and deal with them—but Matthias appeared to vanish from the face of the earth. We now know that he flung
himself on the mercy of the *Drug Enforcement Agency,*
and by their offices, on a dark and sinister conspiracy of
spies."

(Shocked muttering.)

"There is worse. As you know, with the aid of those of
our younger generation who have enlisted and served in
the American armies, we have gained some knowledge
of, and eventually access to, their atomic bombs. The
weight and complexity of these devices, and the secrecy
that surrounds their activation, transport, and use, defied
us for many years, but in the second year of Alexis's reign
we finally infiltrated"—(muttering)—"a master sergeant
in the Marine Corps, yes—enlisted and received special
training—man-portable devices, designed for smuggling,
with which to sabotage the enemies of the Anglischprache
empire overseas in time of war—the, ah, Soviet Union.
And these devices were stored securely, they thought, but

without doppelgangering, as is to be expected of the ignorant. It was a delicate but straightforward task to build a bunker from which a world-walker could enter the storage cells—the hardest part was obtaining a treaty right to the land from the Teppeheuan, and the maintenance schedule for the bombs. From then on, of the twelve weapons, we ensured that six were stored on our side at all times, and rotated back into the Pantex store when they were due to be repaired.

"Then Matthias stole one of them."

(More shocked muttering.)

"Order! Order, I say!"

"Thank you, my lord. If I may continue?"

(Pause.)

"Matthias ven Holtzbrinck was *trusted*. Nobody suspected him! He was Duke Lofstrom's keeper of secrets. I must confess that in all fairness *I* thought him a man of the utmost probity. Be that as it may, Matthias ordered the removal of one of the weapons, and then hid it somewhere. We don't know where because he covered his tracks exceedingly well: Perhaps one of the dead could tell us, but . . . anyway. Need I explain what the king-president's men thought of their ultimate witch-weapon being stolen? I think we can guess. My sources tell me that they began negotiations with the duke with a threat, and that their spies have already been apprehended in the Gruinmarkt. Don't look so shocked. Did you think our missing soldiers had betrayed us and sought refuge? Captivity and slavery—they have ways of compelling a world-walker"—(muttering)—"We face a determined enemy, and they showed just *how* determined they were at the Hjalmar Palace."

"Then it was an atomic bomb?"

"Yes."

(Uproar. Three minutes . . .)

"Order! Order, I say!"

"My lady? You have the floor."

"This is insupportable! Gentlemen, we have known for many years that one day the Anglischprache would learn of our existence. But we cannot allow them to, to think they can tamper at will in our affairs! Sending, without warning, an atomic bomb, into a castle invested only hours earlier by the pride of our army, is a base and ignoble act. It is dishonorable! To live with this threat hanging over us is intolerable, and I submit that it is unthinkable to negotiate as one ruler to another with a king-president who would deliver such a stab in the back. If negotiations were in hand then they acted with base treachery. We act, now, as the largest faction of the Clan, and as rulers of the kingdom of Gruinmarkt, though the peace is not yet settled. We must secure our kingdom from this threat; if there is one thing I have learned in more than sixty years of politics and thirty years of war, it is that you cannot sleep peacefully unless your neighbor can be relied on to obey the same law as you do. The Americans are now, like it or not, our neighbors. We must therefore compel them to obey the law of kings."

"My lady. What are you suggesting?"

(Coldly.) "One act of treachery deserves another. Do we not have arms? Do we not have a kingdom to defend? The American king-president—or rather, the power behind his throne—has declared war upon us and through us upon our domain and all those who live in it. We must make it clear that we will not be trifled with. The time for petty affairs of finance and customs is over. We must hurt the Americans, and hurt them so badly that their next king will not meddle lightly in our affairs.

"My lords. We have, in the course of this civil war, already found it necessary to kill one self-proclaimed king: even, one who would have reigned by blessing of the Sky Father. We must not, now, balk at the death of another lord who is an even greater danger to us than the Pervert. We must settle this matter with the Americans before they think to send their atomic bombs into the heart of Niejwein,

aye, and every stronghold and palace in the land. And the
best way to compel their rulers to negotiate in good faith is
to demonstrate our strength with utmost clarity. My lords,
you must decapitate the enemy. There is no alternative. . . ."

(Uproar.)

END RECORDING

8

high estate

❦

There was a country estate, untouched by war, separated from the clinic in Springfield by about three blocks and two-and-a-half thousand years of divergent history. Brill had picked up a courier from somewhere nearby and driven Miriam round to a safe house on a quiet residential street; whereupon the courier had carried her across, back into the depths of someone else's history.

It was, in many respects, like her time as an involuntary guest of Baron Henryk. There was no electricity in the great stone-walled house, and no central heating or water on tap, and she was surrounded by servants who spoke to her only in hochsprache. Brill had left her in the hands of the maidservants, and she'd felt an unpleasant tension as the chattering women dressed her in clothes from the landholder's wife's chests. *Trapped again*: She felt a quite unexpected sense of panicky claustrophobia rising as they fussed over her. It had been hard to stand still, giving no sign of her urge to bolt and run: She forced herself to recall Brill's oath. *She won't leave me here,* she told herself.

To distract herself she fought her unease by trying to puzzle out their story. The landholder, she eventually concluded, was away in the wars, a relative of the Clan families: He'd sent his dependents to safety for the duration, leaving the staff behind with instructions to look after whomever the council billeted on them. Which meant they were expecting to host one Lady Helge, house and braid and surname unspecified, not Miriam—a woman from another world. *You let yourself get trapped again,* a little corner of her worried. *They laid out a trap and let you walk right into it.*

But there were significant differences from Henryk's idea of hospitality, despite the primitive amenities and unwanted expectations. Her bedroom door had a lock, but she had her own key. The afternoon after her arrival, trying to dispel the anxiety and claustrophobia of being Helge again, she'd ventured from her room to look around the grand hall and the main rooms of the estate. When she'd returned she found the battered suitcase she'd borrowed from Erasmus sitting beside the canopy bed. A quick inspection with shaking hands revealed her laptop and the revolver Burgeson had given her. And not only had they let her keep the locket James Lee had given her—Brill had winked, and given her a second, smaller locket on a gold bracelet. None of these things were of any immediate use, but collectively they conveyed a powerful message: *The trap has a key, and you are not a prisoner.*

She'd sat on the bed, holding the laptop and shaking, carefully stifling her sobs of relief lest the servants waiting outside take fright. When she'd calmed down sufficiently to function again, she checked over the small pistol, reloading it with ammunition from its case. She let the hammer down on an empty cylinder, and slid it into a pouch she'd found cunningly stitched inside the cuff of her left sleeve; *I can make this work,* she told herself. *I've got to make this work.*

The one common drawback of both her own plan, and her mother's, was that they depended on her living as the Countess Helge voh Thorold d'Hjorth. Not playacting in fancy dress, but actually being a lady of the Gruinmarkt—at least unless and until Iris's hastily improvised junta secured its grip on power, or the US military figured out a way to claw a hole in the wall between the worlds. Which could happen tomorrow—or in ten years' time.

The alternatives were all worse: a gamble on the questionable mercies of the DEA's witness protection scheme, an even riskier gamble on Erasmus and his ruthless political allies. Between her mother's Machiavellian proposal and the naïve optimism of the young progressive faction, there was at least some room for her to get a grip on events. "As long as Henryk doesn't rise from the dead I'll be alright," she muttered under her breath. (*Keep telling yourself that,* mocked her inner skeptic. *They'll find some other way to screw you. . . .*)

If Roland were still alive, and had actually been the knight in shining armor he'd looked like at first, she wouldn't have to sort everything out for herself. But first he'd disappointed her, then he'd died trying to live up to her expectations, and now there was nothing to do but press on regardless. *No more heroes,* she resolved. *I'm going to have to do this all on my own again, damn it.* Which, semirandomly, reminded her of the old song. "What do I have to do to get a CD player in here?" she asked herself, and managed a croak of laughter.

A tentative voice piped up somewhere behind her, near the door: "Milady, are you alright?"

Miriam—Helge—turned her head. "I am—well," she managed in her halting hochsprache. "What is it?"

The servant, a maid of the bedchamber—evidently of a higher status than a common or garden serving woman—studiously ignored her reddened eyes. "Milady? I beg you to receive a visitor downstairs?" The maid continued for another sentence, but Helge's hochsprache was too patchy to catch more than a feminine prefix and an implication of status.

"In a, a minute." Helge reached for one of the canopy posts and levered herself upright. "Speak, tell, her I will see them." She took a step towards the heavy oak dresser with the water jug and bowl that stood in for a sink. The door closed behind her. "Ouch." She'd kept the ankle boots she'd acquired in New London because they fit her feet better than any shoes in milady's wardrobe, but she'd been wearing them all day and her feet were complaining. She examined her face ruefully in the precious aluminum-framed mirror. "I'm a mess," she told it, and it winced, agreeing. "Better clean up."

Five minutes later, Helge closed her door and marched onto the landing at the head of the grand staircase, a wide wooden platform that circled the inside wall of the central hall. She gripped the handrail tightly as she descended. *It wouldn't do to fall downstairs, I might lose the baby.* She tried not to succumb to the fit of dark humor: She had a feeling that if she aired that particular joke she might scare people. Not, she was determined, that she was going to bond even remotely with the kid. *That* would be too much like collusion. *I wonder who wants to see me?*

The butler, or equerry or whatever, was waiting at the foot of the stairs with a gaggle of maidservants lined up behind him. "Milady." He bowed, almost sweeping the floor. "Her ladyship awaits you in the green lounge."

Miriam nodded acknowledgement. *Who?* Two unfamiliar servants waited outside the door he indicated, standing at ease with almost military precision. "Introduce me," she said.

"Aye, milady." The equerry walked towards the door, which opened before him. "This is Lady Thorold—"

"We've met," said Helge. She swept past the startled equerry.

Olga met her halfway in a hug. "Helge! You look well. Have they been looking after you?"

. "Well enough so far." She hugged Olga back, then took a deep breath and stepped aside to look at her. With her hair up, wearing an embroidered riding habit, Olga almost looked like the blond ingenue Miriam had mistaken her for when they'd first met, almost a year ago. "You're looking good yourself." She took another deep breath, feeling the knot of anxiety begin to loosen. "But how have you been? Brill tried to bring me up to date on some of the details, but . . ."

"It has been difficult." Olga looked slightly pained for a moment, then her brows wrinkled into a thunderous frown. "But leave that for later! I come to see you, and I find you in a yokel's barn with peasants for attendants and no guards for your back—how long have you been left alone here?"

"Oh, I've only been here since this morning—"

"Only this morning? Well then, I probably need not execute anyone just yet—"

"Wait!" She held up a hand. "Brill was sorting things out for me. What are you going on about?"

"It was Lady d'Ost?" Olga's anger faded. "She told me about your . . . arrangement. She left you here?"

"Yeah. But she was supposed to be back later in the day. Think she ran into trouble?"

"Possibly." Olga walked over to the heavy oak sideboard that stood against one wall and opened a small valise to pull out a CB handset. "I'll just check. One-two, one-two. Stefan, wer' ist?" A burst of crackling hochsprache answered her. Miriam didn't even try to follow the conversation, but after a minute's back and forth Olga was content to shove the radio back in her bag. "My men will ask, when they finish walking the perimeter. It could be just one of those things. . . ." Olga shrugged, delicately. "But we cannot leave you here without a staff, especially once the servants work out who you are. At a minimum you need your own ladies-in-waiting—at least two of them, to supervise the servants and look to your needs. I am able to detach Lady Brilliana from other duties, so she can serve, again. . . . Then you need a lance of guards under a suitable officer, and a communications officer with a courier or two at his disposal. I'd be happier if we could add a doctor or at least a properly trained paramedic, a coachman and two grooms, and either a full kitchen staff or at least a poison-taster. The full household we can leave until later, this is an essential minimum—"

"Olga." Miriam—shoving Helge out of her mind—took a deep breath. "Why?"

"Why?" Olga raised an eyebrow. "Because you're *carrying the heir,* dear. We have a special word for a woman who does that. We call her *the queen.*"

"This glorious nation of ours was not built by the landed gentry or the bastard sons of George; it was built by the sweat and love of men like you. And its future is in your hands."

Erasmus squinted at the faces behind the fulminating glare of the limelights as the scripted applause rolled on, trying to hold an impassive expression of determination on his face. "Thank you, citizens! And long live the commonwealth!"

The applause grew louder, sounding genuinely enthusiastic. Hungry men clinging to their best hope of a solid meal, a cynical corner of his mind observed as he bowed his head, then stepped back from the lectern and walked to the back of the stage to make way for the next speaker.

"I thought that was well enough received," he told the fellow on the bench seat behind the backstage curtain. "What do you think?"

Ronald Smith, the Assistant Commissioner for Justice, nodded thoughtfully. "A good tub-thumping rant doesn't go amiss," he conceded. "Who's on next?"

"Brian MacDougal." Burgeson frowned as he sat beside Smith. "Which means he'll harangue them for three hours on the price of flour while their stomachs are rumbling."

"I ought to go back to the front bench." Smith showed no sign of moving.

"I ought to go back to the office." Burgeson's frown deepened. "There'll be new slanders and rumors from the Patriot Club to rebut before the congress is over, if I don't mistake myself. . . ."

"No, you don't." Smith fumbled in his coat pocket for a while before pulling out a villainously stained clay pipe. "They're getting ready for something big. I can feel it in my bones. We'll have to break some heads before long, or they'll be electing a king to ride us like nags. Francis or Sir Hubert, most likely." Both of whom were popular with the elitist thugs of the Patriot Club and their opportunist red-shirted street runners—the shirts were dyed to conceal the bloodstains of their victims, as Burgeson had announced in one of his more lurid editorials, and for once he was making none of it up.

"They'll break the assembly if they do that."

"The assembly's doomed anyway, Erasmus. As long as Sir Adam sticks to his and our principles and the New Club continue to demand amnesty for John Frederick, there's going to be no compromise, and the taller the debate grows, the more bitter its fruit will be."

"You sound as if you want to compromise. Or am I misunderstanding you?"

Smith grunted as he fumbled with his lighter. "No, I believe there *will* be a compromise, eventually, whether we want it or no; the only question is, whose terms will it favor? The alternative is open strife, and as that would only benefit our enemies . . ."

He pulled the trigger. Sparks snapped and fell into the barrel of his pipe.

"I think you underestimate our resources and our prowess," Erasmus murmured as Smith drew on his weed. "We have a majority of the navy behind us." The rigid stratification and harsh discipline of the service, combined with a recent decline in the quality of rations and an influx of conscripts, had turned the navy into a tinderbox of pro-Leveler sentiment. "In fact, I think we'd have a majority of the people behind us, if the assembly would get round to holding the elections we were promised for our support." Erasmus smiled thinly. "We know we hold the people's mandate, that's why they're carrying on this rearguard action in the popular committees. And the sooner we stop gassing at each other and patting ourselves on the back"—his nod towards the front of the stage, where citizen Mac-Dougal had commenced his peroration on the price of bread, took in the invisible audience of party delegates—"the better. This is what did for us the last time round, and if we don't seize the day it'll do for us—"

He paused. A messenger boy was tiptoeing towards them, eyes wide. "Citizen Burgeson?" he piped quietly.

"Yes, lad?"

"Electrogram from the Westminster Halls!" He held the message slip out, stiff-armed.

"Hmm." Burgeson took the message and read it as fast as he could in the backstage twilight. Then he pocketed it and rose. "It has been good to talk to you, citizen Smith, but I'm needed elsewhere." He smiled faintly. "Do keep me informed as to the substance of citizen MacDougal's bakery, will you?" Then he turned to the messenger boy: "Go tell the postmaster to signal that I'm on my way."

Burgeson emerged blinking from the basement of the commandeered theater where the party caucus was in full swing. Two militiamen in the gray and green uniform of the Freedom Riders challenged him. "Citizen Burgeson. Please tell Citizen Supervisor Philips that I am ready to leave on urgent business and require transport."

"Sir!" One of the guards hurried off; the other stood by. Erasmus pointedly ignored the solecism: Ex-soldiers generally made the best militiamen, even when their political awareness wasn't up to scratch, and with the opposition boasting of two redshirts for every Freedom Rider the Party could muster, only a fool would make an issue of a slip of the tongue.

Presently the guard returned with Supervisor Philips following behind him. Philips, tall, stoop-shouldered, and quavery of voice, wouldn't normally have been Erasmus's idea of a military commander: He reminded him of a praying mantis. (But these weren't normal times, and Philips was, if nothing else, politically sound.) "Ah, citizen Burgeson. What can I do for you?"

Erasmus suppressed a twitch. Drawing himself up to his full height, he said: "I am summoned to the Westminster Halls by Sir Adam."

"Interesting." He could almost see the gears meshing in Philips's mind. "We'll have to avoid the Central Canal and Three Mile Lane, the redshirts are smashing up shop windows and working themselves up." The gears spun to a conclusive stop: "Citizen, please follow me. Meng, go tell Stevens to send the armored car round to the front steps. He's to follow with the motorcycle detachment. Gray, stand guard until I send someone to relieve you." Erasmus fell in behind Philips. "I should like you to ride in the car for your own safety, citizen. Unless you feel the need to arrange a provocation?"

"No provocations today." Erasmus smiled humorlessly, mentally reviewing the message that had dragged him away from the interminable speeches of the party faithful: COME AT ONCE TO DISCUSS PATRIOTS WITHDRAWL FROM ASS BREAK NEED TO RESPOND BREAK. "But there'll be plenty of provocations tomorrow."

Miriam was still vibrating from Olga's arrival two hours later, when the Lady Brilliana d'Ost arrived with all the ceremony due to a lord's daughter, and a small army of servants, stewards, armed guards, and other retainers besides.

They can't mean it, Miriam kept telling herself: *I'm no queen!* She'd met His Majesty King Alexis a number of times, and his mother the dowager queen, but there'd been an empty space in that family tree for some years before Egon pulled his hostile takeover bid. She'd acquired from King Alexis a vague sense of what it was to be a monarch: much like being the CEO of a sprawling, huge, corporation with an activist and frequently hostile board. And the angle that if you screwed up, being fired took on a whole new and alarming meaning.

Olga had dragged her on a tour of the house and its grounds—sucking two bodyguards along in her wake, and using her walkie-talkie to warn other outer guards of their progress—and had tried explaining a huge inchoate bundle of protocol to her, in between showing her round an orchard patrolled by peacocks and a huge selection of outbuildings that evidently made this site suitable for a temporary royal presence—but most of it went right past her head. Too much, too fast: Miriam was still trying to come to terms with her mother's sudden reemergence at the center of a web of diplomacy, and the huge imposition of being pregnant, much less with the whole question of her status here, to grapple with anything else.

In the end, she'd just raised a hand. "Olga. Stop. This is too much for me, right now."

"Too much." Olga paused. "Helge. You need to know this. What is—"

"Back to the house. Please?"

Olga peered at her. "You're not feeling too good?"

"I am *way* overloaded," she admitted. "I'm not ready for this, for any of it. Mom's plan. You're part of it, right?"

"Back to the house," Olga said firmly, taking her in hand. "Yes," she confirmed as they walked, "I have the honor of conspiring with her, as do you. But we are relying on you for so much. If you are overloaded, let me help?"

Miriam sighed. "I'm not sure I can. Being pregnant? That wasn't in my plans. Mom's conspiracy? Ditto. Now you want me to be a queen, which is way outside my comfort zone: It's the kind of job that drives people to an early grave. And then there's the other stuff."

"Other stuff?"

"Don't bullshit me, Olga. Angbard didn't pick you just because of your bright smile and fashion sense. You must have gotten my report through Brill. I *did* meet Mike Fleming in the palace! And he told me—"

"Yes, we know." Olga paused while one of their silent escorts opened the orchard gate for her. "It is a very bad situation, Helge, and I would be lying if I said it was entirely under control. You have been told what happened to Egon's men?"

"Yes." Miriam followed Olga through the gate. "Which means it's only a matter of time. It could all explode in our faces tomorrow, or next month."

"Absolutely. Your uncle—while he lay sick, he told me we needed to put your business plan into action, that it was the only way. But my word carries little weight with the likes of Julius or your grandam. If your mother's conspiracy works, we'll see. But we are riding on a tumbrel with a broken wheel—time is scarce, so we must pursue all our options at once lest we find ourselves treading on air. You as the mother to the heir—that helps. If not with the old aristocracy, then with our own conservatives—*they* recognize the heir, it was their own scheme! And there are other materials that his grace told me to entrust to you, when I can recover them—they are another. We might be able to hold the Gruinmarkt yet, should the American scientists fail to unravel our talent. It could take them years, not months. And we will still need to defeat them in covert battle and recover our hostages from them."

"But it's going to end sooner or later, and probably sooner than we think—"

"Yes, but every month it buys us is a month longer to find a way out of the trap. And we have plans. If the worst should fail to arrive, there is your mother's scheme. And if the worst *does* arrive, we have evacuation plans. We can flee by way of Canada, and then to other nations. We have sent spies to Europe. Your friend in New Britain might supply another option—better, if the Americans announce our existence at large. We've got *many* alternatives. Too many, in fact." The shady garden path approached the courtyard at the rear of the house, the door leading back inside. "Your confusion is our confusion. Brilliana told me you were working on a new plan of business. Work hard; I think we may need it very soon."

Which was all very well, and brought Miriam back to herself, lending her the strength for another try at being Helge. Just in time to open the door onto chaos.

"Move that upstairs! No, not that, the other case! You, yes, you, go find the kitchen! Honestly, where do I get these people? Oh, hi, Miriam!"

The main hallway was full of luggage, heavy trunks and crates, and their attendant grooms, guards, and porters. Brill—Lady Brilliana d'Ost in this time and place, elegant and poised—stood in the middle of it, directing the traffic with the confidence of a born chatelaine. "You'd better wait in the blue receiving room while I get this under control. Which reminds me." She switched to hochsprache: "Sir Alasdair, your presence is required." In English, sotto voce: "Alasdair is in charge of your bodyguards, Helge. Yes he's Clan, a full world-walker, but the offspring of two outer families hence the lack of braid. He's reliable, and unsworn."

"He is?" Miriam murmured, smiling with clenched teeth as a medium-sized mountain of a man shambled across the busy floor, narrowly missing two pieces of itinerant furniture and their cursing porters.

"He is. He's also my cousin." Brill nudged. "Alasdair, I'd like you to meet Helge—"

"Your highness, I am overwhelmed!" The mountain bowed like a landslide, sweeping the floor before Miriam's feet with his hat. "It is an honor to meet you! My lady has told me so much—"

"Oh good." At least the man-mountain spoke English. *Stand up,* she thought at the top of his head in mild desperation.

"Sir Alasdair, you must be able to stand in your liege's presence," Olga interrupted, casting Miriam a sidelong look.

"Of course," Miriam echoed. *Okay, that's two hints. I get the message. Swear your chief of security!*

"Your highness is gracious." Brill winked at her and Olga studiously looked away as Alasdair straightened, revealing himself to be a not-unpresentable but extremely large fellow in his mid-thirties, if not for the starstruck expression on his face.

"If you do not mind, I have to be elsewhere," Olga told Miriam. She nodded at Brill. "You know what must be done?"

"I do."

"Well then." Olga ducked a brief curtsey in Miriam's direction, then sidestepped around the doorway and back into the garden.

"What was that about?" asked Miriam.

"Lady Hjorth is most peculiarly busy right now," Brilliana commented. "As I should be, too, if you do not mind."

Alasdair cleared his throat. "If your highness would care to inspect her guard of honor?"

"I'm not anyone's highness yet," Miriam pointed out. "But if you insist . . ."

"Alasdair and his men will see to your security," Brill repeated, as if she thought Miriam hadn't already got the message. "Meanwhile, I must humbly beg you to excuse me. I've got to get all the servants bedded in and the caravan unloaded—"

"Olga said something about ladies-in-waiting," Miriam interrupted. "Who did you pick?"

"Look no further." Brill raised an eyebrow. "Do you think I would put you in the hands of amateurs? I will find suitable assistants as soon as time permits."

"Oh, thank god." Miriam mopped at her brow in barely feigned relief. "So, I can leave everything to you?"

"You are my *highest* priority," Brill said drily. "You were, even before I swore to you. Now go and meet your guards." She turned and swept back into the chaos in the entrance hall, leaving Miriam standing alone with Sir Alasdair.

"Your highness." Alasdair rumbled quietly when he spoke. "Lady d'Ost has told me something of her time with you. I understand you were raised in America and have little experience of living in civilized manner here. In particular, she said you are unused to servants and bodyguards—is that correct?"

"Pretty much." Miriam watched him sidelong as she took in the details of the room: dark, heavy furniture, tapestries on the walls, an unlit hearth, unpadded chairs built so ruggedly they might be intended to bear the weight of history. Sir Alasdair looked to be a part of these environs, save for the Glock holstered on the opposite side of his belt from his saber. "What, realistically, can your guards do for me? Other than get in my way?"

"What indeed?" Alasdair raised an eyebrow. "Well, there are eight of them, so two are on duty at all times. And when your highness is traveling, all of them will be on duty to cover your path, before and after. We will cover your movements without getting in your way if you but tell us where you wish to go. And when the assassins come, we'll be ready for them."

Assassins? Miriam blinked as Sir Alasdair paused for breath. "Charming," she muttered.

"My Lady d'Ost told me that you have killed a man who tried to kill you. Our job is to see that you never have to do that again."

"Well, that's nice to know. And if I do?"

"Then it will be over our dead bodies," Alasdair said placidly. "If your highness would care to follow me?"

"If you think—" She froze as Alasdair opened the door

back onto the semi-organized chaos in the hall. "Wait, that man. I know him."

She was fumbling with the pouch in her sleeve as Alasdair followed her gaze, tensed, and stepped sideways to place his body in front of her and pull the door closed. He turned to face her. "What about him? That's Sir Gunnar; he's an experienced bodyguard, used to work for—"

Miriam's heart was thundering as if she were trying to run a marathon. She moved her hands behind her back, then tried again to slide her right hand into her left wristband. This time her fingers closed around the butt of her pistol: The man whose true name she had just learned hadn't seen her yet. Talking to another guard, he'd been distracted when Alasdair opened the door.

She swallowed, her mouth unaccountably dry. "Speaking hypothetically—if I ordered you to take that man outside and hang him from the nearest tree, would you do it?" The choking sense of panic was back with a vengeance. *The Ferret,* she'd called him. No-name. *Gunnar.*

"If he were a commoner, yes. But he's one of us," Alasdair rumbled. "A proven world-walker and thus a gentleman, even though he's a by-blow of an outer family lass. You'd need to accuse him of something. Hold a trial." There was an oddly apprehensive note in his voice. *He's afraid of me,* she realized. It was like a bucket of cold water in her face: *Sir Alasdair is* afraid *of* me?

"Well, then I won't ask you to do anything you can't. But if I ordered you to send him a very long way away from me and make sure I never set eyes on him *ever again,* could you do *that?*"

"Of course." The tension went out of his voice, replaced by something like mild amusement. "Do you want me to do that? May I ask why?"

"*Yes.* We have a history, him and me." For a moment she'd been back in Henryk's tower with the Ferret loitering outside her bedroom door, an unsleeping jailer—possibly an executioner-in-waiting, she had no doubt about his willingness to kill her if his master ordered it—cold-eyed and contemptuous. And her racing pulse and clammy skin told her that part of her, a part nobody else could see, would always be waiting in that cell for his key to turn and those pale eyes to flicker across her face without registering any emotion. She flexed her fingers and carefully drew her pistol, then lowered her arm to hide it in a fold of her skirts, careful to keep her eyes on Alasdair's face as she did so. "Did you pick him? Is he a friend of yours?"

"He was on the list." Alasdair's nostrils flared. "One of the top three available bodyguards by ranking. I wouldn't say I know him closely." Miriam stared into his eyes. Wheels were turning there, slowly but surely. "You have relatives who dislike you, my lady, but do you really think they'd—"

"I think we should *find out*." She took a deep breath. "In a moment you're going to open the door and walk towards G-Gunnar. I'll be behind you. Close and disarm him if he so much as blinks. If he draws, you may assume he's an assassin—but if we can take him alive, I have questions I want answering."

"Your highness." Alasdair's nod was cursory, but he looked worried. "Is this wise?"

"Very little I do is *wise,* but I'm afraid it's *necessary.* If you're going to be my bodyguard, you'd better get used to it: As you yourself noted, I'm a target. After you, my lord."

Sir Alasdair turned back to face the door and pushed it ajar. Then he surprised her.

The front hall of the country house was roughly rectangular, perhaps forty feet long and twenty feet wide. The grand staircase started at one side, climbing the walls from landing to landing in turn, linking the two upper stories of the house. At the very moment the door opened, the floor held at least nine porters, servants, guards, cooks, maids, and other workers unpacking the small mountain of supplies that Lady d'Ost had rustled up seemingly out of nowhere to furnish the Countess Helge's entourage. Gunnar was two-thirds of the way across the floor from the door to the blue room, deep in conversation with another fellow, both of them in the livery of guards of the royal household.

Miriam had expected Alasdair to approach his prey directly. Instead, he stood in the doorway for a couple of seconds, scanning the room: Then he broke into a run. But he didn't run towards Gunnar—instead he ran at right-angles to the direct line. As he ran, he drew his sword, with a great shout of "*Ho! Thief!*" that echoed around the room.

Why did he—Miriam raised her pistol, bringing it to bear on the Ferret with both hands—*oh, I see.*

At the last moment, Alasdair spun on his heel before the porter he'd been threatening to skewer—the fellow was frozen in terror, his eyes the size of dinner plates—and rebounded towards the Ferret, who was only now beginning to react to the perceived threat, reaching for a side arm—

"Freeze!" Alasdair shouted. "She has the better of you! Don't throw your life away!"

Miriam swallowed, carefully tightening her aim. *He knew I'd drawn. And he deliberately cleared my line of fire! When am I going to stop underestimating these people?*

The Ferret's face, framed in her sights, was corpse-gray.

"Raise your hands!" she called.

The Ferret—*Sir Gunnar, he's got a name,* she reminded herself—slowly raised his hands. Sir Alasdair stood perhaps six feet away from him, his raised saber lethally close. A healthy man could lunge across ten feet in a second, with arm's reach and sword's point to add another six—the Glock holstered at Gunnar's belt might as well have been as far away as the moon. *If you've got a gun and your assailant has a knife, don't* ever *let them get within twelve feet of you,* she distantly remembered a long-ago instructor telling her.

Miriam took a shuffling step forward, then another, feeling for solid footing with her toes. It got easier to ignore the sensation of her heart trying to climb out through her mouth with practice, she noted absently.

"Disarm him," she heard Sir Alasdair tell the other

guard, who glanced nervously over his shoulder at her—*at her*—then hastily pulled the gun and the sword from Gunnar's belt.

Miriam risked lengthening her stride. Her breath was coming hard. Amusement and hysteria vied for control. She stopped when she was about fifteen feet from her target. "Who sent you here?" she demanded.

"I'm not going to plead for mercy." The Ferret's eyes, staring at her over the iron sights of her pistol, seemed to drill right through her. "You're going to kill me anyway." He sounded curiously resigned.

He'd beaten her, once, to make a point: *Obey me or I will hurt you.* That he'd been following orders rather than giving rein to his own sadistic urge made no difference to Miriam. But—*hold a trial. And accuse him of* what, *exactly?* Of being her jailer after Henryk had violated Clan law and process by *not* executing her for what she'd done? If she gave him a trial, stuff better swept under the rug would come out. Kill him out of hand, and her enemies—the ones who'd tried to have her raped, or killed, or maimed several times over the past year—would find a way to make use of it, but at least he wouldn't be able to rat her out. Likely they'd use it as evidence of her instability or anger—*anger* was always a good one to pin on a threatening woman. But it was nothing like as damaging as what he could reveal.

She licked her lips. "Not necessarily." *Don't tempt me* struggled briefly with a moment of revulsion: *Life is too damned cheap here as it is.* "Restrain him." The other guard was already loosening the Ferret's belt. "Lower your arms. Slowly."

The room was very quiet. Miriam blinked back from her focus through the sights of the gun and realized all the servants had scurried for cover. *Smart of them.* "I hold him covered," Sir Alasdair said conversationally.

"Oh. Thanks." She blinked again, then lowered the gun and carefully unhooked her finger from the trigger guard, which seemed to have somehow shrunk to the gauge of a wedding ring. The guard worked the Ferret's arms behind his back and tied them together with his own belt. She glanced at Sir Alasdair. "Tell him what I told you to do with him. I don't think he'll believe it, coming from me."

Alasdair kept his sword raised. "Her highness ordered me to send you a very long way away from her and make sure she never set eyes on you again. Her exact words." His cheek twitched. "I don't *have* to kill you."

"Highness?" Gunnar's face slumped, defiance draining out of it to leave wan misery behind. "So it's true?"

"Is what true?" she asked.

"You're carrying. The heir."

She stared at Sir Gunnar. "You didn't *know*?"

"My lord did not see fit to tell me." He was pale, almost greenish. Miriam stared at the blue eyes set in a nondescript face, the balding head and wiry frame, trying to remember how scant seconds ago she'd looked at them and seen a monster. *Who's the* real *monster here?* she asked herself.

"It's true," she told him. "And what Sir Alasdair told you is true. You don't have to die; all you have to do is stay the hell away from me. And tell us how your name got on that list."

"What list?" He looked away, at Sir Alasdair. "What the hell is she talking about?"

"Why are you here? Look at me!" Miriam shifted her grip on her pistol.

The Ferret turned his head, reluctantly. "What list?" he asked again.

"The master roster of available bodyguards for council members," Sir Alasdair rumbled. "You were right at the top of it."

"As if I shouldn't be?" Gunnar snorted. "What do you take me for?"

"Wait," said Miriam. "What did you do for Henryk? Officially?"

There was a pause. "I was his chief of security. *Officially.*"

Ah. "And unofficially?"

Gunnar made a small shrug. Now that he wasn't staring down the barrel of a pistol held by an incandescently angry woman he seemed to be recovering his poise. "The same. I *was* his chief of security. Until the Pretender did for him."

"Right." She glanced at Sir Alasdair. "Maybe you'd like to tell him what I asked you *first.*"

"Highness, I think he can guess." Alasdair's smile was humorless, and it wiped the nascent defiance right off Gunnar's face. "I am ordered, and empowered, to act with any necessary force in defense of your person. Do you consider this man a threat to your person?"

It was hard to look at the Ferret's frightened face and still want to see him swinging from a tree. It had been tempting in the abstract, but ven Hjalmar was the real villain of the piece, and beyond her reach if he was indeed dead; in the clarity of the moment she found the Ferret pathetic rather than threatening, an accomplice rather than a ringleader. "Right now . . . no. But he knows things. And I don't trust where he's been, why he's here. It stinks." She glanced at Sir Alasdair. "Escort him from the premises and make sure he doesn't come back, but don't kill him. I need to talk to you later, but first I have other work to do." Her cheek twitched as she looked back at the Ferret. "Payback can be a bitch, can't it? Have a nice day."

Gunnar's control finally cracked. "High-born cunt! The doctor was right about you!" he shouted after her. But she had already turned her back on him, and he could not possibly see her shock. The sound of her guards beating him followed her up the staircase.

BEGIN RECORDING:

"WELLSPRING?"

"MYRIAD?"

"No, I'm the fucking tooth fairy—who do you think? You've missed three calls in a row. This had better be good."

"Oh yes? Well, that stunt you pulled with the physics package could have killed me! What the hell were you *thinking?*"

"Hey, *I* didn't pull the trigger on that one. We're not a monolith; stovepipes melt and shit falls between the cracks. Did you just place this call so you could bitch at me or do you have something concrete?"

(Indignant snort.) "Certainly. Your message in a pipe bomb, up near Concord? It was received loud and clear."

"Really? Good—"

"No, *bad.* You know there was a pocket-sized civil war going on over there? Well, your timing was *brilliant.* You wiped out an entire army. Only trouble is, *it was the wrong one.* You handed the tinkers victory on a plate—they're busy mopping up right now, chasing down the last stragglers. They've even got some kind of half-cocked claim to the throne lined up, and you killed the only legitimate heir! Did you know that? You've just killed off all their enemies, and let them know into the bargain that it's war to the knife."

(Silence.)

"Hello? Are you still there?"

"Jesus."

"The phrase they use hereabouts is 'God-on-a-stick'; but, yes, I echo the sentiment."

"Can you just confirm all that, please?"

"Certainly. When you blew up the Hjalmar Palace the royalist army that was *fighting* the tinkers had just occupied it. *They* had evacuated it a couple of hours earlier. Among the casualties was the crown prince—"

"Hang on. You said the Clan had evacuated the structure. Are you certain of that?"

(Snort.) "If they hadn't, then how come their soldiers are dispersed all around the capital? Oh, they're not stupid—they got the message, you won't catch them all concentrating in a strong-point again. Why?"

"But how? How did they withdraw?"

"The usual way—they world-walked. Or so I infer. They certainly didn't fight their way through the pretender's siege works: Individually they outgunned his army, but quantity's got a quality all of its own, as they say."

(Silence.)

"Are you still there?"

"Yes. Just thinking."

"Well, think faster. I don't have long here."

(Slowly.) "If the nar— If the Clan forces exfiltrated by world-walking, how did they do it? We had the whole area blanketed."

"You did? Well, they must have just gone through another world, then."

"Another"—(pause)—"you're shitting me."

"Huh?"

"Other world, unquote."

"Yes. So?"

"You mean there are more?"

"What?"

"How many worlds, MYRIAD? *How many fucking worlds?*"

"Eh, don't get sharp with me, asshole! I can always put the phone down!"

(Heavy breathing.) "I need to know." (Pause.) "I'm sorry. This is—this upsets everything."

"I thought you knew this shit. Do I have to baby you?"

"Knew—ah, shit. Look, this stuff is new to us. How many worlds are there?"

"How should I know? Last week, there was ours, there was yours, there was the other one the homicidal cousins come from—"

"Homicidal *cousins?*"

"Long story. Anyway, word just in says they've discovered a fourth, and there's a team actively looking for more.

For all I know there are factions or conspiracies who've already gotten there, who've got their own private bolt-holes well stocked for a long siege; but it used to be that everybody only knew about two. I'm guessing that cat's out of the bag, and . . . nobody knows. Could be, four's the total. But are you willing to bet on that?"

"Oh Jesus. WARBUCKS is going to shit a super-tanker."

"Hey, I'm just the messenger. Didn't your other informants tell you?"

"No." (Pause.) "How do they get to these other worlds?"

"Fuck knows. I *think* there's something about using a different symbol, or maybe it's just where they start out from. I really don't—" (Pause.)

"Hello?"

"Someone's coming, got to clear down now. I'll call later."

(Click.)

"Wait—"

(Dial tone.)

END RECORDING

An attorney's office in Providence was an unlikely setting to look for a government-in-exile, but it suited Iris just fine. *The boy's smart,* she decided. *Smart* and *discreet* were interchangeable in this context: Nobody would bat an eyelid at an attorney receiving numerous visitors, some of them shady, some at odd times of day. It was the next best thing to a crack house as an interchange for anonymous visitors, with the added advantage of being less likely to attract attention in its own right.

This would be harder than dealing with Dr. Darling.

"I'll walk," she told Mhara as her young companion opened the minivan door for her. *Bad idea to look weak.*

"Yes, milady . . ."

Something about her tone of voice caught Iris's attention. "Yes?" she said sharply.

"By your pardon, milady, but will you be expecting me to . . . you know?"

Iris sighed. "Absolutely not," she said, in a more gentle tone of voice. "I'm here to talk, not to clean up loose ends; you don't need to worry about conflict of interests. You can leave your kit in the trunk if you want."

"Thank you, milady." Mhara sounded relieved; but, Iris noticed, she made no move to jettison her shoulder bag. "That won't be necessary."

Iris made her way slowly past the unmanned reception desk towards the elevator beyond. Looking up, she noticed the CCTV camera and paused, giving it time for a good look at her. Then she shuffled forward and pressed and held the call button.

"Iris Beckstein," she said. "His lordship is expecting me."

The lift doors opened. Iris gave Mhara an ironic little smile. "After you," she said.

"Thank you milady." Mhara held the lift open for her—redundantly—looking slightly puzzled. "Why is there no security?" she asked as the doors closed.

"You didn't notice, did you?" Iris asked. Mhara shook her head. "This used to be a level two safe house, before they let it out for commercial rent ten years ago. They recommissioned it a few months ago, at a guess, after that bastard Matthias went over the wall. If we weren't expected, the doors wouldn't have opened. And if we'd tried to force the issue"—she raised her walking stick ironically—"the sprinkler system isn't for putting out fires."

"Ugh." Mhara looked at the ceiling, her eyes widening as she noticed the black Perspex hemispheres in two corners.

Naïve, but give her time . . . Iris waited, trying to prepare herself for the coming confrontation.

The elevator car stopped and the doors slid open. "After you."

Iris gestured towards the door opposite, then shuffled after Mhara. A moment later, the door opened. "Your ladyship?" The polite young man in a suit that didn't quite conceal his shoulder holster held the door open. "They're waiting for you in the boardroom."

"Really?" Iris smiled tightly. "Mhara, I'm afraid you'll have to wait outside."

"Certainly, milady—"

"I can see to her comfort."

"You will." Cutting their chatter dead, Iris picked up her pace and hobbled past him, leaning heavily on her stick. It would be the second door on the left, if they'd followed the standard layout. . . .

The boardroom was small, dominated by a huge meeting table surrounded by chairs designed to keep their occupants from falling asleep prematurely. The door's reinforced frame, and the shuttered box on one wall—a discreet cabinet that might equally hide a projection screen or an expensive plasma TV as anything more exotic—were the only obvious signs to distinguish it from a meeting room in any other law firm's office. Iris opened the door with some difficulty and slipped through it with a sigh of relief as a very different polite young man held it open, scowling. "You're late, aunt," he said.

"Heavy traffic on the interstate." She gestured at an empty chair. "If you don't mind, Oliver?" Then she nodded at the room's other occupants. "Ah, Captain. Or should that be Major? I gather congratulations are in order. Julius, was it your idea?"

"No idea what you're talking about!" said the turkey-necked oldster at the head of the table. "But it's good news all the same."

"Yes, well." Oliver, Earl Hjorth, pulled a chair out for her. She lowered herself into it gratefully. "I gather our number one problem has been removed from the map by our number two problem. Or is that a slight oversimplification?"

"Very probably." The possibly newly promoted Earl Riordan put down the document he'd been studying and stared at her, his blue eyes cold as a mountain lake in winter. "If you don't mind waiting, milady, we are expecting one more participant, in a nonexecutive capacity."

"Oh?" Iris asked, as the door opened again.

"Hi, everybody! Am I late? Oh! Iris! How *are* you? . . ."

Olga seemed flustered, but happy to see her—as indeed she should be. Iris suppressed a smile. "No time for social niceties, child! We have a meeting to start."

"Yes." Riordan raised an eye at her. "And what delayed you, my dear?"

"A traffic accident." Olga's smile vanished. "Fatal. On Route 95."

"Ah." Iris glanced sideways as Oliver scribbled something on his notepad.

"Well, we're all here now," Iris commented. "Aside from the absentees. So if you'd care to start? I assume you have an agenda in mind?"

"Yes." Riordan's cheek twitched. "Let's see: attending . . . everyone on the list, yes. Apologies, none. Absent due to death: Henryk Wu-Thorold, Peffer Hjorth, Mors Hjalmar, Erik Herzog, Lars Thorold. *Scheisse* . . . New attendees include Patricia Thorold-Hjorth, Oliver Hjorth replacing Mors Hjalmar, Olga Thorold replacing myself, myself deputizing for Angbard Lofstrom. We are quorate—just barely. The agenda—look under your notepad, it probably got covered up. If you don't mind, as we're starting late, I'd like to begin by calling Lady ven Thorold to report on the current medical prognosis of the principal security officer. Then we'll proceed onto matters arising and work out where we go from there. Olga?"

"Oh. Right." Olga looked almost comically blank for a moment, then reached into her handbag to remove a day planner bulging with notes. "To recap, the duke has been in the high dependency unit for six days now, and he isn't dead. He's even showing some signs of awareness and trying to communicate. That's the good news. The bad news is, he isn't getting any better. Let me just go over what Dr. Benford told me. . . ."

She rattled on for almost ten minutes. "He is much the same," she concluded. "His recovery is slow, and he betrays holes in his memory. He has trouble with names, and his left arm is still very weak."

She put her day planner down and leaned back in her chair, looking almost bored. *Well, she's had longer to adjust to this than the rest of us,* Iris considered. Beneath the blond mop—and Olga could play the blond airhead role for all it was worth when she wanted to—there was a very sharp young mind. *She doesn't think he's coming back.* Iris suppressed a pang of horror. *Oh my brother, why did you have to do this to us* now, *of all times?*

"In short, his grace is unlikely to join Sky Father in his halls this month, but he will probably not be issuing orders in the short term. We may hope that he will recover sufficiently to conduct his private affairs, and possibly even to resume the leadership of Security—but this is likely to take months, or years." She leaned back and crossed her arms, tired and defensive. "All yours, cuz."

"If I may interrupt?" Julius sat up slightly. *Oh, come on*—Iris bit back on her response. Julius had always had a sharp mind behind that slightly vague façade; as one of the last of the elder generation of power brokers still standing, he called for a certain wary respect—but he also had a tendency towards unhurried meandering, which had grown worse in recent years.

"You have the floor." Riordan nodded and made a note on his pad. The cassette recorder at his left hand was turning, red LED steady: Preparing the minutes would be a sensitive job.

"Thank you. As chair of the Council of Families, I would like to note on the record that in view of the current emergency, we cannot allow the seat of principal security officer to remain empty. I therefore propose that until the duke reclaims his throne, or until the council of families votes to replace him, Earl-Major Riordan should continue to execute security policy in his stead. As for the direction of that policy, I believe the best way of ensuring impartiality is to place it in the hands of a committee. Such as this one, assembled as it is to evaluate the situation—I believe all interests are adequately represented? Earl Hjorth?" He turned to Iris. "Your grace?"

Oliver was staring at her, too. Iris nodded slowly, gathering her thoughts. "It could fly. But you've missed someone out," she said after a moment. "And I want to see some limits. . . . Six months, or the death of a member, and it goes to an emergency session of the full council, not just this security subcommittee."

Oliver was nodding, but Riordan looked irritated. "An emergency session could be difficult to arrange—"

"Nonsense. This is a policy committee, not the executive. You have an emergency? *You* handle it. But for policy—we have differences." Oliver stopped nodding. "I won't lend my name to an office that can outlive my approval."

"You're talking coalition," said Julius.

"Yes, exactly." She winked at Oliver. "I don't think any of us want to see a return to the old ways. Let's not leave ourselves open to temptation." In the old days, assassination was a not-unheard-of tool for manipulating the collective will.

Riordan cleared his throat. "You said you thought we were missing a member," he said.

"Yes." She picked up her water glass and took a sip. "There are two aspects to this job: How we pacify our homeland and how we deal with the American authorities. When it comes to the former, it would appear that my daughter is"— she swallowed again—"holding an extremely useful asset. And I gather the central committee"—she nodded at Julius— "have already considered her potential as a tool of state. But, speaking as one who knows her mind, I must warn you that if you think you can use her purely as a puppet you're mistaken. She's a sharp blade; if you don't want to cut yourself, you'll need to get her to wield herself. And the best way to do that is to co-opt her. Offer her a seat on this committee and listen to her input."

"Ah." Oliver picked up his pen, twirled it between his fingertips in thought. "Who do you propose should step down to vacate a seat for her?"

Iris saw Olga begin to open her mouth and pushed on. "I don't. *You*"—she pointed at the earl—"are here to represent your circle. *He*"—Riordan—"is Clan Security. Julius is our council overseer; *she*"—she pointed at Olga, whose eyes widened—"happens to have new party sympathies"—*as close to a lie as I've told all day*—"and as for me, I'm here to make sure nobody poisons my half-brother." Her cheek twitched. "Call me an insurance policy." She crossed her arms and waited.

"I thought you were in favor of marrying her off? Integrating her as fast as possible," Oliver accused.

"That was then, this is now." Iris shrugged. *And what you think has very little to do with the truth of the matter. . . .* "You don't still think I'm trying to undercut your inheritance?"

"Ach." Oliver shook his head. "That's of secondary importance, compared to the mess we've got to clean up! I am prepared to set the matter aside for a period of, say, a year and a day, then submit it to mutually agreed arbitration. In the interests of ensuring that there *is* a future in which I can peacefully enjoy my inheritance, you understand. If you think her claim can be made to stick—"

"We've got some extra help there."

Riordan spoke up. "The betrothal was witnessed. *Not* just by our relatives, and it seems there were survivors. No less a notable than the Duke of Niejwein himself, although how he got away—and he kept what he knew to himself when Egon came calling—"

"Ah." Julius looked relieved. "So we have a friendly witness."

"Not exactly." Riordan looked pained. "Lady Olga? . . ."

"We've got him in a lockup in this world. I had him brought over here as a security precaution—he's less likely to escape."

"Have him witness publicly before his execution," Iris suggested. "Offer him amnesty for his family and estates if he cooperates."

"I know Oskar ven Niejwein," Oliver muttered darkly. *His eldest living son,* Iris realized. "Better hang 'em all afterwards. It's the only way you'd be safe from him."

"No!" Iris's head whipped round as Riordan spoke. "What does royalty trade in?" he asked, meeting her surprised gaze.

"Royalty trades in power."

"Huh." His frown deepened. "I don't think so. Oliver?"

"It trades in law," Earl Hjorth said easily, "its ability to rule well."

"No, that's wrong, too." Riordan glanced at Olga. "What do you think?"

"Consistency?" she offered, with a raised eyebrow.

"Close." Riordan straightened in his chair. "Royalty trades on *belief.* A king is just one man, but if everybody in the kingdom believes in him, with the blessing of the gods, he reigns. *We* know this—we have been touched by this *Anglischprache* world—even if our benighted countrymen remain ignorant. Kings only reign if people believe they are kings. The belief follows the actions, often as not—the exercise of power, the issuing of laws—and is encouraged by consistency in leadership.

"We need Niejwein alive and *believing* we hold the throne by right of inheritance, not conquest, and reminding anyone who asks. If he's dead, people will forget his words if it conveniences them to do so. So I second Patricia Thorold-Hjorth's recommendation that Countess Helge be offered a seat on the security committee. And while we can and must make an example of some of the rebels, Niejwein must live."

"So do we have a general agreement?" Iris asked. "An ad hoc policy committee to sit for six months until relieved by a full council session, ruling in the name of Helge's unborn child, with Helge co-opted as a member of the committee and responsibility for Clan security resting with the major?"

Riordan glanced at the agenda in front of him. "There's a lot more to it than that," he pointed out.

"Yes. But the rest is small print—these are the big issues. I call for an informal show of hands: Is a solution along the lines I just outlined acceptable in principle to you all?"

She glanced around the table. Riordan nodded. "Votes, please. Non-binding, subject to further negotiation on the details," he added, heavily. "So we know whether it is worth our while to continue with this meeting."

Hands began to go up. Iris raised hers; a moment later, Oliver Hjorth grimaced and raised his.

"I see nobody objects." Riordan nodded. "In that case, let us start on the, ah, small print. I believe you submitted a draft list of actions, my lord Julius? . . ."

9

CORONATION

❦

It had been a busy three weeks for Mike Fleming. An enforced week of idleness at home—idleness that was curiously unrestful, punctuated by cold-sweat fear-awakenings at dead of night when something creaked or rattled in the elderly apartment—was followed by a week of presenteeism in the office, hobbling around with a lightweight cast on his foot and a walking stick in his hand, doing make-work to ease him back into the establishment. Then one morning they'd come for him: two unsmiling internal affairs officers with handcuff eyes, who told him that his security clearance was being revalidated and escorted him to an interview suite on the thirteenth floor of an FTO-rented office building.

The polygraph test itself was almost anticlimactic. It wasn't the first time that Mike had been through one; *and I've done nothing to be ashamed of,* he reminded himself as they hooked him up. He focused on the self-righteous truth: Unless the system was so corrupted that sharing honest concerns with his superior officer was now an offense, he was in the clear.

So the questions about his alcohol consumption, political leanings, and TV viewing habits came as something of an anticlimax.

They sent him home afterwards, but early the next day a courier dropped by with a priority letter and a new identity badge, clearing him to return to duty. So Mike hobbled out to his car again and drove to work, arriving late, to find he'd missed a scheduled meeting with Dr. James and that there was a secret memo—one he wouldn't have been allowed to set eyes on two days earlier—waiting for him to arrive at his desk.

"I'm supposed to give you access to the GREEN SKY files," Marilyn Shipman said, her lips pursed in prim disapproval. Mike couldn't tell whether it was him she disapproved of, or merely the general idea of giving someone, anyone, access to the files. "For transcription purposes only. Room 4117 is set up with a stand-alone PC for you to use, and I can bring the files to you there one at a time."

"Ah, right." Mike gestured at his desk. "I've got a lexicon and some other research materials. Can I bring them along?"

"Only if you don't mind leaving them there." Shipman paused. "Paper goes into the room but nothing comes out until it's been approved by the classification committee. Depending on their classification, I could make an authorized copy and have it added to the room's permanent inventory. But if they're another codeword project . . ."

"I don't think so, but I'll have to check." Mike suppressed a momentary smile at her expression of shock. Some of the spooks who'd ended up in FTO were halfway human, but others seemed to take the form of their procedures more seriously than the actual substance. Like Ms. Shipman, who—he had a mental bet going with his evil twin self—would probably be less offended if he exposed himself to

her than by his momentary forgetfulness about the classification level of his own notebook.

An entire working day (and three meetings) later, Mike
finally got the keys to Room 4117 and its contents, including
his carefully photocopied lexicon and handwritten notes on
hochsprache. There was other material, too: an intimidating
row of nonclassified but obscure works on proto-Germanic
and Norse linguistics. The room itself was sparsely furnished
and windowless, half filled by the single desk. The PC, and
an audio-typist's tape deck, were fastened to it by steel cables, and as if to drive home the point, a framed print on the
wall behind the PC reproached him: SECURITY, IT'S MORE
THAN YOUR JOB THAT'S AT STAKE.

Then Marilyn brought him the box of material he was
supposed to be working with.

"You're kidding me. I've got to sign for a bunch of *cassette tapes?*"

"You got it. Here and here." She pointed to the relevant
lines on the form.

"Some of these look like they've been *chewed* by a *dog.*"

"You're working with primary source material now. You'd
be amazed at some of the stuff we get coming in from Paki-
stan and the Middle East." She paused while he signed the
clipboard. "These are originals, Mr. Fleming. They've been
backed up—they're in the library if anything goes wrong—
but most of our analysts work with primary recordings wherever possible. Just in case anything's missing from the backup
copy. There shouldn't be any problems of that kind, but you
can never be quite sure. As to why it's on cassette tape, I
couldn't possibly say. Perhaps that's all the field officer had to
hand. They're still common in some parts of the world." She
smiled tightly and tapped the yellowing plastic lid on the
secretarial recorder with a fingertip. "Do you remember how
to use one of these?"

"I think I can cope." Mike looked at the headset doubt-
fully. "What's that?" He pointed at a hole that had been
drilled through a red button on the machine's control panel.

"That was the record button. They disconnect the erase head, too, just in case; this one's strictly playback only."

"What, in case I slip and accidentally delete something?"

"No, it's in case you try to record a message for the accomplice you've got working down in library services to smuggle out of the establishment, Mr. Fleming. That should have been in your security briefing materials. We are very methodical here."

"I can see that." Mike picked up the first of the cassettes; a thin patina of dust grayed the hand-scribbled label. "Has this been in your archives for long?"

"I don't know and I couldn't say."

After Marilyn left, Mike sorted through the box. There were ten cassettes in all, and some of them were clearly years old. Most were identified only by a serial number scribbled on one side; a couple of them showed signs of the tape having been crumpled, as if they had unspooled and been painstakingly reassembled from a tangle of twisted Mylar. It had been years since Mike had last bothered with a cassette tape in everyday life; his last two automobiles had come with CD players. They were an obsolete technology, analog recordings on thin ribbons of Mylar tape. It seemed very strange to be working with them again, inside a windowless cell in a huge concrete office block in Maryland. But then again, a little voice reminded him: *They're robust. The equipment's cheap, and doesn't have to look like a spy tool. And you can replace them easily. Why fix something if it isn't broken?*

And so he slotted the first tape into the player, donned the headset, and pressed the PLAY button.

And it made very little sense whatsoever, even on the third replay.

By the third day, Mike had just about worked out what his problem was. It wasn't just his grasp of the language, poor as it was. It wasn't the clarity of the recordings, either—the microphone had been reasonably well placed, and it was of adequate sensitivity. The men (and occasional women) he heard discussing things in what sounded like an office suite—these were regular business meetings, as far as he could tell—were audible enough, and he could make out most of their words with a little effort. Many of their terms were unfamiliar, but as if to balance things out, the speakers used familiar English words quite often, albeit with an accent that gave Mike some trouble at first.

"It's the context," he told the security awareness poster. "Knowing what they're talking about is as important as knowing what they're saying." He waved his hands widely, taking in the expanse of his empire—the desk, the chair, the walls—and declaimed, "Half of what gets said in any committee meeting doesn't get expressed verbally, it's all body language and gestures and who's making eye contact with whom. Jesus." He looked at the box of tapes disgustedly. "Maybe these would be some use to a secretary who sat in on the meeting, fodder for the minutes. . . ."

His eyes widened as he remembered lying on the floor in an empty office, Matthias—source GREENSLEEVES—standing over him with a gun: "If you'd gone after the Clan as a police operation, that would have given the thin white duke something more urgent to worry about than a missing secretary, no?"

Jesus. He stared at the tapes in surprise. *Matthias was their boss man's—the thin white duke's—secretary, wasn't he? These are probably* his *transcripts.* Not that he'd recognized the defector's voice—it had been months since he'd died, and Matt's voice wasn't distinctive enough to draw his attention, not on an elderly tape recording of a meeting—but the implications . . . *GREENSLEEVES didn't bring any tapes with him when he defected, so how did these get here? We have a spy in the Clan's security apparatus, high enough up to get us these tapes. I wonder who they are? And what else they've brought over? . . .*

* * *

In a shack attached to the stables at the back of Helge's temporary palace, a man in combat fatigues sat on a swivel chair and contemplated failure.

"It's not working," he complained, and rubbed his aching forehead. "What am I doing wrong, bro?"

"Patience." Huw carried on typing notes on a laptop perched precariously on one knee.

This experiment was Helge's idea. "The first time I world-walked I was *sitting down*," she'd told him. "That's not supposed to be possible, is it? And then, later, I"—a shadow crossed her face—"I was brought across. In a wheelchair." Her frown deepened. "There's stuff we've been lied to about, Huw. I don't know whether it's from ignorance or deliberate, but we ought to find out, don't you think?"

Angbard had said *get to the bottom of it,* and while the duke was hors de combat, Huw was more than happy to keep on following the same line of inquiry for Helge. "Okay, that's test number four. Let's try out the next set of casters. You want to stand up while I fit them?"

"Yah." Yul stood, then picked up the chair, inverted it, and planted it on the workbench.

Huw put down the laptop then went to work on the up-turned chair's wheels with a multi-tool, worrying them until they came loose. He pulled another set of feet from a box and began installing them. "This set should work better, if I'm right," he explained as he worked. "High density polyethylene is a very good insulator, and they're hard—reducing the contact area with the ground."

"What about the mat?" asked Yul.

"That, too. We'll try that first: you, me, then Elena. Then without the mat."

"You think the mat has something to do with it?"

"I'm not sure." Huw straightened up. "She world-walked in an office chair. We don't do that because it never occurred to anyone. They tried wheelbarrows, and on horseback, back in the day. Even a carriage plus four. All we know is that nobody world-walks in a vehicle, because when they tried to do it, it didn't work. But we do it on foot, wearing shoes or boots. So what's going on? What's different about boots and wheels?"

"Horses weigh a lot," Yul pointed out. "So do wooden barrows, or carriages."

"Yes, but." Huw reached for a mallet and a wooden dowel, lined them up carefully, and gave a recalcitrant caster a whack. "We don't *know*. There are other explanations, like: Most shoes are made to be waterproof, yes? Which makes them nonconductive. Whereas anyone who tried horses would have used one that was properly shod. . . . I just want to try again, from first principles."

"Why not get Rudi to try it in midair?" asked Yul.

Huw snorted. "Would you like to give yourself a world-walker's head in midair, while trying to fly a plane? And what if it works but doesn't take the plane with the pilot?"

"Oh." Yul looked thoughtful. "Could he try it in a balloon? With a parachute, set up to unfold immediately if he fell? Or maybe a passenger to do the world-walking?"

Huw stopped dead. "That's a *good* idea. Hold this." He passed the chair to his brother while he opened up the laptop again and hastily tapped out a note. "You volunteering?"

"What, me? No! I can't skydive! I get dizzy wearing plat-form soles!"

"Just asking." Huw shut the laptop again. "Whoever does it, that intrepid adventurer, they'll get lots of attention from the ladies."

"You think?" Yul brightened slightly.

"Absolutely," Huw said blandly. *Especially from her majesty,* but best not to swell Yul's head. "Hand me that test meter then get the carpet protector. . . ."

It was, he figured, a matter of getting the conditions right.

"There are a couple of possibilities," he'd told Helge ear-lier in the morning, when she'd appeared in the stables, un-announced and unexpected, just like any other country squire's wife making her daily rounds of the estate. "It could be the exclusion effect." It was well known that you couldn't world-walk if there was a solid object in the way in the destination world. "What if the ground pressure of feet or shoes doesn't set up a potential interpenetration, but wheels do? There's a smaller contact area, after all."

"Can women world-walk in stiletto heels?" Helge had thrown back at him, looking half-amused.

"What? Have you—"

"I've never tried. I'm not good in heels, and world-walking in them isn't something I'd do deliberately." She paused. "But it's one for your list, isn't it?"

"I'll do that," he agreed. "Would you like to sit in on the experiment today? You might spot something I wouldn't. . . ."

"I wish I could." A pained expression crept across her face. "They're keeping me busy, Huw, lots of protocol crap and meetings with tedious fools I can't afford not to be nice to. In fact, I'd better be going now—otherwise I'll be late for this morning's first appointment. I think I've got an hour free before dinner, maybe you could fill me in on the day's progress then?"

He'd asked Lady d'Ost about the stiletto thing over lunch: The answer turned out to be "yes—but if you're drunk you'll likely twist an ankle, so you take your shoes off first."

As for the chair and the matters in hand . . . "I'm seeing no conductivity at all," Huw muttered. "Good insulators." Bare feet were insulators, too, of course, albeit not that good, and damp leather shoes were piss-poor, but dry rubber-soled boots or bare feet didn't seem to make any difference to world-walking. "Okay, you want to try these?"

"Alright." Yul sighed and tugged the chair onto the middle of the plastic carpet-protector mat. "I'm getting tired, though, bro." He sat down and glanced at the back of his left wrist.

Huw looked at the floor. "Hey, you're off the target—"

He stopped. Yul, and the chair, had disappeared.

"*Shit.*" *Elena will fucking kill me,* he thought incoherently.

He slid a foot forward, then stopped. Opening the laptop again, he tapped out a quick note. Then he stood on the correct spot—not a foot to one side, where Yul had been—and looked at the knotwork he carried on a laminated badge, ready to world-walk.

The headache was sudden and harsh, a classic interpenetration blast. "Ow." *He's moving about.* Huw swore a bit more, then went and stood precisely where Yul had put the chair, and tried again.

The walls of the shack vanished, replaced by trees and sunlight and a warm summer breeze. Huw staggered, jostling Yul, who spun round with pistol drawn. "Joker's bane, bro! Don't *do* that!"

"Sorry." Huw bent double, the headache and visual distortions coinciding with a huge wave of nausea. He barely noticed the chair, lying to its side. The grass around its wheels was almost knee-length. *Should have surveyed more thoroughly,* he thought, then lost his attention to the desperate problem of hanging onto his lunch.

After a minute, he got things under control. "You going to be alright?" Yul asked anxiously. "Because one of us needs to go back."

"Yes." Huw stayed bent over. "Not just yet."

"I fell over when I came across. I think I bruised my ass."

"I'm not surprised." He retched again, then wiped his mouth. "Ow." Shuffling round, he knelt, facing the tussock Yul had stood in. "We missed an angle."

"We did?"

"Yeah." Huw pointed. "You had a foot on the ground."

"So?"

"So you brought the chair over. And you were grounded. When you sat in it, you were fiddling with one armrest." Huw shuffled towards it. "Right. You had your fingers curled under it. Were you touching it?"

"I think so." Yul frowned.

"Show me." Huw was nearly dancing with impatience.

Hulius raised the chair and sat in it slowly. He lowered one foot to touch the ground, then shuffled for comfort, leaned forward with the fingers of his left hand curled under the armrest.

"Okay, hold that position." Huw contorted himself to look under the armrest. "I see. Were you fidgeting with the post?"

"Post?"

"The metal thing—yeah, that. The fabric on the armrest cover is stapled to the underside of the arm. And that in turn is connected to the frame of the chair by a metal post. Huh. Of course if you try to world-walk home, holding the chair up by the underside of those arms, it'll go with you, as long as the wheels aren't fouling anything."

"You think that's all there is to it?" Yul looked startled.

"No, but it's a start. We go across, we take ourselves—obviously—and also the stuff we're carrying, the stuff we're physically connected to, but not the earth itself. The planet is a bit too big to carry. The question is, how far does the effect propagate? I've been thinking electrical or capacitive, but that's wrong. I should probably be thinking in terms of quantum state coherence. *And* the exclusion effect, as a separate spoiler, to make it more complicated. What *is* a coherent quantum state in a many-worlds Everett-Wheeler cosmology, anyway?"

Yul yawned elaborately. "Does it matter? Way I see it, the lords of the post won't be enthusiastic about folks realizing they're not needed for the corvée. It could be a power thing, bro, to bind us together by misleading us as to the true number of participants required to set up a splinter network. If it only takes two guys and a wheelbarrow to do the work of six . . . that might present a problem, yes? On top of which you're the only relative I know who's mad enough to try to disprove something that everyone *knows* is the way things work, just in case everyone else is wrong. Must be that fancy education of yours." He paused. "Not

that I believe a word of it, but I wouldn't mention it to anyone except her majesty if I were you, bro. They might not
understand. . . ."

The next day, Miriam received the visitor she'd been half
dreading and half waiting for. Rising that morning, she'd
donned Helge like a dress even as her maids were helping
her into more material garments. Then she'd started the day
by formally swearing Brilliana and Sir Alasdair to her service, before witnesses, followed by such of her guards as
Sir Alasdair recommended to her. Then she'd gone out
into the garden, just to get out of the way of the teeming
servants—Brill's self-kicking anthill was still settling down
and finding itself various niches in the house—and partly
to convince herself that she was free to do so. And that was
where her mother found her, sitting on a bench in an orna-
mental gazebo. And proceeded to lecture her about her
newfound status.

   "You're going to have to be a queen widow for a while,"
the Duchess Patricia voh Hjorth d'Wu ab Thorold explained
to her. Wearing a voluminous black silk dress that she had
somehow squeezed into the seat of an electric wheelchair,
which in turn must have taken two strapping couriers to
carry across in pieces, she posed an incongruous sight.
"Probably not forever, but you should plan on doing it for at
least the next nine months. It'll give you a lot of leverage,
but don't misunderstand—you won't be ruling the country.
There's no tradition of rule by women in this culture. We—
the junta—have agreed we're going to present ourselves in
public as a council of regents. They'll be the ones who do
the ruling—making policy decisions—but I've held out for
you to have a seat on the council. You'll have title and nobility in your own right, and the power of high justice, the
ability to arraign and try nobles. You'll sign laws agreed by
the assembly of lords, as a member of the council of re-

gents. Which in turn means the Clan council can't ignore you."

"Yes, Mom," Helge said obediently.

"Don't patronize me and I won't patronize you, kid. The quid pro quo is that there's a lot of ceremonial that goes with the job, a *lot* of face time. You're going to have to be Helge in public for ninety percent of that. Also, the Clan council will expect you to issue decrees and perform administrative chores to order. They say rabbit, you hop—at least at first. How much input you manage to acquire into *their* decisions is up to you, but my advice would be to do it very slowly and carefully. Don't risk overrunning your base, as you did last time. I'm going to be around to help. Our enemies won't be expecting that. And you'll have Brilliana. Olga and Riordan seem to *like* you, Sky Father only knows why, but that's another immense advantage because those two are holding two whole branches of Security together right now. I'd advise against trying to swear them to you—nothing's likely to scare the backwoods conservatives into doing something stupid like the fear that you're trying to take over Clan Security—but Riordan leans our way and Olga is one of us."

"Define *us*," Helge challenged.

"*Us* is you and me and everyone else who wants to drag the Clan kicking and screaming into the modern world." Her mother's cheek dimpled. "*Next* stupid question?"

"So you tell me you've fixed up this situation where I'll have a lot of leverage but I'm going to be a figurehead, and I have the power to basically try the nobility, even pass laws, but I can't go head-to-head with the council, and if I push the limits too hard the reactionaries might try to assassinate me, and by the way, I'm going to be on public display almost all the time. Is that the picture?" Helge stood up. "What else am I missing?"

"Your own power base," Patricia said crisply. She peered at Miriam. "Have you sworn Brilliana yet? Your head of security?"

"Yes—"

"That young whippersnapper Huw? Or his brother and *his* doxy?"

"Ma!—" She sat down again.

"You're not thinking ahead. You need them on your side, they're young and enthusiastic and willing—what's stopping you?"

"Um. An opportunity?"

"Exactly! So manufacture one. Invite them to a party. Better still, invite all the progressives. Be visible."

"But I don't know who—"

"Brilliana does. Rely on her!"

"You think I can do that?" Helge asked disbelievingly.

"No." Her mother grinned wickedly. "I *know* you can. You just need to make up your mind to do it." The grin faded. "But. On to other matters. It's been a long time since we talked about the birds and the bees, hasn't it?"

"Oh, Ma." Helge kicked her skirts out. "I'm not a teen-ager anymore."

"Of course not." Patricia nodded. "But you didn't grow up here. Can I offer some blunt advice?"

"You're going to, whether I want it or not, right?"

"Oh M- Helge. You kill me. Very well, it's this: You're a grown woman and you've got needs. And if you wait until the bun's finished baking and are reasonably discreet, no-body will raise an eyebrow. Once you've been publicly ac-knowledged as the queen-widow, you're . . . in effect you're married, to a dead, absentee husband. Marriage is about prop-erty, and status, and rank, and if you're fool enough you can throw it all away. So don't do that, okay? Take a lover, but be discreet, use contraception. And whatever you do, don't mess with the help, *especially* don't mess with your sworn vassals. Pick a man who's respectably married and owes you no obligation, and what you get up to harms no one. But unmarried men, or vassals? They're trouble."

Helge gaped, speechless. After a moment she managed to shut her mouth. "Mother!"

Patricia sighed. "Kid, the rules are *different* here. What have I been trying to beat into that thick skull of yours?"

"But, but—"

"You're confusing love and marriage. That old song, love and marriage, horse and carriage? It's rubbish." She snorted dismissively. "At least, that's not how any self-respecting aristocracy comports itself. You marry for power and heirs and you take your fun where you find it." For a moment she looked wistful: "That's one of the things I'm *really* going to miss about not living in the United States anymore. But just because a society runs on arranged marriages, it doesn't mean people don't fall in love. Just as long as they're discreet in public."

"Oh god." Helge made to run a hand through her hair, stopped at the last moment as she touched the jeweled pins that held it in place. "That is just so screwed up. . . ."

"I realize it must seem that way to you." The dowager grimaced. "The rules here are *very* different."

"Ick."

"It's not that bad, kid." Patricia's grimace relaxed into a smile. "You're a *widow*. You've graduated from the marriage market, *summa cum laude*."

"I don't need to hear this right now," said Helge. "I am *so* not interested in men right now—"

"But you *will* be, and you need to know this stuff now, before it happens. Unless you want to let being a victim define you for the rest of your life, you're going to look back on this one day and shrug and say, 'but I moved on.' "

Helge stared at her mother sharply. "What do you mean?"

Patricia looked her in the eye. "Your—my husband—was a real piece of work. But I didn't let that get between *us,* between you and me, kid."

Helge looked away. "I'm not—"

"You're *my* daughter. *Mine,* not his. That's all the revenge that's good for me."

After a moment, Helge looked back at her mother. Her eyes were dark, glistening with unshed tears. "I had no idea."

"I didn't want you to. I *really* didn't want to lay that on you." Patricia held out a hand. After a moment, her daughter took it. "But you wanted to know why I want to change the Clan."

"Oh, Mom." Helge rose, then knelt in front of the wheelchair. She laid her head on her mother's lap, hugging her. "I'm sorry."

"Hush. It's not your fault."

"But I thought you—"

"Yeah, I know what you thought. It's the usual Clan mother/daughter rivalry. But like I said, we're not going to play by their rules. Are you with me?"

"Yes," said Helge.

"Excellent." Her mother stroked the nape of her neck lightly. "You and me, kid. Together we'll make this thing work."

In the end, the coup came down to simple economics. The emergency government had neglected to pay their employees for three weeks; whereas Sir Adam's party had, if not put a chicken in every pot, at least put a loaf of bread and tripe in dripping on every table that was spread with yesterday's copy of *The Leveler* in lieu of a tablecloth. They didn't have money but they had plenty of guns, and so they'd sent the party militia to seize control of the dockside warehouses. Wherein they found plenty of bulk grain that had been stockpiled for export, and which they lost no time in distributing to the people. It was a short-term gambit, but it paid off: Nothing buys friends in a famine like a temporarily full belly.

The morning of the coup came three days after the Patriot Club withdrew from the emergency assembly. Patriot gangs had taken to the streets of New London, protesting the Levelers' presence in the debating chamber with paving stones and pry bars. They'd scoured the army barracks, recruiting the wrong kind of soldiers—angry, unpaid young

men, their bellies full of looted beer, looking for someone
to blame. "We can't allow this to continue," Sir Adam had
said, his voice tinny over the crackling electrograph conference call. "They'll cause chaos, and the people will blame
us for losing control of the situation. So they must be stopped.
Tomorrow morning, I want to see every man we've got
turned out and ready for action. The Freedom Riders will
patrol the streets around Parliament and the government
buildings on Grosvenor Street; those of you in charge of
departments will go to your offices with your guards and
secure them against intrusion."

"What about the New Party and the other opposition
groups?" asked one of the delegates on the line.

"I don't think we're going to waste our time worrying
about them," said Sir Adam. "They're either broadly for us
and our program, in which case we will listen to their input before we act—once the emergency is over—or they're
against us, in which case they are part of the problem. The
Freedom Riders will bar access to the Commons while we
debate and pass the Enabling Act; let them protest once
we've saved their necks from the noose. I'm more concerned about the Patriot mob. As soon as they work out
what's going on they'll attempt to storm the citadel, and I
want us to be ready for them."

Which was why, at four o'clock in the morning, instead
of being sound asleep in bed, Erasmus was sitting in the
passenger cab of a steamer, facing backwards, knee to knee
with two strapping militiamen and nose to nose with Supervisor Philips, as it screamed up the broad boulevard fronting the East River at the head of a column of loudly buzzing
motorcycle combinations. They were heading for the Propaganda Ministry offices in Bronckborough, to catch them
at the tail end of a quiet graveyard shift. For lack of any
other distraction, he scrutinized Philips closely; in his long
black coat and forage cap he resembled a hungry crow.

"Soon be over, eh, sir?"

Philips's eyes swiveled sideways, towards the serg- *No,*

underofficer, Erasmus reminded himself—*must keep the new ranks straight—underofficer* who had spoken. "One expects so, Wolfe, unless anyone tipped a wink to the traitors."

"Not me, sir!"

Erasmus suppressed his momentary amusement at the man's discomfort. Someone *might* have done so, despite the Party's control over the Post Office and the central electrograph exchanges, and if that was the case they might be heading straight into a field of beaten fire between heavy machine guns. *In which case we'll pay with our lives.* But Philips's reference to the Patriots as traitors—*that* was interesting. *So easily do our names twist and bite us,* Erasmus mused cynically.

The ministry offices stood at the crest of a north-south ridgeline at the intersection of two broad boulevards lined with plane trees; with clear fields of fire in all directions and no windows below the third floor, it was a characteristic example of the governmental architectural style that had arrived in the wake of the Black Fist Freedom Guard's assassination of King George Frederick's father. The steps fronting the building were guarded, but the railway sidings and loading docks at the back, through which huge rolls of newsprint arrived every evening to print the next day's edition of the *Parliamentary Gazette* were another matter. By the time Burgeson's car drew up beside a gap-doored loading bay, there wasn't a red shirt in sight: All the guards on duty wore the black pea coats and helmets of the Freedom Riders.

"Ah, good." Erasmus unwound to his full height as Philips hurried into the warehouse and conferred with his junior officers. "Underofficer Wolfe."

"Sir?"

"As soon as it's safe, I intend to go to the minister's office. I need guards."

"Yes, sir. Allow me to petition Supervisor Philips?"

Erasmus's cheek twitched. "Make it fast."

The second staff car arrived, disgorging a claque of radical journalists and sub-editors handpicked by Erasmus earlier in the week just as Philips strutted over. "Sir, the building appears to be in our hands for now. There was only a skeleton crew on duty, as the Patriots appear to have been shorting the staff to pay their thugs. I can't *guarantee* there isn't an assassin lurking in the minister's dining room until my men have searched the place top to bottom, but if you'll let me assign you a guard you can have the run of it." He grinned beakishly, as if claiming ownership of a particularly juicy piece of roadkill.

"Good." Erasmus nodded at his editorial staff. "Jonas, Eric, I want you to go to the speaking-room and see that the pulpit is ready for a morning broadcast. I'll be addressing the nation on Voice of England as soon as we have a program. Milo, get the emergency broadcast filler ready to run. Stephen, coordinate with Milo on developing a schedule of news announcements to run round the clock. I will be on hand to read proclamations and announce emergency decrees as we receive them from Freedom House through the day. Jack, the print floor is yours. Let's go to work!"

They stormed through the Ministry building like children in a sweet shop, capering around the huge printing presses and the broadcasting pulpits of the king's own mouthpiece; marveling at the stentorian voice of the state that fate, audacity, and Sir Adam's brash plan had put at their disposal. "'T's going ter be glorious, sorr," Stephen confided in Erasmus as they walked the editor's gallery overlooking the presses that had until recently spun the *Gazette*, official mouthpiece of John Frederick's despotic agenda. His eyes gleamed. "All them years hiding type-trays in us basement, an' it come to this!"

"Enjoy it while you can, Steve." Burgeson grinned like a skull. "Seize the front page!" They came to the door leading to the third floor landing, and the stairs up to the soundproofed broadcasting pulpits. "You'll have to excuse me:

I've got a speech to record for the nine o'clock news, and then I'll be in the Minister's office, working up our schedule for the next week."

"A speech? What's in it?"

"Just some announcements Sir Adam charged me with making," Erasmus said blandly. Then he relaxed slightly: No point in *not* confiding in his new subordinate, after all! "We're taking the People's Palace"—the Houses of Parliament, renamed by raucous consensus earlier in the week— "this morning, to pass an Enabling Act. It'll give the Executive Council the power to rule by decree during the current emergency, and we'll use it to round up the Patriots as soon as they raise their heads and start belling for our blood. The sooner we can get the opposition to shut up for a while, the faster we'll be able to set up a rationing system and get food to the people again. And the faster we do that, the sooner we'll have their undivided support.

"By winter, we'll be building the new Jerusalem! And you, my friend, are going to tell the world that's what we're going to do."

Pomp, circumstance, and matters of state seemed inseparable; and the more tenuous the state, the more pomp and circumstance seemed to surround it, Miriam reflected. "I hope this is going to work," she murmured.

"Milady, it looks perfect!" Gerta, her recently acquired lady of the wardrobe, chirped, tugging at the laces of her left sleeve. "You are the, the model of a queen!" Her English was heavily accented and somewhat hesitant, but at least she had some; Brill had filtered the candidates ruthlessly to ensure that Miriam wasn't left floundering with her rudimentary hochsprache.

I don't feel like one, Miriam thought, but held her counsel. *I feel more like a wedding cake decoration gone wrong. And this outfit weighs more than a suit of armor.* She was still ambivalent about the whole mad scheme; only the certain knowledge of what could happen if this masquerade failed was holding her on course—on course for weeks of state audiences and banquets and balls, and seven months of sore feet, morning nausea, aching back, and medical worries. "Continue," she said tonelessly, as Gerta continued to wind a seemingly endless silver chain around her collar, while three other maids—more junior by far—fussed around her.

She'd lain awake for most of the previous night, listening to the wind drumming across the roof above her, and the calls of the sentries as they exchanged watch, and she'd worried at the plan like a dog with a mangy leg. If this was the right thing to do, if this was the right thing for *her,* if, if . . . if she was going to act a part in a perilous play, if she was going to have another baby—at her age—not with a man she loved, but by donor insemination, as a bargaining chip in a deadly political game, to lay claim to a toxic throne. *Poor little bastard,* she thought—and he would, indeed, be a bastard except for the elaborate lies of a dozen pre-briefed and pre-blackmailed witnesses who would swear blind to a secret wedding ceremony—doomed to be a figurehead for the throne. *Damn, and I thought* I *had problems. . . .*

Miriam had no illusions about the fate awaiting anyone who aspired to sit on the throne of the Gruinmarkt. It would be an unstable and perilous perch, even without the imminent threat of invasion or attack by the US government. *If I wanted the best for him I'd run away, very fast, very far,* she'd decided. But the best for him would be the worst for everyone else: The Gruinmarkt would fall apart very fast if a strong settlement wasn't reestablished. *It would trigger a civil war of succession,* she realized. And her life, and her mother's, and—*nearly everyone I care for*—would be in danger. *I can't do that,* she thought hopelessly, punching the overstuffed bolster as she rolled over in the night. *Where did I get this sense of loyalty from? What do* I *owe* them, *after what they did to me?*

"My lady?" She blinked back to the present to see Gerta staring at her. "And now, your face?"

The women of the Clan, and their relatives in the outer families—recessive carriers of the gene that activated the world-walking ability—had discovered cosmetics, but not modernism or minimalism. Miriam, who'd never gone in for much more than lip gloss and eyeliner, forced herself to stand still while Gerta and a small army of assistants did their best to turn her into a porcelain doll, using so many layers of powder that she was afraid to smile lest her face crack and fall off. *At least they're using imported cosmetics rather than white lead and belladonna,* she consoled herself.

A seeming eternity of primping preparations passed before the door crashed open, startling her considerably. Miriam, unable to simply turn her head, maneuvered to look: "Yes? Oh—"

"My lady. Are you ready?" It was Brilliana, dressed to the nines and escorted by two young lords with swords and MP5Ks at their waists, and three more overdressed girls (one to hold the train of her gown, the others evidently for decoration).

Miriam sighed. "Gerta. Am I ready?"

Gerta squawked and dropped a curtsey before Brill. "My lady! Another half hour, please? Her grace is *nearly*—"

Brill looked Miriam up and down with professional speed. "No. Stick a crown on her and she's done," she announced, with something like satisfaction. "How do you feel, Helge?"

"I feel"—Miriam dropped into halting hochsprache—"I am, am ready. I am like a hot, blanket? No, sheet, um, no, dress—"

Brill smiled and nodded—somehow she'd evaded the worst excesses of the cosmetological battalions—and produced a small crystal vial with a silver stopper from a fold in her sleeve, which she offered. "You'll need this," she suggested.

Miriam took it and held it before her face, where the flickering lamps in the chandelier could illuminate it. "Um. What is it?"

"Crystal meth. In case you doze off." Brill winked.

"But I'm pregnant!" Miriam scolded indignantly.

"Hist. One or two won't hurt you, you know? I asked a *good* doctor." (Not, by her emphasis, Dr. ven Hjalmar, who Miriam had publicly speculated about disemboweling—especially if, as Gunnar had implied, he was still alive.) "The damage if this act of theater should go awry is far greater than the risk of a miscarriage."

"I thought you had an iron rule, don't dabble in the cargo. . . ."

"This isn't dabbling, it is your doctor's prescription, Helge. You are going to have to sit on that chair looking alert for more than four hours without caffeine or a toilet break, and I am warning you, it is as hard as a board. How else are you going to manage it?"

Miriam shook one of the tablets into the palm of her hand and swallowed. "Uck. That was vile."

"Come now, your grace! Klaus"—Brill half-turned, and snapped her fingers—"Menger, attend! You will lead. Jeanne and you, you will follow me. Sabine, you take my train. We will practice our order on the way to the carriage. Her grace will walk ten paces behind you, and you—yes, Gerta—arrange her attendants. When we arrive at the palace, once we enter the hall, you will pass me and proceed to the throne, Helge, and be seated when the Green Staff is struck for the third time and Baron Reinstahl declares the session open. I'll lead you in, you just concentrate on looking as if I'm not there and not tripping on your hem. Then we will play it by ear. . . ."

They walked along the passageway from the royal receiving room at a slow march. Brill paced ahead of her, wearing an ornate gown dripping with expensive jewelry. The walls were still pocked with the scars of musket balls. The knights Brilliana had brought to her dressing room paced to either side, and behind them came another squad of soldiers—outer family relatives, heavily armed and tense. It was all, Miriam thought, a masque, the principal actors wearing costumes that emphasized their power and wealth. Even the palace was a stage set—after the explosion at the Hjalmar Palace, none of the high Clan nobles would dare spend even a minute longer than absolutely necessary there. But you had to hold a coronation where people could *see* it. The whole thing, right down to the ending, was as scripted as a Broadway musical. Miriam concentrated on keeping her face fixed in what she hoped was a benevolent half-smile: In truth, her jaw ached and everything shone with a knife-edged crystal clarity that verged on hallucination.

Before them, a guard detail came to attention. A trumpet blatted, three rising notes; then with a grating squeal, the door to the great hall swung open. *The hinges,* Miriam thought distantly, *they need to oil the hinges.* (The thought gnawed at her despite its irrelevance—glued to the surface of her mind by the meth.)

"Her grace the Princess Royal Helge Thorold-Hjorth, widow of Creon ven Alexis du"—the majordomo's recitation of her name and rank rolled on and on, taxing Miriam's basic hochsprache with its allusions and genealogical connections, asserting an outrageous connection between her and the all-but-expired royal family. She swayed slightly, trying to maintain a dignified and expressionless poise, but was unable to stop her eyes flickering from side to side to take in the assembled audience.

It looked like half the surviving fathers of the Clan had come, bringing their sons and wives with them—and their bodyguards, for the rows of benches that rose beneath the windows (formerly full of stained glass; now open to the outside air, the glaziers not yet rounded up to repair them) were backed by a row of guards. Here and there she could pick out a familiar face amidst the sea of strangers, and they were all staring at her, as if they expected her to sprout a second head or start speaking in tongues at any moment. Her stomach clenched: Bile flooded into the back of her mouth. For an instant Miriam trembled on the edge of panic, close to bolting.

Brill began to move forward again. She followed, instinctively putting one foot in front of the other.

"The throne, milady," the girl behind her hissed, voice pitched for her ear only. "Step to your left, if you please."

There was another cantonment of benches, dead ahead, walled in with wooden screens—a ladies' screen, Miriam recognized—and within it, a different gaggle of nobles, their wrists weighted with iron fetters. And there was a raised platform, and a chair with a canopy over it, and other, confusing impressions—

Somehow she found herself on the raised chair, with one of her maids behind each shoulder and the lords Menger and Klaus standing before her. A priest she half recognized (he'd been wearing a pinstriped suit at the last Clan council meeting) was advancing on her, swathed in robes. A subordinate followed him, holding a dazzling lump of metal that might have been a crown in the fevered imaginings of a Gaudí; behind him came another six chanting subordinates and a white calf on a rope which looked at her with confused, long-lashed eyes.

The chanting stopped and the audience rose to their feet. The calf moaned as two of the acolytes shoved it in front of the dais and a third thrust a golden bowl under its throat. There was a moment of reverential silence as the bishop turned and pulled his gilt sickle through the beast's throat; then the bubbling blood overflowed the basin and splashed across the flagstones to a breaking roar of approval punctuated by stamping feet.

The bishop raised his sickle, then as the assembled nobles quieted their chant, he began to shout a prayer, his voice hoarse and cracked with hope. *What's he saying*—Miriam burped again, swallowing acid indigestion—*something about sanctification*—she was unprepared when he turned to her and, after dipping a hand into the bowl, he stepped towards her and daubed a sticky finger on her forehead. Then the second priest knelt beside him, and the bishop raised the crown above her head.

"It's the Summer Crown," he told her in English. "Try not to break it, we want it back after the ceremony."

When he lowered his arms his sleeves dangled in front of her. The hot smell of fresh blood filled her nostrils as the crowd in the bleachers roared their—approval? Amusement? Miriam closed her eyes. *I'm not here. I'm not here. You can't make me* be *here.* She wished the earth would open and swallow her; the expectations bearing down on her filled her with a hollow terror. *Mom, I am* so *going to kill you.*

Then the bishop—*it's Julius, isn't it?* she recalled, dizzily—receded. She opened her eyes.

"Milady!" hissed the lady-in-waiting at her left shoulder. "It's time to say your words."

Words? Miriam blinked fuzzily, the oppressive weight of the metal headgear threatening to unbalance her neck. *I'm meant to say something, right?* Brill had gone over it with her: She'd practiced with Gerta, she'd practiced with a mirror, she'd practiced until she was sure she'd be able to remember them. . . .

"I, the Queen-Widow Helge, by virtue of the power vested in me by Sky Father, do declare this royal court open. . . ." her memory began.

Oh, that, Miriam remembered. She opened her mouth and heard someone begin to recite formal phrases in an alien language. Her voice was steady and authoritative: She sounded like a powerful and dignified ruler. *I wonder if they'll introduce me to her after the performance?*

BEGIN TRANSCRIPT
(Cockpit voice recorder):

(Rotor noise in background.)

"Climbing two five to flight level three zero, ground speed 150. GPS check."

"GPS check, uh, okay."

"TCAS clear. Ready to engage INS."

"INS ready, fifty-mile orbit at three zero."

"Okay. How's the datalink to that—that—"

"FLIR/DIMT is mapping fine."

"Right. INS engaged. Racetrack. You boys ready back there?"

"ARMBAND is ready."

"Ready."

"Coming up on way point yankee one in fifty seconds, boys. On my mark, activate translation black box."

"Arming translation circuit . . . okay, she's ready on your command."

"Mark."

"We have translation."

"Radar altimeter check, please. What's the state of ARMBAND?"

"Sir, we've got two translations left, three hours to bingo time—"

"Tower, mike-mike-papa-four, do you read."

"Two translations, three hours, check. You gentlemen will doubtless be pleased to know that as we've only got fuel for 140 minutes we'll be going home well before then."

"Inlet temperature four. External temperature ten and dropping, was fifteen. Cloud cover was six, now four. Holy shit, *the ground*—it's completely different—"

"FLIR/DIMT is mapping fine. Uh, INS shows six meter z-axis anomaly. INS red light. INS red light. Looks like he took us with him okay."

"Tower, mike-mike-papa-four, do you read."

"INS reset. INS breaker reset. Damn, we're back to dead reckoning. Speed check."

"Ground speed 146. Altitude three zero nine zero by radar altimeter. Lots of trees down there, whole lotta trees."

"Okay, let's do an INS restart."

"Captain, confirmed, tower does not respond."

"FLIR/DIMT lock on north ridge corresponds to INS

map waypoint 195604. Restarting. Restarted. Returning to orbit."

"Tower on crest of ridge via FLIR. Got battlements!"

"Fuel, nine thousand. Throttle back on two, eighty percent. Okay, you've got an hour from my mark."

"Got any candidates on IDAS?"

"Not a whisper. It's dead down there. Not even cell phone traffic. Why am I getting this itchy feeling between my shoulder blades?"

"Time check: three hours twenty-nine minutes to dawn. Altitude four one hundred, ground speed 145, visibility zero, six on FLIR. Stop worrying about MANPADs, number two."

"Roger. Waypoint yankee two coming up, turning on zero two zero."

"I'm still getting nothing, sir. Trying FM."

"Use your judgment."

"Fuel eighty six hundred. Throttle on eighty, inlet temperature three."

"Quiet as the grave. Hey, some traffic on *shortwave*. Twenty megahertz band, low power. Voice traffic . . . not English."

"Waypoint yankee three coming up, turning on zero nine zero. Climb to flight level five zero."

"Okay, that's enough. We're in class E airspace on the other side, so let's get out of here. ARMBAND?"

"Ready to roll whenever you call, captain."

"Okay, we're going home. Prepare to translate on my mark—"

END TRANSCRIPT

(Cockpit voice recorder)

10

⽼eceptive practices

❦

A week had passed since the bizarre coronation ritual, and it had been a busy period. Miriam found herself at the center of a tornado of activity, with every hour accounted for. There were banquets with lord this and baron that, introductions until her cheeks ached from smiling and her right hand was red from scrubbing: Their kisses left her feeling unclean, compromised. The dressmakers had moved in, altering garments borrowed from some remnants of the royal wardrobe and fitting her for gowns and dresses suitable for a dowager queen-widow and a mother-to-be. Brill had found time, for a couple of hours every day, to bring a bottle of wine and sit with her while she explained the finer points of political and personal alliances; and Gerta engaged her in conversational hochsprache, nervous and halting at first, to polish her speech. (Which, with total immersion in a sea of servants, few of whom spoke English, was beginning to improve.)

Being Helge was becoming easier, she found. Practice

had diminished the role to a set of manners and a half-understood language that she could summon up at need, rather than a claustrophobia-inducing caul. Perhaps she was getting used to it, or perhaps her mother's private crusade and promise of mutual support had given her the impulse she needed to make it work. Whatever the cause, the outcome was that whenever she paused to think about her position Miriam was startled by how smoothly her new life had locked in around her, and with how little friction. Perhaps all she'd needed all along was a key to the gilded cage, and the reassurance that people she could trust were minding the door.

It had not been Miriam's idea to put on the gilded robes of state today, to sit on an unpadded chair in a drafty hall and read aloud a variety of prearranged—bloodcurdling and inevitably fatal—sentences on assorted members of the nobility who had been unlucky enough to back the wrong horse. But it had shown up on her timetable for the week—and Brill, Riordan, and her mother had visited *en masse* to assure her that it was necessary. They'd even hauled in Julius, to provide a façade of Clannish unity. "You need to sit in on the court and pronounce judgment, without us whispering in your ear all the time," Brill explained, "otherwise people will say you're a figurehead."

"But I *am* a figurehead!" Miriam protested. "Aren't I? I get the message, this is the council's doing. It's just, I don't approve of the death penalty. And this, executing people just because they did what Egon told them to, out of fear—"

"If they think you're a figurehead, they won't fear you," Iris explained, with visibly fraying patience. "And that'll breed trouble. People hereabouts aren't used to enlightened government. You need to stick some heads on spikes, Helge, to make the others keep a low profile. If you won't do it yourself, the council will have to do it for you. And everybody will whisper that it's because you're a weak woman who is just a figurehead."

"There are a number of earls and barons who we definitely cannot trust," Riordan added. "Not to mention a duke or two. They're mortal enemies—they didn't act solely out of fear of Egon's displeasure—and we can't have a duke sitting in judgment over another duke. If you refuse to read their execution order we'll just have to poison them. It gets messy."

"But if I start out by organizing a massacre, isn't that going to raise the stakes later? I thought we were agreed that reinforcing the rule of law was essential. . . ."

"It's not a massacre if they get a fair trial first. So give them a fair trial and fill a gibbet or two with the worst cases, to make an example," Iris suggested. "Then offer clemency to the rest, on onerous terms. It worked for dad."

"Really?" Miriam gave her mother a very old-fashioned look. "Tell me more. . . ."

Which had been the start of a slippery-slope argument. Miriam had fought a rearguard action, but Helge had ultimately conceded the necessity of applying these medieval standards of justice under the circumstances. Which was why she was sitting stiff as a board on a solid wooden throne, listening to advocates argue over a variety of unfortunate nobles, and trying not to fall asleep.

For a man with every reason to believe his fate was to be subjected to *peine fort et dure,* the Duke of Niejwein was in remarkably high spirits. Or perhaps the reddening of his cheeks and the twinkle in his eye were signs of agitation and contempt. The resemblance he bore to the Iraqi dictator Ali Hassan, who'd been on all the news channels a few weeks ago when the Marines finally got their hands on him, was striking. Whatever the case, when he raised his fettered hands and spat something fast at Miriam she had no problem interpreting his intent.

"He says he thanks you for your hospitality but it is most unnecessary," murmured Gerta.

"Tell him he's welcome, all the same." Miriam waited while her assistant translated. "And I view his position with sympathy."

"Milady!" Gerta sounded confused. "Are you sure?"

"Yes." Miriam glared at her. *I am your queen, damn it. Even if I'm fronting for a committee.* "Do it."

"Yes, milady." Gerta addressed the duke; he seemed confused.

"Have another sweet," Miriam offered the Duke of Niejwein by way of her translator.

It was, Olga had explained, the polite way to do business with noble prisoners: Offer them candied peel and a silk rope to sweeten the walk to the scaffold where, if his crimes were deemed minor, he could expect the relative mercy of a swift hanging. But Niejwein, for some reason, seemed not to have much of an appetite today. And after having sentenced two earls to death earlier in this session—in both cases they had massacred some of her distant relatives with more enthusiasm than was called for, and Riordan had been most insistent on the urgent need to hang them—she could see why. The earls and their retainers were hired thugs; but Niejwein, as head bean counter, had expedited Egon's reign of terror in a far deadlier way.

"We wanted to speak with you in private," Miriam added, trying to ignore the small crowd of eavesdroppers. "To discuss your future."

Niejwein's short bark of laughter turned heads; more than one guard's hand hovered close by a weapon. "I have no future," Gerta translated.

"Not necessarily. You have no future without the grace and pardon of the crown, but you should not jump to conclusions about your ultimate fate."

For the first time the Duke of Niejwein looked frightened. And for the first time Miriam, watching him, began to get an edgy feeling that she understood him.

Niejwein was outwardly average: middle-aged, of middling stature, heavy-faced, and tired-looking. He sat on a stone bench before her, arms and legs clanking with wrought iron whenever he moved, wearing a nobleman's household robes, somewhat the worse for wear, ingrained with the grime of whatever cellar they'd warehoused him in for the run-up to her coronation. He'd been there a week ago, Miriam remembered, staring at her with hollowed eyes, among the other prisoners in the guarded block on the floor of the great hall.

He'd never been much of a warrior or a scholar, according to Brill. She'd asked for—and, for a miracle, been given—Angbard's files on the man, and for another miracle they'd been written in English. (Angbard, it seemed, insisted on Clan secrets being written in English when they were to be kept in the Gruinmarkt, and in hochsprache if they were to be used in the United States.)

Oskar Niejwein was a second son, elevated into his deceased brother's shoes after a boar hunt gone wrong and a lingering death from sepsis. He'd distinguished himself by maintaining and extending the royal estates and by tax farming with a level of enthusiasm and ruthlessness not spoken of in recent memory. It was no wonder that Egon hadn't sent him into the field as a commander, and no surprise that Riordan's men had seized him with such ease—Niejwein had all the military acumen of a turkey. But that didn't make him useless to an ambitious monarch planning a purge: quite the opposite. As the old saying had it, knights studied tactics, barons studied strategy, and dukes studied logistics. Oskar was an Olympic-grade tax farmer. Which meant . . .

"Your majesty plays with me," said Niejwein. "Have you no decency?"

Miriam kept her face frozen as a ripple of shock spread through her audience. That was *not* how a vassal should address a monarch, after all. *How do I deal with this without looking weak? . . .*

(Iris—showing a coldly cynical streak Miriam had seldom seen any sign of back home—had laid it out for her in the privy council meeting the morning after the coronation performance: "There are certain rules you've got to obey in public. You can't afford to look like a patsy, dear. If they

give you backchat it either means they're scared to death or
they think you're weak. The former is acceptable, but if
it's the latter, you must be ruthless. The rot spreads rapidly
and the longer you leave it the harder it becomes to fix the
damage. Put it another way: Better to flog them on the spot
for insubordination than let things slide until you have to
have them broken on the wheel for rebellion.")

"We are not playing games," Miriam said evenly. "We are
simply trying to decide whether you can be of use to us. But
if you insist on seeing malice in place of mercy, you *will* seal
your own fate." She waited while Gerta translated. The color
drained slowly from Niejwein's cheeks as she continued:
"We understand that circumstances placed your neck under
our brother-in-law's boot. We are prepared to make allowances—to a degree. A prudent woodsman does not chop
down all the trees in his forest when autumn comes; he har-
vests the old and rotten, and keeps the healthy for another
year. Only the rotten need fear the axe in this demesne."

She'd stiffened up again, sitting on this damnable hard-
as-a-board throne. Shifting her thighs, she leaned forward
as Gerta worked through to the end of the speech. "Are you
a rotten bough?" she asked, raising an eyebrow. "Or would
you like a chance to demonstrate how sound you are?"

Abruptly, Niejwein was on his knees; she didn't need the
blow-by-blow translation to grasp the gist of his entreaties.
Her hochsprache was still stilted and poor, but she got the
sense that he'd only gone along with Egon's mad usurpation
out of terror while unaware of her majesty's survival, and
he was of course loyal to the crown and he'd be her most
stalwart vassal forever and a day if, if only, if—

*Damn, he could give lessons in crow-eating to the CEO
of a Fortune 100 corporation facing a record loss-making
quarter.* Miriam managed a faint, slightly perplexed smile
as Gerta tried to keep up with the storm of entreaties. Right
now, with a royal pardon dangling before his eyes, Niejwein
would promise her just about anything to keep his head
atop his shoulders and his neck unstretched. Which meant

that she'd have to take anything he said with a pinch of salt big enough to pickle a sperm whale. Her eyes narrowed as she considered her options. *I can't kill him* now, *even if he deserves it*—not without looking capricious. But in his undignified hurry to ingratiate himself, the duke was impressing her with his unreliability. *Why would he misjudge me like that?* she wondered. Chalk it up to another of the gaps between Gruinmarkt and American mores: The political over here was *very* personal indeed, as everybody kept reminding her.

"Enough." She raised her right hand and he stopped so suddenly he nearly swallowed his tongue. Miriam took a deep breath. "Rise, your grace. We will not hang a man for a single honest mistake." Two *mistakes in a row and I might change my mind. . . .* "We would, however, be delighted if you would stay here as our honored guest, while we restore the kingdom to order. Perhaps your wife and eldest son would care to join us as well. We shall take full responsibility for their safety." In hochsprache, there were no separate words to distinguish *safety* from *security*. "And we would be pleased if you would attend us in session with the council of regents to decide in what manner you can assist us in securing the realm."

There. She waited for Gerta to translate, watching the succession of expressions flit across Oskar ven Niejwein's face, starting with stark relief, then fading into apprehension as he realized just how onerous his rehabilitation was to be. *You, your wife, and your eldest son are to be hostages under the Clan's control. You will devote precisely as much time and money to cleaning up this mess as the council demands. And if you don't play along, we've got you where we want you.*

Well, it beat the usual punishments for high treason, which included the aforementioned *peine fort et dure,* or just a straightforward impalement-and-burning-at-the-stake, the traditional cutting of the blood eagle being considered too barbaric for this effete and gentle age.

Miriam suppressed a slight shudder as Niejwein bowed deeply, then bowed again, stuttering a mixture of gracious thanks and praise for her mercy, insight, wisdom, deportment, wit, and general brilliance. She merely nodded. "Take him away," she said, for the benefit of his jailers, "to suitable accommodation for a high noble whose loyalty to the crown is beyond question." Which was to say, a cell with a view.

It took three more weeks of ceremonial duties, horse-trading with noble descendants of real (but successful) horse thieves, sitting in court sessions and trying to show no sign of discomfort when her judges pronounced bloodcurdling sentences upon the recalcitrant few—not to mention diplomacy, shouting, and some pigheaded sulking—but at last they agreed to book her into a suite in a boutique hotel near Quincy, with an ob-gyn appointment for the following day. The ob-gyn exam was the excuse; the real purpose was to give her a weekend off, lest she explode.

"I think you can take two, or at most three days off before too many questions asked," Riordan had said. "Then it will be getting close to Hedge-Wife's Night and you'll be expected to officiate—"

"Four," said Brill, just as Iris said: "Two." They stopped and glared at each other warily, like cats sizing each other up for a fight.

"People." Miriam rubbed her forehead tiredly. "I've had too much of this." She waved a tired hand, taking in the high ceiling, the ornate tapestries and rugs that did little to soften the wood and plaster of the electricity and aircon-free room, the discreet chamber pots. They were in private, having exiled the servants for the duration of the brief discussion; they'd be back soon enough, like the rats in the walls that kept her awake in the dead of night with their scuttling and fighting. "I need to decompress, just for a couple of days—"

"We can bring doctors to you, there is no need for you to go to them. If we are secure by winter, then you can retreat to the Winter Palace and spend most of your time in Manhattan," Iris pointed out.

"That's months away. And anyway, you can hold down some of my appointments right now if I'm not here," Miriam told her. "Her grace, the dowager Duchess Patricia Thorold ven Hjorth, mother of the queen-widow, who is indisposed due to her confinement. Isn't that the formula?"

Iris grunted, displeased. "Something like that," she conceded.

"Admit it, *you* want some time off, too, don't you?"

Her mother shook her head. "Coming back to this life hasn't been easy. If I give up now . . ."

After much haggling they had arranged that an anonymous carriage would leave town in the morning with Miriam inside, disguised as an anonymous lady-in-waiting of noble rank. An hour later, by way of the Clan's highly organized courier service, Miriam—wearing jeans and a cotton blouse, feeling almost naked after weeks in court gowns—checked into a four-star hotel near Quincy, with no servants and no visible guards, and and no pomp, ceremony, or stench of open sewers outside the windows.

(That the Clan owned the hotel via a cut-out investment company, and that it was carefully monitored for signs of external surveillance, and discreetly guarded by much better than normal security, was another matter entirely. There was a tacit agreement: As long as Miriam agreed not to test the bars on her cage, everyone could pretend they didn't exist.)

It had come as a welcome, but monumental, relief to have *electricity* and *air conditioning* and *toilets* and *jacuzzis* and *daytime television* and other miracles that had not yet reached the Gruinmarkt. Or even New Britain. It was enough to leave her head spinning and half-dizzy with sudden culture shock: Aside from her brief stay in the safe house out west, she'd been living in strange, backward cultures for months on end. *I ought to start with a shower,* she thought, almost salivating with the pornographic luxury of it. *And turn the air con up to max. And I'll wash my hair And then* . . . the phone rang.

"What the—" She looked round, then made a dive for the room phone. "Yes?" she demanded.

"Ms. Beckworth?" (That was the name.) "This is the front desk, you have a visitor. . . ."

Oh hell. Miriam glanced at her watch. *Twenty minutes.* "Can I talk to them, please?"

"Certainly, ma'am. . . ."

"Miriam?"

"Olga?" Miriam sat down hard on the edge of the bed.

"Hi! It's me! I heard you were in town and figured I'd drop in. Mind if I come up?" There was a bright, slightly edgy tone to her voice that set the skin on Miriam's nape crawling.

"Sure, pass me back to reception and I'll tell them. Okay—"

A couple of seconds later the handset was back on its cradle. Miriam stared at it, hard. "Shit," she muttered. Her vision blurred; *it's one thing after another.* Her carefully fostered illusion of stolen time wavered: *What's happened now?*

There was a knock on the door. Miriam, far less trustful than she'd been even a couple of months ago, checked the spy hole: A familiar face winked at her.

"Come in."

"Thank you." Olga smiled reflexively. Then, as the door closed, her smile slipped. "Helge, I am so terribly sorry to impose on you, but we need to talk. Urgently."

"Oh hell." Miriam sat down again, her own face freezing in a smile that mirrored Olga's in its insincerity. "I guessed." *Something's come up in the past three hours, damn it, and they want my input, even though I'm just a front for the policy committee.* Plaintively: "Couldn't it wait?"

"I don't think so." Olga took a deep breath. "It's about your mother."

"Shit. She's not ill, is—"

"No, it's not that." Olga paused.

"Yes?" Miriam's vision blurred as her heartbeat settled back to normal. Iris's multiple sclerosis hadn't been far from her mind for years, now; she'd thought she'd gotten used to the knowledge that sooner or later she'd have a really bad relapse, but all it took was Olga's ambiguous statement to drag her to the edge of an anxiety attack. "It's not her health?"

"No." Olga glanced around the room, her expression wooden. "I think—there is no easy way to say this."

"Yes?" Miriam felt her face muscles tense unpleasantly.

"Your uncle. When he was ill. He told me to collect certain documents and, and bring them to you."

"Documents?" Miriam sat up.

"About the"—Olga licked her lips—"the fertility clinic." She stared at Miriam, her expression clear but unreadable. "You know about it."

"Know—" Olga shook her head. "Only a bit. His grace told me something, after the, the war broke out. It has been closed down, Helge, the program ended and the records destroyed."

"My uncle," Miriam said very slowly, "would *never* destroy that program."

"Well." Olga wet her lips again. "Someone did."

"Eh." Miriam shook her head. "I don't get it."

"His grace shut down the program, that's true enough. He had the records copied, though—taken out of the clinic, physically removed to a medic's practice office pending transfer to Niejwein. He wanted to keep track of the names, addresses, and details of the children enrolled in the program, but while there was fighting in Niejwein it was too risky to move the records there. And it was too risky to leave everything in the clinic. So."

"You'd better tell me what happened," Miriam said deliberately.

"I went to see Dr. Darling." Olga shivered for a moment,

then walked across the room and sat down in the solitary armchair. "He's dead. It was a professional hit, almost a month ago. And his office was cleaned out, Helge. The records are missing."

"But he—" Miriam stared. "Where does Mom come into this?"

"I had orders to get those records to *you*." Olga looked unhappy. "And your mother took them."

Miriam rolled her eyes. "She was in the same town at the same time, right?"

"Yes." The set of Olga's shoulders relaxed. "On its own that would not be conclusive, but—"

"You're telling me my mother, who spends half her time in a wheelchair these days, assassinated a doctor, stole several thousand sets of medical records, and made a clean getaway? And why? To stop me from getting my hands on the *breeding program's records?*" Her emphasis on the last three words made Olga wince.

"I am uncertain as to her motive. But—your mother knew of the program, no? And you must needs be aware of her views on the balance of powers within our circle of families, yes?"

Miriam sighed. "*Of course* I know what she thinks of—of all that stuff. But that breeding program was just plain odious. I know why they did it, I mean—we're dangerously short on world-walkers, and if we can use a fertility clinic as a cover to spread the recessive trait around, then pay some of the first generation women to act as donors—but I tend to agree with Mom that it's destabilizing as hell. And ethically more than questionable, too. But why would she destroy the records or kill Darling? Was there something else we don't know about?"

"I don't know." Olga looked troubled.

"Then why don't you ask her?" Miriam crossed her arms.

"Because." Olga bit her lip. "She killed Dr. Darling," she said, conversationally. "She had her woman Mhara do it, in direct contravention of Security protocols. The other thing,

Helge, that you did not let me get to, is that there was another witness present."

"Really?" Miriam's shoulders tensed.

"Dr. ven Hjalmar," said Olga.

"I want him dead." Miriam's voice was flat.

Olga shook her head. "We need to find out why she killed Dr. Darling first. Don't we?"

"But—" Miriam changed tack. "Brill thought ven Hjalmar was dead," she said. "In fact, she told me so."

"Hmm. There was some confusion after the palace— Perhaps she was not in the loop?" Olga leaned back and met Miriam's eyes. "I am telling you this because Mhara's first loyalty is to Security; she was most upset when she learned her actions were unauthorized. What is your mother doing, Helge? How many games is she playing?"

"I . . . don't . . ." Miriam fell silent. "Dr. ven Hjalmar," she said faintly. "Is she cooperating with him?"

Olga stared at her for a long time.

Summer in the suburbs. The smell of honeysuckle and the creaking of cicadas hung heavy in the backyard of the small house on a residential street in Ann Arbor; there was little traffic outside, the neighbors either already in bed or away from their homes, dining out or working late. But inside the house, behind lowered blinds, the lights were on and the occupants were working. Not that a casual interloper would have recognized their activities as such. . . .

Huw sat in front of a laptop in the day room at the back of the house, staring at the running Mathematica workbook through goggles as it stepped through variations on a set. Wearing an oxygen mask, with a blood pressure cuff on his upper arm and a Glock on his belt, he squinted intently as the program flashed up a series of topological deformations of a familiar knot.

On his left wrist, he wore an electronic engineer's grounding strap, which he had attached to a grounding spike in the backyard by a length of wire—and tested carefully. Two camcorders on tripods monitored his expression and the screen of the laptop. The medical telemetry gear was on order, but hadn't arrived yet; it would have to wait for the next run. There were other watchers, too, equipped as best as he'd been able to manage in the time available.

"Ouch." Huw tapped the space bar on the keyboard, pausing the run. "Sequence number 144. I definitely felt something there." He glanced round. "Elena? You awake back there?"

"This thing stinks." Her voice buzzed slightly. "And I give you seven more minutes until changeover time, my lord. Would you mind hurrying up and getting it over with?"

Huw stretched, rotating his shoulder blades. "Okay," he agreed. "Resuming with sequence number 145 in three, two, one"—he tapped the space bar again—"ouch! Ow, shit!"— and again. Then he reached down and hit the start button on the blood pressure monitor. "That was a definite . . . something. Ow, my head."

The machine buzzed as the cuff inflated. Thirty seconds passed, then it began to tick and hiss, venting compressed air. Finally it deflated with a sigh. "Shit. One fifty-two over ninety-five. Right, that's it for this run. I got a *definite* ouch."

Huw closed the workbook, then removed his goggles and unclipped the oxygen mask. "Ow." He rubbed at his cheeks and the bridge of his nose, where the rubber had chafed. "How are you coping?"

"Help me out of this thing?" Elena asked plaintively.

Huw stood up, detached the grounding strap, and stretched again. "Okay, let's see . . ." Elena was fumbling with the gas regulator under her visor. "No, let me sort that out." A moment later he had the visor unclipped and her helmet swinging open.

"That's better!" She took a deep breath and began to unfasten her gloves as he attacked the straps holding her backpack in place. "Are you sure the real thing will be lighter?"

"No," Huw admitted. "And that's if we can get our hands on one in the first place. I think we're going to end up having one custom made." Pressurized suits with self-contained air circulation weren't widely sold, and some of the suppliers he'd approached had responded with alarming questions; the line between civilian and certain military uses was rather thin, it seemed. "Here, you should be able to get your helmet off now."

"Oh, that's nice." Elena began to work at the high-altitude suit's catches. It had been a random find in a somewhat peculiar store, and had taken almost a week to restore to working order; so far it was the only one they had, which had put a serious cramp on experimentation until Huw had bitten the bullet and decided to work with an oxygen bottle and goggles as minimal safety precautions. "How do you feel?"

"Head's splitting," Huw admitted. "Hmm. Let me just check again." He ran the blood pressure monitor again. It was roughly the same—alarmingly high for a fit twenty-something—but he was standing up and moving, rather than slouched over a computer: *Good.* "I think I'm coming down."

"It was definitely a tingle? Stronger than the last?"

"I think," Huw paused for thought, "I'm going to skip forward a couple of notches, see how far this sequence runs. I got two weak ones, then this"—he winced—"like tuning in an old radio."

"A radio? A radio tuned to new worlds?"

"Maybe." He detached the blood pressure cuff and walked over to the archway leading to the kitchen. "I'm more interested in knowing what class of knot we're dealing with."

"What kind of? . . . But it's a knot! How many kinds *are* there?"

"I don't know." Huw glanced at the coffee machine, then

the wine bottle sitting next to it. "Huh. Where's—" The door chime pinged for attention.

"I'll get it." Elena was out of the boots and gloves; she'd managed to unzip the pressure suit as far as the crotch, revealing the rumpled tee shirt and jeans she was wearing inside it. Huw shook his head. "That'd better not be the Jehovah's Witnesses; they're going to think we've got a *really* weird family life."

"You say that like it's a *bad* thing—oh hello there!" Her voice rose to a happy chirp as Huw looked round. "Come in, be you welcome! He's in the kitchen, over there, *Huw*—"

Making a snap decision, Huw palmed the corkscrew and picked up the bottle. Turning, he paused in the doorway. "Sigfrid? What are *you* doing here?"

Sigfrid—lanky, tall, with a mustache that resembled a corpulent caterpillar asleep on his upper lip—unslung his shoulder bag and grinned. "Eh, his lordship the major sent me. Said you needed spare hands for some kind of project?"

"Well." Huw raised the bottle. "It's about time. Do you know if he was sending anyone else?"

"No." Sigfrid looked uncertain. "At least, he didn't tell *me*."

"Right." He turned to Elena: "Can you phone Yul? Tell him to pick up food for four this time." Back to Sigfrid. "So what have you been doing in the meantime?"

"Oh, you know." Sigfrid shrugged his jacket back from his shoulders and let it slide to the floor. "I was with his lordship of Markford's household when the pretender went on his rampage? So I had a busy couple of weeks. First a siege, then an evacuation through the backwoods, then lots of running around, hurry up and wait, until they stuck me in Castle Hjorth with the guards detachment."

"But you're here now." Huw nodded to himself. "Want to fetch some glasses?" Elena was on her mobile phone. "Top cupboard, to the left of the kitchen sink." Sig was never the scholarly sort, but he was bright enough to learn. "Let me fill you in on what we're trying to achieve here."

"Surely. The major said something about trying to *find other worlds*. Does that mean? . . ."

Huw nodded. "Yes. And tomorrow we're going to try to open up another one." He pulled the cork free with a pop. "We live in interesting times!"

On their first day in the enemy capital, the reconnaissance team checked into their hotel and commenced operations. Disguised as a family of Dutch tourists, Sir Gunnar ven Hjorth-Hjalmar, accompanied by his married younger cousin Beatrice and her infant son (the elder was back at the family estate, in the care of his nurse), purchased day passes on the double-decker tourist busses that rumbled incessantly through the boulevards and avenues of the city. Sitting on the top deck with a camcorder glued to his right eye, his "wife" gaping in bucolic awe at the colonnaded classical buildings and low office blocks to either side, Gunnar found it amusing to contemplate the police and security check-points that swarmed defensively around the federal build-ings. *They call* this *security?* he asked himself ironically. *Hmm. Target-rich environment, maybe.*

"What's *that?*" asked Beatrice, pointing at the Washing-ton Monument. She spoke hochsprache, the better to aid the disguise; a strawberry blonde with a two-year-old on her hip wasn't anybody's idea of an Al Qaida terrorist. She hadn't spent much time over in the Anglischprache world, beyond the minimum required for the corvée, and her emulation of an awestruck tourist was entirely genuine—because Niej-wein, the largest city with which she was familiar, was less than a tenth the size of downtown Washington, D.C.

"It is a memorial to their founding king-emperor, the duke who led their armies during their rebellion against the right-ful king over the water." Gunnar sniffed. "He refused to take the throne, but their aristocrats honor him to this day."

"How very stupid of him," Beatrice agreed. "Was he mad?"

"I don't know." Gunnar zoomed in on the monument, then panned slowly sideways to take in the neoclassical palaces of bureaucracy to either side of the wide plaza and the shallow pool. Eight and nine stories high, none of them exceeded the height of the spire. *Interesting,* he noted. "Mark a waypoint, please."

Beatrice fumbled obediently in her handbag, then produced a tissue and wiped little Anders's nose. Anders bubbled sleepily as his mother wadded up the tissue with mild distaste and stuffed it back in her bag, along with the GPS machine. "He will need cleaning soon," she told Gunnar.

"It cannot be helped. A single man, making notes and filming, would attract attention."

"Of course, cousin. But we will need to stop the carriage to do so."

Gunnar panned back across the Mall, slowly scanning a frontage of museum buildings. "There are public toilets in all the museums and public buildings here, well-kept and as luxurious as any palace back home."

"Good." She glanced behind her. "These buildings. The *people* own them?"

"Only indirectly. Just as they rebelled against their king and replaced him with none, so they tried to abolish their aristocracy. It grew back, of course, but not in the same image—so there is a ruling class here, but its members are not named count this or lord that."

"How very confusing! How is one to recognize a superior? . . ."

"You don't." Gunnar ignored her evident discomfort. "It's *very* confusing at first. But eventually you learn to spot the signs. Their wealth, for one thing. And the way the laws that leash the ordinary people slip past them. They don't carry arms; other people carry arms for them, it's a sign of how rich and powerful this empire has become." *Too many words,* he thought. The words wouldn't stop coming; relief at being here, at not worrying about being murdered by the bitch-queen back home, had loosened his tongue.

Beatrice shifted Anders across her lap. "It's huge," she said, her voice wavering slightly.

"Of course. This city, Washington, D.C., has nearly two-thirds the population of the entire Gruinmarkt. And it rules over everything from the outer kingdom in our west through the badlands and the mountains to the Sudtmarkt and the Nordmarkt—well, part of the Nordmarkt belongs to these Americans' northern neighbor, but that kingdom is also vast, by our lights. But it is still a kingdom and it is still run by a king-emperor of sorts, albeit one of their elite who is formally proclaimed by his peers to rule for four or eight years. And we know how to talk to power."

"Huh. My tutor told me their king-emperor is elected, that the people choose him. Is this not so?"

"It looks like that, yes, but it's not so simple. The little people are presented with two contenders, but the ruling elite would never tolerate the candidacy of an outsider. Sometimes a contender tries to *look* like an outsider, but it's purely a rabble-rousing pretense. This current king-emperor doesn't even go that far; his father was king-emperor before last."

"Huh. Again, how stupid! Sir Gunnar, I think we should move now, before Anders disgraces himself. If it pleases you?"

Gunnar lowered the camcorder and switched it to standby. The tour guide was still droning on in a nasal voice, mangled by the loudspeakers behind the windshield at the front of the open upper deck of the bus. "Yes, let us do so." The bus swayed as it moved forward then turned in towards the curb. "Follow me."

The sky was clear and blue, the sun beating down on the sidewalk as Beatrice stepped off the bus with Anders, waiting while Gunnar—determinedly staying in character—collected the push-chair. As he unfolded it, Anders sent up a sleepy moan: Beatrice bounced him, shushing. "Please let us get him indoors."

"In a moment." Gunnar glanced round. The bus had

stopped close by a huge concrete and stone facade—back home, it would have been the stronghold of a noble family, but here it was most likely a museum of some sort. "Ah yes. We'll try there." *Holocaust Memorial Museum?* Gunnar had a vague recollection that it might be connected with some historic massacre in these Anglischprache folks' history, but that didn't matter to him; it was a museum, so obviously it would have toilets and baby changing facilities. "Record a waypoint. And another one in the baby-changing room, if the machine functions adequately indoors."

The museum had security guards and one of those annoying contraptions that let them peer into visitors' possessions next to a metal detecting arch. Gunnar was sufficiently familiar with such precautions to have left his weapons back at the hotel, but they still irritated him, reminding him that he was not free to comport himself as an arms-man in this place. If the business of governance was to maintain a monopoly on lethal force, as his baron had once asserted, then the Anglischprache clearly understood this message. Still, discreet signs pointed to the toilets beyond the obstruction, and the little one's needs must be attended to.

Gunnar cooled his heels in the atrium for a few minutes while his sister-in-law dealt with the child. It was a peculiar museum, he decided, very strange—more like a mausoleum. This holocaust was clearly a most unsavory affair, but why dwell on it? It was confusing: It didn't even seem to have happened to the Anglischprache themselves, but to some other people. So why bother commemorating it with a museum? *But it's in the right place,* he reminded himself. *And it'll be easier to get onto the roof than any of the government offices. If it's high enough . . .*

Beatrice finally emerged from the rest room, carrying a quieter Anders. Gunnar smiled, trying to look relieved. "I think I would like to go upstairs here," he told her quietly. "Let's go find the elevator and ride it to the top. Did you get a waypoint?"

"I'm sorry cousin; the machine balked. I think the walls are too thick."

"Then you will try again on the highest floor. And I shall look for access doors to the roof. If there's a window, I will film landmarks through it, to estimate the elevation."

"You have plans for this place?"

"Oh yes, indeed." Gunnar nodded. "We're well into Sudtmarkt territory here, but for what I think we shall be doing, that should be no obstacle."

"You want to doppelganger a *museum?*"

"It's a possibility—I want to look at some shops, too. As long as the land is accessible, it will fit my needs. And I don't recall any cities in the middle of swamps down there. The Sudtmarkt can be bullied, bought, or bribed, and along with elevation that's all that matters."

A month had passed since the disastrous mission into Niejwein; Mike had been back in the office for two weeks, alternating between interdepartmental meetings and frustrating sessions in room 4117 when he got an e-mail from the colonel: Tomorrow we're taking a day trip to the Otis Air National Guard Base on Cape Cod. I've got a meeting there, and there are some folks I want to introduce you to.

The aircraft hangar was dim and cavernous after the bright daylight outside. Mike blinked, slightly dazzled, at the thing squatting on the stained concrete in front of him. It seemed misshapen and malformed, like a fairy-tale dragon sleeping in its cave. It was green and scaly, sure enough, and spiky—a huge refueling probe jutting lancelike from the chin beneath its cockpit windows, and infrared sensors bulged like enormous warts from the deformed forehead beneath the hunched shoulders of its engine cowls.

Dragons, however, did not traditionally have high-visibility warning tags dangling from their rotor blade tips, or an array of maintenance trolleys and tractors parked around them. And dragons most especially didn't have a bunch of Air Force officers chattering next to the huge external fuel tank slung from their port winglet.

Mike had hobbled halfway to the chopper before anyone noticed him. An arm waved: "Mike. Over here, I want you to meet these folks." He picked up his pace as much as he dared. "Gentlemen, this is Mike Fleming. Mike is a special agent on assignment to our organization from DEA. His specialty is getting under enemy skin. He's our HUMINT guy, in other words, and he picked up that broken leg in the same line of work as you guys—only on foot. Mike, this is Lieutenant John Goddard, and Captain Simon MacDonald. They're in charge of flight operations for this little test project—staff and execution both, they sit up front in the cockpit." More faces and more introductions followed, warrant officer this and tech specialist that, the guys in charge of making the big helicopter work. Mike tried to commit them all to memory, then gave up. The half dozen guys and one or two women in fatigues standing around here were the crew chiefs and flight crew—it took a lot of people to keep a Pave Low helicopter flying.

"Pleased to meet you." Mike shook hands all round. He caught Eric's eye. "I'm impressed." Which statement, when fully unpacked, meant *How the* hell *have you been keeping this under wraps?* The implications weren't exactly subtle: *So this is Dr. James's breakthrough. What happens next?*

"Good," said Smith, nodding. Quietly: "I told them you're not up to serious exertion, they'll make allowances. Just try to take it all in." He paused for a moment. "Simon, why don't you give Mike here the dog and pony show. I'll go over the load-out requirements with John and Susan in the meantime. When Mike's up to speed, we can meet up in the office, uh, that's room R-127, and share notes."

"Yes, I'll do that, sir." MacDonald turned to Mike and waved a hand at a door some way back along the flank of the green monster. "Ever seen one of these before?" he asked breezily.

"Don't think so. On the news, maybe?" Mike followed the captain across the stained concrete floor towards the door, going as fast as he could with his cast. The chopper was huge, the size of a small airliner. Blades big enough to bridge a freeway curved overhead in the dimness. The fuel tanks under the stubby wings proved, on closer acquaintance, to be nearly as tall as he was, and as long as a pickup truck. "I don't know much about helicopters," he admitted.

"Okay, we'll fix that." MacDonald flashed a smile. "This is a modified MH-53, descended from the Jolly Green Giant. Back about twenty years ago it was our biggest cargo helicopter. This one's been rebuilt as an MH-53J, part of the Pave Low III program. It's still a transport chopper, but it's been tailored for one particular job—low-level, long-range undetected penetration of enemy airspace, at night or in bad weather, in support of special forces. So we've got a load of extra toys on this ship that you don't normally see all in one place."

The side door was open. MacDonald pulled himself up and stood, then reached down to help Mike into the cavernous belly of the beast. "This is a General Electric GAU-2/A, what the army call an M134 minigun. We've got three of them, one in each side door and one on the ramp at the back." He walked forward, towards the open cockpit door. "Night, bad weather, and enemy territory. That's a crappy combination and it means flying low in crappy visibility conditions. So we've got terrain-following radar, infrared night vision gear, GPS, inertial navigation, an IDAS/MATT terminal for tactical datalink—" He stopped. "Which isn't going to be much use where we're going, I guess. Neither is the GPS or the missile warning transponders or a whole load of stuff. So I'll not go over that, right? What you need to know is, it's a big chopper that can fly low, and fast, at night, while carrying three infantry squads or two squads and a dozen prisoners or six stretcher cases. We can put them down fast, night or day, and provide covering suppressive fire against light forces. Or we can carry an outside load the size of a Humvee. So. Have you got any questions?" He seemed amused.

"Yeah." Mike glanced around. "You've crossed over before, as I understand it. How'd it go?"

MacDonald's face clouded. "It went okay." He gestured at a boxy framework aft of one of the flight engineer's positions. "I'd studied all the backgrounders—but still, it wasn't like anything I'd expected." He shook his head. "One thing to bear in mind is that it would be a really bad idea to do that kind of transition too close to the ground. The air pressure, wind direction, weather—it can all vary. You could be in a world of hurt if you go from wet weather and low pressure to a sudden heat wave without enough airspace under your belly." He registered Mike's expression. "You get less lift in high temperatures," he explained. "Affects rotary-winged ships as well as fixed-wing, and we tend to fly low and heavy. With all the graceful flight characteristics of a grand piano, if we lose engine power or exceed our load limit." He sat down in the pilot's chair. "Go on, take a seat, she won't bite as long as you keep your hands to yourself."

"I don't think I'd fit. Not 'til I get this thing off my leg." Mike leaned across the back of the copilots' seat, staring at the controls. "Last time I saw this many screens was when I had to arrest a share trader—it's like a flying dealer desk!"

"Yeah, that's about right. Of course, if any of it goes wrong it adds a whole new meaning to the phrase, 'my computer crashed.'" MacDonald grinned. "Look, out there. And down. Get a feel for the visibility. What do you think our main problem is going to be?"

"What do I—oh." Mike frowned. "Okay, there's no GPS where we're going. The Clan don't have heavy weapons, at least nothing heavier than machine guns—as far as we know. Unless they've somehow bought some missiles, and they're pretty much limited to whatever they can carry by hand from one side to the other. So—" He glanced up at the rotor blade arching overhead and followed it out into the middle distance. "Hmm. Where we're going there are a lot of trees.

And the places we want to get inside of are walled. Is that going to be a problem?"

"You ever seen *Black Hawk Down*?" It was a rhetorical question. "We've got ways of dealing with trees. What we really don't like—our second worst nightmare—is buildings with armed hostiles overlooking the LZ. In general, just don't go there. The ground pounders can secure the target *then* we can land and pick them up. The alternative is to risk us taking one on the rotor head, in which case we all get to walk home."

"What's your worst nightmare?"

"MANPADs," He said bluntly. "Man-portable air defense missiles, that is. Not your basic SAM-7, which is fundamentally obsolete, but late-model Stingers or an SA-16 Igla—that's Russian-made and as deadly as a Stinger—can really ruin your day. From what I've been reading, your bad guys could carry them across, they only weigh about twenty kilos. We've got countermeasures and flare dispensers, of course, but if they've bothered to get hold of a bunch of MANPADs and learn how to use them properly we could be in a world of hurt."

Mike nodded. "That wouldn't be good."

"Well." MacDonald slapped the top of the instrument console affectionately. "It's not as bad as it sounds. Because they won't be expecting anyone to come calling by chopper. It's never happened to them before, right? So they've got no reason to expect it now. Plus, we have God *and* firepower on our side. As long as the ARMBAND supply holds up we can ship over spec-ops teams and their logistics until the cows come home. You do not want to get between a Delta Forces specialist and his ticket home, if you follow my drift, it doesn't give you a good life expectancy. So it's all down to the guys with the black boxes."

"I don't know anything about that side of things." Mike shrugged. "For that, you need to talk to the colonel. But I would guess that we've got a bunch of GPS coordinates you can feed into your magic steering box of tricks; sites the

Clan used as safe houses in this world, so they're almost certainly collocated with their installations in the other place. We don't know what they look like over there, but that's beside the point if we know where to find them."

"Well, it also helps to know what we're meant to do when we get there." MacDonald grinned briefly. "Although that oughta be obvious—otherwise they'd have sent someone else. So what *do* you know that you can tell me?"

"I don't. Know, that is. What you're cleared for, for example." Mike paused. "I'm just the monkey—Colonel Smith, he's the organ-grinder. You've been over to the other world, you've got the basics, right? But this is new to me. Until this morning, I hadn't had more than a hint that you guys even existed."

"There are too many Chinese walls in this business. Not our fault."

"Yeah, well, you know this didn't come out of nowhere, did it?" Mike decided to take a calculated risk. "The folks who live over there found us first. And they're not friendly."

"No shit? I'd never have guessed."

"Well, that's the punch line. Because the target where they live—it's another version of North America, only wild and not particularly civilized. I've been over there on foot and, hell, we're not getting very far if we get stuck down there. So I would *guess* that's where you guys come in. But I don't know for sure because nobody's told me"—He shrugged—"but I think we're about to find out. Maybe we should go find that office now. Find out what the official line is."

11

PARTY TO CONSPIRACY

❧

Throwing a party and inviting all your friends and family was not, Miriam reminded herself ruefully, a skill that she'd made much use of over the past few years—especially on the scale that was called for now.

For one thing, she had status; as a member of the council of regents that had assembled itself from the wreckage of the Clan Council's progressive faction, and as a countess in her own right, she wasn't allowed to do things by half. A low-key get-together in the living room with finger food and quiet music and a bring-your-own-bottle policy was right out, apparently. If a countess—much less a queen-widow—threw a party, arrangements must be made for feeding and irrigating not only the guests, but: their coachmen, arms-men, and servants; their horses; their hangers-on, courtiers, cousins, and children in the process of being introduced to polite society; her *own* arms-men and servants; and the additional kitchen and carrying staff who it would be necessary to beg, borrow, or kidnap in order to feed all of the above. Just the quantity of wine that must be brought in beggared the imagination.

"Old King Harald, he had a reputation for bankrupting any lord who made trouble for him. He used to invite himself and his court to stay for a couple of weeks, paying a house call—with six hundred mouths to feed." Brill grinned at Miriam over the clipboard she was going through. "Two thousand three hundred bottles of spiced wine and eighty casks of small beer is *nothing* for a weekend retreat, my lady."

"Oh god. Am I going to bankrupt myself if I make a habit of this?"

"Potentially, yes." Brill lowered her clipboard. "You must know, a third of the royal budget was spent on food and drink for the court. I know this sounds insane to you, but this is the reality of our economy—peasants produce little surplus, knowing that it can be taken from them in taxes. However." She made a note on her checklist: "Four oxen, two hundred turkey-fowl, twelve pigs, a quarter-ton of fresh-caught cod, six barrels of salted butter, two tons of wheat . . . yes, you can afford this from your household funds. Monthly, even. It increases your outgoings tenfold, but only for three days. And once you have demonstrated your hospitality, there is no reason to hold such entertainments merely for your courtiers: Say the word and those you wish to see will visit to pay their respects. Next week's festivity demonstrates your wealth and power and establishes you on the social circuit."

"You make that sound as if it's something I'm going to have to repeat."

"My lady." Brilliana's tone was patient rather than patronizing: "Nothing you do now can divert you from your destiny to become a shining star in the social firmament—well, nothing short of raving at the moon—but how seriously the other stars of the stratum take you depends on how you comport yourself in this affair. Many of your peers are shallow, vapid, prone to superficial gossip, and extremely malicious. Yet you—or I—cannot live without their sanction. Your status as queen-widow depends on their consent and their consent is contingent on you being the queen-widow they expect—in public."

"Huh. By throwing a huge party I give them lots of stuff to gossip about, though." Miriam frowned. "But if I *don't* throw a huge party they'll gossip anyway, with even less substance and possibly more malice because I haven't stuffed their stomachs with good food. I can't win, can I?"

Brill nodded. "My humble advice is to treat it as a matter of gravest business, and to attend to every plaint and whine that your supplicants—and you will have many—bring to your attention. Then ignore them, as is your wish, but at least let them talk at you."

"I'm not going to ignore them." Miriam picked moodily at a loose thread on the left sleeve of her day-dress. "Damn it. You remember my Dictaphone? I need it, or one like it. Make it one that runs on microcassettes, and make sure there's a spare set of batteries and spare tapes for, oh, let's go mad and say twenty-four hours. Add a pair of desktop recorders with on/off pedals to the shopping list, and another laptop, and some kind of printer. We've got the generator, right? Let's use it. Can you find me a couple of people who know how to use a keyboard and speak both English and hochsprache who we can trust? I need an office staff for this job. . . ."

Brill closed her mouth with a snap. "Uh. An office?"

"Yeah." Miriam's smile flickered on for a moment. "You've framed it for me: This is a political do, isn't it? And I'm a politician. So I'm going to listen to everybody, and because I can't take it all in, I'm going to record what they say and respond later, off-line. But somebody's got to type up all those petitions and turn them into stuff I can deal with."

"You need secretaries." Brill picked up her clipboard, flipped over a page, and began making notes. "Trustworthy—I know. Second sons or daughters of allies? To assist the queen-widow's household? I believe . . . yes, I can do that. Anything else?"

"Yes. I want a photographer."

"A photographer." Brill frowned. "That is very unusual? . . ."

"Yes, well. If anyone makes trouble, tell the truth: I need to learn to recognize people, and because I'm new around here and don't want to give offense by *not* recognizing people the second time I see them, I want photographs with names attached. But otherwise—hmm. It's a party. People are on display, right? So have a photo printer to hand, and offer to take portraits. Do you think that would work?"

"We don't have a photo printer. . . ." Brill trailed off. She blinked, surprised. "You offer portraits, while you compile mug shots? . . ."

"Old political campaign trick, kid, Mom told me about it. She did some campaigning back in the eighties when she was married to—" Miriam stopped, her throat closing involuntarily. *Dad,* she thought, a black sense of despair suffocating her for a moment. "Shit."

Brill stared at her. "Helge?"

Miriam shook her head.

"Hara!" Brill snapped her fingers. "A cup of the slack for my lady, at once." The maidservant, who had been hiding in some dark recess, darted away with a duck of her head that might have been a bow. "Helge?" Brill repeated gently.

"A memory." Miriam stared at the backs of her hands. Smooth skin, unpainted nails—nail paint was an alien innovation here—and she remembered holding her father's hands, years ago; it seemed like an eternity ago. A happier, more innocent lifetime that belonged to someone else. "You know how it is. You're thinking about something completely different and then—bang."

"Your father." Brill cleared her throat. "You do not speak of Lord Alfredo, do you."

Miriam sighed. "The man is dead, and besides, it was in another country a long time ago." She glanced at Brill. "He died nearly ten years ago. He was a good man." She tried to swallow. "It seems so long ago. I'm being silly! . . ."

"No you're not." Brill laid her clipboard down as the door opened. It was the maid, bearing a tray with a bottle and two cups on it. "You've been driving yourself hard today, my lady; a cup and a pause to refresh your nerves will not delay you any more than overtiring yourself would do."

"A cup." Miriam focused on the tray as Hara placed it on the table and retreated, bowing. Over the weeks she'd been working on her ability to ignore the omnipresent servants; or rather, to avoid embarrassing anyone—herself or them—by recognizing them as social individuals. Long habit of politeness vied with newly learned behavior as she held herself back from thanking the woman (which would only commence both of them on a possibly disastrous social minuet of interaction that might result in the maid losing her job or being flogged for insolence if she misspoke). "Pour one for yourself, Brill. I'm—you're right. Anyway, what am I meant to be doing next?"

Brilliana produced a pocketwatch from her sleeve. "Hmm. You were due for a fitting half an hour ago, but that doesn't matter. The seamstresses already have all the toiles they need, they can embroider while they wait. Hmm again. There is the menu to consider, and your household's clothing, and the fireworks, and small gifts and largesse, but"—her gaze flickered to Miriam's face—"we can do that tomorrow. Milady? Right now, you're going to take a break. Please?"

Ding-dong.

The doorbell chime died away. The short dark-haired woman swore quietly and put down the vegetable knife she'd been using on a handful of onions. "What now?" she asked herself rhetorically, wiping her hands on a towel as she walked towards the front door. Last week it had been the Jehovah's Witnesses, the week before . . . *well, at least it won't be* them. They *never ring.* They just appeared in her living room, disturbingly self-possessed and always armed.

"Yes?" she said, opening the door.

"Hi, Paulie," said Brilliana, smiling hesitantly.

Paulette gaped for a moment. "You'd better come in." She took in Brill's companion: "You, too?"

"Thank you," said Olga, as they retreated into the front hall. She closed the door carefully. "Miriam sent us."

"Looks nice," Brill added offhand as she looked around. "That wallpaper, is it new?"

"I put it up six months ago!" Paulette stared at her in exasperation and muted fear. At her last visit, Brill had hinted darkly about the extremes the Clan would go to in order to preserve their secrecy. "How is she? Did you find her?"

"Yes." Brilliana grimaced. "Luckily I found her before things went too badly awry. And there is gold at the end of this tunnel."

"Politics! Who needs it?" Olga chirped brightly, momentarily slipping into her well-practiced airhead role. "One needs must be patient while these things work themselves out. But in any case, we thought we ought to visit. It's well past time we had a talk."

"Um." Paulette backed towards the kitchen. "Sure. How would you like to do it over an iced tea?"

"I'd like that just fine."

Ten minutes later, with mugs in hand, they were seated around the coffee table in the lounge. "Have you had any official visits?" asked Brill. "Men in black, that sort of thing?" She said it lightly, as if half-joking, but Paulette knew how serious it was.

"No, nothing I've noticed. No visits, no strange minivans, none of that sort of thing."

"Fine." Brill sounded reassured. Olga, however, looked thoughtful.

"Don't you want to check the phone lines?" she asked, unable to help herself.

"Already done." Brill's smile was unsettling. "I left a device behind on my last visit. It would have told me if there was any sign of tampering."

"We hope," Olga added, with a disturbing smile.

"Oh." Paulette took a mouthful of her drink to stop herself saying anything she might regret later. "Well that's alright then." Brill showed no sign of noticing any irony. "So you came to have a little chat. After nearly six months of nothing at all." She squinted at Brill. "And you brought Olga. How nice." Sarcasm was risky, but Paulette was a realist: If the news was really bad, these two wouldn't have invited themselves in for a social. There had to be a *value proposition* in play here, an offer too good to refuse. But at least they were here to make an offer, not to simply shoot her out of hand. The Clan were comparatively civilized, for a bunch of barely postmedieval gangsters.

"She sent us," said Olga. "She told us to tell you, you were right. But that is not why we are here. It appears the US government has noticed us."

"Oh." Paulette put her glass down. "Shit."

There was a moment's heartfelt silence.

"Just *how much* have the feds noticed you guys?" Paulette asked carefully, meaning: *Am I likely to get any of that attention?*

"Thoroughly." Olga looked tired for a moment. "Brill?"

"There's an entire new federal agency devoted to us." Brill took a mouthful of tea, frowned. "Super-black, off the books, siphoning money off the war appropriations and the NSA and the CIA, as far as we can tell. They've captured couriers and used them as mules to get into our world. Most recently they"—she swallowed—"used a backpack nuke to send us a message."

"Oh Jesus." There didn't seem to be anything else to say to that. "That's not policing, that's *war.*"

"Exactly," Brilliana said heavily.

"Which leaves us with problems." Olga picked up the thread. "We can no longer do business over here as usual"—*business* being the somewhat less legal side of the import-export trade—"and furthermore, this mess coincided with a political upset back home. Everything's up in the air."

"And you're off the reservation," Paulette said drily.

"Yes, there is that." Olga glanced sidelong at Brill. "There's no telling how long it'll last." Brill shook her head slightly. "But anyway . . . we came to apologize for dragging you into this mess."

"Isn't it a bit late for that?"

"Not necessarily. We can cut you loose. You were never directly involved in our principal business operations. There's no record of you outside of a few handwritten ledgers in Niejwein, and the office Hel- Miriam bought, and there's no sign that the feds are aware of what she was up to on her own behalf. I think if we cover your tracks we can be confident that they won't stumble across you." She halted awkwardly for a moment. "The flip side is, if they identify you as a person of interest, we won't be able to do anything to protect you. We won't even know."

"Ah." Paulette contemplated screaming, but it didn't seem like it would do any good. "What *could* you do to help?"

"Well, that depends." Olga put her hands between her knees, clearly uneasy. "Whatever happens next, the Clan will no longer be acting as, as an extradimensional drugs cartel anymore. The feds consider us to be a hostile government: Should we not act upon our status? Furthermore, the changes among the all-highest mean that they are not entirely wrong. Anyway, I didn't come here merely to say we are cutting you loose."

Here it comes. "What have you got in mind?" Paulette asked wearily. "And is it going to just evaporate under me again, three months down the line? . . ."

"That wasn't Miriam's doing." Olga grimaced. "You should not underestimate the power of the enemies she made. She spent months under house arrest. Later, you can ask her yourself if you are so inclined. But this is different."

"In what way is it different?" *Why am I doing this?* Paulette asked herself. *Am I trying to get myself sucked in again?* It was true, the money had been good—and Miriam was a friend, and it beat the ordinary daily grind she'd had before, and the tedious admin job she'd had to take up since; but the downside, attracting the attention of the government, and not in a good way, was almost enough to make her short-circuit the process and say "no" immediately. Only residual curiosity was keeping her going.

"Miriam has both a secure position and a plan," said Olga. "She is in a position where, if she plays her hand correctly, she can set policy for the whole Clan. I am not entirely clear on her design, but she said I should tell you that unlike the old trade, this one is both legal and ethically sound. She said it would also need a lot of organizing at this end, materials and books and journals and specialist expertise to buy in . . . and to be firewalled completely from the Clan's historic operations. Is that of interest to you?"

Paulette nodded. She'd visited New Britain once at Miriam's behest, found it a strange and disorienting experience, like a trip to another century. "Well, it's a plan. But what makes this time different?"

Olga glanced at Brill, as if for support. "She's the queen," she said.

Paulette blinked. "Queen," she repeated. It was the last thing she'd have expected to hear.

"Yes. You know, woman who sits on a throne? Sometimes wears a crown?"

"Eh." Paulette blinked again, then looked at Brilliana. Who was watching her, a flicker of tightly controlled amusement twitching her lips. "She's not joking, is she?"

"Power is no joking matter." The younger woman's eyes were cold. "We've just fought a civil war over it. And now Helge is carrying the heir to the throne—long story, you do not need to look shocked—we would be fools not to seize the moment. And we need a new world to exploit, now that this one has shown itself hostile. That much has now become glaringly clear even to the most reactionary of the conservative wing."

"Okay." Paulette licked suddenly dry lips. She could feel her heartbeat. "So what's in it for me?" *If you say* old time's sake *I may just punch you* . . . this was the proverbial offer too good to refuse. *No way will they just let me go now.*

"A tenth of a point of gross," said Olga. "But you don't have to say yes now. Miriam is holding a meeting in a few days of her accomplices and confidantes. If you are interested, you may attend." She slid a business card across the table. "Phone this number no later than four o'clock tomorrow afternoon and say yes or no, then follow the post officer's instructions; they will see you across. The nature of the business, and your role in it, is such that if you choose to decline the offer, you have nothing to fear—you could spill everything you know, and the US government would learn nothing of use. Oh, and she sends you this. You can treat it as a nonreturnable advance against wages." She slid a checkbook across the table to rest atop the card. "Half a million bucks in the account, Paulie. Try not to spend it all at once."

It was just another summer party, held on the afternoon of a muggy, humid summer day twelve miles outside of Niejwein, in the grounds of a fortified mansion out near what would—in another world—be Lincoln, Massachusetts. Summer parties were a seasonal fixture among the aristocracy of Niejwein, required to live in proximity to their ruler and lacking in any kind of civil society that might host more public entertainments; but this was also the first Miriam had ever held. *Just a summer party,* Miriam reminded herself, glassy-eyed, as yet more carriages and their obligatory escorts of footmen and mounted guards drew up, disgorging men and women in the peacock finery of the nobility: It was more like the Academy Awards, minus the onlookers and the network television presence, but with added cockfighting behind the woodshed.

Sir Alasdair had a third of his men dispersed around the perimeter of her commandeered residence, another third staking out the doppelganger house in Lincoln, and the remaining cadre of guards on alert downstairs. Brilliana had the receiving line under control, looking for all the world like the lady of the house herself—and leaving Miriam (again wearing the persona of Helge, Prince Creon's putative widow) free to focus on those she wished to talk to. Two teenage scions of the inner family lines, Barbara and Magraet, had been introduced into the household for transcription and translation and ensconced in a back room with a bottle of wine and a supply of spare batteries and Dictaphone tapes. And Earl Riordan—no, *Baron* Riordan, a reward by order in council for his support, paid out of the estates of several drastically pruned noble family trees—had sent her a dozen hard-eyed Security agents in the livery of waiters and other domestics. There'd be no trouble here, clearly. "It's all under control," Brill had assured her that morning. "Just relax and enjoy the affair."

"Relax? In the middle of *this?*" Miriam had taken in the organized chaos.

"Yes, Helge, it's your job to be serene. Leave the panicking to me." And Brill had left her to the mercy of her wardrobe staff, who had spent weeks preparing their idea of a party dress for her, and who had never heard of the word *excess*.

Which left her standing still in an attempt not to perspire in the stuffy warmth of the blue receiving room, trying to smile and make small talk and juggle a glass of wine and a peacock-feather fan that barely stirred the air in front of her. She was surrounded: With Sir Alasdair standing discreetly to one side, and a permanent floating mob of relatives and hangers-on trying to approach her from the front, she was unable to move, reliant on the two ladies-in-waiting hovering nearby.

"—The effect on the harvest will, unfortunately, be bad, your highness, with so many destitute; the pretender's army ate what they could and burned the rest, and banditry and famine follow such as night follows day."

Miriam—*no, Helge*—smiled politely as Lord Ragnr and Styl droned on, talking *at* her rather than *to* her, but most accurately delivering his report to the small condenser mic hidden in her corsage. "And how much has been lost, exactly?" she nudged, shaking her head minutely as Sir Alasdair raised an eyebrow and mimed a shoving motion.

"Oh, lots! I myself counted—" That was Lord Ragnr and Styl's vice, Miriam remembered. In another world he'd have been an adornment to a major accountancy firm's boardroom. In this one, he was a liability to his profession (lord oath-sworn to Duke Lofstrom and ruler of some boring fishing villages, a small chunk of forest, and a bunch of peasant hamlets; performance appraisal based on ability to hunt, drink, and kill the duke's enemies). But she'd listened to him before, and he seemed to think this gave him license to bend her ear in future, and what he had to say was deeply tedious but clearly a matter of profound importance for the business of future good governance. And so, she stood and smiled, and listened to the man.

"—By your leave, my lord?" Miriam blinked back to the present as Sir Alasdair gently interrupted. "My liege, your grandam is about to be announced."

"She is?" Miriam felt the color draining from her cheeks. *Well shit!* "You're certain about that?" *I thought she was dead!*

"Absolutely." Sir Alasdair's expression was imperturbable: She noted the colorless wire coiling from his left ear to the collar of his tunic.

"Oh. Well." She took a breath of musty, overheated air. "My lord, you must, please, forgive me? But I have not seen my grandmother since before the insurrection, and"—*if I clap eyes on her before I die of old age it's too soon*—"I really must pay my respects." *I'd rather piss on her grave, but I suppose I'd better find out why she's here.*

Ragnr and Styl seemed disappointed for some reason,

but took it in good spirit, and after much backing and flowery commiseration she was free. More backing and sidling and some whispered instructions and her ladies-in-waiting formed a flying wedge, or at any rate a creeping one. As they moved towards the door with Miriam in their wake she recognized a gaggle of familiar faces. "Sir Huw?" she called.

"Milady!"

She smiled, unforced: "Did you bring your results?"

Huw nodded. "I'm ready to speak. Whenever you want me to."

"Good. Upstairs, half an hour?"

Huw ducked his head and vanished into a knot of younger Clan members. Miriam blinked as she noticed Elena, almost unrecognizable in a red gown with a long train. *Are they an item*? Miriam wondered, before dismissing the question. Where's Mom? *I need her advice before I confront Hildegarde.*

"Milady?" It was Gerta, pressed into service as an attendant. "If it please you . . ."

"I need to circulate," she mouthed over her shoulder. "Sir Alasdair? . . ."

The press around her began to give way as she made progress towards the main hall. Despite the open doors and windows the air was no less close, thanks to the milling clusters of visitors and their attendants, and the copious quantities of rose water and other perfumes with which they attended to their toilet. Out here in the countryside, the humidity and stink of summer was a mere echo of conditions in the capital; though the gods had little to say against bathing (unlike the early Christians), the smell of old sweat and unwashed clothing was unpleasantly noticeable.

"Make way for her grace!" called one of her servants. "Make—"

"So the rumors were accurate. You *did* survive."

Miriam turned to face the speaker. "I could say the same of you. Grandmother."

The grand dowager Duchess Hildegarde was in her eighties, one of those octogenarians who seemed to persist through a process of mummification. She stared at Miriam, her eyelids drooping as if in disinterest. "I find that interesting," she said flatly. "The odds were not in your favor."

For a moment Miriam flickered back to that bewildering and fearful night, remembering James Lee's evident flattery—and offer of a locket bearing the Lee clan's deviant knotwork: In retrospect an incitement to defect. She managed a polite smile. "I try to make a habit of beating bad odds."

"Hah. You'll continue to face them, girl, as long as you keep playing your fancy games. You ignore the old ways at your peril; others cleave to them, and your fingers can be burned just as easily by the fire you didn't light. Although you do seem to have a fine talent for getting others to rescue you from situations of your own devising. But on another matter, have you seen your dam? I must have words with her. We need to clear the air."

Her grandmother's offhanded condescension didn't surprise Miriam; but the suggestion that the air needed clearing was something else. "What's there to talk about? I thought you'd disowned her!"

"Well." Hildegarde's cheek twitched into something that might have been a grimace. "That was then; this is politics, after all."

"On the contrary, this is my party, and I'm shocked, absolutely shocked, that anybody might want to discuss matters of politics here." Miriam glared at her grandmother. "Or haven't you worked it out yet?"

Hildegarde looked her up and down. "Oh, Patricia raised you well," she breathed. "And I could ask exactly the same of you, but you wouldn't listen. Best save my breath. You'll understand eventually." Then, before Miriam could think of a suitable response, she turned and shuffled aside.

"What was *that* about?" asked Brill, materializing at her elbow: "I could have sworn—"

"I wish I knew." Miriam stared after the dowager, perturbed. "I have the strangest feeling that she was trying to send me some sort of message I'm meant to understand. Only somebody forgot to tell me how to mind read."

"She is"—Brill stared at the broad shoulders of the dowager's arms-men—"a most powerful and dangerous lady."

"And what makes it worse is the fact that she thinks I ought to be on her side." Miriam curled her lower lip.

"Really?" Brill glanced sidelong at her. "I was going to say, I believe she thinks she is looking out for *your* best interests. Being your grandam, after all."

Miriam shrugged uncomfortably. "Save me from people acting in my best interests. Without asking first," she added.

"I wouldn't—" Brill paused and cupped a hand to her left ear. Like Sir Alasdair, she was wearing a wire. "Ah, Baron Isserlis is soon to arrive, my lady. I must leave you for a while. Where should I tell him you want to meet, again?"

"With the others: in the red room, upstairs, at six o'clock. That's where I told Laurens to put the projection screen and laptop, anyway."

"If that goes for all of them? . . ."

"It does. Except for the obvious exceptions."

"The B-list."

"Wine 'em, dine 'em, and keep 'em out of my hair while I'm making the pitch." Miriam fanned herself. "Can you do that?"

Brill smiled. "Watch me," she said. "It's your job to relax and enjoy yourself. Then give a good presentation!"

In a mosquito-infested marsh on the banks of a sluggish river, a draft of peasants from the estates of the Earl of Dankfurt had assembled a scaffold. The scaffold, of stout timber with a surface of planking, bore a winch and some additional contrivances, and despite its crude appearance it had been positioned very carefully indeed. Blood and sweat had gone into its location, and the use of imported surveying tools to measure very precisely indeed its distance and altitude relative to the four reference points where Clan couriers had established accurate GPS locations before crossing over from Washington D.C.

(Accurately locating anything in the Sudtmarkt was problematic, but where there was a need—and urgency—there was a way: and with four reference points, theodolites, and standardized lengths of chain, positioning to within a couple of inches at a distance of up to a mile was perfectly achievable. Besides, Gunnar had insisted on three-inch accuracy with the icy certainty of punishment from above to back him up. And so it was done.)

"This is the entry point?" asked the visitor.

"Yes, my lord." Gunnar turned and gestured towards a nearby copse of trees, climbing the gentle slope. "And right over—there, past the tree line—you should just be able to see the tower for the department store on Pennsylvania Avenue. Site three is, I'm afraid, not visible from here, being on the other side of the river, but construction is complete. We carried out our intrusion tests yesterday shortly after closing time and everything worked perfectly."

"Intrusion tests?"

"A courier, outfitted with cover as a tourist, to make sure our proposed sites were workable. They crossed over ten minutes after the museum closed, to ensure there were no human witnesses, then made their way out when the alarm system went off. Their story was that they'd been in the rest room and hadn't noticed the time. Along the way, they check for motion detectors in the rest rooms, that sort of thing, to ensure a witness-free transit point."

"Excellent. And the others?"

"Shops are a little bit harder to probe, so I checked the store in reverse, myself—I crossed over from the other side. Found we were three inches too low on this side, so I raised the platform accordingly. We will have to risk their store security noticing that they lost a shopper, but they are most likely to assume that I was simply an artful thief."

One of the visiting lord's companions was making notes in a planner; another of them held a large parasol above his lordship's head. His lordship looked thoughtful for a few seconds. "And how do you probe the third site?"

"Ah, well." Gunnar froze for a few seconds. "*That* one we can't send a world-walker into. We can fool store security guards who are looking for shoplifters, but soldiers with machine guns are another matter. We will just have to do it blind and get it right first time. On the other hand, I managed to get a verified GPS reading and a distance estimate to the façade from the car park by pretending to be lost tourists, and the outer dimensions of the building itself are well-known. I am certain—I place my honor on it—that site three is within four or five feet of the geometric center of the complex, at ground level."

"What about the subway station?"

"It's been closed since 9/11, unfortunately, otherwise that would be ideal. Damned amateurs with their box-cutters . . ."

"Leave me. Not you, Gunnar."

Gunnar stared at his visitor. "My lord?"

The parasol- and planner-bearers and the bodyguards were also staring at his lordship. "All of you, go and wait with the carriage a while. I must talk with Sir Gunnar in confidence."

Heads ducked; without further ado, the servants and guards backed away then turned and filed towards the edge of the clearing. His lordship watched with ill-concealed impatience until the last of them was out of easy earshot, before turning to Gunnar.

"You must tell me the truth, sir. I'm informed that our superiors have a definite goal in mind, for which they require certain assurances. *Both* our necks—and those of others—are at risk should this scheme fail. If, in your estimate, it is doomed, please say so now. There will be censure, certainly, but it will be nothing compared to the punishment that will fall on both of us should we make the attempt and fail."

Gunnar nodded thoughtfully. "Your staff, how many of them? . . ."

"At least two spies, for opposing factions."

"Ah, well that makes it clear, then." Gunnar took a deep breath. "This is a huge risk we're taking. And you just revealed your internal security coverage. You know that, don't you?"

"The spies in question will have a boating accident involving alligators around sunset this evening." His lordship smiled humorlessly. "We—my superiors—have chewed the plan to pieces. Our other choices are no better. The pretender saw to that with his betrothal-day massacre and the radicals have been happy to complete his work. But. My question. Can you make it work?"

"Well." Gunnar raised his hat to run fingers through his hair. "I believe so, given the men and the machines. Sites one and two are not professionally secured. The Anglischprache, they rely too much on machines to do the work of men. I will need a team of four world-walkers for each of those two sites, including two Security men who can kill without hesitation if necessary. And the, ah, janitor's carts we discussed. They will need to synchronize their time in advance, and if anyone is out of position it will fail. And you will need to supply the devices and they must work, and at least one man on each team must be trained in setting their timers. But I am, um . . . I believe we have a one in fifty chance of failure for sites one and two. It's a solid plan."

"And site three?"

Gunnar wiped the sweat from his forehead. "Site three is the tricky one. Unlike one and two, it's going to happen in full view of a whole bunch of soldiers who have been on the alert for terrorist attackers for the past two years, ever since a couple of hundred of their comrades were slain. We need two world-walkers—one to get them in, and one to get himself and his partner out—and the device must be pre-set with a very short timer, no more than one minute. And even then, I would only give the insertion team a fifty-fifty chance of getting out in one piece. The only thing in its favor is surprise."

"Hmm."

"What about team four?" Gunnar asked slyly.

"Team four?" His lordship raised one sculpted eyebrow. "There is no team four."

"Really?" Gunnar fanned himself with his hat. "I find that hard to believe, my lord. Or perhaps our superiors are holding something in reserve? . . ."

His lordship snorted. "They're targeting the White House, the Capitol, and the Pentagon—what more do you want?"

"That bitch in Niejwein."

His lordship winked. "Already taken care of, Sir Gunnar. But I advise you to forget I told you so. Too much knowledge can be a dangerous thing."

Room 4117 was scaring Mike. Not the room itself, but what its contents implied.

Matthias's—source GREENSLEEVES's—voice featured prominently in his dreams as he doggedly plowed through the box of cassette tapes, transcribing and backing up, listening and rewinding, making notes and cross-checking the dictionaries and lexicons that other, more skilled linguists were working on with the detainees FTO had squirreled away in an underground dungeon somewhere. FTO had access to some of the NSA's most skilled linguists, and they were making progress, more progress in weeks than Mike had made in months. Which realization did not fill him with joy; rather, it made him ask, *why has Dr. James stuck me in here to do this job when there are any number of better translators available?*

There were any number of answers to that question, but only the most paranoid one stood up to scrutiny: that this material was toxic or contagious, and only a translator who was already hopelessly compromised by exposure to secrets and lies should be given access to it. Mike had worked with source GREENSLEEVES in person, had been infiltrated into a Clan palace in the Gruinmarkt, and knew some of the ugly little truths about Dr. James and his plans. *James wants me here so he can keep an eye on me,* Mike realized, staring at the calendar behind his monitor one afternoon. *He gets some use out of me and meanwhile I'm locked down as thoroughly as if he'd stuck me in one of those holding cells.* He shivered slightly, despite the humid warmth that the air conditioning was fighting a losing battle to keep at bay.

The further into the tapes he got, the dirtier he felt. Someone—probably Matt, but he had an uneasy feeling that there was someone else in the loop—had wired a number of offices, both in the Gruinmarkt and, it appeared, in locations around the US. And they'd recorded a whole bunch of meetings in which various deeply scary old men had talked business. Much of it was innocent enough, by the standards of your everyday extradimensional narcoterrorists—move shipment X to port Y, bribe such a local nobleman to raise a peasant levy to carry it, how many knights shall we send, sir?—but every so often Mike ran across a segment that made him sit bolt upright in alarm, doubting the evidence of his own ears. And some of this stuff went back *years.* These recordings were anything but new. And bits of them, mixing broken English with hochsprache, were unambiguous and chilling in their significance:

"Another five hundred thousand to the Partnership for a Drug-Free America," said the old guy with the chilly voice and the accent like a fake Nazi general in a 50's war movie. "Feed it through the top four pressure trusts."

"What about the other items? . . ."

"Commission those, too. I believe we can stretch to sixty thousand to fund the additional studies, and they will provide valuable marketing material. Nobody looks at the source of this funding too closely, the police and prisons lobby discourage it." A dry chuckle. "The proposal on drug-screening prisons will be helpful, too. I think we should encourage it."

Mike paused the tape again and sat, staring at the computer screen for a while. The skin in the small of his back felt as if it was crawling off his spine. *Did I just hear that?* He wondered bleakly. *Did I just hear one of the biggest cocaine smugglers in North America ordering his accountant to donate* half a million dollars *to a zero-tolerance pressure group? Jesus, what is the world coming to?*

It made economic sense, if you looked at it from the right angle; it was not in the Clan's interest for the price of the commodity they shifted to drop—and drop it surely would, if it was legalized or if the pressure to keep up the war on drugs ever slackened. But for Mike Fleming, who'd willingly given the best years of his life to the DEA, it was a deeply unsettling idea; nauseating, even. *Bought and sold: We're doing the dealers' work for them, keeping prices high.*

His fingers hunted over the keyboard blindly, stabbing for letters as he stared through the glass screen, eyes unfocused. Eventually he stopped and pressed PLAY again.

"—Tell them first, though: They'll need to make suitable accounting arrangements so that it doesn't show up in the PAC's cash flow if they're audited."

A grunt of assent and the conversation switched track to inconsequentialities, something about one of the attendees'—a count's—daughter's impending wedding, gossip about someone else's urgent desire to obtain the current season of *Friends* on tape or DVD. And then the meeting broke up.

Mike hit the PAUSE button again and massaged his forehead. Then, glancing mistrustfully at the screen, he scribbled a note to himself on the legal pad next to the mouse mat: *LOOK INTO CREATIVE ACCT. RE. PAC PAY-OFFS?* And: *COUNT INSMANN'S DAUGHTER'S MARRIAGE -> POLITICAL IMPLICATIONS.* It was a tenuous enough lead to go on, but the Clan's political entanglements were sufficiently personal that it might be—he was willing to concede to himself—that the wedding gossip was actually the most important news on this tape.

Then he pressed PLAY again.

Whatever device Dr. James's mole had been using to bug these meetings seemed to be sound-triggered, with about a thirty-second delay. Mike waited for the beep as the machine rolled on to the next recording, ready to laboriously translate and transcribe what he could. It was the old man, the duke, again, talking to a woman—younger, if Mike was any judge of such things, but . . .

"I'm not happy about the situation in D.C., my lady."

"Is there ever anything to be happy about in that town, your grace?"

"Sometimes. The trouble is, the people with whom we do business change too fast, and this new gang—this *old* gang, rather, in new office—they get above themselves."

"Can you blame them? They are fresh in the power and glory of the new administration. 'The adults are back in charge.'" (A snort.) "Once they calm down and finish feeling their oats they will come back to us."

"I wish I could share your optimism."

"You have reason to believe they'll be any different, this time?"

(Pause.) "Yes. We have worked with them before, it's true, and most of the team they have picked works well to protect our interests. For example, this attorney-general, John Ashcroft, we know him well. He's sound on the right issues, a zealot—but unlikely to become dangerously creative. He knows better than to rock the boat. An arms-length relationship is sufficient for this term, no need to get too close . . . our friends will keep him in line. But what concerns me is that some of the other positions are occupied by those of a less predictable disposition. These Nixon-era underlings, seeking to prove that they could have—yes, like the vice president, yes, exactly."

"You don't like the current vice president? You think he is unfit?"

"It's not *that*. You know about the West Coast operation, though—"

"Yes? I thought we terminated it years ago?"

"We did. My point is, WARBUCKS was our partner in that venture."

(Long pause.) "You're joking."

"I'm afraid not. He's one of our inner circle."

"But how—it's against policy! To involve politicians, I mean."

(Sigh.) "At the time, he was out of office. Swore blind he was going to stay out, too—that's when he began developing his business seriously. The complaints of financial opacity in Halliburton that came out during the Dresser Industries takeover—whose interests do you think those accounting arrangements served? And you must understand that from our point of view he looked like the perfect cutout. Respectable businessman, former defense secretary with heavy political and business contacts—who'd suspect him?"

"Crone Mother's tears! This should *not* have been allowed."

"May I remind you again that nobody saw it coming? That if we had, it wouldn't have happened?"

"What are you going to do about it?"

"What we always do, when they're too big to take down: I'm afraid we're going to have to pay him tribute."

"It's going to be expensive, Angbard. He's their king-in-waiting—indeed, he may actually be their king-emperor in all but name. The idiot child they've placed on the throne does not impress with his acumen. Someone must be issuing the orders in his stead."

"Oh, I wouldn't be so sure, my lady; he's strong-willed and I'm told he's not as stupid as he looks when the glare of the public gaze is shuttered. And I am not certain you're right about the cost of tribute, either. WARBUCKS is as rich as one of our first circle, and from his office in the Old Executive Office Building he has more power than many of our relatives can even conceive of. So we cannot buy him with money or cow him with threats—but there is a currency a man of his type craves, and he knows we can pay in it."

"What—oh. I see."

"He is, it seems, setting up his own private intelligence group—by proxy, through Defense—this Office of Special Plans. He is one of those seekers for power who have a compulsive need for secrecy and hidden knowledge. We know exactly how to handle such men, do we not?"

"As long as you're cautious, Angbard. He knows too much already."

"About us? We won't be feeding him tidbits about *us*. But the fellow has enemies, and he knows it, and as long as we make ourselves discreetly indispensable we'll be safe from investigation by any agency he can touch. We've never had a vice president before, my lady; I hope to make it a mutually profitable arrangement."

(Pause.) "As long as he doesn't turn on us, your grace. Mark my words. As long as he doesn't turn on us. . . ."

The tape clicked to an end. Mike stared at the poisonous thing, unwilling to rewind it and listen again. It wasn't as if he hadn't had his suspicions, but . . . *this is Art Bell Show material*, he told himself. *The vice president is in cahoots with the Clan?*

Slowly a new and even more unwelcome supposition inserted itself into his mind. *No. The vice president* was *in cahoots with the Clan. Now he's*—Mike flashed over on a vision of Dr. James, in a meeting with WARBUCKS himself, giving orders from his shadowy web—*now he's set on destroying* them. *When Matthias defected he didn't realize the reports would end on WARBUCKS desk and WARBUCKS would have to kill him and turn on the Clan to destroy the evidence of his collusion*—

The thoughts were coming too fast. Mike stood up tiredly,

stretched the kinks out of his shoulders, glanced at the clock. It was four in the afternoon: a little early to go home, normally, but . . .

Shit. The Clan take politics personally—when they figure out what's happened they'll treat it as treachery. And if I even hint that I know this shit, the vice president will try and have me rubbed out. What the hell am I going to do?

Buy time. Sign myself out as sick. And hope something turns up. . . .

12

COUP

☙

iriam cleared her throat. *Begin with a cliche:* This was the part she was edgy about. "I expect you're all wondering why I asked you here," she said, and smiled. Deathly silence. She studied her audience: forty or so of the most important movers and shakers of the inner families, mostly allies of the progressive faction. They were rapt, waiting for her explanation and uninclined to social chatter. *Oh well, moving swiftly on . . .* "It's been a year since I turned up with a plan and a business and asked my uncle to call a meeting of the Clan Council."

Heads nodded. Many of them had been at that particular meeting.

"You probably think I asked you here today because a lot has happened in the past year. In particular, *that* plan is dead in the water. I'm not going to assign blame or complain about it. Rather, I'd like to describe the situation we face right now, and propose a new plan. It's drastic, because we're in a bad position, but I think we can make it work.

It'll mean major changes to the way we live, but if we go through with it"—she shrugged—"we'll be in a better position, going forward." *Too much padding,* she thought nervously.

She leaned over the laptop—sitting on a lectern borrowed from the shrine to the household deities—and tapped the space bar. PowerPoint was running, but the projector— "Someone check that—"

Huw poked at the projector. "It's on," he confirmed. A moment later the screen beside her (a bleached, lime-washed canvas stretched flat within a monstrously baroque gilt picture frame) flickered to life.

"Okay." Miriam focused on her notes. She'd spent almost twelve hours working on this presentation, far less than the subject deserved but as much as she'd been able to steal between her other duties over the past week. "Here's what we know for sure: Almost ten months ago, Sir Matthias, who had been participating in at least one little conspiracy against his grace the duke, vanished. We've subsequently learned that he handed himself in to the DEA in return for immunity"—shocked muttering from the back of the room told her that not everybody present had known even that much—"and the DEA handed him on to some kind of black intelligence team called the Family Trade Organization. They're the folks behind the series of raids that shut down the east coast network. A number of us have been compromised, including myself and her grace my mother. FTO subsequently captured at least two of our number and coerced them to act as mules, and at least one of their agents was in the grounds of the Summer Palace earlier this year when the pretender made his bid for the succession."

She paused. The muttering hadn't died down. "Can you save it for later?" she called.

"Silence!" This a deep bellow from Sir Alasdair, at the back corner of the room. "Pray continue, milady."

"Thank you. . . . As I was about to say, anything we decide to do now has to take account of the facts that the US government is aware of us; considers us to be a threat; has developed at the very least a minimal capability to send operatives over here; and we can presume that the explosion at the Hjalmar Palace was also their work. And the news doesn't get any better from there. Um."

Next slide. "Now, I'm going to assume that we are all familiar with the long-lost cousins and the rediscovery of their, ah, home world. Before his illness, his grace the duke observed that one extra world might be an accident, but two were unlikely to be a coincidence; accordingly, he tasked Sir Huw here with conducting some preliminary research into the matter. What Sir Huw established, very rapidly, was that our early attempts to use the cousins' variant knotwork design on the east coast in the United States had failed because of a doppelgangering effect of some kind. The cousins' knotwork does, in fact, work, if you go far enough south and west. The world Sir Huw and his fellows discovered was—well, we don't know that it's uninhabited, but the presence of ruined buildings suggests that it used to be inhabited. Now it's cold; Maryland is sub-arctic, with pine forests, and there's residual radioactivity around the ruins—" She paused again, as the chatter peaked briefly. "Yes, this is, *was,* a high-tech world. *Very* high-tech."

She ran the next slide. A photograph of a shattered white dome on a forested hillside. Fast forward again: structures inside the dome, indistinct in the gloom but clearly showing how enormous it was. Next slide: a sealed metal door set in a concrete wall. "On the other side of this door, Sir Huw discovered hard vacuum." Next slide: a view down into the valley, thick mist swirling around the crack in the dome's side. "A door into an apparently endless vacuum. The cloud you're looking at is condensation where the air pressure around the dome drops. It's too dangerous to approach closer, or we'd have gone back to try and seal it—our people were lucky to get away alive—but it's not any kind of vacuum pump *I've* heard of. Our best guess is that it's a gate that maintains a permanent connection between two worlds, rather than the transient connection we make when we world-walk. But we have no idea how it works or why there's no, uh, world there. Maybe there used to be and the gate needs to be anchored in some way? We don't know."

The chatter had subsided into a stunned silence. Miriam glanced round the shocked faces in front of her. "Sir Huw has also conducted some topological analysis on the family knotworks," she said forcefully. "He generated a series of variants and checked them—not to world-walk, but to see if he could feel them. He generated them using Mathematica. It turns out that the family knots can be derived by following a fairly simple formula, and there are three constants that, if you vary them, give rise to different knots that give him the family headache." Next slide: a polynomial equation. "Apparently, this is the key to our ability—it's the Alexander polynomial describing the class of knots to which ours belong. No, I don't understand it either, but it turns out that by tweaking some of these coefficients we get different knots that include the two we already know of.

"Any given knot, starting in any given world, seems to act as a binary switch: Focus on it and you can walk from your starting world into a single destination determined by the knot you use."

Someone had thoughtfully placed a wine goblet by her laptop. Miriam paused to take a sip.

"There's more. The conventional wisdom about how much we can carry, about the impossibility of moving goods using a carriage or a wheelbarrow? It's somewhat . . . wrong. It's true that you can't *easily* carry a larger payload, but with careful prior arrangement and some attention to insulators and reducing contact area you can move about a quarter of a ton. Possibly more, we haven't really pushed the limits yet. I suspect that this was known to the postal service but carefully kept quiet prior to the civil war; the number of world-walkers who'd have to cooperate to establish a rival corvée, independent of our Clan authorities, is much smaller than the conventional wisdom would have it.

If this was widely known it would have made it harder to control the young and adventurous, and consequently harder to retain a breeding population. So the knowledge was actually suppressed, and experimentation discouraged, and during the chaos of the civil war everyone who knew the truth was murdered. Maybe it was a deliberate strategy—knowledge is power—or just coincidence, or accident. It doesn't matter; what I want to impress on you is that there are big gaps in our knowledge, and some of them appear to have been placed there deliberately. Only we've begun to piece things together, thanks to the recent destabilization. And the picture I'm building isn't pretty."

She hit the key for the next slide. "You heard—a year ago you heard—my views on the Clan's business and its long-term viability. Smuggling drugs only works as long as they stay expensive, and as long as the people you're smuggling them past don't know what's going on. We've seen evidence of a technology to build gates between worlds, and if there's one thing the US government is good at, it's throwing money at scientific research and making it stick. They know we're here, and I promise you that right now there is a national laboratory—hell, there are probably ten—trying to work out how world-walking works. Worst case, they've already cracked the problem; best case . . . we may have years rather than months. But once they crack it, we, here in the Gruinmarkt, we're *finished*. Those people can send two million tons of heavy metal halfway around the world to kick in doors in Baghdad, and we're right on their doorstep."

She paused to scan the room again. Forty pairs of eyes were staring at her as if she'd sprouted a second head. Her stomach knotted queasily. "I think we need to get used to the idea that it's *over*. We can't stay here indefinitely; we don't have the leverage. Even if we can negotiate some kind of peaceful settlement with them—and looking at the current administration I'm not optimistic—it'd be like sleeping with an elephant. If it rolls over in its sleep . . . well. We

need some ideas about what we *can* do. New Britain is a
first approximation of an answer: It's got vastly more resources than the Gruinmarkt, Nordmarkt coastline, and
we've got contacts there. I propose that we should collectively go into the technology-transfer business. We've got
access to American libraries and know-how, and if we put
our muscle into it we can jump-start a technological revolution in New Britain. Operating under cover in the United
States has brought very mixed results—it's encouraged us
to act like criminals, like gangsters. I propose that our new
venture should be conducted openly, at least in New Britain. We should contact their authorities and ask for asylum.
We *could* do it quietly, trying to set up cover identities and
sneak in—but it would be much harder now that they're in
the middle of a war and a major political upheaval. If we
were exposed by accident, the first response would likely be
harsh, just as it has been in the United States.

"But anyway. That's why I invited you here today. Last
year I told you that I thought the Clan's business was unsus-
tainable in the long term. Today, I'm telling you that it has
become a lethal liability in the present—and to explore an
alternative model. I can't do this on my own. It's up to you
to help make this work. But if it doesn't, if we don't pull ourselves together and rapidly start up a new operation, we're
going to be crushed like bugs. Probably within a matter of
months."

She took another sip from her wineglass. "Any questions?"
A hand waved at the back, then another. The first, Huw, was
one of her plants, but the other . . . "Earl Wu? You have
something to say?"

"Yes," rumbled the Security heavy. "You are an optimist.
You think we can change our ways, yes? We will either have
to run from the Americans, or negotiate with them."

Miriam frowned. "Isn't that obvious? There's nothing
else—"

"—They will want to strike back," Carl interrupted. "Our
backwoods hotheads. They are used to power and they do

not spend enough time in America to understand how large the dragon is that they think they have cornered." He tapped his forehead. "I got my education in the US Marine Corps. And I know these idiots, the ones who stayed home."

"But how *can* they strike back?" Miriam stared at him. Brooding and grim as a warrior out of a Viking saga, Carl exuded absolute certainty and bleakly pessimistic skepticism.

"They can aim a sniper's rifle as well as anyone. And there are always the Clan's special weapons." A ripple of muttering spiraled the room, rapidly ascending in volume. "Whose principle military value lies in *not* using them, but the conservatives have never been good at subtle thinking."

"The Clan's—" Miriam bit her tongue. "You've got to be joking. They wouldn't dare use them. Would they?"

"You need to talk to Baron Riordan," said Carl. "I can say no more than that. But I'd speak to him soon, your majesty. For all I know, the orders might already have been signed."

It was early evening; the store had closed to the public two hours ago, and most of the employees had long since checked out and gone to do battle with the rush hour traffic or the crowds on the subway. The contract cleaners and stock fillers had moved in for the duration, wheeling their handcarts through the aisles and racks of clothing, polishing the display cases, vacuuming the back offices and storerooms. They had a long, patient night's work ahead of them, as did the two-man security team who walked the shop floor as infrequently as they could. "It creeps me out, man," Ricardo had explained once when Frank asked him. "You know about the broad who killed herself in the third floor john ten years ago? This is one *creepy* store."

"You been drinking too much, man," Frank told him, with a snort. "You been listenin' to too many ghost stories, they ain't none of your business. Burglars, *that's* your business."

"Not slipping and breaking my fool neck on all that marble, that's my business," Ricardo grumbled. But he tried to follow Frank's advice all the same. Which was why he wasn't looking at the walls as he slouched, face downturned, past the rest rooms on the third floor, just as the door to the men's room gaped silently open.

D.C. played host to a whole raft of police forces, from embassy guards to the Metro Police to the secret service, and all of them liked to play dress-up from time to time. If Ricardo had noticed the ghost who glided from the rest room doorway on the balls of his feet, his first reaction might have been alarm—followed by a flood of adrenaline-driven weak-kneed shock as he registered the look: the black balaclava helmet concealing the face, the black fatigues, and the silenced pistol in a military holster.

But Ricardo did not notice the mall ninja stepping out into the gallery behind him. Nor did he notice the second man in SWAT-team black slide out of the toilet door, scanning the other way down the aisle between knitware and ladies' formals with his pistol. Ricardo remained oblivious—for the rest of his life.

The first intruder had frozen momentarily in Ricardo's shadow. But now he took two steps forward, drawing a compact cylinder from his belt. One more step, and Ricardo might have noticed something for he tensed and began to turn; but the intruder was already behind him, thrusting hard.

The security guard dropped like a sack of potatoes, twitching as the illegally overcharged stunner pumped electricity through him. At the thud, the second intruder twitched round hastily; but Ricardo's assailant was quick with a hand signal, and then a compact Syrette. He bent over the fallen guard and picked up his left hand, then slid the needle into a vein on the inside of the man's wrist and squeezed the tube. Finally he looked round.

"Clear," said his companion.

"Help me get this into the stalls and position him."

Together they towed Ricardo—eyes closed, breathing slowly, seemingly completely relaxed—back into the men's room. A quick crisis conference ensued.

"You sure about this?"

"Yes. Can't risk him coming round."

"Shit. Okay, let's get him on the seat and make this look good. On my word—"

"God-on-a-stick, he's heavy."

"Roll his sleeve up, above the elbow, while I find the kit."

"You're really going to do this."

"You want to explain to the earl why we didn't?"

"Good point. . . ."

There was a janitor's trolley in front of the row of washbasins, with a large trash bin and storage for cleaning sundries. Drawing on a pair of disposable gloves, the second intruder retrieved some items from one of the compartments: a tarnished Zippo lighter, a heat-blackened steel spoon, a syringe (already loaded with clear liquid), and a rubber hose.

"Right, let's do this."

Ricardo twitched slightly and sniffed in his sleep as the men in black set up the scene. Then the syringe bit cold into his inner arm. "Wuh," he said, dozily.

"Hold him!"

The first intruder clamped his hands around Ricardo's shoulders; but the guard wasn't awake enough to put up any kind of struggle. And after drawing blood, his executioner was finished. The intruders stepped back to examine their handiwork: the ligature around the upper arm, the empty syringe, the addict's works on the floor by his feet.

"Shit. Never had to do that before."

"Neither have I. Easier than a hanging, isn't it?"

"Uglier, maybe. Let's get this shit over with."

Leaving the cubicle and its mute witness behind, the two men removed their masks and gloves and unhooked their holsters, stowing them in the janitor's cart. "Okay, we've got six minutes before his number two notices that he hasn't finished his round—if we're unlucky. Let's go find the freight elevator and get out of here."

Intruder number one wheeled the heavy janitor's cart out of the toilet block while his partner stood watch. This was the riskiest part of the procedure: The security guard was a known quantity, and one they'd been prepared for, but if they ran into a real cleaner they'd have to play things by ear. Too many disappearances in one night and someone, in the morning, might think to ask urgent questions. But they didn't run into anyone as they wheeled the cart over to the un-marked door leading to the service passages behind the shop floor, and the battered and scraped freight elevator arrived without undue fuss.

The sales floors—the sections of the store open to the public—occupied the first through fifth floors, but it was an eight-story building. The upper levels housed a restaurant, then administrative offices and storage rooms for stock and old documents. When the elevator stopped on the eighth floor, intruder number one was the first to exit. He glanced both ways along the empty corridor. "Clear."

"Alright, let's shift this."

Together they wheeled the cart along the corridor to-wards the building's northeast edge. Most of the rooms on this level were offices, prized by the store managers for their view of Penn Avenue; none of these would do. But where there are offices there are also facilities—mail rooms, sluices for the janitors, storerooms. And presently the intrud-ers found what they were looking for: a locked door which, once they opened it using the guard's master key, proved to conceal a small, cluttered closet stacked with anonymous brown cardboard boxes. The odor of neglect hung over them like a mildewed blanket. "This one's perfect—hasn't been cleaned in weeks."

"Good, let's get this thing in here. . . ."

Together they manhandled the cart into the room, then busied themselves moving and restacking the boxes, which proved to be full of yellowing paper files. By the time they finished, the cart was nearly invisible from the doorway, concealed behind a stack of archives. "Okay, setup time. Let's see. Epoxy glue first . . ."

Intruder number one busied himself applying fat sticks of epoxy putty to the wheels of the cart. By the time he finished, anyone attempting to remove it would find the wheels more than reluctant to budge, another mild deterrent to anyone wondering what an abandoned janitor's cart was doing in the back of a storeroom. Then intruder number two went to work on the contents of the trash can, with a pen-sized flashlight and a checklist with an olive drab cover bearing the words TOP SECRET.

"Power lead one, positive . . . safety to 'armed.' Countdown, see table three. Yes. Yes, that's right. Power lead three to input four. Armed. Timer self-test—green. PAL code is the default, eight zeroes. Let's see if that works. Okay, that works. Timer master key to 'set.' Here goes . . ." The intruder carefully twisted a butterfly nut, unscrewing a small cover that concealed a thumbwheel. The detonation controller on the device predated LEDs: no bright lights and digital countdown here, just six plastic dials and a push button to latch the timer into place. Finally, after checking his wristwatch and double-checking his calculation he replaced the cover. "Okay, switching safety to 'live.'" He winced slightly as he twisted the switch, but the only thing that happened was that a dull red pilot lamp next to the main power switch went out. "That looks okay. You got the putty?"

"Here."

He took the tube of epoxy putty, squeezed a strip out, and kneaded it into place over the thumbwheel securing the timer wheels, then under and around the safety switch. Once the putty hardened, it would take a hammer and chisel to free up the controls—and the device itself was tamper-resistant: pulling out wires or cracking the case would trigger it.

Intruder number one looked at him with wide, spooked eyes. "You realize what we've just done, cuz?"

"Yeah. Let's get the hell out of here!"

Methodical as always, his last action before they caught the elevator back down to the toilet—and thence to the wooden scaffold in a swamp in the Sudtmarkt—was to lock the door, and then empty half a tube of Krazy glue into the keyhole.

The guard would, of course, be discovered, but the body of a junkie was unlikely to trigger a tear-down search throughout an entire department store. The locked door might be noticed, but if so, would either be ignored or generate a low-priority call to Facilities, that might or might not be responded to the same day. The rearranged boxes might be noticed, but probably wouldn't be—nobody cleaned inside that room on a regular basis. And the out-of-place janitor's cart might irritate someone into trying to move it, but in that case they'd discover its wheels were stuck and its contents were inconveniently heavy. *True stealth,* intruder number one's superior had explained, *is made of lots of little barriers that are not apparent to the enemy.*

If anyone penetrated the final barrier and actually looked inside the waste bin in a janitor's cart in a locked room on the top floor of a department store, they might discover a sleeping horror.

But they'd have to do it fast: The timer would count down to zero in less than eighteen hours.

"What have you not been telling me?"

Miriam leaned on the back of the visitor's chair in the wood-paneled office, unwilling to sit down or comply with the usual polite rituals of an office visit. For his part, the office's owner looked equally unhappy. Miriam's arrival (accompanied by a squad of personal retainers, including both Brilliana and Sir Alasdair) had clearly disrupted his plans for the day.

"Lots," Riordan snapped. Then he paused to visibly gather his wits. "Please excuse me, this is *not* a good time. . . ."

"It never is." Miriam's stomach churned. Dyspepsia was a constant companion right now, along with weird aches and odd food cravings. And she'd had to ride piggyback on one of her guards to get here, which indignity didn't improve her mood. "I'm talking about the special weapons. I gather there are *complications*."

Behind her, Brilliana shifted from foot to foot; Riordan leaned back in his chair, steepled his fingers, and stared at her. It was a mannerism blatantly modeled on Angbard's style. *The poor bastard's as out of his depth as I am*, she realized. *We're both aping the absent experts.*

"Someone blabbed," he said flatly. "Tell me. I need to know."

"It was—" Brill stopped abruptly at Miriam's look.

"You don't need to answer him," Miriam told her. "Baron." She fixed him with a stare of her own—this one not modeled on anyone, even her mother. "Here are the facts as I know them. Some idiot a generation ago sneaked a couple of our people through an Army or Air Force technical school and got them qualified in the care and handling of special weapons. More recently, someone else, also an idiot, decided that having a brace of special weapons to hand was a good idea; just knowing where to steal them in a hurry wasn't good enough. Angbard trusted Matthias, Matthias had the keys to the kingdom, and when he defected he took at least one of the weapons as a fallback insurance policy. The Family Trade Organization sent it back to us, up near Concord. But it wasn't the only weapon we'd stolen, and they want the others back. So where *are* they? *You* know who's supposed to be in charge of them. What's going on?"

Riordan wilted suddenly. "My lady. Please. Have a seat."

"You've lost them, haven't you?"

"Scheisse," murmured Sir Alasdair. "Sorry."

Riordan glanced at her bodyguard, then back at Miriam. "Not . . . exactly. I'm not in charge of them. The Clan Council entrusted them to someone else."

"Oh." Miriam rolled her eyes. "You're going to tell me that after Angbard's fuck up and in the absence of a track record showing where you stood they didn't see fit to entrust you with them. So they gave them to that fuckup Oliver Hjorth to sit on."

"Oliver's not a fuckup." Riordan's tone was distinctly defensive. "I appreciate that you and he got off to a very bad start, that he's seen fit to align himself with a faction that you have a predisposition against, and all the rest of it. But he is neither stupid or lazy, much less unreliable. Usually."

"Usually."

It hung in the air for a moment, before Riordan replied. "Nobody has seen him for two days."

"Nobody has—" Miriam blinked. "You're kidding. You're *Clan Security*. You're telling me you've lost track of the official the Council put in charge of half a dozen atom bombs?"

"Milady—" It was Brill.

"What is it?"

"He can't—" Her eyes were pleading.

"Nobody can keep track of every member of the inner families," rumbled Alasdair. "We don't have the manpower." Miriam looked round, to see him watching Riordan. "Nevertheless . . . something happened, did it not?"

"I was awaiting a report," Riordan said reluctantly, "before calling a meeting of the Committee of Regents. And the full Council, if necessary. It is not just his lordship who is proving hard to contact."

"Who's missing?"

"Oliver, Earl Hjorth. Baron Schwartzwasser. His lordship of Gruen, Baron ven Hjalmar. About half a dozen past and present soldiers of this very office who are absent without leave, two-thirds of the Postal Committee, various others—don't look so shocked; it's a goodly cross section of the conservative faction, but not all of them. I happen to know that Baron Julius is sitting on the bench in the royal assizes today, and when I raised the matter he professed ignorance convincingly. My lady, they might be attending a private party, for all I know. Their political views are not a sufficient reason to condemn them, in the absence of any other evidence."

"But you don't know where the bombs are." Riordan looked pained. Miriam leaned towards him. "And there are *rumors*," she hissed. "A lot of whispering about revenge and honor. I'm not deaf, I've got ears to hear this stuff with. What do you think is going on?"

Riordan tensed, and she thought for a moment that he was about to reply, but at that moment the door opened. "I said we weren't to be—oh. My lady." He rose to his feet as Miriam turned.

"Helge? What are you doing here?" Olga glanced round angrily as she closed the door. "I see." She focused on the office's owner. "My lord, we need to talk about Plan Blue, *right now*. Helge, I beg of you, please excuse us—"

"It's too late for that." Riordan frowned. "Helge was just asking me about—about Plan Blue."

"Plan Blue?" Miriam echoed.

Alasdair cleared his throat. "Is that the contingency plan for—" He cleared his throat again, and raised an eyebrow.

"Oh *scheisse*," said Brill, despair in her voice.

"The bastards have activated it," said Olga, her voice tightly controlled. "And I do not recall being invited to a plenary session to approve such action. Do you? It's unforgivable!"

"Plan Blue?" Miriam repeated.

"Excuse me." Riordan nodded at her. "My apologies, my lady, but I must make a call." He lifted the telephone handset and began to dial, then paused. "That's funny. There's no tone."

"Give that to me." Miriam reached for it. The handset was dead, mocking her. "Um, you've got a dead line. Could you have been cut off by accident, or is that too improbable?"

"Enemy action," said Sir Alasdair. "My lady, over here." He moved swiftly, gesturing Miriam away from the window and moving to stand where she'd been a moment before.

"Otto Schenck admitted it to, to one of my sources," Olga added as Riordan poked at his desktop computer, a frown spreading on his face. "Boasted, belike, he said they're going to send the enemy their king's head on a plate—"

"It's not going to work," Brill whispered.

"What's not going to work?" Miriam rounded on her tensely. "What are you talking about?"

"Why now?" Brill frowned. "Why are they doing this *now?*" She looked at Miriam. "It's something to do with your grandmother, my lady. Her visit the other day. That was no coincidence!"

"What do you—"

"We need to get out of here!" Brill raised her voice, piercing and urgent. "Listen, everybody! This is a setup! We need to leave the building *right now!*"

"Why—" Riordan was standing up.

"She's right, *go, now!*" Olga grabbed his arm.

"My lady. This way." Alasdair yanked the door open and pulled Miriam along behind him.

"But where are we—" Miriam stopped arguing and concentrated on not stumbling as he powered along the corridor towards a fire door. "Alasdair! *No!*" Visions of claymore mines flashed through her mind as he stopped dead.

"Oh, I don't think so," he assured her with a sharkish grin. "I checked this one before you arrived. Besides, I don't think they want to *kill* us. Immobilize us and send us a message, perhaps, but they're not going to risk killing the heir." He shoved down on the emergency bar and pushed the door open. In the distance behind them, a tinny siren began to wail. "After me, if you please."

Sir Alasdair ducked round the door, then pronounced the area clear. They piled down the fire escape to the car park at the back of the small office building, Brill and Olga trailing behind. "What exactly is Plan Blue?" Miriam demanded breathlessly. "Where's Riordan?"

"He's got other things to do," said Olga. "My lady Brilliana, please take your mistress somewhere safe."

"Where—"

"—Plan Blue?"

"Plan Blue is the usage case for the Clan deterrent," Brill explained as they climbed into Sir Alasdair's Explorer. "A decapitation strike at the enemy."

"Oh Jesus. Tell me that doesn't mean what I think it means."

"I fear I cannot."

"Olga, what is Riordan doing?"

"He's going to find a phone." She grinned, humorlessly. "Oh, there he is now. . . ."

Miriam turned her head to see Riordan round the side of the building, holding a briefcase. He was walking towards them. Olga popped the door.

"Drive," he said, climbing in. "I've got to make a call. Once it connects, they'll be trying to trace us, so on my word pull into a car park so I can ditch this thing."

Brill stared at the case as if it contained a poisonous reptile. "Is this safe?" she asked.

"No." Riordan didn't smile. "You were right about it, Olga."

The truck was already moving as Riordan opened the briefcase. "What's that?" asked Miriam.

"A special phone." Brill pulled a face. "Not safe."

"Indeed." There was a tray in the case, with a cell phone—in several pieces—nested in separate pockets. One of them contained a small, crude-looking circuit board with a diode soldered to it; another contained a compact handset.

"Why did we leave the office?" asked Miriam.

"Can't use this phone while stationary," Riordan grunted. "And the opposition cut our lines. A nuisance measure, I think, but the timing is worrying; I think they were watching you to see if you would take their bait. And you did."

"Bait?" She shook her head, bewildered.

"You came to see me, about Plan Blue. I do not believe that is an accident."

"Bastards," she mumbled under her breath. Louder: "It was your man Carl."

"Thank you," Riordan said gravely. "Alright, I am going to talk to the enemy now." He picked up the handset, flicked a switch on the small circuit board, and poked at the exposed keypad of the vivisected phone. "Dialing . . ." The sound of a ringing phone filled the truck's cab, coming from a speaker in the briefcase.

"Hello?" The voice answering the phone was cold.

"I was told that you can send a message to the White House," said Riordan. "Is that correct?"

Miriam's skin crawled as she waited for the reply.

"Correct," the voice said drily. "To whom am I speaking?"

"You can call me the Chief of Security."

"And you may call me Dr. James. Are you calling to surrender?"

"No, I'm calling to warn you that your meddling has produced an overreaction from our conservative faction. They've activated a plan which—*fuck.*"

The line had gone dead; simultaneously, the LED on the circuit board had lit up, burning red.

"They did it," Brill said, fascinated. "The *bastards.*" Her actual word, in hochsprache, was considerably stronger.

"Next drive-through, please," Riordan called to Sir Alasdair. "I am afraid you are right, milady."

"What was that?" Miriam asked, staring at the LED.

"Something one of our artificers put in to replace the ten grams of C4 wired across the earpiece," said Olga. "Is it not an ingenious little assassination weapon?"

"But we"—Miriam stared in horror—"we were going to warn them!"

"Maybe they don't want warning?" Sir Alasdair commented.

"But we—" Miriam stopped. "We've got to do something! Do you know where the bombs are?"

"No," said Olga.

"That's the whole point of Plan Blue," Riordan added. "It's a procedure for deployment. Nobody knows everything about it; for example, I don't know the precise target locations. It was designed so that it can't be disrupted if the commanders are captured, or if one of the bomb emplacement teams is captured."

"But that's insane! Isn't there any way of stopping it?"

"Normally, yes, if the chain of command was operating. But someone appears to have decided to cut us out of the loop. I fear we are facing a coup assisted by people inside Security, my lady. I have some calls to make. . . ."

"We can warn them," said Olga, causing at least three people to ask, "how?" simultaneously.

"Your friend, Mr. Fleming," she added, glancing sidelong at Miriam. "He is inside their security apparat."

"So was that, that man. On the phone." Miriam stared at Riordan, who was busily unplugging components in the briefcase and fiddling with something that looked alarmingly like a pyrotechnic flare.

"Yes, but Fleming will know how to bypass him," Brill said thoughtfully. "He will know how to escalate a bomb threat and sound a general alert. His superior may be playing insane games, but I believe he is still trustworthy."

The Explorer turned a corner. "Stopping in a minute," called Sir Alasdair. "Are you ready?"

"Yes," said Riordan, depressing a button on the flare and closing the briefcase. He latched it shut, then spun the combination wheels. "We have two minutes until we require a fire extinguisher."

"You won't need them." Alasdair was already slowing, his turn signal flashing. "Okay, go." The car park outside a 7-Eleven was deserted.

Riordan popped the door, lowered the briefcase, and then kicked it away from the truck. "Go yourself," he said. He was already opening another mobile phone, this one reassuringly unmodified. "Duty chief? This is the major. I have some orders for you. The day codes are—"

Miriam rubbed her temples. "Anyone got a cell phone?" she asked.

"I have," said Olga. "Why?"

"Unless you can't live without it, I want to call Mike."

"But we can—"

"I said *I want to call Mike!*" Miriam snarled. "When I've spoken to him you can put me back in my padded box to gestate while you get down to finding those fucking bombs and arresting or shooting whoever stole them, but *I* should be the one who talks to Mike."

"Why—"

"Because I'm the only one of us he's got any reason to trust," she said bleakly, "and I'm afraid I'm going to burn him."

The clinic room could have been a bedroom in a chain hotel, if not for the row of sockets on the wall behind the bed—piping in oxygen, vacuum, and other, less common utilities—and for the cardiac monitor on a stand beside it, spreading leads like creepers to each of the occupant's withered branchlike limbs. Outside the sealed window unit, the late afternoon sunshine parched the manicured strip of grass that bordered this side of the clinic; beyond it, a thin rind of trees dappled the discreet brick wall with green shadows.

The man in the bed dozed lightly. He'd been awake earlier in the day, shaking in frustration as the speech therapist tried to coax words out of his larynx, and the effort—followed by an hour with the physiotherapist, working on the muscles in his damaged left arm, and then a light lunch served by a care assistant who carefully spooned each mouthful into his mouth—had tired him out. He'd been in his late sixties even before the stroke, his stamina reduced and his aches more noticeable with every morning. Since the stroke, things had only gotten worse. Afternoon naps, which he'd once disdained as suitable only for kindergartners, had become a regular daily fixture for him.

Something—a small movement, or an out-of-place noise—brought him to consciousness, though he could not say why. Perhaps the shadow of a bird fluttering before the window glass disturbed him, or footsteps in the corridor outside: In any case, his eyelids flickered open, staring at the ceiling overhead. "Urrr." He closed his mouth, which had fallen open as he slept, and reached for the bed's motor controller with his left hand. His eyes twitched from side to side, scanning the angles and planes of the space surrounding him, looking for intrusions. His thumb twitched, pushing the headboard motor control, and the bed began to whine, raising him towards a sitting position.

"Good afternoon, old man." The visitor closed the clinic room door carefully, then approached the bed, standing where its occupant could see him.

"Urr . . . doc." Surprise and doubt sparked in the old man's eyes. "Doc-tor!"

"I wanted to take a last look at you. You know, before the end."

"You. End?" The visitor had to lean close to make out the words, for Angbard's speech was garbled, the muscles of his lips and tongue cut loose by the death of nerves in his brain. "Wher' guards?"

"They were called away." The visitor seemed amused. "Something to do with an emergency, I gather. Do you remember Plan Blue?"

"Wha—"

The visitor watched as Angbard fumbled with the bed's controller. "No, I don't think so," he said, after a moment. Reaching out, he pulled the handset away from the duke's weakened fingers. "Your aunt sends her regards, and to tell you that our long-standing arrangement is canceled," he said, and stood up. "That may be sufficient for her, but some of us have been waiting in line, and now it's *my* turn."

"Scheisse!"

The duke made a grab for the emergency cord, but it was futile; he was still deathly weak and uncontrolled on his left side, and his right hand clawed inches short of the pull. Then the visitor grabbed the pillow from behind his head and rammed it down onto his face. It was a very uneven struggle, but even so the old man didn't go easily. "Fucking lie down and *die*," snarled the visitor, leaning on him as he tried to grab the duke's flailing left hand. "Why can't you do something right for once in your life?"

He was answered by a buzzer sounding from the heart monitor.

Breathing heavily he levered himself off the bed; then, lifting the pillow, he shoved it under the duke's lolling head before turning to stare at the monitor. "Hmm, you do appear to have lost your sinus rhythm altogether! Time to leave, I think." He stared at the corpse in distaste. "That's a better end than you deserved, old man. Better by far, compared to the normal punishment for betrayal. . . ."

He breathed deeply a few times, watching the buzzing heart monitor. Then Dr. ven Hjalmar opened the door, took a deep breath to fill his lungs, and shouted, "Crash cart, stat! Patient in cardiac arrest!" before turning back to the bed to commence the motions of resuscitation.

Mike had been accumulating leave for too long; taking some of it now wouldn't strike anyone in human resources as strange, although it was a fair bet that someone higher up the tree would start asking questions if he didn't show up for work within a week.

In the meantime he went home, still numb with shock from the disclosures buried on the cassette tapes. It was, he thought, time to make some hard choices: Collusion between officials and the bad guys was nothing particularly new, but for it to go so high up the ladder was unprecedented. And it would be extraordinarily dangerous for someone at his level to do anything about it. Or not—and that was even worse. *Dr. James is in WARBUCKS's pocket,* Mike reminded himself. *And he gave me those tapes, not some other, more qualified analyst. If I'm lucky he did it because he considers me trustworthy. More likely . . .* A vision kept flickering in his mind's eye, of Colonel Smith, in all candor, telling Dr. James, "Mike's a bit squirrelly about you. Nothing to worry about, but you should keep an eye on him." And Dr. James, with that chilly reserved look in his eye, nodding and making a note by his name on the org chart: *disposable resource.*

Mike was under no illusions about the taskmaster Dr. James worked for: a determined, driven, man—*ruthless* would not be an exaggeration. He had a fire in his belly and a desire to bend history to his will. With his doctrine of a unitary executive and his gradual arrogation of extraordinary powers granted by a weak presidency, he'd turned the office of vice president into the most powerful post in the government. And he had good reason to silence anyone who knew of his covert connection to the Clan: good reason, even, to silence the Clan themselves for good. *He's an oilman, and he knows they're sitting on all the oil that was ever under Texas, untapped,* Mike realized. *And now he's got a machine for getting there. It's crude today, but who knows what it'll be like tomorrow? He's got to be thinking, who needs Iraq, anyway? Or Saudi Arabia?*

Mike wasn't naïve: He knew that the most addictive drug, the deadliest one, the one that fucked people up beyond redemption every time, was money. *And I'm between an addict and the most powerful fix in history. . . .*

That afternoon and evening, he meticulously searched his apartment, starting by unplugging all the electrical appliances and checking sockets and power supplies for signs of tampering. Then he began to search the walls and floors, inch by inch, looking for bugs. And while he searched, he thought.

The picture looked grimmer the longer he looked at it. Thinking back, there'd been the horror-flick prop they'd found in a lockup in Cambridge, thick layers of dust covering the Strangelovian intrusion of a 1950s-era hydrogen bomb, propped up on two-by-fours and bricks with a broken timer plugged into its tail. Nobody ever said what it had been about, but the NIRT inspectors had tagged its date: early 1970s, Nixon administration. *What kind of false-flag operation involves nuking one of your own cities? How about one designed to psyche your country up for a nuclear war with China?* Except it hadn't happened. *But the Clan have a track record of stealing nukes from our inventory.* Mike shuddered. And WARBUCKS had backed BOY WONDER's plan to invade Iraq, even after Chemical Ali had offed his cousin Saddam and sued for peace on any terms. And according to some folks who Mike wasn't yet prepared to write off as swivel-eyed loons, the oil had something to do with it.

He slept uneasily that night, his dreams unusually vivid: an injured princess in a burning medieval palace, her face half-melted by the nuclear heat-flash, telling him, "I'll call when I can," as he tried to pull his leg from a man-trap and reached down to lever apart its jaws, only to find it was a skull, a skull biting his legs, Pete Garfinkle's skull, horribly charred by the bomb that had set this off, and if he couldn't get away the next nuke would fry him—

The next morning he rose, late and groggy, and went back to work. Around ten o'clock he finally found what he'd been looking for: a pinhole in the living room wall that had been all but concealed by the frame of a cheap print that had come with the apartment. Mike passed it by, continuing his search. It would be perfectly obvious what he was doing, and there was no point in showing any sign of having discovered the camera. Either it was being monitored, in which case they'd simply replace it with another the next time he went out, or the survey had been terminated, in which case there was nothing to worry about. He leaned towards the latter case (keeping a watch on an apartment was an expensive business, requiring at least six full-time agents on rotation) but he had to assume the former, especially if Dr. James considered him unsound. *He could have farmed it out to Internal Affairs, told them I'm suspected of espionage,* he thought bleakly. In which case, he was providing them with lots of circumstantial evidence that he was overdue for a vacation in Club Fed; but that couldn't be avoided. Federal prison might actually be an improvement over the alternatives, if WARBUCKS decided Mike needed to be silenced.

He'd finished the bug hunt—without finding any additional devices—and had moved into the washroom to process the pile of shirts and underwear that had been building up, when the phone rang.

Swearing, he made a grab for the handset and caught it before the answering machine cut in. He was half-expecting a recorded telesales announcement for his pains, but years of fielding out-of-hours emergencies had made him wary of dropping messages. "Mike?" asked a woman's voice. "Are you there?"

"Yes"—it took a moment for the voice to register. "Don't say your name!" he said hurriedly. "The line is probably being monitored."

"And this cell phone is going down a storm drain as soon as I end the call." She sounded nervous.

"Is it about the talk we had? Because if so, there've been some changes—"

"No, it's not about that. Listen, Olga told me what you told her."

"*Olga* told"—he paused, his tenuous train of thought perilously close to derailment—"what's your situation?"

"I'm okay, my mom's okay, and we know about the surprise in the cell phone your boss left for us." Cold sweat drenched Mike's back as she continued relentlessly: "It's about the nukes. Your boss didn't stay on the line long enough to let us pass on the news that all this *send them a message* shit has just blown up in a big way. The conservative faction are attempting to stage a coup and as part of their preparations they've stolen"—a pause—"no, they've *deployed* at least three, possibly four, of the bombs in their possession. Hang on"—the line went silent for a few seconds—"word is that *they* have decided to send *you* a message, and you've probably got less than twenty-four hours to find it."

"If this is some kind of joke—"

"No, hang on, I'm relaying stuff. The target is probably Washington D.C., and the bombs only dial up to about one kiloton each. The bad guys are inside our chain of command; they activated a contingency plan and changed the targets. We're currently trying to reestablish control and find out where the new target locations are, and as soon as we figure that out I will phone this land line number and pass the information on. I want you to know that we're treating this as treason and it is not our intention to blow up any cities. Have you got that?"

"Wait, *listen!* Did you try telling—did you talk to Dr. James? Did you talk to him—"

"Yes, that's the name. Can you pass this—"

Mike tried to swallow, his mouth was dry and sticky, and his heart was hammering. "Dr. James works directly for the vice president. WARBUCKS has been in collusion with someone in your inner families for a very long time—more than ten years—and he wants you all dead. There are tapes . . . I'm not trusted, I'm a disposable asset. Just saying. If what you're telling me is true, Dr. James doesn't care about losing a city block or two—it would make it easier to justify what's coming down the line. Think of Pearl Harbor, think of 9/11. If I pass this up the line, they'll bury it and I'll show up in the morgue one morning."

"Shit." Her voice cracked. "Mike, I'm going to have to put the phone down in a minute, I've been on the line too long. What can we do?"

"Find the bombs. Drag them back to the Gruinmarkt and dump them in a swamp or something." He stared bleakly at the kitchen sink. "I'm going to put the answering machine on now and go out. Got to go outside the chain of command and talk to some folks who might be able to do something useful."

"If there's anything we can do—"

"Just find the fucking bombs!" he snarled, and slammed the handset down on its charge point so hard that the battery cover pinged off.

"Shit." He breathed deeply, staring at the phone. Coming from anyone else, he'd have questioned the sanity of the bearer of such news—but he knew Miriam. And he'd let his mouth run away with him, blabbing the truth about the tapes Dr. James had him listening in on. Never mind the pinhole camera: The phone line *was* bugged and even if nobody was monitoring it in realtime, the word would be out soon.

Mike went through into the living room, and then his bedroom, as fast as his cast would let him. (It was still itching, but nearly ready to come off; give it two weeks, said the doctor he'd seen the week before.) He collected his jacket and a small go-bag from under the bed, which held (among other things) a gun, a couple of fully charged and never-used cell phones, and a handwritten paper address book. "Who first?" he asked the air as he headed for the front door. *I could try the colonel again,* he thought dismally. Or . . . *Agent Herz. She might go for it.* But whether she'd listen to him was another matter: *They'll put the word out on me within an hour.* That left the usual channels—he could go talk to the FBI or his former boss at the DEA field office in town, but again: *They'll think I'm crazier than a fruitbat once Dr. James gets through with my rep.* He opened the front door.

I'm going to have to go to the press, he thought, and raised the remote on his car key chain, and had already begun to press the button just as a second thought crystallized in his mind: *James is an old hand. What if he's playing by the pre-Church Commission rules—*

In the aftermath of the explosion, every car alarm within three blocks began to sound, accompanied by a chorus of panicking dogs and, soon enough, the rising and falling of sirens; but they were too late.

And two hours and fourteen minutes later, in a locked storeroom on the top floor of a department store on Pennsylvania Avenue, a timer counted down to zero. . . .

THE WAR BETWEEN UNIVERSES
REACHES ITS CLIMAX

CHARLES
STROSS

THE TRADE OF
QUEENS

BOOK SIX OF THE MERCHANT PRINCES

A dissident faction of the Clan, the alternate-universe group of families that has traded covertly with our world for a century or more, has carried nuclear devices between the worlds and detonated them in Washington, D.C. Now they want to exterminate the rest of the Clan and keep Miriam alive only long enough to bear the heir to the throne of their land in the Gruinmarkt world.

"The world-building in this series is simply superb, in other words—it is engaging, crystal-clear, and disturbingly real."
—SyFy.com

"[These books] are, first and foremost, great fun."
—PAUL KRUGMAN, *New York Times* bestselling author of *The Great Unraveling*

HARDCOVER   tor-forge.com   978-0-7653-1673-8